ADRIFT

Praise for Sam Ledel

Worth a Fortune

"The romance burns tantalizingly slowly as Ledel takes the time to thoroughly explore the ways her well-shaded heroines both complement and clash with each other. This remarkable emotional maturity does not come at the expense of heat, however; when the love scenes come, they steam up the pages. It's subtle, lovely, and stirring. Starred review."—*Publishers Weekly*

"Loved this! It was exciting, down to earth and totally unexpected. Nothing outrageous, just a wonderful connection between two women who find their world has completely changed following the Second World War. I adored the way both of them had to learn new things, take new changes, risks, and try things that weren't known to them, only to find themselves reconnecting in a most lovely way." —*LESBIreviewed*

Rocks and Stars

"I think Sam Ledel told a great story. I adored Kyle even though a few times I wanted to shake her and say enough, girlfriend. I wish the ending was a bit longer, but that's the romance addict in me. I look forward to Ledel's next book."—*Romantic Reader Blog*

Daughter of No One

"There's a lot of really smart fantasy going on here…Great start to a (hopefully) long running series."—*Colleen Corgel, Librarian, Queens Public Library*

"It's full of exciting adventure and the promise of romance. It's sweet, fresh and hopeful. It takes me back to my teenage years, the good parts of those years at least. I read this in a few hours, only stopped long enough to have lunch. I hope I won't have to wait too long for the sequel—I have high hopes for Jastyn, Aurelia, their friend Coran, Eegit the hedgewitch and Rigo the elf."—*Jude in the Stars*

"A fantasy book with MCs in their very early twenties, this book presents a well thought out world of Kingdom of Venostes (shades of The Lord of the Rings here)."—*Best Lesfic Reviews*

"Sam Ledel has definitely set up an epic adventure of star-crossed lovers. This book one of a trilogy doesn't leave you with a cliffhanger but you are definitely going to be left ready for the next book...As a non-fantasy lover, I adored this book and am ready to read where Ledel takes us next. This book is quality writing, great pacing, and top-notch characters. You cannot go wrong with this one!"
—*Romantic Reader Blog*

"If you're a huge fan of fantasy novels, especially if you love stories like this one that contains a host of supernatural beings, quirky characters coupled with action and excitement around every tree, winding path or humble abode, then this is definitely the story for you! This compelling story also deals with poverty, isolation and the huge chasm between the royal family and the low-class villagers. Well, fellow book lovers, it really looks like you've just received a winning ticket to a literary lottery."—*Lesbian Review*

Broken Reign

"Sam Ledel has created a fascinating and at times terrifying world, filled with elves, sirens, selkies, wood nymphs and many more... Going on this journey with both young women and their fellow travellers still has this fresh and exciting quality, all the more so as new characters joined the story, some just as intriguing."—*Jude in the Stars*

The Princess and the Odium

"The world-building in the whole trilogy is fantastic, and even if it feels familiar now that we've been navigating it with the characters for a while, it's still surprising and unsettling. All in all, *The Princess and the Odium* is a fitting end to a well-written YA fantasy series."
—*Jude in the Stars*

By the Author

Wildflower Words

Worth a Fortune

Heart of Stone

Adrift

Rocks and Stars (Young Adult)

The Odium Trilogy

Daughter of No One

Broken Reign

The Princess and the Odium

Visit us at www.boldstrokesbooks.com

ADRIFT

by

Sam Ledel

2024

CREDITS
Editor: Barbara Ann Wright
Production Design: Stacia Seaman
Cover Design by Tammy Seidick

Acknowledgments

Thank you to Sandy and the Bold Strokes Books team. A big thank you to my editor, Barbara Ann Wright, for always triple-checking the research in these historical tales. You push my stories to their potential, and they would not be what they are without you.

Thanks also to the beta and sensitivity readers who looked at the early drafts. A special thanks to Ashley Lynn Hengst for your insight and constructive feedback on these characters. My appreciation goes out to everyone, from my partner to friends to family, who listened to the early ideas for this story and encouraged me. Your support means everything.

PROLOGUE

Seaside, San Diego, California, 1923

Cool night wind twisted itself in Janeth Castro's braid as she stood watching the shoreline. A candle flickered in its tray just inside the open window of her bedroom. Her gaze went from it to the dark night that had settled over the rocky cliffside. She stiffened at the sound of waves crashing, then grimaced. *You would think I'd be used to it by now.* She glanced sideways as if the floral,-patterned wallpaper eyed her judgmentally.

Her second-story vantage point provided the ideal view every other Friday night for the incoming boat. It was always small, usually a dory, carrying three or four men, rising and falling with the Pacific's taciturn waves.

Shadows engulfed the cliff line. Janeth fiddled with the end of her necklace, her fingers running absentmindedly over the thin gold cross. Finally, the dory's lantern flickered over the water, then disappeared between the rocks. She tucked the necklace beneath her nightgown and lowered the pane, leaving it open only an inch above the sill.

Crossing the modest space, her bare feet treading quietly over a plush Persian rug, she dimmed the lights, black smoke drifting up as she turned each wall lamp latch. It cast her room in an eerie glow, encasing the bookshelves, her twin bed, and the small piano in pale light. Striking a match, she lit another candle, placing the wax-laden tray atop her bedside table. Her mother's rosary hung above a wood-framed black-and-white photograph. Victor's wide smile seemed to glow in the dim light.

Janeth had the timing down to the minute. As she settled onto the piano bench, a distant dull scraping sounded below, deep in the belly of her uncle's great home. She thumbed through the sheet music, reminding herself to ask about more modern selections at breakfast tomorrow. She trailed her fingers over the keys, then began to play as the echo of voices sounded downstairs.

It took only two compositions. Then would come the dull thud of the cellar door closing. After that, she would return to the window to catch the lantern light retreating toward the black horizon. Then it would be done.

As her thumb sank against the C key, a shout from downstairs broke the melody. She paused, listening. It was a man's voice but didn't sound like her uncle. She eyed the door to her bedroom she'd left cracked open, then continued to play. Another shout. This one was from her uncle, and Janeth swallowed at the fear in his voice.

She stiffened, fingers hovering over the keys. She replayed her uncle's words from six months prior, after she had decided to call his great mansion home: "Stay upstairs, Janeth, dear. These men…well, it's not a meeting for a lady such as yourself."

Another angry yell was followed by a crash, like one of the antique chairs being overturned. She stood, the piano bench scraping on the floor before it jammed against the rug.

Something was wrong.

Quietly, she moved to the door and peered out. From her room, the hallway and stairwell that climbed down the center of the cavernous house was dark, the ornate furnishings, oil paintings, and fine statues all shrouded in a blanket of black. Janeth crept into the hall. The grandfather clock ticked on indifferently against the wall opposite the top of the wide, carpeted stairs, marching closer to the midnight hour.

She listened, clutching the top of her floor-length silk nightgown as she slowly descended the stairs. Over the polished wood banister, she peered toward the library tucked into the southeast corner of the home. Lamplight shone from beneath the sturdy oak door and through the two-inch opening where it had been left ajar. The voices were clearer now.

Her uncle's voice quivered. "This is *not* the agreement."

Another man's voice, gravelly and clipped, replied curtly, "I don't care, Mr. Mills."

"But Marquez, he—"

"Marquez isn't in charge anymore. I am."

Standing outside the library door, Janeth held her breath as her uncle said, "I can't. I'm sorry, Raymond. It's too much."

"It's what you owe."

"No," her uncle said, his voice stronger, but Janeth could still hear his trepidation. "I won't stand for this. It's brutish. I refuse to—"

A bang echoed through the house. The shock of the sound reverberated through her body, and she covered her mouth to hide her gasp. The anxiety that had trickled down her spine upstairs scorched into a bright panic.

The floorboards creaked behind her. She could hardly turn before a hand was over her mouth. She tried to scream as another hand yanked her left arm behind her back, and she was shoved into the library.

Blinking at the brightness, Janeth struggled against the man who held her. She tried to take in her surroundings as she wriggled against him. A pair of young men, no older than her, with sepia skin and black hair framed a tall, broad-shouldered blond man holding a pistol.

"Janeth."

Her gaze flew to the corner bookcase, the one that opened to reveal the dank, dark stairwell leading to the cellar. In front of it, her uncle lay with his back against the mahogany shelves, his legs splayed in front of him. It seemed as if he'd been shoved backward, a look of surprise on his pale, lined face. A small tear in his pressed pants, several inches below his right knee, seeped with blood. Equally dark red specks covered his fine shoes. His white hair, thick with oil, stuck up in the back where his head must have hit the books now in disarray behind him. His thin mustache twitched when he winced.

The man holding her lowered his hand from her mouth. Janeth pushed against his tattered striped shirt, the sweat stains clear in the soiled blue material around the low neckline. "Uncle." She tried to go to him, but the man pulled her back. He cackled, the stench of stale tobacco hitting her face from behind yellow teeth. He made her face the room and replaced his hand over her mouth when the blond man, Raymond, spoke, his blue eyes fixed on her.

"Golly, fellas, what do we have here?"

"Leave her out of this," her uncle said, reaching for the wound to try to staunch the bleeding.

"Now, Mr. Mills, it seems to me your niece is trying to meddle in a man's affair."

Janeth could smell the gunpowder fresh from his pistol in his right hand. Old suspenders held up tattered brown pants beneath a blue shirt that looked eager to burst from his barrel chest. Heavy boots, like the ones she'd seen fishermen at the cannery wear, made dull thuds on the floor when he walked toward her.

Her uncle reached out. "Don't touch her."

Janeth, wide-eyed, tried again to escape the man's arms. Raymond rubbed his strong-looking, stubbled chin. He smiled, then nodded for the man to release her. Janeth stepped away but was restricted to the space between Raymond and his crony. "Your uncle is right," he said, stepping closer and using the end of the pistol barrel to move her bangs out of her eyes. He squinted, muttering curiously, "Uncle." He glanced over his shoulder.

Janeth wondered if he noticed the stark differences between the two of them. She lifted her chin, hoping he didn't sense her fear. He turned back to her, a newfound knowledge sitting in his sneer. "This is no business for a lady." His brown eyes reflected her as his gaze flitted from her to the men behind her. "Not even one like you."

"Please," she said, gesturing to her uncle. "Let me help him."

Raymond puckered his chapped lips, his gaze scraping down her figure. She pulled her nightgown closer at her neck. The gesture drew his eyes to the small silver band on her left ring finger. He frowned, eyeing her again. Eventually—apparently making a decision—he bowed and let her pass.

"Your tie," she said and helped her uncle untie the bow in his starched collar. Swiftly, she wound it around his lower leg. He cringed when she tightened it.

"Now," Raymond said. "Where's our money?"

"I paid you." Her uncle shot Janeth a look, and she helped him stand. Fumbling, he managed to lean against a leather wing back chair. Meanwhile, the men grumbled from across the room.

"No, Mr. Mills. The price has gone up."

"I've been paying the same amount for two years with Marquez."

"As I said, Marquez isn't in charge anymore." Janeth shifted to keep her uncle propped up, watching Raymond's grip tighten around the pistol. He turned to his men. "I fear the old man is getting senile, fellas." To her uncle, he nearly shouted, "Marquez is gone. I'm in charge now."

"You cannot waltz into my home and place of business and ask for ten percent more than what I've been paying since the beginning. There's an order to these things. We had an arrangement."

"There's a new order now, Mr. Mills."

Janeth could hear the shudder in her uncle's breath before he spoke. She wondered if he noticed the way Raymond's finger twitched near the pistol's trigger.

They stood in silence for what seemed like an eternity. "Janeth," her uncle finally said, "fetch my pocketbook from the desk." Nodding, she glanced across the room before helping settle her uncle against the chair. Once she was sure he could hold himself up for a moment, she scurried to grab the pocketbook. "The twenty-dollar note," he added, sending a glare at Raymond. Her uncle must have registered the shock on her face when she paused. "You heard me," he said firmly.

Her hands sweaty, she pulled out the note and handed it to Raymond. He held it up to the light, tugging on it as he seemed to scrutinize it. He handed it to one of the men, who stuck it in a clip attached to his shirt pocket.

"That wasn't so hard, was it?" Raymond clapped, looking satisfied. "Change can be difficult, Mr. Mills, but I know this is the start of a wonderful relationship." He grinned widely, his gaze flitting across the fine possessions scattered throughout the library. "I look forward to working with you."

Her uncle only stood there looking defeated and overwhelmed, his face a mask of pain. Raymond nodded to Janeth. The man who had shoved her into the room winked, then followed the others through the bookcase doorway.

Her uncle spat, and as Raymond moved to go, he muttered, "Good for nothing pig."

At the desk, Janeth dropped the pocketbook. Raymond turned, his face hard. Before she could move, he fired the gun.

"Uncle!"

Her uncle fell, clutching his side as he tumbled over the chair onto the floor. Blood spilled between his fingers just below his waist.

Janeth fumbled forward, pulling his jacket off and pressing it against the wound. She looked up at Raymond, whose face was blank, but his eyes were cold.

"That was your last warning, Mr. Mills," he said, his voice even. He met Janeth's gaze. She shuddered at his smile as he tipped an imaginary hat and said, "Good evening, miss."

Once they were gone, Janeth laid her uncle on the rug, finding a throw pillow to rest beneath his head. "I need to call the physician," she told him, hating the way her voice wavered.

He nodded, his watery gaze tracing the ceiling. "Very good, my dear. Very good." She found a book to lay atop the jacket, hoping to keep pressure against the wound. She flew to the drawing room that hosted the candlestick phone, cursing the size of the house as she ran into doorways and stumbled between great marble statues.

As she waited for the operator to connect her, Janeth worked to ease her breathing. She reminded herself this had always been a possibility. Her uncle had told her about the nature of this business when she'd moved in. She had always known it could come to this. She had never thought it ever really would.

Making the choice to live with the most prominent bootlegger in southern California had given her a lot. It gave her a home she could have only dreamed about as a child. It gave her money. It gave her security.

Now, all of that lay on the precipice of being stripped away, gathering into a desperate pool of blood on the other side of her home.

In the hum of the phone, Janeth tightened her grip on the telephone base. She determined then and there that she wouldn't let this life slip away. This couldn't be it. She'd come too far, been through too much, for this to be the end. No, she decided as the physician's voice came through the line. No matter what, she wasn't going to let this go.

CHAPTER ONE

San Diego, California, 1925

"Alice Covington?"

"Present." Alice hurried forward, the toe of her worn heel catching on a day-old newspaper, half-crumpled and dirty as it tumbled across the sidewalk. She caught the date among the smudged black print: May 11, 1925. She scooted between a pair of young women studying pamphlets as a series of cars sped down the street to her right.

The woman who had called her name—a matronly lady whom Alice thought could be anywhere between forty and sixty—frowned down her sharp nose. The small knot of dark gray hair on her head reminded Alice of a bird's nest with a single egg. She was surprised the woman didn't wear a hat. Besides being a fine deterrent from the bright California sun, it was still quite fashionable for women to wear one. Not that Alice would dub herself fashionable, but she tried to pay attention to the storefronts and magazines. She reached to her own periwinkle blue cloche hat as if to reassure herself it was still there. Then she nervously fiddled with the end of her bob haircut peeking out beneath it and gave the woman a smile. "Yes, that's me. I'm Alice."

The woman lifted her chin higher, her frown deepening. Dark eyes narrowed. "Age?"

"Twenty-four." The woman's eyes flickered to Alice's ungloved hands. Quickly, she added, "My father dropped me off earlier this morning." Behind her, the other girls tittered amongst themselves. The lie seemed to satisfy the matron. Alice had seen the other women dropped off by their husbands or fathers when she'd trudged her way into downtown from the railway yard three miles away just after dawn. Her parents had told her where to find this group. After two weeks of scouring the papers and posters plastered to telegraph poles, this had been the one: a young women's group gathering to preach on the corners of San Diego's busiest streets.

"The Young Woman's Holy League," her mother had called them, one of many groups that had sprouted out of the Temperance Movement since the implementation of Prohibition five years prior. They were groups determined to eradicate America's deadliest enemy from its shelves. These groups also received ample funds from the well-to-dos of big cities to fund their rallies and conventions. Thus, they were the perfect next target for Alice and her parents.

Alice hadn't wanted to go this morning when her father had stumbled into her room, calling out that it was time for her to leave. Alice had been dog-tired. Her mother and father had been up all night with new friends in the room next to hers, drinking and dancing until sunup. Now, they were asleep, passed out in bed, and here she was, stifling a yawn as she realized the old woman was looking for a wedding band on her finger.

She harrumphed when she didn't find one. "Take this." She handed Alice a pamphlet, the one she'd seen the other women poring over. "Wait for further instructions after I check the other girls in."

Nodding, Alice scanned the large print on the manilla parchment above a giant cross hovering over half a sun. She recognized a few words: "street," "save," and "sin" among them. Hurrying to the back of the crowd, she chewed her lip as she worked to make out the rest.

The crowd of fifteen were all young women in similar outfits to Alice's: knee-length gingham dresses with either checked patterns or solid pastels with large, white, flat collars. They wore low, dark-colored heels that had a strap running across the top of their stockinged feet. Alice's stockings featured a tear on the back of her left thigh, and she tugged at the hem of her dress to make sure it was covered. She had high hopes that her new hat helped her look the part, despite her dress being several years out-of-date.

A conversation to her right caught her ear:

"Mary, how did you convince me to be part of this?" Alice glanced sideways to find a young woman with fair skin and mud-brown hair cut into a stylish bob standing coolly with one hand on her hip as she read the open pamphlet. Her heart-shaped face featured strong cheekbones. "I can think of ten different ways to spend my weekday rather than standing in this heat to…what are we doing, exactly?"

Alice raised a brow, then slid her gaze to the brooch on the woman's yellow jacket. It shimmered in the sunlight, and Alice quickly determined it was lovely but not real garnet. She turned her attention to the other woman—Mary—as she drifted closer to listen.

"It's what everyone at church is doing. We couldn't *not* come." Mary appeared the opposite to her companion both in demeanor and looks as she seemed to hide behind her pamphlet rather than peering out over the busy sidewalk where they stood at the cross streets of Broadway and Columbia. Her blue eyes seemed dazed by the red streetcar that ambled past. "We have to fight the evil within our city, Dorothy. What would the others think if we didn't join?"

Dorothy rolled her eyes, then leaned closer, adding behind a raised hand, "I hear there will be a young gentleman's group here every other Thursday."

Mary turned, seemingly startled. "Gentlemen? But Dorothy…is that appropriate?"

At this, Dorothy gave her a gentle *thwap* with her pamphlet. "Come now, Mary. We're Daughters of the Holy League, not nuns."

Alice grinned. As the remaining young women were being checked in, she pretended to be studiously reading her pamphlet when she walked right into Mary.

"Oh, I do apologize," Mary said, looking alarmed.

"No apology needed. I'm a regular klutz with two left feet." Alice widened her grin, and Mary gave a sheepish smile, her freckled cheeks blushing as Dorothy stepped forward.

"How do you do? I'm Dorothy Martin." She paused, her head tilting slightly. "I don't recognize you." Alice noticed they were the same height, and both of their five-six frames seemed large compared to miniature Mary. Alice could see the top of her fine red hair half pinned behind her ears.

Alice focused on Dorothy, extending her hand. "How do you do? I'm Alice. I only just moved to San Diego a month ago from Oklahoma."

"Oklahoma." Mary whispered the word as if unsure it was proper to say. "Oh my."

Dorothy, meanwhile, looked amused. "This is Mary Wagner. How'd you hear about us?"

Alice frowned, then Dorothy gestured to the pamphlet. "Oh." The honest answer sprang to her mind first. *My mother has her sticky fingers in anything that can get us a quick buck.* But like always, she tampered the truth with a quick, easy lie. "My parents...well, my mother knows the matron." She hitched a thumb toward the old woman.

"Madame Enfield?"

"They're friends from girlhood."

Mary nodded, seemingly enraptured. Alice wondered if she wasn't a bit dim or simply sheltered to the ways of the world. Dorothy, meanwhile, seemed to scrutinize her. Sensing a string of questions readying themselves, she spoke quickly to move the conversation along. "Hard to believe the old bird was ever as young as us."

Mary went wide-eyed again and covered her mouth to stifle a laugh, throwing her gaze to Dorothy at the remark. Alice knew it wasn't proper to say such things, but something about Dorothy told her she could get away with it. Dorothy's sly smile confirmed this.

"That is a truth if I've heard one." Dorothy gestured for Alice to follow. "Come on. She's about to show us our spots for the day." Mary giggled and looped her arm through Alice's.

"I'm so glad to know you, Alice," Mary said, glancing around furtively as if making a new friend was an entirely scandalous thing to do on a Monday morning.

Well, it might as well be, Alice mused. Mary bumped her with her hip as they moved through the crowd, and the accidental gesture sent a flare of panic through her chest. She glanced over her shoulder, a sense of doom hitting her like the bright sun, making her dizzy. She spotted her mother in the doorway of the corner store, watching, and Alice's heart sank. Quickly, she smiled at Mary and pulled her arm away, pretending to dissect the pamphlet once again. Another look over her shoulder saw the storefront awning flicker, revealing a woman who looked nothing like her mother. It was only a trick of the light. Exhaling, Alice shook the uncertainty from her shoulders and followed her new friends to the front of the group.

CHAPTER TWO

It's a pleasure, as always, Mrs. Castro, to do business with you." Mr. Aldridge bowed, the shiny circle of skin atop his head gleaming beneath the overhanging oil lamps in his office. He kissed the top of her hand and replaced his hat.

Janeth smiled. Mostly in relief that his false teeth decided to remain inside his mouth today. Pulling her hand back, she said, "And to you, sir. Please give my regards to your wife, and thank her for the pineapple upside-down cake recipe. Mr. Mills found it to be absolutely exquisite."

He beamed, hands settling into the pockets below the high waist of his brown pants. They stood facing one another in his cramped office doorway. Behind him, customers milled about the front of his drug store, and snippets of conversations drifted in the background.

"How is the old chap these days?" Mr. Aldridge frowned thoughtfully, pulling out his pocket watch to glance at the date. "It's been some time since I've seen him."

"Oh, he's fine, thank you kindly for asking. I'm more than happy to run these errands for him. He's so busy keeping the books and things, as you might imagine." He nodded knowingly, and Janeth added, "A man like him shouldn't be bothered with daily chores."

Mr. Aldridge smiled. "He's lucky to have you, my dear." A store clerk called to him from behind a counter lined with brown-tinted bottles of varying shapes and sizes. Janeth started for the office door as he said, "Pardon me, I'd better see to that. Thank you again."

"I'll see you in a month. Glad to know Hugh was timely in his deliveries once again." They both glanced at the corner of his office where a crate held paper-wrapped bread loaves packed tightly in neat stacks, each one hollowed out to host a slim bottle of rum. They shared a knowing smile, and Janeth folded the banknote he had handed her, carefully slipping it into her handbag. She followed him through the store toward the street. A slender woman with an auburn bob tucked beneath her hat eyed her curiously. "What a lovely hat," Janeth said, careful to enunciate clearly.

The woman seemed surprised at first, then smiled. "Why, that is kind of you to say."

Outside, Janeth breathed deeply, a sense of satisfaction settling in her chest. The woman's inquisitive gaze, however, lingered in her mind. She glanced at the store window, checking her reflection to see if her hair had fallen loose. Finding everything in place, she sighed and brushed her fingers through her dark bangs. It was the same reason they always stare, she reminded herself.

The streetcar ambled around the corner. She hurried to the designated loading spot located outside the tall, brick-lined First Bank of California a block away to catch it. Downtown absolutely bustled with people today. She didn't blame everyone for being out on a day like this as she navigated rows of folks strolling easily in opposite directions on the sidewalk. It was another gorgeous day in southern California, something she had been glad to learn was a regular occurrence upon moving here. Though her hometown of San Ignacio in Durango, Mexico, received more rainfall, the generally temperate climate and sunny skies had become like an old, much needed friend when she'd arrived alone five years ago.

Storefronts had their doors open, merchants greeting customers jovially as ladies in fine dresses and gentlemen in suits with shiny leather shoes accompanied them. Most of the men downtown reminded her of her uncle, Mr. Mills, or younger versions of him she'd seen in photographs. Like her uncle, money seemed to waft off these men like their heady colognes. She'd grown accustomed to keeping company with such people since taking over deals for her uncle. Still, seeing everyone out and about, spending money willy-nilly—like the woman she'd skirted past being trailed by a pageboy hidden behind half a dozen hat boxes—reminded her this hadn't always been her world. Part of her wondered if she could really claim it, even now.

She climbed onto the streetcar at Kettner Boulevard and settled onto a seat, passing men in morning suits with wide trouser legs below a variety of brown, black, and blue single-breasted jackets covering vests and pressed white shirts. Each one wore either a bowler hat or a fedora. The women wore knife-pleated skirts that fell past their knees, all with low heels adorning feet delicately crossed at the ankle. Their blouses were brightly colored to match their skirts, featuring wide sleeves that fell to their biceps. Nearly all wore their hair cropped short in line with the latest fashion trend. Again, Janeth brushed her hand through her curled bangs, suddenly aware of how long her hair still fell when she let it out of its pins at night.

An old woman with white hair and strong perfume looked her up and down from the seat across the aisle. Janeth ran a hand over her belt, then reached up to her pearl drop earrings. She smiled, then turned her attention to the street as the car started south.

She mentally went through her to-do list as the other passengers chatted amongst themselves or read the paper. All three client visits had been successful. Hugh, her assistant and the nephew of Mr. Mills, had made deliveries the day before to each of the men she'd spoken with today, bottles of Mexican tequila and rum enclosed clandestinely within hollowed loaves of bread or bottles labeled as various tonics. Once she was home, the banknotes in her handbag would join the others in the safe near the accounting ledger in her uncle's office. *Her office, really.* She noted that she still needed to visit Mr. Cadena, but she could do that after dropping by her brother's store first.

A police officer directing traffic raised his hand at the next cross street, and the streetcar paused to let a horse-drawn cart pass. They were at the corner of Broadway and Columbia Street when a raucous chorus of voices drew Janeth's attention away from the two- and three-story business buildings.

A group of maybe fifteen young women huddled near the edge of the sidewalk. One woman held a makeshift wooden cross high over her head. Many of the others simply raised their open hands skyward as if in praise. One particularly tiny redhead held a basket out for passersby to drop money into as the group shouted in unison: "Save your souls! Just say no!" A hand-painted sign held staunchly by a matronly woman pictured a liquor bottle smeared with an angry red slash.

Janeth watched them until the streetcar mercifully rumbled on. The older woman on the streetcar tossed a coin to the group, which the redhead quickly snatched up for the donation basket. Janeth frowned, shaking her head. More and more of these groups were popping up around the city. The Temperance Movement was like a hydra; as soon as one group dispersed due to lack of funding, two more popped up in its place.

Don't they know abstinence rarely works? She reached up, feeling the fine material of her dress below her neckline. Beneath it, she found the end of her necklace and the raised edge of her thin gold cross. Old memories of Victor drifted to the front of her mind. The two of them ran together outside, stumbling over one another in her family's field. The sun was warm on her skin, and she recalled the gentle lilt of Victor's infectious laughter, the playful shine to his eyes. Closing hers, Janeth replayed the time from her youth. The time that had felt magical and unparalleled when she was sixteen and utterly in love.

The streetcar jerked forward as it turned down the next road, shaking Janeth into the present. No, she thought as the memory disappeared with the sounds of the Temperance group behind her. *People will always find a way to the things they crave.* This was something Mr. Mills had known when the laws had changed and Prohibition came into effect. People wanted what they always had, no matter the attempt at keeping it out of their hands. She and her uncle were more than happy to be the ones to meet their demands.

The Daughters of the Prohibition movement could protest all they wanted. Janeth wouldn't let them stop her. She had a bootlegging business to run.

CHAPTER THREE

At midday, Daughters of the Holy League had been preaching on the streets of downtown San Diego for five hours. Alice's feet ached from standing so long, and her throat was hoarse from all the chanting. Not to mention, she was starved. Dorothy, too, seemed ready to call it a day—huffing in annoyance between hymns—when Madame Enfield gave a long whistle and called them to congregate.

"What a feeling," Mary said, smiling like she'd just stepped out of a fast-moving car, her breath quick and her cheeks flushed.

"It certainly was busy," Alice replied, eyeing the small basket of coins and banknotes Mary held. Several of the other girls added their own collections to the basket before bidding good-bye to the matron.

"I could go for lunch. You girls want to join me? I'm meeting my women's group for tea over at Baley's Café on Third Avenue." Dorothy fanned herself with a handkerchief and turned to Alice. "You a supporter of suffrage, Oklahoma?"

A faint warmth hit Alice in her chest at the nickname. "Of course. Men shouldn't have all the fun." Dorothy smiled approvingly as she adjusted her hat. Meanwhile, Mary counted the donations. Despite the grumble in her stomach, Alice added, "I can't today, though. I promised my parents I'd help them unload the rest of our furniture that arrived from the move."

A frown turned down Dorothy's face before she shrugged. "That's good of you. Another time, then."

Alice nodded, glad her new friend didn't see the lie in her words. Her family didn't own more than what they could carry on their backs and never had. Dorothy turned to speak to the matron, and before Mary could do the same, Alice grabbed her by the elbow. "I can take that for you, Mary."

"Oh, but I was just finishing counting." She stared at a five-cent piece, then dropped it among the others. "I don't remember where I left off."

Smiling, Alice gently pulled the basket from her. "I'll recount for you. I'm a bit of a whiz with numbers. Besides, I imagine you want to get along with Dorothy."

Blinking, Mary looked around, her mouth open in surprise to see her friend across the street, waving at her. "Oh, well, yes. Thank you, Alice." She pulled her into a hug. Alice stiffened as Mary said, "It's so nice to make your acquaintance. I do hope to see you again," before she scurried away.

A handful of girls were still speaking to Madame Enfield about the next meeting—Alice heard mention of next Saturday in a place called Seaside—when she spotted the matron peering over their heads, no doubt in search of the final collection basket. Quickly, Alice waved to her. Then, as a trio of older gentlemen walked past on the sidewalk, she dropped the basket, giving an exaggerated "Oh," as the contents spilled out.

One of the men bent to assist her, and she added a layer of saccharine to her voice when she said, "Oh no, thank you, I've got it. Silly me." He harrumphed and continued. Keeping her back to the matron, Alice gathered the money, except for six coins she tucked inside the side wall of her shoe and a five-dollar banknote she shoved down her blouse, tucking it into her bra. She was careful to match each movement with the legs of passersby.

She hurried over to Madame Enfield, panting. "I'm sorry, the basket slipped. I found it all, though." She shook the basket to prove her point, the coins jingling among the paper notes. "Looks like we did well."

Madame Enfield took the basket, the cynical look she'd worn all day still firmly on her face. "Yes. We live to spread the word of God another day." She squinted, looking from the money to Alice.

Feeling uncomfortable, Alice turned to go. "Have a nice day, matron." She shoved her hands into her pockets and dove into the crowd, eager to disappear.

❖

The walk back to the railroad yard seemed longer than it had in the early morning hours. Once she was several blocks away from the picket site downtown, Alice ducked into an alley and moved the coins from her shoes to her dress pockets. The satisfying chink of the metal was like a song as she continued north, then east through the streets. She pictured the tattered cigar box beneath her bed, hidden inside the old suitcase she'd brought here. With today's earnings, she'd have nearly twenty dollars saved up since she'd started her own stash two years ago.

A man in a fedora tossed his lunch bag into a wastebasket outside a sundry store. She slowed and, checking her surroundings, dashed her hand in to fetch the brown paper sack. Sniffing the fried crust of the half-eaten fishcake, she muttered, "Better than nothing," and scarfed it down.

Later, the rumble of a distant train shook the ground beneath her feet as she ran across the line of tracks. The first row of shanties— small rooms built of plywood and sheets of tin or scrap metal—stood like wayward vagabonds on the inland side of the railyard. Most of the people residing here were like Alice: new to town and uncertain what the future held. It was a feeling she knew well.

The third row of homes beyond the tracks was more substantial. Many of them were run-down, fort-style buildings left behind from original rail workers. Most were plain-looking, with cracked windows atop unkempt plots of land. She headed into the fourth one on the opposite side of a dirt road, across from a dilapidated shelter where a scruffy dog chased two small children, both cackling with glee in the weed-filled lawn. She pushed inside the door of the latest place she called home.

The stench of stale cigarettes and beer hit her like a slap to the face.

"Alice, there you are." Her mother sat at the beige card table propped near an old stove, a long cigarette poised in her hand and a shining coat of red on her nails. The polish sat next to a bottle of Coca-Cola sweating beside an ashtray already half-full. Smoke hovered above the oil lamp in the table's center. The larger window behind her was cracked open, though no breeze blew through to relieve the stuffy air inside.

"Hello, Mother." Alice hung her hat on a nail jammed into the wall next to the door. The window next to it was dirt-smudged, a small circle cleared to let in faint sunlight.

"Hiya, Dumplin'," her father called from the corner where a twin bed had been arranged. He stood before a low vanity, a hand-sized mirror hanging above it. Shaving cream was lathered on half his face and down his neck when he turned to face her, an old razor in his left hand. He'd already done his hair; Alice caught a whiff of the pomade that helped to part his thick sandy locks down the middle, tugging the strands back and pressing them flat behind his ears.

Alice smiled and started for her room, a ten-by-seven extension of the one she stood in but with no window. She was imagining being able get out of her shoes when her mother's chair scraped along the hard floor. She was in front of Alice in a flash, forcing her to a halt a few paces from the doorway as she stood with one hand on her slender hip. To anyone else, she looked casual, relaxed. But Alice saw how calculated her posture was, how her cocked hip cut Alice's pathway.

"How was the holy girls' group?"

"It was fine." Alice shot a look to the corner where her father was cleaning off his face. He pulled suspenders over broad shoulders clad in a clean white undershirt. Her mother, meanwhile, took a long drag from her cigarette, looking down at Alice, her hazel eyes narrowed.

Her mother was beautiful. A strange fact, since Alice deemed her mother one of the most conniving people alive. A mismatch, perhaps, in the grand design of things. Or perhaps her mother had figured out early how much she could get just from her looks and hadn't seen a need to be particularly kind. Alice had always thought her mother could have been a stage or even screen star. "Margaret Covington" popped easily into her mind, the name in bright lights on a theatre marquee. Though her mother had never spoken of any such dreams, Alice wondered if she'd had the chance to get to California sooner in life, how things might have played out.

A diet of cigarettes and booze had kept her figure lithe, even at forty. A rose-colored negligee clung like it was made for her. Despite having only woken a short while ago, her short, curly hair—its shades of strawberry catching in the light—looked impeccable. Thin eyebrows arched over a perfect nose as pink lips took another long, thoughtful drag.

"Meet anyone interesting?" her father called, now working on tying his shoes. He looked like a well-to-do gentleman today, donning a textured cream sweater and wide-legged pants. Alice figured he was headed to the upper-crust beach towns on the coast or perhaps a betting room in the Gaslight District. John Covington, the clever chameleon who'd taught his daughter how to be anyone on any given day, as long as she wasn't herself.

Alice glanced from him to her mother. "Not really."

"No new friends?" Her mother stepped closer, smoke hitting Alice with each word.

She shook her head.

"Well, that's all right, Dumplin'." Her father tossed her a wink over her mother's shoulder, and Alice gave him a smile. The left side of his face lifted higher in a matching one, one of their many similar physical traits. "Crooked as the day you were born," her mother always said of their lopsided grins.

Again, Alice moved to go, but her mother didn't relent. She stepped back and reached an arm across the open doorway. She leaned against it, keeping Alice in front of her, a captive she wasn't done with yet. "Alice," she said, sighing before holding out her hand, palm up. Her gravelly voice slunk toward her, unhurried. "You didn't come back empty-handed, did you?"

Alice shifted. The cigarette smoke snaked into her nostrils, burning like the feeling in her mind. Her mother stared, the embers on the end of her cigarette flaring when she lifted it to her mouth.

Her father moved to the table, snatching a bite of bacon. Alice noted the smell of eggs between tendrils of smoke. She was certain only scraps were left in the frying pan. From behind them, he said encouragingly, "You know the drill, Dumplin'."

Clenching her jaw, Alice dug into her pocket. She dropped the fistful of change into her mother's waiting hand. When she gestured to the other pocket, Alice only stared back as she handed the separate stash of coins over.

"That's our girl," her father said, his voice laced with pride and what sounded like relief as her mother moved to hand him the money.

Dejected, she unclenched the fist that had tightened at her side. "I'm going to change," she said.

In the doorway, so close to the quiet and freedom of her room, her mother called, "Wait."

Closing her eyes, Alice froze. She took a slow breath, then turned. "Yes?"

Her mother's lips lifted in a smile, though it was the smile of a cat eager to pounce upon cornered prey. Alice felt small as her mother walked toward her, a sense of pleasure seeming to grow on her face with each measured step. "John, dear. Our daughter is trying to pull one over on us."

Her father looked up from the coins stacked neatly on the table. "Dumplin'?"

Her mother's eyes were bright now, eager with flares of red like the end of that godforsaken cigarette. "Hand it over now, sweetheart."

It felt like her stomach leapt into her throat. Alice hated this, hated how shrewd and unrelenting her mother was. Those same qualities had kept them alive when times were anything but easy, but the older Alice got, the more that fire was directed at her. She knew the watchful eye locked on her had to do with what had happened in Oklahoma. Still, she hated it. Whatever crumb of peace or prosperity Alice found for herself, it was only minutes before her mother swooped in, claiming it as her own. Clenching her jaw, Alice held her gaze, fighting back the lump of tears gathering in her throat.

Reluctantly, she reached into the neck of her dress and found the banknote. Her mother took it, studying it. She ran the edge beneath her nose, inhaling. A satisfied look filled her porcelain face. Then, as if remembering Alice was there, that happiness dissipated, the rouged cheeks pulled into a steely look. She quirked her head to the side, waving the note. "You know, Alice, I saw the dress you had torn from that catalogue on the train ride in to town. The red one with a wide neckline."

The sense of doom that had settled over her was pierced as Alice recalled the beautiful way the dress had fit the model in the magazine. She had determined she would save up for it, along with the matching hat, hoping to have enough before they went out of style or weren't manufactured anymore.

Her mother was still talking. "I had popped into a little shop on

Seventh Street last night." She strolled to the corner opposite the bed behind the card table where a skinny wardrobe stood, faded cherry blossoms evident on the old wooden doors. It had been left behind by the previous tenants. Her mother reached in, then pulled out the dress Alice had been daydreaming about. "And what do you know, there it was."

Alice stepped forward. *It couldn't be.* She smiled, her head swimming. "Mother, I—"

"I saw it, and well, I just had to try it on. Turns out," she added slowly, "it fits me like a glove." Her mother looked from the soft, vibrant material of the shift dress to her. "You know how much I love red, Alice dear."

The words stuck in her throat. Alice blinked, a feeling like she'd been punched making her dizzy as her mother held the dress up to herself. She gave a twirl, humming. Alice watched her for a time as she spun, giddy as any young girl. The burning in her mind returned. She wasn't sure how she didn't scream as her mother grinned at her father, who nodded, oblivious.

She forced herself to turn away. Her mother laughed as Alice hurried into her room, the dark corners of the space pulling her into its grasp.

When she glanced over her shoulder, her father's head was down as he counted the coins. He didn't seem to even know what had just transpired between his wife and daughter. Her mother was dancing now, singing some jingle from the radio, ash from her cigarette nearly singing the end of the dress. Alice found the door and, with every ounce of energy she had, quietly closed it.

On the other side, her mother's laughter echoed.

CHAPTER FOUR

A fter switching streetcars at Imperial Avenue, Janeth sat back on the wooden seat, reminding herself to relax while the shifting landscape rolled by as she rode farther south toward Logan Heights, Barrio Logan to local residents. The multistory buildings of downtown fell behind her, and the land opened in wide swaths of patchwork neighborhoods. Streets broadened, and the business fronts became less refined but more welcoming as family-owned stores splashed with bright colors dotted the coastal desert that scraped over this part of the county.

Fewer cars drove past, and men and women walked at a leisurely pace compared to downtown. At this point, she was only one of four people left on the streetcar as it slowed to a stop at the corner of Logan Heights's main street. A man around her age in a flat cap bid good afternoon to her before hurrying past. Two women, maybe in their late twenties like her, spoke to one another in Spanish. Their dresses weren't as modern as her own but still lovely. Their raven hair caught the sunlight.

She stood and let them pass toward the front of the car, calling, "Good day," in Spanish. Both of them turned, their eyes wide. The shorter of the two looked from Janeth's rouged cheeks to her fine hat before seeming to gather herself and replied in kind.

Janeth waited an extra few seconds before following them out of the streetcar. She thanked the driver, then stepped onto the newly paved street. All around her, the sounds of Barrio Logan rang out. Livestock sang a never-ending cacophony behind ranch-style homes plastered with white stucco and vibrant tiled roofs. The steady clop of mules marched along the edges of the street. Spanish flowed between each building like a river.

She waved to an older gentleman coming out of her sister-in-law's family market, though she couldn't recall his name. Pretending to look at something in her handbag, she passed him and ducked into the store. "Elena, you're supposed to be with your brother. Get away from there." Janeth's sister-in-law, Maria, flew out from the back room, her deep blue skirt kicking up to reveal low heels. A flowing yellow blouse with sleeves that fell to her elbows revealed tan forearms. Her dark eyes quickly found the two dark heads that were her children scurrying out from behind a trio of barrels near the edge of the storefront.

"Mama, can I have a mango?" Janeth's seven-year-old niece, Elena, asked as she reached for the piece of fruit, already determined to secure the sweet treat.

Her mother grabbed the fruit before she could and gently led her toward the back of the store. "Only if you keep your brother behind the counter."

"Jorge, this way." Elena took her brother's tiny hand before he could reach over into the barrel of pinto beans. His four-year-old stature made it a difficult task. At the same time, Maria clucked her tongue as she swept her gaze over the produce stands. "And what happened to the dragon fruit?" she asked. "It looks like someone tried to swim in it."

Janeth was about to say hello when Maria—still wrangling her children—called over her shoulder, "Hi, Janeth, love. Give me one minute while I collect these little monsters."

"We're not monsters, Mama," Elena protested, reaching for the mango still in her mother's hand.

From an open door that led to the delivery room behind the store, Janeth's younger brother, Leo, emerged. "And what is this I hear about little monsters roaming my store?"

"Your store?" Janeth teased. "Here I thought Mr. Martinez was the owner."

Leo scooped up Jorge before he could scurry back to the front. Elena stood patiently as her mother inspected the mango, then handed it to her. In English, he said, "I'm assistant manager now, sister, didn't you hear?"

Janeth passed the floor-to-ceiling shelves on the right side of the store, each one packed tight with glass jars hosting colorful spices. "Is that right? I had forgotten since you told me yesterday. And the week before that."

"Don't forget the week before that, too," Maria called from the back room before she reappeared with a bag of lentils. She and Janeth exchanged grins as she refilled the barrel among the other dry beans near the opposite side of the store.

Leo shook his head, but his dark eyes twinkled. He made Jorge, wiggling in his arms, face him and said seriously, "Can you believe them? We're outnumbered, my boy. It's us against these women."

Elena licked her lips, mango juice already on her chin. "I'm a girl, Papa."

He gasped, wide-eyed. "A girl? My, you are right. Pardon me, miss," he said, then bowed, making Jorge cackle with glee. Elena giggled behind her bite of mango. Setting Jorge down, he added, "All right, you two. I have a very important job. Head to the back and help me count the bags of flour."

"Yes, Papa." Elena grabbed her brother's hand and tugged him behind her.

"I don't know how to count past twenty," whined Jorge.

"No time like the present to learn." Leo watched them go, smoothing the green apron he wore over a long-sleeve white button-down and black pants. Janeth leaned against the wooden counter that stretched across the modest corner store. A two-by-two portion had been cut out for them to pass through.

"They look more and more like you every day, Maria," Janeth said, adjusting her handbag on the counter and nodding toward her niece and nephew.

Leo winked. "Thank God for that. Can you imagine this nose on their little faces?" He turned in profile, sticking out his strong chin to exaggerate his features.

"You always think your nose is like a bird," Maria said, moving past and giving him a bump of her hip. "And your ears like an elephant."

Janeth pursed her lips to keep from laughing. Her brother's features were larger than her own, his dark brown hair was often slicked back with oil; doing so could make his ears look bigger than they were. His large nose he'd inherited from their father. His wide, expressive eyes also didn't seem to match his otherwise slight build. Their parents had always hoped his stature would fill in with the physical work on their land growing up, but Leo was destined to be slender. He'd been self-conscious of this when they were younger, but moving to San Diego and meeting, then marrying, Maria had settled any anxieties he felt about his appearance. She was quite beautiful, Janeth thought, and kept her silly brother in line most days.

"I see your eyes in Elena," Maria said to her, sidling up to Leo on the other side of the counter and exhaling sharply to kick some of the hair from her face. She'd cut it to fall just above her shoulders, the thick brown strands curling in toward her delicate chin that accentuated her round features well. "They got our complexion, though. Eternally sun-kissed."

Janeth smiled but quickly said, "I've got some new inventory." She pulled out a slip of paper from her handbag. "These are last week's numbers."

Leo unfolded the paper, a thoughtful line settling in his brow. Maria continued in Spanish despite Janeth conversing in English. "All business you are today."

"It's been busy. I need to get back to Mr. Mills before sundown."

"How is the generous benefactor these days?" Maria asked, checking over her shoulder to see Elena and Jorge plopped atop flour bags in the store room.

"The same. The doctors say bed rest is still needed. He gets out for a walk now and then, but he remains in some pain."

The front door swung open. At the same time, a car backfired on the street. Janeth jumped and for a moment was back in the library, running to her uncle, a fresh gunshot wound in his hip.

"He's lucky he's alive." Leo was still looking over the numbers and had found a stubby pencil to make adjustments. Maria pressed a hand to his arm before going to help the gentleman who walked in and was eyeing the peppers. "And he's lucky to have you stepping in to run things."

"I can handle most of the runners who deliver things. But Raymond." She closed her eyes and took a breath. "I loathe each time I see him."

Leo glanced up, sympathy in his gaze. He knew as well as Janeth that after what had transpired eighteen months ago, Seaside had their eyes on her uncle's mansion. Mr. Mills had needed to stay home to recover. Police couldn't know the reason for his injury. They'd had to make up a story of intruders. Janeth had felt embarrassed as she'd lied about how she'd left a back door open before retiring for the night. The fact that nothing was stolen and the purported intruders were somehow scared off by a young woman and an old man was far from convincing. It was Mr. Mill's standing in the community—Uncle, as she'd come to call him—that helped quell gossip. Still, she heard the whispers. Rum smuggling was common all along the coast these days. She only hoped Raymond's visits continued like they had since: uneventful in every way.

"He's overcharging for the product," her brother said, pulling Janeth back to the present.

"Raymond? I know. Do you want to have that conversation with him?"

He snorted. "Only after you give him a piece of your mind first." He winked.

"That would be something." She pondered the image of telling Raymond exactly what she thought about him. "One day, maybe."

"One day." Leo scratched out one of the numbers she'd written at the bottom of her page. "You missed a couple things. This is the actual income for last week." He turned the paper so she could read it.

Her eyebrows went up. "Not bad."

"Not bad at all."

"Considering the protests are gaining in numbers."

"The Prohibitionists? They're just a bunch of uptight women who need other things to occupy their time."

"I don't disagree," she replied, remembering the protest she saw earlier today.

He straightened, hands in his pockets, wearing an impressed look. "Well, they're not doing any harm to these numbers." He added, "You must also have a knack for charming the white men of San Diego."

She scoffed and shot him a look. The way his eyes seemed unfocused, more like they were seeing through her, gave her pause. Ever since she'd taken this position with Mr. Mills, she'd sensed her brother had more to say about the situation than he was letting on. While he'd been the first one to encourage her to move in with Mr. Mills, something about the way he talked about him, and the other people she did business with, contained an undercurrent. A tinge laced his words that Janeth couldn't pinpoint.

She took the paper back. "I do all right. My customers are people like you and me."

Maria joined them, the gentleman she had helped gone. "We all may be people, but there is a difference between us."

Janeth turned, surprised at her apparent knowledge of their conversation.

"Those men and women you sell to on the other side of downtown are not the same as us."

Discomfort tickled Janeth's shoulders, but she kept a smile on her face. "Silly me. Here I thought I sold the same products to you as I did to Mr. Jamison in La Jolla." She swallowed. "We all seem to want the same thing these days, do we not?"

Leo gave a chuckle—perhaps to break the tension—when Maria placed a hand on her hip. "We? And which side of we do you fall on, Janeth?"

She held Maria's gaze. She clenched her jaw and pulled herself up taller. "The side that is doing what is best for me and for my family." She articulated the last part carefully in Spanish, her tongue less familiar with the language these days.

"Family." Maria looked at her a moment more, then her face relaxed. "Of course."

"Well," Leo said, moving to usher Janeth toward the front. She didn't miss the look he gave Maria as he said, "We have the delivery from your young man in the back. There are a lot of events coming up here, baptisms, weddings. I'm sure we can move the supply quickly."

"Good." Janeth let him lead her out the door. She was as eager to get away from Maria as he seemed to be. Outside, they both took a breath. Nearby, an older man readied his mule and cart packed tight with bushels of tomatoes. The streetcar ambled to a stop at the opposite corner.

Her brother gave an apologetic smile. "You know Maria means no harm."

Janeth exhaled. "I know."

"Her sister had an incident last week," he added, lowering his voice and tossing a furtive gaze to passersby. "She was working in Coronado, helping at the hotel, when a couple of white men approached her."

A sinking feeling pit itself in Janeth's stomach. "Did they…"
He shook his head. "No. It was only words, thank God, but it left her shaken."
"Of course." She nodded. The sinking feeling turned into a tightness in her chest. She knew the risks anyone with darker skin ran in mixing with white society. She also understood Maria's thoughts on her position among those people. Janeth bit her lip, uncertain whether to feel angry at her sister-in-law or guilty at her ability to drift between worlds with ease.

Her brother reached out, rubbing her arm. A group of women greeted him, then hurried into the store. "Well, I better get back." He started to go, then added, "It's nice to have you here, Janeth. The kids love seeing you. You should come by again next week."

She nodded but was already thinking about the days ahead as she tried to shake off the unease from her brother's story. There was a visit from the physician for her uncle, the appointments to follow up on deliveries, and Raymond loomed on the horizon with the next shipment. "I'll try."

He smiled. Then, seeming to remember something, his face fell. "Janeth, I completely forgot. I'm sorry."

She had waved to the streetcar that she was on her way when she turned. "Sorry?"

He stepped closer, pulling her into a hug. "It's been seven years. Yesterday, right?" She stood awkwardly for a moment, trying to understand. "I miss him, too."

Victor. The memory washed over her like the tall waves that crashed into the cliffs each night. "Oh yes." She hugged him back, blinking over his shoulder. "Thank you, Leo."

He let her go, giving her one last reassuring look before disappearing into the store.

On the streetcar, she sat in a daze the entire ride toward the coast. Seven years. Could it be? Reaching up, she felt for the cross beneath her dress and closed her eyes. Heaviness dug into her limbs. That same heaviness had lessened so much since his death. She felt like herself more often than not these days. And now…

Janeth's eyes flew open. Two things startled her simultaneously, and she wasn't sure which was more alarming: the fact that she had forgotten the date or that losing her husband didn't hurt like it once had.

CHAPTER FIVE

The next Saturday, Alice found her way to Seaside with the Daughters of the Holy League. She'd donned her nicest spring dress, a coral-colored piece that fell straight from shoulders to calf. If anyone looked closely, they'd note the uneven stitching along the waist and bust where her mother had let it out as Alice had gotten older. She had nabbed her mother's brown belt from the wardrobe while she'd slept and decided a white hat would do to match her shoes. Her father had approved the outfit as he scoured the papers on her way out the door, scarfing down a stale bread crust.

As she descended the trolley they'd taken from downtown to the coast, the wind whirled vigorously, pulling strands of hair across her face. Dorothy was answering her earlier question as their group gathered on the sidewalk.

"It's not that I mind coming to these. My church supports the movement, and as a member..." She gave a wry smile, then lowered her voice. "All I'm saying is, I do enjoy a glass of wine now and then. And my husband loves his sherry." She sighed, shooting a look to Madame Enfield trudging down the train car steps behind them. "I simply wish the church would throw their support into the Suffrage Movement as much as they do Temperance."

Alice nodded but was distracted by the dazzling glimmer that seemed to shimmer off every surface in Seaside. She blinked, raising her hand to shield her eyes from the glare. The hillside they stood on looked out over paved streets that sloped steadily downward toward the beach. She and her father had wandered to the water when they'd first arrived in San Diego, and Alice had been in awe then, too. The feeling remained as her eyes adjusted, and she stood slack-jawed as the waves crested, running up to the shoreline dotted with people in their bathing suits, sporadic umbrellas opened wide and sunk into the sand for loungers seeking a shady reprieve.

"Oklahoma, you comin'?" Dorothy was several feet away, standing with Mary. Madame Enfield turned to eye her. She snapped out of it and hurried to follow the group to the beach.

They wound down the road a quarter mile toward a boardwalk. "Seaside boardwalk is famous," Mary told her as they gathered around to listen to instructions next to an elaborate iron sign. It was held aloft by two sturdy poles set wider than a house, the arc of the letters running across it overhead reading "Seaside Carnival" in bold red. Beyond it, the boardwalk split into two trackways twenty yards apart that snaked toward the sand. Those trackways were intersected by two others, each wide enough to host tents that Alice presumed were the featured carnival attractions. To the right, just next to the far-right trackway, a modest-sized Ferris wheel spun lazily, its base nestled into the grassy stretch between the pavement and the sand. "Folks come here from all over just to ride that," Mary added, following Alice's gaze.

"That's where my husband asked for my hand three summers ago," Dorothy chimed in, nodding to the top car on the ride. A warm smile filled her face, and a pang hit Alice in her chest. A flash of Gladys sitting next to her on the park bench in Oklahoma City sprang up from the depths of her mind. Her dark hair had shone in the sun. Her lips had been the most perfect shade of red that day.

Shaking the memory away, Alice replied, "It's nice here."

"Ladies, your attention, please." Madame Enfield clapped, beckoning them closer. "We will work in shifts. Five of you take the west side, over near the bungalows along the cliffs. Five of you will stay here to catch folks wandering into the carnival. The rest will meander through, handing out pamphlets to those along the beach. We'll work in thirty-minute shifts, then rotate."

A scattering of "Yes, madam" rode through their group.

"We'll start on the beach," Dorothy called out, pulling Alice and Mary closer. She beckoned for two other girls to join them. Madame Enfield nodded, then turned to sort out the others.

"Come on, girls," Dorothy said to them under her breath. "I smell seasoned chestnuts, and I simply must have some."

"Wait. The pamphlets!" Mary hurried after her. The other two girls wandered toward the water, leaving Alice to follow. The wooden trackway creaked beneath her, and she peered between the planks to the sand several feet below. The sparse crowd on the beach ahead was surprising, but she figured it was still early, not even ten thirty. Several men passed her, heading back toward the street, hands in their trouser pockets. One walked with a cane landing easily at his side. A few children—boys in gray short pants and girls in lacy cotton dresses—sprinted by on their way to the water. A pair of young women in day dresses strolled, unhurried, after them beneath parasols.

Five large white tents were lined across the trackway running perpendicular to her path. She started past the first one where a tall, bearded man poured a slick-looking red syrup over a mound of shaved ice before handing it to a young woman in an orange swim dress. The next tent hosted another man, though this one was hardly taller than her with the voice of a giant. He tried to entice her into a ring toss game, dozens of glass bottles packed tight inside a large wooden crate. Alice smiled but knew how unlikely it was to win. She continued on.

At the third tent, she caught up to Dorothy. Mary was hurrying after their comrades, waving flyers after them. Both women seemed more interested in the young men in swim shorts wrestling one another near the water. "Care for any?" Dorothy asked, gesturing to the man shoveling roasted chestnuts into small paper bags.

Alice inhaled, the spices reminding her of the store she'd first met Gladys in. Reluctantly, she shook her head. "I forgot my pocket money today." She'd hoped to pickpocket a few folks after this event, already having spotted a few well-to-do looking gentlemen with wide jacket pockets rife for the taking.

"Nonsense," Dorothy said, waving for the man's attention. "It's my pleasure."

"Dorothy—"

"Oklahoma," she said sternly, though a lilt of playfulness lined her tone. "If we're going to be friends, it's best you know now: I refuse anyone's refusal to accept my gestures of payment. How are we as women supposed to move up in this world if we act like only men can pay for things?"

Alice grinned, accepting the bag of chestnuts offered to her. "I can't argue with that."

Nodding approvingly, Dorothy munched on her treat. Alice tossed several in her mouth, her stomach squirming in anticipation. She closed her eyes, relishing the sweet and savory combination.

Mary appeared, a worried look on her face. Sand stuck to her heels as she said, "Dorothy, I don't know what to do. Everybody I hand a pamphlet to either tosses it in a bin or starts using it to keep the warm air at bay." She demonstrated by fanning herself with one. Alice snorted, then glanced away at Mary's confused look.

"Oh, very well, then. Leave it to me." Dorothy sighed. "We'll see you over there, Oklahoma. You should take this in for a minute, being a first-timer and all." She winked, and Alice swelled with the notion of having a new friend in this place.

A shout from the Ferris wheel pulled her attention as the girls headed for the beach. Alice shielded her eyes to watch a pair of young women, maybe school-age, laugh and kick their feet as the car steadily moved skyward. She admired the way one of them held on to the other's forearm in anticipation of the ascent.

A captivating scent of lilac wafted past attached to a woman Alice spotted on the trackway. Her dark brown hair was styled in an underpin, gentle waves evident beneath the floral-patterned cloche hat that dipped lower on the left side of her face. She wore a powder blue blouse and matching skirt that fell just past her knees. Her stockings were sheer and ran into a pair of black low heels. The *clack* as they landed on the boardwalk hypnotized Alice, who could only stand and watch this woman walk to the final tent, a cotton candy stand.

It took the shine of a bracelet that the woman wore on her right wrist above a gloved hand to pull Alice from her stupor. She noticed the handbag next. Was it really silk? Alice scoffed. Only wealthy women would bring a silk handbag to the beach. Her heart skipped a beat when the woman set the handbag at her feet before leaning over the counter to speak to the man working behind it.

Alice glanced around. Dorothy and Mary were thirty yards down the beach. Behind her, the cliffside group was up the hill that hosted small, brightly painted bungalows overlooking the water. Turning, she spotted Madame Enfield near the fair's entrance with the third group.

She would have to be quick. She couldn't keep the handbag. Dorothy, surely, would notice she hadn't come with one. No problem, she decided, tucking the bag of chestnuts into her pocket and slowly walking along the opposite side of the trackway, analyzing the woman's position. She could swipe it, duck into a changing booth on the sand, snatch what she could, then replace the handbag before the woman even knew what had happened. She looked deep in conversation with the man, and their words were growing more heated. Alice couldn't quite make out what was being said, but the woman placed a hand on her hip. Again, Alice laughed. People with money would argue over anything, including a carnival confection.

She scanned her surroundings again. A group of young men were starting her way from the opposite end of the trackway. Slowly, she drew closer to the cotton candy stand. The man working it didn't seem to notice, still in conversation with the woman, who had her back to Alice.

Two feet away, Alice pretended to examine her shoe. She knelt close enough to the handbag that it was within arm's reach. The conversation above her was still heated. Briefly, she heard, "Mr. Preston, I must insist that Mr. Mills receive his payment today. We've been overly gracious with the deadline."

Alice fiddled with the strap of her heel. Glancing up, she found the line of the woman's stocking. She followed it up her calf and let her gaze linger on the hem of her skirt.

Focus, Alice. She forced her gaze to the handbag. As the woman continued to berate the man, she reached out and grabbed it, then hurried toward the end of the trackway just as the group of young men passed. She fell in behind them, easily taken for part of their group to anyone looking on. She pulled open the handbag. A dollar was folded near the top. She pulled it out and shoved it down her blouse.

The men took a right toward the Ferris wheel. Feeling pleased, she looked up only to collide with a troupe of sweaty, sand-covered college boys. They rushed over the trackway in two waves, the first running past her—through her, more like—as they shouted for the second to catch up. One of them collided with her shoulder, jostling her. She stumbled back, dropping the handbag. Another rammed into her, pushing her forward, and she turned, trying to keep an eye on her latest treasure. A sea of limbs and loud voices surrounded her until the boys moved on.

"Well, pardon me," she shouted after them in a huff, adjusting her hat and flattening her dress. She blew a strand of hair from her face, hoping they could feel the glare she leveled at the back of their heads as they wandered on, oblivious. She sighed, then recovered the handbag. As she straightened, though, she realized how empty the trackway was. Her body grew hot as she felt somebody watching her. Turning, she realized that the woman and the man behind the cotton candy stand were staring at her.

The woman lifted her chin, a concerned line between her arched brows that framed a stunning pair of deep brown eyes. Alice considered running. But she would have to explain to Dorothy why she had a handbag. Her mind spun with other options, all of which seemed ridiculous, and she cursed herself. Her mother's voice screamed in the back of her mind. *Rule number one: don't let the target see your face.*

"Miss, are you all right?"

Alice blinked. The woman was still watching her. Alice leaned sideways, her body in a war with itself on which direction to go. The carnival sounds seemed distant as the ocean and sky compounded, pressing down as a sudden tug pulled at her chest. She clutched it to quell the rapid beating of her heart.

"Miss?"

Alice gripped the handbag, though she was certain the woman had to have noticed it. Her gaze remained locked on Alice's face. What was happening? She had done this a hundred times. Perhaps the sun was getting to her, marring her vision and typically quick thinking. *Rule number two: never speak to the target.*

Alice replied, "I'm fine, thank you."

Dammit.

"You don't look fine." The woman seemed to hesitate. She turned to say something to the man, who seemed relieved to be through with whatever discussion they were having. The woman stepped closer. "Are you quite sure?"

Alice stepped back. Lilac hit her again, this time wrapped around the air in a breeze. The woman's light brown skin was touched with rouge on her prominent cheeks. Delicate-looking pearl earrings dangled from her earlobes. She was beautiful, and Alice couldn't stop herself before she presented the handbag between them. "Is this yours?"

The woman's eyes widened, her pink lips parting in surprise. She turned to the stand, looking at the spot where her handbag had been, then spun back to Alice. "Oh, well, yes. How did you—"

"I saw someone take it," Alice said quickly. She pointed down the trackway vaguely. "One of those boys. An easy prank is my guess. The fella ran into me, got scared, dropped it, and took off."

The woman listened, glanced around, then refocused on Alice. She seemed to contemplate the story for a moment, a slight tilt to her head as she frowned. Alice pulled herself up, noticing the dimple in the woman's chin. It was adorable.

Focus, Alice. Confidence was key in getting out of sticky situations. She'd already broken two rules. She needed to get away from this woman, who took back the handbag slowly.

"Well, I'm glad you were here." She smiled, her eyes still curious but brightening. Alice could only nod. She stepped back when the woman said, "You're sure you're fine? Here, there's a bench just over there." She pulled the handbag string over her left wrist, then reached out. Alice stiffened, and the woman stopped. Her brows shot higher beneath coiffed bangs.

"I'm here with friends," Alice managed to say. God, what was she doing? Why was she still talking to this woman? She met her gaze, and the tug in her chest seemed to settle as the world realigned itself. A warm spark reached out from the woman's eyes, and Alice felt a deep, nearly forgotten longing spike near her ribs.

"Well, you may want to find them and have them escort you home. I'm afraid you look rather pale, Miss…" Her voice trailed off. Alice realized she was waiting for her name.

You've fudged this one, Dumplin', her father's voice said. She could hear the disappointment in his tone. *You're on your own now.*

Alice swallowed, glancing toward the shoreline to see Dorothy waving at her. "I should be going. You're right. I ought to get home."

The woman's bottom lip jutted in a small pout at not getting a name. Alice glanced at the handbag. The clasp was still open. She started when the woman reached a hand out, resting it on her arm. "You're certain you're all right? Those men didn't do anything to hurt you, did they?"

Lost, that was how she felt. Alice felt utterly lost. Sweat gathered under her arms and on the back of her neck, the sun seeming to burn above her head from its seat in the cloudless sky. Was the sun always this bright? She closed her eyes as more warnings rang in her mind. Her mother's voice grated like rusty gears in her head. She'd never failed a job this grandly, not since she was too young to truly understand her parents' profession and the rules that came with it. Rules meant to keep her out of the eyes of the law. Rules to keep her with her parents, rules set in place to keep her working another day.

"I'm fine," she said quietly, pulling her arm back.

When she met the woman's gaze again, it held a look Alice didn't know what to make of. The woman smiled softly before saying, "Well, thank you again for returning this." She pressed a hand over her chest. "I'm Janeth, by the way."

Alice stood, certain she seemed like a dunce, too dumbstruck by her own failure to form a response.

"Please take care of yourself," Janeth added, giving Alice's shoulder a pat before she turned to go.

For a time, Alice stood watching her. Her breathing slowed, but her throat dried as her gaze landed on the way Janeth's skirt clung to her hips and the confident stride she walked with. When Janeth turned back, Alice blushed at being caught watching her. Janeth only smiled and waved. Stiffly, Alice waved back.

The world seemed to tilt again. Alice was floating, adrift, confused by what had transpired. *I gave back the handbag?* What on earth had compelled her to do such a thing? She could have run. She could have tossed it beneath the trackway and said she saw someone else walk off with it. She could have done so many things. Anything except what was good, what was right.

Janeth disappeared into the crowd, but Alice only stood there, recalling Janeth's brown eyes. She inhaled sharply, the lilac fading, already a memory. A crushing feeling hit her as she knew exactly why she'd done what she had. And that reason broke every rule in the book.

CHAPTER SIX

A fter climbing the steep stairs leading to the white gabled front door of the great Mills mansion, Janeth called, "I'm back."

In the foyer, the marbled floor shined in the sunlight. She closed the large door, but the space remained flooded with late afternoon light from the windows at her back. She set her hat and handbag on the long table lining the wall separating the foyer from the sitting room to her right. Removing her gloves, she eyed the handbag.

The woman from the boardwalk lingered in her mind. How strange she had seemed. Perhaps she had been lost, Janeth wondered, or unwell. She had noticed the dollar note was missing on the walk home. To her surprise, she'd felt only sympathy. Something about the woman—perhaps the startled look in her hazel eyes—had given Janeth pause and kept her from fetching a police officer to notify him of the petty theft.

Her uncle's voice called from across the house, "In here, Janeth."

"In the library again," she muttered, passing the base of the grand stairs to the library in the back of the house. The scenic oil paintings along the walls gleamed, and she made a note to have the frames polished soon.

She found JP sitting in his wingback chair, a leatherbound ledger open in his lap. His sun-spot-riddled, wrinkled forehead had been crinkled in thought and smoothed some at her presence. He smiled, revealing teeth yellowed near the gums from years of smoking despite Janeth's efforts to temper the habit. "How was the day?"

She started to reply but hesitated. The encounter at the boardwalk sat with her still. She brushed the incident aside, though, and replied,

"Dandy. Besides Mr. Preston, that is. He says he'll have our money next week."

"That's grand." JP coughed, then studied his numbers. "He's good for it."

Janeth straightened the blanket on the leather couch opposite him and reshelved several books lying about the room. She pushed closed the wall of shelves that served as the false door to the cellar, reminding herself to take a closer look at the floor latch. It had trouble catching at times, leaving the passageway open unbeknownst to them. "You are far too lenient with that man. This is his fourth extension in as many months."

"I knew his father and his father before him. They're honest men." At her look, he added, "He's working two jobs. Three if you include our product pushing. His weekdays are spent in the cannery, you remember. Then he's in that sugar stand on weekends."

Admitting defeat, she sighed. "Very well."

As she finished tidying the space, he added, "You just missed Hugh, by the way." He set the ledger on a side table and moved to stand. She hurried to him, offering her arm as he pushed up. She passed him his cane. His long, knobby fingers clutched the gold eagle's head at its top to steady himself. His watery blue eyes found hers, and she caught his teasing gaze.

"You know I've no time for frivolity, least of all with your nephew. He's developed quite the reputation, I'll have you know."

Hugh Mills, a recent alum of UCLA, was like a ghost. A handsome ghost, so claimed Maria after his first delivery of rum and tequila to the market last fall. Janeth admitted Hugh was a handsome fellow, if overeager in his conversation, mainly with young women. He lived up the hill on Temple Street with his mother and father, who had hoped he would fall directly into prominent employment following his graduation. Hugh seemed perfectly content to enjoy life, unabashedly spending his inheritance on things like sailing excursions, trips up the coast, and European getaways. His charm landed him in favor of the young, unmarried women of San Diego, and he often found himself in romantic entanglements he had no apparent interest in resolving.

His parents, seeking structure for their wild son, had turned to JP for support. He'd employed Hugh to keep him busy, as busy as possible, that was. The phantom-like hours Hugh kept meant Janeth hardly saw him as he came and went during odd times and never lingered. Much to all their surprise, he had taken to the position of assistant in their rum-smuggling business quite well, making covert deliveries to customers around the county quietly and efficiently.

"Let me get this straight," Hugh had said last September, leaning back in a dining room chair when JP and Janeth had presented him with the opportunity. His blue eyes had twinkled beneath sun-bleached hair slicked back behind his ears. "I'm to help you smuggle *illegal* goods to the citizens of San Diego, at odd hours, sometimes with little notice, and I'll be paid for my troubles?"

"Precisely," JP had said, hands matter-of-factly behind his back.

Hugh, seemingly unable to hide a grin, had crossed his arms over his blue sweater, his alma mater's letters in bold yellow on the chest. He pointed to the back of the house toward the garage carriage. "I get to use the Bentley for deliveries." It wasn't a query but a statement.

Janeth had gone wide-eyed, but JP didn't miss a beat. "Deal."

Entitled cad, Janeth had thought as Hugh had shaken JP's hand before sending her a wink.

Despite her initial misgivings about his supercilious personality, Hugh had proven his worth. He was always on time, seeming to like the late hours and getting to mingle with customers. The vagueness of his occupation gave him an air of mystery to women, and he played it up to gain their affections. Janeth was certain the only reason he didn't pursue her was the ring on her hand. She'd heard of his dalliances with any young thing in a skirt. "Who would have thought?" her uncle had said two months after hiring Hugh. "A natural salesman, that one."

Presently, JP laughed. "A young man's heart is obligated to other, more carnal reasonings, my dear. There's little we can do about it. Believe me."

She snorted but was glad when he changed the subject to the weather. Since Leo's reminder of Victor, she had felt like she was floating, untethered from the great love of her past and unsure where any future might lead. Talk of Hugh was a reminder about how the outside world viewed her: a widow in need of a husband. The pressure to find someone new had lessened since moving in with her uncle. The cannery where she had worked before had featured an assortment of men, young and old, more than eager to offer her a chance at love. Each offer was rebuffed, though, her heart unready. Only in the last year had it seemed to mend itself. Still, she wasn't sure she wanted to risk putting it out there again, despite the fact she was pushing twenty-eight.

"Hugh did bring by my medicine," JP was saying, switching topics again. He limped over to the desk near the floor-to-ceiling bookshelves.

Janeth moved to close the heavy green curtains on the south-facing windows, then turned on the three oil lamps ensconced on the walls. "A new tonic from the physician?"

"Yes. The previous one was atrocious. I felt like the living dead after each dose." He shook his head, his gruff voice seeming to tremble at the memory. "Dreadful stuff, truly dreadful."

"Are you certain it's not the prospect of turning sixty that has you acting your age?"

He guffawed, and she laughed. "Balderdash. If it weren't for this damned bullet in my side, I'd be fit as a fiddle."

She smiled as he hobbled through the doorway, still carrying on about his war wounds, as he called them. Of course, it hadn't been a battle that had left half a bullet in his hip or taken out a sizable dent in his left tibia. Their business had been the catalyst. No, she corrected herself, it had been Raymond. Mad Raymond had left JP Mills with incurable pain, bound to his home, the mere act of walking a great torture for him. At the same time, that life-altering night had given Janeth a window, a foot into a world she was certain few other women could call their own.

In the front dining room, JP settled into a chair upholstered with a vertically striped pattern. At the head of the table, he prepared his next pipe, tugging back the sleeves of his red velvet robe. Crossing the wood floor, she clucked her tongue and turned on the electric lamp. The snap of the bright light made both of them jump.

"I still don't know what to make of that," he muttered, gesturing to the light.

"Nor do I," she admitted. A handful of other families had transitioned to the newest trend: electric power. Over the last few years, things like telephones, electric lamps, and refrigerators graced the homes of the well-to-do along the southern coast. Janeth still didn't fully understand how all of those items worked, despite explanations from the installation teams. As their eyes adjusted to the light cast over the mahogany table, she briefly wondered what her parents would have thought of her living in a home with such modern luxuries. They probably had seen the drastic changes her life had undergone the past few years, she reasoned, looking down on her since they passed only months apart in 1922.

JP spoke around the mouth of his pipe. "There's a cut of lamb in the icebox."

She pulled two plates from the china cabinet, along with silverware and wineglasses for two. "That does me no good, Uncle. We can't very well eat frozen meat."

"Yes, I forgot to set it out." At her raised brow, he pointed his pipe at her. "I may be nearly sixty, but I'm still in my right mind. I was merely busy with the numbers."

Laughing, she said, "Very well. Yesterday's potatoes with cheese it is. I may be able to find some bread in there, too."

As she moved into the kitchen at the back, JP called, "Don't forget the caramel custard for dessert."

Later, Janeth idly swirled the drizzle of sweet caramel around her plate. The color reminded her of the eyes of that young woman from the boardwalk.

"Janeth?"

"Hmm?" She looked up, not realizing how far away in thought she was.

"I asked if you needed help with this Friday's incoming shipment. They'll be in late, so I'm told."

"Oh." She straightened, taking a sip from her wine to gather herself. "No. It's Hernandez and his men. They're harmless."

He nodded. "Very good." A flicker of something crossed his worn face.

Janeth set her glass down, reaching a hand out toward the other end of the table and resting it on the white lace tablecloth. "Uncle, I know you wish to be up with me to receive the product, but the doctor insists you rest come sundown. It's not good to be on that leg longer than necessary."

"I know." He tapped the table near his plate where the potatoes gathered in a listless heap.

"I can handle myself," she assured him. "Raymond is the only one who worries me."

His face fell more, his fist tightening. "If I were a younger man…"

Janeth chuckled. "You would 'show him how a real man acts in business,'" she quoted. The line had become a mantra of sorts since the incident. Her uncle was proud, and he felt ashamed since Raymond had gotten the better of him that night. JP Mills was a respected man in San Diego, and his becoming chained to his home—only able to hobble to the park for a short walk—left him embarrassed. She could imagine the shame. The extravagant Mr. Mills who, only a decade ago, had hosted decadent seaside galas and practically lived downtown, was now confined to his elaborate mansion. He was known as a gracious benefactor in upper-crust society, and Janeth would agree. He had plucked her from obscurity at the fishing cannery and given her this new life. For such a man to become a shadow of his grandiose self...

Still, she saw the fire reignite in him when it came to the business. He might have been crippled in body, but his spirit remained strong.

They sat in silence for a time while Janeth finished her food. Whatever anger her uncle had felt thinking of Raymond seemed to subside, and he threw back the last of his brandy and stood, using the table to help himself up. "This was delicious, Janeth, dear. I'll see you in the morning."

"Good night, Uncle." She watched him disappear into the hall. The wall clock ticked on as her mind drifted to the next shipment coming from Mexico. Those thoughts beckoned to old memories, and Victor's face swam before her. She leaned back, her gaze settling on the candelabra lit on the table's center. Victor's genial laugh echoed in her mind. To her surprise, the sadness that often accompanied those memories didn't come. In their place was an acceptance, a knowing that time in her life had come and gone.

She found the cross, pulling her necklace from beneath her collar. Her mind shifted as her husband's laughter changed to the shouts of the Temperance protestors. Those transformed into the stilted voice of the woman from the boardwalk. Janeth recalled the way her short blond hair was tugged across her face in the breeze. Curiosity swelled within her for the woman, though she wasn't sure why she couldn't rid herself of the seemingly insignificant meeting.

Shaking herself from her thoughts, Janeth glanced again at the caramel drizzled across the custard. The woman's eyes filled her mind a moment more before she closed her own, forcing the image away. She slowly began to clear the table.

Later that night, Janeth was scanning her uncle's ledger at the desk when there was a knock from the other side of the bookcase. She opened the door and glanced at the wall clock through the dim lamplight across the room. Hernandez entered, two men at his heels dragging in a large wooden crate. He greeted her in Spanish.

"Good evening," she replied.

"Always with the English," he teased.

"Habit, I'm afraid."

He stood back as his men opened the crate. As she inspected the latest supply, Hernandez ran a hand through his dark hair. She noted the nervous gesture, then asked, "Is something wrong?"

"We had a run-in with Raymond earlier today."

Her lip rose at the mention of his name. She replaced the coffee tins filled with tequila bottles into beds of straw. "What did he want?"

Hernandez gestured for his men to take the crate downstairs. Once they were gone, he said, "He's getting greedy."

She snorted. "He already was."

He smiled at her comment, but his face fell again. Calloused hands dug into his trouser pockets. Janeth had always considered Hernandez a kind man, one of the more soft-spoken rum ringleaders they did business with. Upon their first meeting, she'd learned he hailed from a small town in Sonora. He had a strong build and handsome features, and he always seemed to treat his men with respect. Unlike Raymond.

"He's approached several of us over the last few weeks. Wants to buy us out."

"Buy you out?"

"Like he did with Marquez."

Janeth had always wondered what had transpired to bring Raymond into their lives.

Hernandez continued: "His offer isn't a good one. Doesn't surprise me. He underestimates our worth. He doesn't understand most of us do this for our families." He held her gaze, and she nodded. "We know it's dangerous. But it's good money. Raymond…" He trailed off, seeming to search the room for the right words. "He does this for himself."

Janeth wasn't sure what to say. She'd been worried about Raymond since their first meeting. Her ire for him only grew each time he was here. "What would you suggest?" she asked, going to the drawer and finding his payment. "For how to deal with him?"

As she handed the money to him, he held her hand. His dark gaze met hers. "We hope you and Mr. Mills will be on our side if things take a turn."

Cold ran between her shoulders. "What do you mean?" A scuffle amongst rumrunners wasn't unusual, but his tone implied something grander. Something that could draw attention and be very bad for business.

"Hopefully, I don't mean anything," he said, pulling back his hand and putting the money in his pocket. "Raymond is trying to gain numbers. We're going to see that he doesn't." His tone was light, but Janeth could feel the undercurrent of warning in his words.

She nodded. "Understood."

He bid her good night, then hurried down the cellar stairs. She closed the door after him, listening for the click of the latch. A draft swept through the library, and she pulled her house jacket tighter. "Raymond," she muttered, an inkling of fear running down her arms. She forced the thought of him from her mind, then turned off the lamps and went to bed.

Chapter Seven

*T*he picture show theater was nearly vacant for the Sunday matinee of Three Weeks. *In the second-to-last row, tucked into the compact seats, Alice bumped Gladys with her knee.*

Gladys shot her a mischievous grin, the light from the black-and-white film glinting off her playful brown eyes. Tossing a glance over her shoulder despite knowing there was no one behind them, Alice reached her left hand to find the hem of Gladys's skirt. When her forefinger slipped beneath the material, finding Gladys's thigh, Gladys leaned sideways and whispered, "Al, be careful."

"No one can see us," she countered, finding her gaze. Alice wanted desperately to reach up and tuck the stray lock of brown hair behind Gladys's ear. She bit her lip to quell the urge, though that drew Gladys's gaze.

While the picture played on, filling the twenty-row theater with music as Aileen Pringle's and Conrad Nagel's characters mooned over one another, Alice reluctantly sat back. A man near the front of the theater wrapped his arm around the woman he accompanied. Alice watched, a surge of anger rising at the sight. The ease with which men could touch women was utterly unfair. All she wanted was to do the same. For a moment, she considered it but knew Gladys wouldn't approve. She was always the more cautious one.

Instead, she sighed and crossed her arms. Her right hand came to rest below her left elbow, hidden. Scooting closer, her fingers found Gladys's waist just above her belt.

In the dark, she heard Gladys inhale sharply. The sound shot a sense of deep longing through Alice. She yearned to wrap her arm around Gladys and pull her close, to disappear into the soft velvet light that encased them and created a world of their own in the corner of the small theater. Briefly, she wondered if the space inside the screen was any different from their own. Could she take Gladys with her, slip between the cellophane images, and run away to a place where they could be free? Was such a world even possible?

Gladys's voice called, "Al, wake up."

Alice frowned, turning as the theater fell away, and Gladys disappeared with it into the dark.

"Wake up, Alice." Someone shook her shoulder hard, and she was startled back into the present. Her mother's voice tore her from her dreams as the smell of cigarette smoke hit her. "Get up. You'll be late to the picket."

"Picket?"

Her mother threw a dress at her as Alice sat up, blinking the sleep from her eyes. "We told you about it yesterday. Jesus, Alice." Her shoes and blue hat were tossed toward her next, landing unceremoniously at the foot of the bed. "You're going to the same place as last weekend. This one will have five of those groups meeting together. It's an important one. If you can get in with the matron's colleagues, we can find out where the next fundraiser will be before anyone else. That'll give us a leg up." Her eyes shined. "That money will be ours for the taking."

Alice nodded, tossing the tattered blanket off and moving to the washbasin near the doorway. As she washed her face, still clinging to the memories of Gladys, she felt her mother's eyes on her. She dabbed her face dry, turning.

A drag from her mother's cigarette was followed by a look Alice couldn't pinpoint. For a moment, she thought she saw something akin to what other parents had to feel for their children: affection, appreciation, love. Her mother's eyes flickered, though, and the look vanished. Her lips pursed, and she said, "Get a move on," before she left Alice alone in her dark room to prepare for another day.

❖

"Did I miss anything?" Alice asked, hurrying up to Dorothy after pushing her way through the sea of fifty women with picket signs. The group stood on the sidewalk at the base of a sloping front lawn before a great, coral-colored Seaside mansion. Or was that a castle? Alice had never seen a castle, but the house was grand enough, and its perch atop the green knoll seemed to fit the bill. She stared at its two towering stories, its rows of windows like great spying eyes framing an elegant, white-gabled front door.

"Nothing really," Dorothy replied, handing her a sign that read: *Lips that touch liquor shall not touch ours.* Alice, pleased she could make out the message, caught Dorothy's mischievous look. "Clearly, I can't hold this one, but maybe it's a better fit for you." Alice smiled, wondering if Dorothy caught the knowing in her own gaze as she continued. "Madame Enfield has been busy with the other old birds since we started." She winked at using Alice's terminology.

The matron stood stoically near the front of the protest, framed by two other old women wearing fine frocks and dour expressions. They must have been who her mother was mentioning, the other leaders of the movement. Alice wondered how to start a conversation with them when Mary appeared, looking startled but excited with a picket sign as tall as her.

"Alice, you made it. Isn't it gorgeous?" She gestured to the house atop the hill.

She nodded, glancing again at the gleaming rooftop and immaculate front lawn. Rosebushes lined the steep front walkway. The ocean waves crashed in a gentle roar at their backs below the cliffsides on another idyllic day. This house definitely had the best view of the Pacific, and she turned to catch sight of a freight ship far out to sea, a hazy outline on the horizon against the blue sky.

"The story behind it is a doozy," Dorothy said, moving closer to be heard over the chants from the rest of the women. "They say this mansion is the home of the most prominent rum-smuggler in San Diego."

"So they *say*," Mary interjected, looking around as if spilling government secrets, not local legend.

Dorothy gave her an incredulous look and pointed toward the sandy slope below. "They use these cliffs here as a cover."

"Cover?" Alice asked, intrigued. "What do you mean?"

"You know," Dorothy added, glancing around and ignoring a disapproving look from some of the nearby protesters. "A cover to receive the very thing we're here protesting."

Alice looked from the great house to the cliffs behind them. The long stretch of sandstone, with its ribbons of brown and tan rock that ended in a steep drop to jagged rocks below, seemed unmoved by such a tale. Even she found it a little hard to believe. She had stood near the edge with her father a few weeks before. The water had churned endlessly, a brutal beating against the cliffs that created mesmerizing eddies full of seaweed and foam. She doubted any boat would be able to navigate such a maze of rock and make it through unscathed. At her frown, Dorothy added, "They say there are secret tunnels right below our feet."

Still finding this hard to believe, she asked, "Why hasn't anyone looked into that? Surely, local law enforcement would have heard such a theory and tried to catch an incoming boat."

Dorothy smiled, seemingly pleased at her interest in the story. "They say Mr. Mills, the resident of that grand home, has his hands in police pockets."

"Dorothy," Mary said, hitching her sign higher, "what a thing to say."

"Mary, why else would we be here, protesting at this house?" Dorothy replied. "Obviously, nothing has been done about it."

"But the police raid bars," Mary countered, "they shut down those sinful places. Those…speak-easies." She said the last word in a near whisper.

Dorothy shook her head, an amused look on her face. "To keep up appearances. They have a hand in this whole thing. They reap the benefits of liquor coming in while 'closing' certain bars on a regular basis, regular enough to keep groups like ours at bay. Haven't you noticed others always pop up in their place?" She sighed. "Mary, you know how I feel about this stuff. We're better off spending our effort on a fight that we can win: suffrage."

"Are you saying this is wasted time?" Alice asked, a lurch of unease in her stomach. This was the entire point of her family being here. What if the protests ended? Where would she be dragged to then?

"Ladies, signs up!" Madame Enfield appeared nearby, her face stern. "Now is not tea time. The weaknesses of men don't adhere to gossip, only prayer."

"Yes, madam," they muttered. Dorothy shot her another look, and Alice looked from the ocean to the great house, curiosity rising as she raised her sign and joined the chants.

❖

"There's at least forty, maybe more, protestors down there, Uncle." Janeth stood at the second-story-landing window. Glowering, she tried to count again, the sea of women and signs seeming to move, circling the base of the hill like the whirlpools near the rocky shoreline at low tide.

From his room in the southeast corner of the home, directly above the library, her uncle called, "Let them be, Janeth dear. It's not the first time we've had a protest."

"It's the first time we've had one this large," she called over her shoulder, one hand still holding back the blue satin curtain to peer out. "This has to be several groups. I recognize one of the older women from last month's gathering."

The steady dull thud of her uncle's cane echoed through the hall, and she turned to watch him walk slowly past the top of the staircase to join her. The hunch in his shoulders made him shorter than her by an inch. His wrinkled face fell into a thoughtful frown as they stood watching.

"What if they're on to us?" she asked, her throat dry. They'd had to tread carefully since the incident with Raymond. She knew gossip had streamed through the city, overflowing the restaurants and local businesses with lore for eager lips. It was an open secret that people were smuggling liquor from other countries during Prohibition, but she had been pleased that thus far, it remained only that, an intangible story leaving people to guess as to where the product was being brought in.

"Nonsense," her uncle said, turning to head downstairs. "They have no proof."

"*Yet*," she said loudly over her shoulder before spotting the same tiny redhead amongst the group whom she'd seen three weeks prior at the protest downtown.

Her uncle's shining black Bentley rounded the street corner to the west. Hugh blared the horn, scattering a few of the protesters who had wandered into the road. He rolled down the window to wave at them as he turned up the drive, stopping with a screech just outside the car carriage behind the house.

After giving up on counting how many protestors there were, Janeth hurried downstairs to find Hugh in the drawing room with her uncle, who was settled in a chair with the newspaper and his pipe. She opened the drapes just wide enough to see, determined to observe the protest until it was done, as if doing so would keep them from storming the premises.

"Good day, Mrs. Castro," Hugh said, propping their uncle's cane next to him and passing him his box of tobacco.

"Hugh," she said as cordially as possible.

His bright smile stretched wider as he joined her near the window, moving the curtain aside to better see. She glared, reaching to tug it back into place, not wanting to draw attention. "Quite the bluenose gathering," he mused. "If I didn't know better, I'd say those dames think we're up to something."

"We are up to something," she said, eyeing his maroon sweater paired with brown trousers. His thick blond hair was slick with pomade, his mustache freshly trimmed, and his rosy cheeks shaved. A red mark on his neck caught her gaze, which she quickly averted at the notion of how he came to acquire it.

Their uncle chimed in. "They'll be gone by noon. Come have a smoke, Hugh, before your next delivery."

"I'd love to, but," he said slyly, still peering outside, "I see a couple of real dishes down there. I can't very well ignore such charming gals when they're right outside our door." He grinned widely and moved to the empty fireplace, scanning his reflection in the large, gold-framed mirror above it.

"Most of them are probably married, no doubt," Janeth called, unsure why she felt the need to defend these women from him. His reputation, she told herself, was the reason she needed to keep him inside. No woman should have to endure courtship that inevitably ended in disappointment.

"Most, you say?" he replied, smoothing his sweater. "I like those odds." He winked and hurried from the room. The sound of the front door opening, then closing, sounded in the hall. From the window, she watched him trot down the steep walkway, then practically leap past the final step, landing in a showy pose in front of a trio of blond women. One of them blushed, but the others elbowed their companion, seeming to remind her of the task at hand.

"Uncle, do you really approve of this?"

He puffed on his pipe, not looking up from the paper. "I see no harm in it. Besides, he'll distract them. They'll realize we're only a little family minding our own business in here and move on."

Grumbling, she watched Hugh stroll along the sidewalk, greeting several of the women. One of the matronly ladies moved toward him, but he seemed unfazed, bowing genially and striking up a conversation. Behind the old woman, a younger protester with short, mud-brown hair was helping the petite redhead readjust her sign. Janeth inhaled sharply when she spotted the same woman from the boardwalk behind them, a sign raised high above her head as she chanted with the group.

Her throat went dry. What was she doing here? She thought back to the Seaside carnival. She'd been so preoccupied with speaking to Mr. Preston that day that other details of the boardwalk were fuzzy. Closing her eyes, she conjured the scene, trying to recall the people at the beach. There had been several groups of well-dressed women around, women not dressed for the beach, all toting pamphlets. Had these groups been there that day, too?

Turning to her uncle, she started to share such a revelation, but the words stuck in her throat. It was merely a coincidence, surely, that this woman was here again. But when Hugh drifted toward her, working his way through the throng of protestors to say hello, Janeth quickly said, "He's going to get himself arrested for harassment," and rushed into the foyer. She grabbed her hat and jacket and tore outside.

The chants were magnified in the open air, the high pitch of women shouting, "Save your soul! Just say no!" hit her like the bright sun as it climbed higher across the cloud-dotted midday sky. Her long skirt confined her stride, and she carefully stepped down the walkway, keeping her eye on Hugh. Near the sidewalk, she heard the whistle of a policeman. The ocean crashing, seagulls cawing overhead, and the dissonance of Temperance shouts were dizzying. It was only when she reached the sidewalk that Janeth had no idea what she was really doing down there and realized she had willingly thrown herself into the face of the enemy.

An angry-looking brunette, her sign equally red-faced, stepped in front of her, shouting, "The devil drinks whiskey. Throw it out to sea!"

Janeth grimaced, pushing past her and ignoring her fiery gaze. Some of the protestors turned to aim their shouts at her while others tightened around the base of the walkway, aiming their jeers at the house. The officer spoke to one of the elderly women, and Janeth could only hope he was telling them their time was up. Most protests were given an hour, maybe two, before local residents had enough of the raucous gatherings. Spotting Hugh, who had cornered the blonde from the boardwalk, Janeth pushed between the same brunette and redhead she had seen from the window and pulled up beside him.

"Hugh, there you are," she said, trying to collect herself and putting on a smile. Perspiration sat on the back of her neck.

The woman turned at the sound of her voice, her hazel gaze going wide. She was average in height, about two inches taller than Janeth, but still small compared to Hugh's five-ten frame. "Mrs. Castro, I was just making the acquaintance of this charming daughter of the Holy League."

Janeth's smile tightened. Of course Hugh had found one of the few women without a ring on her finger, something she noticed too, as the woman didn't wear gloves. Her blue cloche hat seemed new, but her dress was several years out of fashion. Still, her sandy-blond hair was cut in line with the latest trend, and the clothes fit her figure well. Her face was handsome, a strong brow set above lovely eyes and thin lips. Another reason, surely, Hugh had set his sights on her.

Behind them, another whistle from the policeman sounded. The chants became uneven, and one of the matrons called out for her followers to assemble across the street near the cliffs.

Hugh frowned. "Is the party over already?"

"Looks like it," the woman said. Janeth noticed her hand resting deeply in her left pocket, and her gaze stayed low.

Hugh peered over the heads of the scattered crowd. "I'd love a word with your matron. Surely, she'll spare you for a minute." He smiled and sidled up to the woman, one hand behind the small of her back in an attempt to pull her aside.

Janeth stepped closer as the protest dispersed around them. "Hugh, don't you have that appointment you need to get to?" She tried to keep her voice light, but something about the way Hugh pushed himself toward the woman made her skin crawl.

He glanced at his pocket watch, sad realization drawing over his face. "I suppose you're right." He stepped back. Janeth noticed the brunette and redhead approaching. The brunette eyed Janeth, then Hugh. "Well, it was a pleasure to make your acquaintance," he said to the woman, placing a quick kiss on her hand before sauntering away. He bowed again to the matron, then waved and jogged up the walkway back into the house.

Left alone, a surge of something foreign and exciting filled Janeth. She smiled, raising a hand to block the sunlight. She found she had a lot of questions, but none of them seemed to find her tongue. Instead, she said, "Apologies. Hugh is rather insistent, I'm afraid, especially when it comes to fetching young women." The woman, whose gaze had been searching the group she'd come with, zeroed in on Janeth at that comment. Her cheeks warming, Janeth stepped closer. "I must say, it's nice to see you again. You seem well."

The same look from the boardwalk drew over the woman's face, the look of a startled fawn that had found its way onto an icy lake. Her hand was still firmly planted in her pocket, and the large sign seemed to be weighing on her right arm. She lowered it, then asked, "You live here?"

Janeth blinked at the question. "Yes."

The woman looked past her toward the great house. Janeth wished she could read her thoughts as the brunette and redhead approached.

"Oklahoma," the brunette said, looking harried. "Time to go. We're reconvening at Baley's downtown to talk about the fundraiser in October."

"Come on, Alice," the redhead said. "My father will kill me if he learns a police officer was here."

The brunette started to usher the woman, Alice, away, but Janeth reached out. That exhilaration from before drove her to extend their time, and she tried to think of a valid reason to delay her departure. "Wait, Alice." The woman flinched at the sound of her name but paused. "I have something of yours. From the boardwalk."

"Boardwalk?" the brunette asked, one brow raised. "You know each other?"

"Please," Janeth said, looking at Alice, "it's just inside. It'll only take a moment."

A contemplative look fell over Alice's face, and she slowly stepped away from her friends. The protesters were reorganized a block away now. The matron called, and the brunette turned, waving.

"I'll catch up, Dorothy," Alice finally said. She handed her the sign. "Baley's?"

"Yes, on Third Avenue downtown." She hitched the sign over her shoulder, shooting Janeth a curious look. "See you there, Oklahoma."

The others left, and the exciting feeling from before intensified. A strange sensation overcame her, as if she was floating. She reached out her hand, smiling. "Alice." She said the name slowly, a satisfied warmth caressing her tongue as it left her lips. "It's nice to meet you."

CHAPTER EIGHT

It was the scent of lilac that hypnotized Alice. The smell swept over her as soon as Janeth had found her in the crowd. Now it pulled her like a siren up the steps toward the house she had protested in front of not five minutes before. Suddenly, she was inside the grandest home she'd ever stood in. Not even Gladys's house in Oklahoma City had been this impressive.

"Alice. Please, come in."

The wide door closed behind her, and Alice stood on a marble floor that shone like a jewel. She tried to take everything in: the gleaming floor, the towering staircase thirty feet ahead, the blue-and-yellow patterned wallpaper behind fine artwork, and wall lamps that emitted dim light. She smelled tobacco smoke somewhere nearby, along with potpourri that she spotted in a glass vase on an ornate table near the base of the stairs. As Janeth removed her hat and jacket, looking at Alice expectantly, she remembered the two dollar notes she'd nabbed from that man—Hugh—outside and readjusted her hand in her left pocket.

The thought that broke through the haze of lilac and glare of the fine furnishings found its way out as she asked, "Why am I here?"

A small line creased Janeth's brow. She clasped her hands in front of her. Alice quickly scanned her fine blouse, royal blue with buttons down the front, that was tucked into a knife-pleated black skirt that covered her shoes. Her posture was impeccable, and her deep brown hair was parted down the middle, the tail of a braid falling below her shoulders. She seemed to contemplate her answer before saying,

"As you probably know, I don't actually have anything of yours."
She paused. "I suppose, I wanted to see how you were after our last
meeting."

How strange, Alice thought, eyeing Janeth, then glancing to the
door. She needed to go downtown and get back to the Daughters of
the Holy League. She needed to learn details about the fundraiser. The
thought of arriving home empty-handed, with no new information
for her parents, was the last thing she needed. At the same time, she
was curious. She had imagined Janeth was a wealthy woman from the
snippet of interaction they'd shared at the boardwalk, though she hadn't
imagined her being *this* wealthy. "I'm fine," she replied slowly.

"Good." Janeth smiled, and seemed unsure what to say next. She
bit her lip, which drew Alice's gaze. She wore a dark shade of lipstick
that complemented her dark eyes and rouge-dabbed cheeks. Even
under the dim light of the foyer, she was stunning. She stepped closer,
leaving only a foot of space between them. Alice stepped back but ran
into the door as Janeth tossed a furtive glance over her shoulder, then
said quietly, "I know it was you."

She swallowed, at first to quell the urge to lean closer and fall
deeper into the lilac perfume Janeth wore. Recovering, she asked,
"Pardon me?"

"You took the dollar note from my handbag that day. On the
boardwalk in Seaside."

Alice's pulse quickened. God, what was she thinking, coming into
this house? This was too dangerous. She shot her gaze to the side room
where the smoke continued to waft from. Whoever was in there could
be listening. What if Janeth called the cops? Alice clenched her jaw,
trying to stay calm. This was her plan, she thought as a shot of panic
flew down her back. She felt for the doorknob. Janeth had lured her
here as a trap, to keep her here until the law arrived to take her away.

"I suppose I'm curious," Janeth was saying, her voice low as she
remained standing dangerously close. "Why did you do it?"

Fear withered to confusion. "I…" Alice started to speak, but the
quick lies fell flat. Fortunately, an elderly gentleman's voice called
from the next room.

"Janeth, dear, did Hugh leave?"

Janeth held her gaze a moment more, bright curiosity rampant in her eyes, then widened the space between them and called, "Yes, I just heard the Bentley start. He'll be back some time tonight."

"Can you check the icebox? The meat should be out, but I can't recall. I just set my next pipe."

Alice couldn't be sure, but she thought the look that crossed Janeth's face was one of disappointment before she called, "Yes, Uncle. Just a moment." She lowered her voice and to Alice said, "Will you come by again? I…" She licked her lips, her gaze thoughtful. "I'd like to understand things better."

Alice took a breath. She hadn't called for the police. Surely, she would have by now if that had been her plan. What was this woman playing at? She glanced around the great house again. An idea struck her: if she did return, there was more than enough here for the taking. Surely, a house like this had piles of money sitting behind locked drawers that could easily be picked. She could pilfer something. She'd just have to be smart. Smarter than she had been thus far around this woman. "I don't know."

"Next weekend? Come by Saturday, won't you? My uncle will be out for his walk at one." She smiled, and Alice hated how her stomach flipped at the sight. "We can do lunch."

Do lunch? Alice had only heard fancy women say things like "do lunch." Well, she reasoned, if anything, it was a free meal. She'd have to craft a tale for her parents, but something told her to say yes. "All right."

Janeth's smiled widened. "One o'clock? I'll see you then."

Alice nodded as Janeth hurried away into the next room, talking to the older gentleman. She stared a moment more at where Janeth had stood, then quietly slipped out into the sunlight.

Dazed, Alice found her way to Baley's Café. In her seat next to Dorothy, she tried to listen as Madame Enfield droned on about the fundraiser, a "splendid occasion for the devout women of the church to come together in the fight against Satan's latest test." She could hardly follow more than a sentence of her speech, though, as her mind remained in Seaside.

Janeth was one of the most confusing women she had ever met. Typically, a woman showing that much interest in her would mean one thing: the same thing it had meant between her and Gladys. She bit her lip with the thought, but a tinge of guilt followed. She straightened in her seat, glancing sideways, knowing how indecent her thoughts were. Fortunately, Mary wasn't paying her any mind, looking enraptured by Madame Enfield while the rest of the women, only about half the group from the beach, nodded along over teacups settling in white saucers in the quiet café.

Alice took a bite of the cookie that had been served with her tea, chewing slowly. Janeth didn't strike her as *that* kind of woman. Her inquiries into Alice's motivations seemed genuine in their naivety. Though, she thought, recalling the way Janeth had stood so close, the lilac perfume twisting around her like a vise, her earnestness did seem…hungry.

After an hour of munching on tea cakes—a first for Alice and admittedly underwhelming as she forced down the cucumber and cheese concoction Dorothy had sponsored—Alice stood as the lecture came to a close.

"That's an hour I'll never get back," Dorothy muttered, resting her floral handbag in the crook of her elbow.

"Dorothy," Mary scolded, pushing in her chair, "truly now."

Dorothy snorted. "We have five months until the fundraiser. This could have waited until they have a venue, at least."

Alice laughed, but her mind buzzed with satisfaction. She had come away with something insightful: the funds raised by the collective donors would be presented at the closing of the fundraiser ceremony. This would satisfy her parents and allow them to begin a scheme to get to the money. Alice felt the dollar notes in her pocket when a pair of gentlemen near the back of the restaurant caught her eye. They stood smoking beneath a tall electric lamp with a fringed shade. The outline of a billfold could be seen in one of their breast pockets.

"I'll see you next time," she said to Dorothy, who was dragging Mary toward the front. "I'm going to use the washroom before heading out."

"See you in a week, Oklahoma. Next protest is in National City on Sunday. Main Street."

"See you there," she called. She lingered for a minute, pushing in chairs and smiling at the waitstaff who came to clear the tables. Smoothing her skirt, she moved toward the back of the restaurant. Once she was certain the women from the group were gone, and the men were deep in conversation, Alice went to work.

❖

"Hi, Father," Alice said, closing the door once she got home. The air inside their house was clearer today, the back window open. A fresh pitcher of tea sat on the card table, sweating in the late May heat, and she grabbed a cup to pour some.

Her father sat in the opposite chair before a pile of dollar notes: ones, fives, and tens neatly stacked in front of pillars of coins. His hair sat loose around his forehead, and he looked like he'd just had a bath. His wide-leg pants were hitched high with a belt beneath a faded white undershirt.

"Hiya, Dumplin'." He looked up, smiling. Then he raised a finger to his mouth, hitching a thumb over his shoulder. Alice followed it to the bed in the corner. Her mother lay stretched out on her back, snoring lightly beneath a faded quilt. "She had a busy night at the Dime Club. Charmed two oil barons in town from New Mexico. Suckers had over fifty bucks on 'em between the two of 'em. Didn't see it comin'." He chuckled, taking a bite from a ham and cheese sandwich, brushing the crumbs on his shirt, then rearranging the coins.

Alice relished the tea as it cooled her off after the morning in the sun. "Sounds like a good night."

"It was." He recounted the stacks, his gaze flickering to her. "How'd you do?"

She reached into her right pocket, then placed three dollar notes and a fiver next to his plate.

He grinned widely. "Attagirl." He swiped the money like an eager badger, adding it to his piles, then counting them once again.

She glanced to the corner where her mother slept and wondered if even in her sleep, she knew Alice had the two dollar notes from Hugh hidden in her left pocket.

"It'll be another busy night for us, Dumplin'," her father was saying. "We're heading to the Gaslamp District again. I've got an in with the fella who runs the blackjack table in the back of Willy's restaurant. I'm up twenty-two bucks." She whistled low and smiled. "Your mother will be downtown. She met a woman who sells fabricated Persian rugs. We'll see what we can do there."

"How're the games faring?" she asked, gesturing to the large walnut shells laid in a row of three on the table. Her father was an expert at sleight-of-hand, and he utilized variations of "Find the Bean"—when someone had to try and track a bean beneath a shell that her father would move in a specific pattern for the participant to follow—as a means to quick and easy money on street corners.

"Going well," he replied. "So far."

She nodded, her thoughts drifting ahead to next weekend. She still wasn't sure if she should go back to Seaside. What angle was Janeth playing?

Her father's voice cut into her thoughts. "How was the Holy League?"

She looked up, then took a sip of tea. "Oh. Fine. They don't have a venue for the fundraiser yet. Seems like a big event, though." She proceeded to share the details she'd acquired from the café.

"That's great. Good start." He moved to the wardrobe to pull out his worn leather briefcase. He placed it on the card table. Alice watched him undo the numbered lock, then pull out a tin not unlike the one she kept under her bed. He started to place the stacks of money inside as he spoke. "Keep your ear to the ground. Your mother has a good feeling about this one. That's why she sent you into that group. If we can get our hands on a Temperance fund…" He paused, looking at the bills, then her, his eyes sparkling. "Well, we'd be set for a while. Wouldn't that be grand?"

"Swell," she said, turning her glass on the table. He must have noticed the drop in her tone as he paused, one hand on his hip.

"Somethin' wrong?"

"No."

He watched her a minute, then tossed a look over his shoulder to the bed. Sitting, he lowered the lid of the briefcase to better see her. "Dumplin', listen…I know San Diego wasn't on your list." She swallowed, staring at her glass. "You know why we had to come here."

Looking up, she found his sympathetic gaze. "I liked Oklahoma City, same as you," he said, his voice low as he reached out to squeeze her hand. "Well," he added, pulling back, "maybe not exactly the same as you."

She pulled her hand into her lap. Images of Gladys overwhelmed her. She blinked, but the memories bombarded her like flies in springtime, and she couldn't keep them away. She saw the doctor's car parked in front of Gladys's house, then the psychiatrist's small glasses, his beady eyes cold as he stood in her doorway.

A lump lodged in her throat. Her father kept his voice low. "We had to go. You know that. Your mother…" He glanced over his shoulder again. "It was that or leave you behind. Commit you to those doctors." He closed the lid with a hard click, his watery gaze finding hers. "We couldn't lose you, Dumplin'."

She could hardly look at him, the flashes of their last day in Oklahoma searing through her mind like a scalding burn. Tears stung her vision as her father sighed and sat back in his seat. "But now, everything's peachy. We're here, you're here, and nothing like what happened there is gonna happen again."

Alice sniffled, looking at the ceiling to keep her tears from coming. Immediately, the image of Janeth swam before her, standing close in the foyer of her home. Lilac filled the room. Alice inhaled and closed her eyes. Then, she forced a smile. "Right. It won't happen again."

"Good," he said, replacing the briefcase in the wardrobe, the table cleared. "Well, get some rest. We need you in Coronado tomorrow."

She nodded and headed for her room. The pain of Oklahoma settled into a deep ache between her shoulders. She kicked off her heels and slipped out of her skirt and blouse, then collapsed on the bed. Closing her eyes, she saw Gladys. But it wasn't the Gladys from their clandestine date to the movies; it was last-day Gladys. Fearful, screaming, broken Gladys being torn from her life as Alice could only stand back and watch, her own heart shattering as her father dragged her away before it was too late.

Rolling onto her side, Alice hugged the pillow. For a moment, she thought she caught the scent of lilac once again. It was gone in an instant, though, and Alice reminded herself she couldn't allow such fanciful thoughts. Janeth could only be one thing to her: another job.

It was too risky to feel anything for anyone ever again. Her life could have been thrown away in a moment after Oklahoma, but it had been spared. She couldn't waste a second chance on impossible dreams.

She reminded herself who she was: the daughter of swindlers, a master fingersmith, and ultimately, nobody. A nobody whose job it was to help her parents in their schemes. Nobody, she told herself, tears returning, but the woman who deserved the hand she had been dealt. And there was nothing she could do to change that.

CHAPTER NINE

Janeth played the final notes of her latest piano piece, lost in the melody. When the grandfather clock in the hall struck the hour, she paused, taking a deep breath before moving to the window. She waited for the dory's lantern to appear over the waves. The sun was setting, casting glorious hues of orange and red over the horizon between streaks of dissipating clouds. She wondered at the beauty of it all, clinging to it as she fought the urge to turn away from the picturesque scene. How could such a breathtaking creation still bring so much pain?

She reached for the cross at the end of her necklace. It wasn't often anymore that the anger consumed her. It had been years since she had accepted the idea that God could be so cruel. Why create a passage between land on waters that could turn cold and crushing in a moment, swallowing boats and ships like meaningless pebbles, dragging them down to the murky seabed? What made people like Raymond, whose shadowy figure she could see in the dory as it navigated the seaside cliffs, immune to the ocean's wrath while others were powerless to fight it?

Shaking her head, she blew out the candle on the sill and dimmed her wall lamps. Her evening dress hung on the door, and she slipped out of her nightgown and into the dress. Glancing at Victor's photo on the side table, she smiled. It faltered, though, as Alice sprang to mind. She frowned and lifted her gaze to the mirror, quickly adjusting the stud earrings and brushing her bangs. *I wonder what Alice is doing now.* It had been several days since their last encounter, but Alice lingered in her mind.

The distant scraping of the cellar door below broke through her musings, and Janeth hurried downstairs.

"Set it over there, fellas," Raymond said after she'd let him in.

The lights dazzled Janeth a bit. All the wall lamps were turned up high, casting shadows across the green wallpaper and rows of leatherbound books. Two well-muscled men placed a pale yellow crate labeled "Matriculation Materials" next to her uncle's desk.

Raymond looked up and said, "The lady has to make sure everything is there."

She smiled curtly. "I've told you, I'm more than happy to meet you in the cellar. Your men needn't carry that all the way up here." She cut her glance at the open cellar door, a false front of shelves, ajar to reveal a dank passageway featuring a spiral of cement stairs that led to their vast basement below. Admittedly, Janeth would rather *not* be down there, especially with Raymond, but she wasn't about to let him in on that fact.

One of the men pulled a small crowbar from his pocket and pried open the top of the crate. Raymond coughed, then ran a hand over his slick hair. "We wouldn't want you to tire yourself out, Mrs. Castro."

She felt his eyes on her as she approached, peering over the crate. The scent of ocean spray and seaweed drifted from the goods inside as she inspected the shipment. Pulling her pale pink shawl tighter around her shoulders, she quickly counted the tightly packed rows of books layered with barnyard straw. None of the books featured titles. She grabbed one, examined it, and pulled the fake exterior apart to reveal the top of a bottle sticking out from the false plaster pages. She sniffed the open top, and the scent of agave tequila hit her.

Nodding approvingly, she replaced the top and set the book in the crate. "Everything looks to be in order."

Raymond had wandered to her uncle's desk, his fingers grazing the small lamp and flipping through the books that lay open across it. His piercing eyes didn't seem to take any of the words in. Rather, they only seemed to rove eagerly over the fine possessions. He wore the same pair of pants he'd always donned in their meetings over heavy boots that left marks on the floor. His shirt looked new, or Janeth reasoned, at least not as stretched out like his other one. His chin needed a shave, but she was glad his gaze didn't linger on her like it often did as he said, "Go on, boys, take that downstairs for the lady."

They replaced the crate top and lugged it through the passageway. Janeth watched them go, then moved carefully to the desk. Raymond knew where they kept the money: in the top right drawer. The key, though, was in Janeth's hands. Raymond stood in front of it, turning to her and wearing an annoying grin.

"If you'll excuse me," she said, pointing to the drawer.

He didn't move for a few seconds, only smiling wider at their proximity and no doubt the expectant look on her face. "Where's our dear Mr. Mills this evening?"

"He wasn't feeling well, I'm afraid. He retired early."

Raymond clucked, turning to the bookshelf behind the desk where the cigar box rested. He opened it, pulling out a Cuban and running it under his nose, inhaling deeply. "What a pity. I had hoped he'd be up for a reunion."

Janeth glared, resisting the urge to reach out and snatch the cigar from him. Eventually, Raymond replaced it and, to her relief, stepped around her so she could open the drawer. She didn't miss how he put himself between her and the library door, though.

She bit her tongue as she unlocked the drawer. His first visit after the incident had seen her furious with him. How could anyone think shooting an old man was right, especially in business? That night, no sooner had she uttered a sentence expressing such sentiments, however, that he had cornered her, his pistol in its holster on his right hip, just as it was now.

"You'll find I prefer my clients complacent, Mrs. Castro," he had said behind a sinister smile. "I would hate to have to end this partnership so soon."

Fear had overcome her, practically paralyzing her on the spot. Later, when she'd told Leo what had happened, he'd told her how lucky she had been.

"Don't be reckless, sister. A white man's temper is not to be tested."

Presently, Raymond watched her as she pulled open the drawer. Once she found the pocketbook, he seemed satisfied and wandered to the leather sofa near the middle of the room. He plopped onto the center seat, leaning back to rest his left arm across the cushions while she readied the payment.

"You've been here how long, Mrs. Castro?"

She hesitated at his question. Since she'd taken over handling shipments for her uncle, Raymond had never bothered getting to know her. Not that she had minded that fact. Wondering what changed, she replied, "Five years."

He scratched his temple. "Five years, huh? I thought you'd been here longer. Your English is better than all the fellas I work with."

"I've lived with Mr. Mills for nearly three years. I've been in the United States for five."

"What'd you do before here?" He tilted his head. "I never saw you in the Gaslight District at one of those...establishments. There's a lot of ladies like you down there." His voice lilted suggestively, and he raised a brow.

Her skin itched at his insinuation. "I worked in the cannery near the harbor. I saved enough money to rent a room, then lived with my brother when he immigrated."

"Brother?" He puckered his lips, tossing his gaze to her. "I bet he doesn't have your looks." She closed the pocketbook and replaced it in the drawer. She crossed the rug, and he stood. "Tell me this, Mrs. Castro. How is it a woman like you ends up here, in this kind of a house, wearing such fine frocks as this." He picked at the end of her shawl, making her step back. "Don't seem fair. No offense."

She smiled, lifting her chin. She knew from the moment she'd met Raymond that he'd felt this way. She could see it in the way he seemed to bask in the light of the library, how he lingered near the marble busts at the back window, and how he seemed desperate to sit on that couch like it was his each time he was here.

"Mr. Mills is a generous man," she said, the money at her side. "I was fortunate enough to fall into his good graces. He and I have more in common than people think."

He must have only heard part of what she said. He stepped so close, she could smell the faint odor of beer and sweat from his neck. His voice lowered, he asked, "And were you generous in return, Mrs. Castro, to old Mr. Mills?"

Her eyes widened. Words burned her tongue behind her teeth in a retort, but she bit them back. He was trying to get a rise out of her, she knew it. Anything to give him a reason to step forward and do something rash.

Willing her hand to steady itself, she held the money between them.

"Your payment." He held her gaze a moment more. She wondered what he was thinking as she measured the distance between them and how far it was to the library door at her back. Finally, thankfully, he took the money. "Now, if you please, I've got to go and check on Mr. Mills."

Smiling again, he gave a small bow of his head. "See you next month, Mrs. Castro." He tossed her a wink, then disappeared into the dark.

CHAPTER TEN

O n Saturday, Alice rose to the smell of coffee. She pulled on her worn stockings and a forest green skirt with a rippled hem that fell just below her knees. She paired it with an old cream-colored blouse featuring buttons down the front. It wasn't her nicest outfit, but it was comfortable. The skirt hadn't come with pockets originally, but her mother had taken scissors to it three years before and had stitched one into either side just below her hips. Her "working skirt," as her mother called it. Her blue cloche hat didn't match, but it was cleaner than the other one, so she tugged it over her head, slipped on her heels, and hurried into the main room.

"Close that curtain, will ya?" her mother said, her back to Alice as she poured steaming coffee into a chipped mug at the small stove. "Can't stand that light this morning."

Alice grimaced, noting the gray skies outside, but followed orders and found her own cup. Her mother moved slowly, as if each limb was being tortured, and sat at the card table. Her father snored in the corner.

"Late night?" Alice asked, examining a speckled, week-old banana and deciding it was good enough to eat.

Her mother leaned forward, resting her elbows on the table with the mug hanging between her hands as she took a long, slow sip. Her gaze found Alice over the top of it. Ignoring the question, she asked, "Where are you off to? I thought the Holy League was next weekend."

"It is. I heard there's going to be a college visit to the Seaside carnival. Lines of young people with cash sitting in their pockets for the attractions." Her mother's eyes lit up, a smile lifting lips still stained with color from last night. "Can't miss a job like that," Alice added for good measure. She had concocted the lie a few days ago, reciting the line over and over until it sounded natural.

Setting the mug down, her mother leaned back. The left shoulder strap of her negligee fell, and she found her packet of cigarettes behind the half-empty tea pitcher. She pinched her brow, squinting, then lit a match. Before bringing it to the cigarette she said, "Don't lose sight of the main event, Alice. Next weekend is the priority."

Alice took another bite of the banana, scrunching her nose at the taste, and started for the door. "I won't."

"And Alice," her mother called, "don't come back unless you've got at least five dollars in those pockets I gave you. Understood?"

Swallowing, Alice took a breath. "Yes, Mother." She tossed the banana peel into the waste bin and hurried out the door.

Later, Alice stood on the corner of Sunset Cliffs Boulevard. The gloomy skies stretched all the way from the railyard to the shore here, and the waves crashed against the sandstone cliffs, the sound jarring as wind whipped around her skirt. She wished she'd thought to bring a jacket, but she had been eager to get out of the house. Not surprisingly, the seaside carnival below the hill was nearly vacant. She spotted one couple on the Ferris wheel. Otherwise, the cold day and cloudy sky had kept visitors inside. Her gaze trailed to Osprey Street to the right of the carnival where trinket shops and restaurants lined opposite sides of the paved road. She imagined any visitors, including the fictional college boys, were inside enjoying a drink and fried fish.

She licked her lips, admittedly eager for the lunch Janeth had claimed she was invited to. Alice still wasn't sure what to make of the invitation. She'd never been to a ladies' lunch before. The thought that she should have brought something crossed her mind, but she laughed. What could she have brought? The half-rotten banana?

She walked several more blocks until she reached Marseilles Street. She waited there, a few houses away from the Mills mansion, as the coral home's front door opened. An elderly gentleman dressed in pressed black pants and a heavy-looking red sweater used a cane to hobble out onto the front porch. He steadied himself as Janeth appeared next to him, leaving the door slightly ajar behind her. She wore a simple navy dress with straight lines, the hem falling below her knees. Matching heels carried her forward. The sleeves of her dress were long, and she had tied a white, polka-dotted scarf in a loose knot that rested below her bosom. Her cloche hat was fitted as she helped the gentleman down the steep stairs toward the sidewalk at the bottom of the lawn.

Alice stood back, watching as Janeth seemed to listen to the man chatter; about what, she couldn't hear over the roar of the sea. When they reached the sidewalk and turned left, away from Alice, a middle-aged woman appeared over the next hill and waved. She met them and took the older man's arm, and the two disappeared down the hill. Alice crossed Monaco Street as Janeth hurried back to the stairs, her head down.

Now only a few yards away, Alice called out, "Hello."

Janeth looked up, startled. "Oh, Alice." She smiled. "Good afternoon."

Alice moved closer and pointed behind Janeth. "Is that your uncle?"

She turned as if he were still there, then said, "Yes. His daily exercise. Well, weekly, if we're being honest." She smiled. "Doctor's orders. His sister lives three blocks that way, so she comes and walks with him when I can't."

Alice nodded.

Janeth seemed unsure what to say. Finally, she gave an exaggerated shiver and said, "My, can you believe this weather? Please, do come in. Lunch is ready for us."

Us. It was an inconsequential word, but Alice's stomach flipped nonetheless, and she cursed herself for it.

Inside, Alice removed her hat. Janeth hung it on a coatrack. "This way." She led them past the left side of the massive staircase that climbed up through the middle of the house, its gleaming railings beckoning her to explore. She could only imagine the fine things that lay upstairs. They walked through a small hallway featuring a door Alice imagined must lead to a washroom, then took a right behind the stairs. The hallway opened again. To the right was the main foyer where she'd entered. To her left was where Janeth went, and Alice scurried after her into a dining room.

The high walls gleamed as the gas lamps reflected off them. Along the opposite wall loomed an enormous china cabinet with five shelves packed tight with polished dinnerware. Waist-high pedestals adorned all four corners of the room, each boasting tall flowerpots with elegantly arranged mixtures of birds-of-paradise, cattails, and tulips. In the center of the room was a mahogany table large enough to seat eight. Stalwart, polished oak chairs were arranged neatly around it beneath a stunning chandelier.

"Please, take a seat." Janeth motioned to the middle chair on the long side of the table. It and the head were the only two with places set. Alice pulled out the chair as Janeth added, "My uncle takes his lunch at noon. He'll be gone an hour." What was that in her voice, a glint of excitement? Surely, Alice had heard wrong.

Settling into the tall, upholstered chair, she examined the salad nestled in an ornate bowl. Glancing at the absurd amount of silverware framing it, she found the crystal glass filled with ice water and took a sip. Janeth had found her seat catty-corner and was looking pleased. Alice wondered at the space between them, shrugging it off quickly. The seating choice was probably something wealthy people did. If one had enormous amounts of space, why not use it? Alice was surprised that she wasn't at the opposite end of the table, leaving them to shout at one another. "What's for lunch?" she asked.

Janeth beamed, removing a silver ring from around the paisley napkin next to her plate. Alice did the same as Janeth replied, "Chicken a la King. To start, though, I thought a Waldorf salad sounded like perfection on a day like this. A nice balance to the gloom outside."

Looking down, Alice decided the sliced red apples, pieces of grilled chicken, and celery tossed in mayo seemed palatable enough. She smiled. "Like the hotel?"

Janeth, who had taken a bite of hers, went wide-eyed. "You know it?"

Alice crunched into a piece of celery, enjoying the tang from the apple juice that coated it. "Saw pictures in a magazine once." Gladys had loved *Woman's Home Companion*, flipping through modern interest stories and gushing over what the models wore.

An amused look crossed Janeth's face. "How wonderful." She took another bite, then a sip of water before adding, "My uncle doesn't care for it. Hence, why I prepared it for when he would be out."

"You made this?" Alice looked around. "A house like this, I thought you'd have a cook."

Janeth chortled, then seemed to collect herself. "Oh no. Uncle had several employees before I lived here. A cook, a maid, a driver…but he lost the need for them in 1920 and was on his own for a while."

"You haven't always lived here?" Alice took another bite, finding she quite enjoyed this salad, though the lack of green leaves remained odd. She glanced at the seat between them. Perhaps this spot did belong to someone else. Maybe Janeth had moved in here with a husband. A woman of her beauty surely had one. She seemed around Alice's age, maybe a little older.

A contemplative look filled Janeth's gaze. She rested her left hand at the edge of the table, her fork pointed delicately above the fine white tablecloth. Alice caught the glint of a wedding band.

Yep, husband.

"No." Janeth hesitated, then lifted her chin as if posing for a painting. The light from the candelabra shone in her hair, the dark shades mesmerizing. Alice noted hues of deep crimson in the brown locks Janeth had rolled and pinned behind her ears. She seemed like she wanted Alice to study her closer, so she did. She took in her skin, her dark eyes, the brown irises nearly black. Her nose seemed perfectly placed above full lips dabbed with lipstick. Alice was torn back to their conversation as Janeth spoke again, but it wasn't in any language she knew.

"I beg your pardon?"

Janeth laughed, looking down. Alice wondered at her amusement. "Nearly everyone sees it right away. I moved to San Diego five years ago. I grew up in a small town in Durango, Mexico."

Mexico? "Oh." Alice swallowed, some of the celery sticking in her throat. She'd never met anyone from Mexico. On the train ride into town, they'd passed citrus groves and fields of strawberries and asparagus. She'd seen people working those fields, people with eyes and hair like Janeth's, but their skin was tanned. Alice reasoned it was from hours spent in the sun each day.

"My uncle, as you may have suspected by the look of him, isn't my true uncle. Mr. Mills took me in. He…" Her voice faltered, and she fingered the edge of her water glass. "Well, I suppose he was tired of being alone and wanted somebody around who understood him."

The comment seemed intended to explain things, but it only left Alice with more questions. She didn't know a lot, but she knew that people from other countries, especially women, rarely lived in places such as this. Why did Mr. Mills invite Janeth to live here? Her mind went back to the wedding band. "Does your husband live here, too?"

Janeth stared as if she hadn't quite heard the question. Alice, chewing, glanced around. It seemed like a fine thing to ask. She was about to repeat herself when Janeth shook her head. "No. He's not here."

"He's in Mexico, then?"

Janeth swallowed a bite, studying the water glass she turned slowly. Finally, her gaze lifted, and Alice saw a distant sadness in it. "My husband died seven years ago."

Alice's throat went dry. "Oh," she muttered, feeling awkward. "I'm sorry."

Janeth took another drink, then gave an odd laugh and waved like she was trying to shoo the topic away. They ate quietly for a time until she asked, "Did you like the apples? They're from my brother's market. He works and lives in Logan Heights with his wife and their two kids."

"They're delicious." Alice pushed the salad bowl forward, and Janeth stood, carefully pushing out her chair.

"Here, let me serve you." She moved around to pull the large ceramic platter closer.

Steam drifted upward when she lifted the lid. Alice's mouth watered just looking at it. Several pieces of finely roasted chicken sat on a large bed of seasoned rice dotted with slices of tomato. "That looks amazing."

"I hope it's good. If not, blame my brother. He supplied the chicken, too."

Alice laughed. Janeth leaned closer to scoop a chicken thigh and rice onto her plate. Alice sat back from the scent of lilac wafting gently past at Janeth's proximity.

When she sat again after serving herself, Janeth said, "I fear I've commandeered the conversation thus far." She threw a glance at a wooden cuckoo clock on the opposite wall. "And here we're already halfway through the hour. Please, Alice, I'm dying to know more about you."

Alice squirmed as she chewed, savoring the taste. She hadn't had a meal this nice since…she couldn't remember. She shrugged. "There's not much to know."

"Come now, don't be modest." Janeth glanced over her shoulder despite Alice being certain they were the only two in the house. She leaned forward and said in a hushed tone, "Tell me about the dollar note."

Alice averted her gaze and took a bite of rice to give herself time to think. She chewed slowly. The truth wasn't an option. Rather, it was a matter of choosing the best lie. "It's my mother," she said slowly, "She's...she's not well."

Janeth frowned, her left hand over her downturned mouth as she said, "Does she need treatment?"

Alice looked sideways, scooting the food around on her plate. "The doctors aren't sure. But medicine is expensive. You looked like somebody who could spare the change. I...I guess I was feeling desperate."

Shaking her head, Janeth said, "Alice, I'm so sorry." She was quiet a moment. "I suppose I'd do the same thing if I didn't have the means." She tilted her head, and Alice tried not to smile at the way her brow furrowed. "Is that why you're in San Diego? To attend the medical facilities here? They're some of the best in the country."

Relieved that Janeth seemed content to fill in the blanks of her story, Alice nodded.

Janeth took another contemplative bite, brushing the fingers of her free hand through her bangs. "You were with those groups, the Temperance women, the last times I saw you."

Damn, thought Alice. How was she going to explain that? "It's a good cause."

At this, Janeth's brow shot up. "Is it?"

The tone of her voice had changed, and Alice eyed her a moment before replying, "My friend's church is involved. I go to show my support."

Janeth opened her mouth like she wanted to respond but seemed to decide against it. They ate in silence for a time. Alice watched the clock tick toward one forty-five as she finished the last of her chicken. "So you came to San Diego with your mother and father...anyone else?" Her gaze flickered to Alice's left hand.

Alice swiped at the corner of her mouth, then remembered she had a napkin and used that to get the pieces of rice stuck near her lips. "No, it's just the three of us."

"That woman, one of your friends from the Temperance group, called you 'Oklahoma.'"

"That's where I'm from. Well, most recently."

"I've never been there." Janeth sat back, seeming to be done with her food as she rested her fork delicately across her plate. "What's it like?"

Immediately, Gladys's screams filled Alice's mind. The psychiatrist's car engine rumbled. The heavy doors slammed shut, muffling Gladys's cries. She inhaled sharply. "It's fine."

Janeth gave a small smile. "You don't like to talk about yourself very much, do you?"

"Not much to tell." Alice studied her spoon, feeling nervous under Janeth's gaze. When she looked up, she found a curious look in Janeth's eye, and she seemed to tear herself away from their gaze as she stood. "Well, I must have you try the Jell-O before you go. It's lime flavored, if you can imagine."

Alice watched her disappear from the room and bring back a silver bowl. A large, round, green Jell-O mold shook as she placed it between their seats. Alice reached for the serving spoon at the same time as Janeth. A warm hum vibrated over her skin when their hands met accidentally, and Alice pulled back. She looked up, startled, to find Janeth wearing a look of wonder that shifted quickly to confusion. She caught Alice's eye. Was that a blush filling her cheeks?

"Pardon me," Janeth said, a sheepish smile lifting her lips, her gaze averted.

Alice motioned for her to go ahead, and she sat back, willing more space between them. They ate the dessert in silence, Alice commenting once, "It's really good," to which Janeth answered, "Wonderful."

A tense silence enveloped them as the clock struck the hour. As if on cue, voices echoed from outside. Janeth cleared her throat. "Well, that will be my uncle. Always on time." She glanced around, and Alice wondered if she was avoiding eye contact with her as she stood.

In the hallway near the door, Alice grabbed her hat. "Thank you for the lunch." She needed to get to the carnival or at least find some tourists in Seaside to grift before heading back home. The desire to stay here just a little longer settled over her shoulders, though. Her stomach was blissfully full, she was warm, and her chest swam with something else she couldn't name.

"It was my pleasure," Janeth said. She stood between Alice and the door, her hands wringing. *Is she nervous?*

"Well." Alice wasn't sure what to say. How did people excuse themselves from fancy luncheons?

"Well, I..." Janeth started, then bit her lip. "I have a bit of a confession."

Alice straightened. She looked toward the next room, then the tall windows behind Janeth, wondering if she could break through them. Of course, she scolded herself, tire me with a full meal, *then* call the cops. *I'm such a fool.*

"I don't have many friends here in San Diego. I'm not a recluse, mind you. I just...well, I find you're someone whose company I quite enjoy. Would you...I mean...what I'm trying to say is..."

"You want to see me again?"

Janeth's cheeks flushed, Alice was certain this time. "Would you mind? I know you have your Temperance friends to meet, and your mother to look after."

Alice frowned, recalling her earlier fabrication. "Right."

"But what do you say to a walk next Tuesday? Hugh will be here tending to Mr. Mills for a while. I can get away between my—" She cut herself off, looking nervous. "Between my other calls. I'd love it if you could join me downtown."

Downtown was too close to her parents' jobs, even if it was during the day. "How about a walk by the ocean?" She gestured to the door. "I love to look at the waves rolling in, especially if it's a clear day."

A strange look filled Janeth's face, but it was gone nearly as quickly as it had appeared. "I wouldn't count on the weather in June, I'm afraid. The fog can get so thick, one can hardly see what's right in front of them."

Confused at her deflection, Alice offered, "All right. Why don't you show me around Seaside? Besides today, I've only been here with the Temperance groups."

Janeth, seeming to prefer this idea, matched her smile just as the front door started to open. "It'd be my pleasure to show you around, Alice."

"Janeth, dear, I'm home." The old gentleman limped inside, cane first. His sister waved and hurried down the hill, leaving him to close the door. They stepped aside to let him in. Upon seeing Alice, he started. "Oh. Janeth, I beg your pardon. I didn't know we had company."

"I'm just leaving," Alice said, eager now to get outside. The tension between her and Janeth had grown thick, and she wasn't sure how much longer she could stand there in the middle of it.

"This is Alice," Janeth said. "Or Miss…"

"Covington," Alice finished for her, reaching for Mr. Mill's free hand. "It's nice to meet you, Mr. Mills. You have a fine house."

He smiled, squinting as if he couldn't really see her. "It's a pleasure to make your acquaintance, Miss Covington. Any friend of Janeth's is a friend of mine."

She smiled as he hobbled past. "Well," she said to Janeth, "I'll be going now."

Holding the door open, Janeth said, "See you on Tuesday?"

Alice turned, catching the hopeful look in her gaze. *God, she has beautiful eyes.* A small voice called from the back of her mind: *What are you doing, Alice? Don't be stupid.* Alice shoved the warnings aside, though. Janeth wasn't like that. She had been married, for crying out loud. All they would be was friends. A friend could do her good. After everything with Gladys, it was nice to meet someone who seemed interested in her. Somebody who wasn't tied to the job she had to do with the Temperance group.

"See you Tuesday," she replied. Then, feeling light, she turned to go.

CHAPTER ELEVEN

The next day, Janeth had just collected the most recent payment from Mr. Preston in Seaside and was admiring a handbag in the store window of a boutique on Second Street downtown. Mr. Aldridge was next on her to-visit list to make sure Hugh had once again made the appropriate deliveries. She was considering the collection of fake berries pinned on a wide-brimmed sun hat when a familiar reflection caught her eye.

Turning, she found her brother leaving a hardware store. "Leo!" She waved, then called again. He smiled and waved back, then hurried across the street, dodging an agitated driver and garnering a whistle from the corner policeman. "What are you doing downtown?" she asked after greeting him. He placed a quick kiss on her cheek. His scent was musky with cologne and the underlying odor of garlic, no doubt from sorting some earlier this morning.

"Maria sent me to put in an order for more wood beams. The ceiling near the back of the store is beginning to sink from the humidity. So queer, this weather lately." He looked skyward, then gave a sideways glance before adding, "We also need some to cover a window while we wait for her cousin Helio to replace the glass."

Janeth had been listening, though her gaze had wandered to a young woman whose hair resembled Alice's. The comment pulled her back to their conversation. "Replace the glass? Whatever for?"

Her brother gave a tight smile at a glare he received from an older gentleman passing by. He leaned closer to her, then said, "Another brick."

Janeth's hand found the end of her necklace. "No. Not again."

"It was only Maria and me inside, thank God. The kids were with Maria's mother down the street." He shook his head, a dark look drawing across his face. "No note this time, either."

"Did you see who it was?"

"Just their backs as they ran and caught the trolley. They hit Estevan's restaurant and Mr. Ruiz's fish market, too."

A seething anger filled her. Her right hand clenched at her side. "Leo, I'm sorry."

"It's only glass," he said. "Glass is replaceable."

Shaking her head, she motioned for him to follow. "Come on." They walked half a block before she asked, "Did the police do anything?" At his incredulous look, she said, "Leo, if you don't call for them, how are they supposed to help?"

"Janeth, you know they won't do anything. Those men who vandalized our property may very well have brothers who are police. They don't care."

The anger swelled in her chest. She forgot, more and more lately, it seemed, how different things were for her brother and sister-in-law. Her life had expanded with Mr. Mills, but it had also been condensed into a bubble. A bubble of safety and confused looks but no questions or slurs and angry jeers when it came to her ethnicity. A flare of guilt sang in her throat for the life she lived in comparison. "If you need help replacing the glass," she said slowly, "in the payment, I mean—"

"We're fine, Janeth." Her brother's voice was curt, but he straightened and smiled. "Thank you."

They slowed in front of a restaurant Janeth recognized from a time she'd met Hugh there to go over the logistics of his deliveries when he had first started working for them. It was small, the wood front painted blue and gold, with red letters on the glass proclaiming fresh soup and warm bread for patrons. Her stomach growled, and she said, "It must be nearly the lunch hour. Come sit with me?" she asked. "I'd love to hear about what the kids have been doing this week."

She started inside. To the host—a young man with red hair and pale blue eyes in a short vest and black pants—she said, "Two for lunch, please." He nodded and disappeared to fetch menus. Turning, she found Leo still outside. Frowning, she pulled open the door. "What are you doing?"

He looked at her in a way she hadn't seen before, like she'd sprouted another head. "Janeth."

"What?"

"Madam, the table is—" The host wore a look of surprise when he spotted Leo in the doorway. He swallowed then said, "I'm afraid the tables are full."

Janeth frowned, stepping closer to peer into the restaurant. She found at least five open tables. "What do you mean? I see several right there."

The host stared at Leo, who put his hands in his pockets. It took Janeth a moment to realize what was going on. When she did, she lifted her chin and asked, "You're certain the tables are full?"

Sweat shining on his pale forehead, the host nodded. "I'm afraid so, madam."

She harrumphed. "Well, that is unfortunate. And this being one of my uncle's favorite locations to dine. I'm sure you've heard of him: Mr. JP Mills."

The host's sweaty face went even paler, though Janeth wasn't sure how that was possible. "Mr. Mills of Seaside?"

"Yes," she said, pretending to rearrange the contents of her handbag. "What a pity I'll have to tell him and all his close friends this establishment has gone downhill. Very well." She snapped her handbag closed and turned on her heel.

Outside, Leo walked slowly behind her. When she stopped to wait for him, he said, "Why did you do that?"

"I couldn't let it be, Leo. Truly now, the audacity of that man. Not serving us like that."

"It wasn't *us* he wasn't willing to serve." She caught his gaze. "Why did you even think I could go in there with you?"

"I…" She paused. The people walking by downtown seemed to stare. The men in fine suits, the ladies in slimming day dresses…they all walked past, their light gazes scrutinizing them, wondering at the dark-haired siblings standing in broad daylight downtown. She stepped out of herself and saw things: she saw how they were the only ones for blocks who looked like them, how people stared, not at her but at Leo. She saw the furtive gazes sizing him up, wondering when he would return to where he came from.

"I'm sorry," she finally said. "I wasn't thinking."

Hands still in his pockets, he eventually smiled and shrugged. "How Mr. Mills lets you keep the books with that mind of yours, I'll never know."

Grateful the tension had broken between them, she laughed. He wrapped an arm around her, and they continued another block.

After stopping in to see Mr. Aldridge—while Leo waited outside—Janeth walked with him to the corner to wait for the trolley that headed to Logan Heights.

"You're sure you don't want to come by for dinner?" Leo said, his posture much more relaxed now, Janeth noted, as he anticipated home.

"No, I'm afraid not tonight. I've got another shipment to get ready for this Friday. The cellar needs rearranging, among other things." It was a bit of an excuse, and she smiled at the idea of being home, alone in her room in the peace and quiet. The notion gave her a sort of thrill. She found she wanted to return to her own space to replay her luncheon with Alice. Already, she was dying to see her again. A new friend, to her surprise, was quite an exhilarating notion. She found Leo's gaze and realized he wore an amused look. "What?"

His smile turned sly and questioning. "Have you met a man?" he asked.

She raised a hand to her necklace, scoffing. "Brother, you've lost your mind. Whatever gave you such an idea?"

He tried to stifle his smile, shrugging. Behind him, the trolley rounded the corner. "Since Mr. Aldridge's, you've been walking with a lightness to your step. Your tone seems gayer than usual. You seem anxious to, I don't know, write a letter to a new paramour?"

She laughed, hoping it didn't sound forced. "Nonsense. Wherever would I even meet someone?"

"Maybe Hugh finally wore you down."

"Come now, Leo."

"Or one of those wealthy white men you do business with."

"You know I've no taste for those men."

The trolley slowed, and Leo headed toward it. He pretended to scrutinize her. "If you say so. But something is different. I'm your brother, I know these things."

She undid the silk scarf around her neck as the sun seemed

suddenly warmer. She waved it at him but also to push the notion away as the trolley trudged onward. Then, she dabbed her neck, glancing around, aware of people everywhere.

"Met someone," she muttered, beginning her walk toward Seaside. But no sooner had she spoken the words than Alice filled her mind. Well, she reasoned, she *had* met someone. But that someone was a woman. A friend. Somebody new whom Janeth found utterly intriguing. She hurried, giving in to the joy of the feeling Alice brought her, and practically glided all the way home.

CHAPTER TWELVE

It was the day she was to meet Janeth, but first, Alice had business to do. She climbed to the cliffside bungalows she'd spotted the first time the Daughters of the Holy League had been in Seaside. This morning, she'd gotten up early to catch the trolley, not feeling like walking after several busy days featuring, among other things, a Temperance protest in National City on Sunday. Madame Enfield continued in her scrutiny, and Alice cursed the matron's intuition. She had nicked a pair of dollar notes and some change from the donation basket before leaving the rest to Mary. Sweet, naive Mary, who never questioned Alice when she volunteered to count their collection, but Madame Enfield's piercing gaze seemed to follow her every move.

Add to that, Saturday night had seen her dragged downtown by her parents, her mother shoving her into her most tattered dress.

"Here," her mother had said, smearing charcoal she'd collected from the railyard beneath Alice's eyes and across her cheek. "This will really get their sympathy." Alice had stood there in their ramshackle dwelling, letting her mother fashion her into the perfect beggar. She had tried not to be envious of her parents' fine garb for their rendezvous at the gambling halls.

The costume had worked, of course, and she'd managed to hide away seventy-five cents while leaving six dollars and ten cents to her father early Sunday. She'd slept a couple hours before finding her way to the Temperance protest, then had snuck out while her parents slept on Monday to pilfer a few pockets on the trolley. Admittedly, despite how tired she was, she found it hard to sleep Monday night in anticipation of her day in Seaside with Janeth.

At the same time, she'd been overcome lately with a surge of defiance, a notion that she needed to embrace every opportunity to get money of her own. Her mother's voice tore open her pockets in her dreams. The cliffside bungalows above Seaside were ideal for a quick job: isolated, sleepy spots, likely empty of tenants when the sun was out and the water enticing. Now, she walked casually and quietly toward the one farthest from the road, tucked away on the cliffside near smatterings of scrub brush and small trees. It was the perfect spot for a quick pick, one that was all her own.

The home was painted green. The side of the house that faced her featured a white front door and three wooden steps leading to a porch with a wooden chair. Around the corner of the bungalow, toward the north-facing cliffs hanging above, she found a window attached to what she assumed was the bedroom. Just inside, she spotted a table hosting several necklaces and a lady's perfume bottle. Alice glanced over her shoulder as the wind blew past, then slowly opened the window just enough to reach inside.

Light music drifted from the room. Someone was home. No matter. She reached in and quickly grabbed the first piece of jewelry—a thin gold chain with a long black pendant—and shoved it into her pocket. Then, she closed the window and hurried away.

Grinning, Alice pulled back her shoulders, wondering how much the necklace might go for. If anything, perhaps she could offer it as payment for a new dress or hat. Something her mother couldn't take away from her.

Later, Alice was ankle-deep in the sand, the small grains wiggling between her stockinged toes when she heard Janeth call her name. Turning, she found her waving from the boardwalk fifteen yards away near the edge of the carnival.

"Hello." She waved back, then beckoned Janeth to join her.

Janeth, who had lifted a hand to shield the sun beyond the rim of her hat, seemed to frown. She pointed behind her toward town. Wind rippled over her day dress. It was red with a wide neck and large white collar that collected in a bell-shaped scarf above her bosom. A band of white also ran just below her waist across the dress, and matching heels completed the ensemble. Janeth's hat was the inverse, white with a red band. She seemed utterly fashionable, and a feeling of admiration filled Alice at the sight. That and something else, something startlingly familiar, as she wondered if Janeth was wearing the same lilac perfume.

"Come on," Alice called, kicking up sand in a teasing manner toward the boardwalk.

Janeth gave a laugh but didn't budge. "Alice," she said over the wind, and Alice caught an uneasy edge to her tone. Sighing, Alice made her way to the boardwalk stairs, brushed off her stockings, and buckled her heels. She looked up expectantly, waiting for Janeth to meet her, but she remained stoically standing in her spot.

Joining her finally, Alice asked, "Got somethin' against the beach?"

Janeth's gaze had been on her ankles but shot up to meet her eyes. "The beach, no. I'm afraid it's the water I'm not fond of." Alice opened her mouth to ask why, but Janeth hurriedly said, "Come. There's much to show you." She looped her arm through Alice's and led her toward the busy streets of Seaside.

"We must stop in here," Janeth said, a balloon of enthusiasm filling her at the sight of Milton's sweet shop on Newport Avenue. The brightly painted storefront beckoned from its corner residence on the busy, tourist-filled block. A bell chimed as three sandy-haired children flew out the front door, the boys in linen shorts intended for the beach and a young girl in a swim-dress chasing after them. A dashing blond couple Janeth presumed were their parents smiled at the gaggle as they waved giant lollipops and hurried back to the beach several blocks away.

Alice, who had practically leapt aside to avoid being run over by the boys, stood in the street studying the shop's window. She didn't wear a hat today, so her hair kept drifting across her eyes. Her hands were gloveless, and the dress she wore was the same as the first time they'd met. She frowned and asked, "Won't this spoil your ladies' lunch?"

Janeth smiled, then laughed at Alice's matching, teasing grin. "You really don't know me, Miss Covington, if that's what you think."

Alice hopped onto the sidewalk now that the coast was clear.

Doing so landed her mere inches from Janeth. She held her gaze and said, "Maybe we can change that."

Janeth swallowed, looking at this woman she wasn't sure what to make of. *She speaks so candidly, like a man.* Clearing her throat, she brushed Alice's elbow to guide her. "Follow me."

Inside, she waved to the shopkeeper, Mr. Milton, who stood behind the counter just inside the door.

"Mrs. Castro! What a delight to see you again." His thick mustache was styled so it came up in a smile to match the one he wore. Blue eyes twinkled beneath bushy eyebrows. A thick waist and belly were contained behind a red-and-white striped shirt beneath a pair of sturdy blue suspenders. His hat was like the vendors' near the carnival: a khaki sun hat with a red band around the base to match his shirt.

"Good day, Mr. Milton." She smiled politely. Her uncle had introduced her to nearly every shopkeeper and restaurant owner in San Diego County when she'd decided to move in with him. A few had eyed her skeptically, but most noted the fetching new clothes, her reserved demeanor, and saw only the newly adopted niece of the wealthy, enigmatic socialite and kept their questions to themselves.

She glanced at Alice, who was walking slowly around the tightly packed barrels brimming with foil-wrapped sweets near the back of the store. Her gaze took in the shelves that lined each wall, where jars upon jars were labeled and filled with a colorful array of taffies, licorice, and hard candies.

Mr. Milton was helping a young woman pay for a box of chocolates as he said loudly, "Mrs. Castro, it's been quite some time since I've seen you in here. A year ago, I believe it was."

"Truly?" she asked, trying to focus on Mr. Milton but flitting her gaze to Alice, wanting to know what she was looking at. She was struck with the urgent need to discover what sort of delicacy Alice preferred.

"Yes, one year and a month." He handed the woman a nickel in change, then raised a pudgy finger to his temple. "I've got a mind like a bear trap. You came in for a few taffies and chocolates."

She smiled, then nodded as the memory returned. "I certainly did. Mr. Mills enjoys the taffy, though I insist they can't be good for his teeth at his age."

He laughed. "Shall I fix you up some of the same?"

"In a minute, if you don't mind." She motioned to Alice, who had been watching her near a stand hosting peppermints in all colors. "I'm showing my new friend around. Whatever she wants is what we'll get."

"Of course." Mr. Milton busied himself restocking some of the jars while Alice continued to peruse. Janeth joined her before the wooden counter separating them from Mr. Milton, whose back was to them as he sorted various sweets. The glass top allowed them views of plates hosting neat stacks of fine chocolates. Each was labeled by a small tented notecard. *White chocolate with strawberry cream. Milk chocolate truffle. Chocolate-covered cherries.*

As Alice seemed to study one of the plates, Janeth asked quietly, "What do you like?"

Alice kept her gaze on the candies. She cocked her head as if thinking. "Well, I tried one of those once before." She pointed to the pretzels drizzled in strips of chocolate. "Those weren't bad."

"Ah, a sweet and savory combination. I know just what to get." She wandered down the counter, and Mr. Milton followed. "Four of these, please."

As he packaged the chocolates, Janeth pretended to busy herself with finding money in her handbag as she eyed Alice still walking carefully along the green-and-white checked floor. Her hazel eyes were bright and curious. Her hands were clasped behind her back but went to her left pocket occasionally, as if reassuring herself it was still there.

Mr. Milton handed Janeth the small paper bag. After paying, she led Alice back outside. A small flutter echoed across her chest as she suggested, "I know a park three blocks down. What say we go enjoy these before I show you a dress shop that I absolutely adore."

Alice agreed. Janeth had noticed she was quiet since leaving the sweet shop. Granted, Alice always seemed quiet. That bright, inquiring gaze swept over wherever she was and whoever she was with, seeming to contemplate five things at once. Janeth wondered if she ever opened up to people. Had anyone been able to break past the furtive first layer of Alice Covington? As they sat on a park bench beneath a large tree, Janeth decided she wanted to try.

"Here we are." The park was a new installation by the city's mayor. It was always busy, placed across from the primary school. The small building stood opposite them, its doors shuttered for the summer.

Several families and groups of children either frolicked across the green lawn or picnicked beneath the shady boughs of a laurel fig tree. Pairs of older men strolled along the edges, conversing.

Alice was scanning their surroundings as they wandered toward a vacant bench. "This is nice."

"Isn't it? I like to bring my niece and nephew here when they come this way."

"How old are they?"

"Elena is seven. Jorge is four." She paused, then asked, "Do you want children someday?"

Snorting, Alice glanced sideways, then seemed to collect herself. A look like she was keeping a clever secret crossed her face as she replied, "I don't think children are in the cards for me."

Janeth's instinct was to console her. It was the reply of every woman she'd known: don't worry, someday, it will happen. But now, after all these years without Victor, Janeth had come to understand the weariness that accompanied such replies. So she only nodded. They sat, and Janeth noticed Alice was doing her best to match her posture.

"What made you want to come here?" Alice asked, her gaze meeting Janeth's. "California, I mean." She gave up on the posture and leaned back against the bench, her ankles crossed easily.

Janeth smiled to combat the sharp, stinging memory that was her reason for leaving Mexico. The image flared brighter, though, marring her vision until she was back there, standing in her yard, shucking corn with her mother when her aunt had come running down the lane, a terrible look across her face. Janeth had gone to her, confused, thinking her cousin had lost another animal to disease or that one of her grandparents had fallen. Instead, she had listened incredulously as her aunt had explained there had been an accident, but not one she could have ever imagined. Victor, his two brothers, and father had been fishing in the ocean when a storm had blown through. All four, each an adept fisherman with years of experience navigating the sea, had perished in mere moments as the water had turned unforgiving and had taken each of them down.

Presently, she raised a hand to the end of her necklace. "I didn't have any reason to stay there," she finally replied. "Not after Victor, my husband, died."

Alice's gaze went to her ring, then back to her. "I see."

"My family was there, of course, but…I suppose I needed something different. My parents, rest their souls, encouraged me to leave. I immigrated here and worked in the cannery over in the shipping yards."

"I knew women who worked in canneries in Mississippi."

"Then you know how the stink of fish lingers on one's clothes, in one's hair, for ages." She gave what she hoped was a more positive smile. "Still, it was a way to earn money as a woman in this new place." Feeling the desire to share more, she explained, "Mr. Mills is good friends with the cannery manager. He often came by to share a brandy and cigar in the office. Sometimes, they'd wander the cannery floor. Mr. Mills took an interest in me."

At this, Alice raised a brow.

Janeth shook her head. "Not that kind of interest. He's a kind man. We had something in common, the two of us. Recent grief. He'd lost his wife in 1915, then his daughter four years later to scarlet fever."

"You reminded him of her."

Janeth shrugged. "Perhaps on some level. I think, more than anything, he was lonely. We were simply two secluded souls, searching for solace. We found some of that with each other. He proposed I come live with him and help him with a few business matters. Three years later…" She waved, gesturing to herself. "And here we are."

Alice's eyes had twinkled when Janeth mentioned matters of business. Janeth moved to place the bag of chocolates between them as Alice asked, "What exactly is Mr. Mills's business?"

Janeth studied the bag, then met her gaze confidently. "He handles imports from Mexico that are featured in many businesses across San Diego County."

"What kind of imports?"

Janeth chuckled, but a sense of unease tickled her spine. She realized how easy it was for Alice to coax words from her. Janeth had intended to get to know Alice more, and here she was again, sharing only about herself. Clever, she thought, this unassuming new friend of hers.

"Oh, you know," she said, waving between them. "Basic goods. It's really quite boring, I assure you." Her voice hitched at the lie. Rum-running was, of course, the least boring business she could possibly imagine. But despite her affinity for Alice, she wasn't sure how she would handle such a truth. Feeling anxious, she opened the bag. "Come now, we haven't even tried one of these yet. I have a feeling you're going to like them."

"What is it?" Alice leaned to look inside, but Janeth pulled the bag back, surprising herself at her own playfulness.

"Well, Alice, since you enjoy a combination of savory and sweet delicacies, I wanted to introduce you to one of my favorites."

Alice was smiling and seemed like she was trying to contain it. "And that is…"

Janeth pulled a one-inch square out of the bag and dropped it into her upturned palm. "Dark chocolate filled with caramel and topped with sea salt."

Alice looked at it and then her. "That sounds expensive."

"It's exquisite is what it is. Here." She moved her palm closer to Alice, her hand even with her chest. Alice leaned back slightly, perhaps at Janeth's hand so close to her, then took the chocolate. As she studied it, Janeth noted the uneven cut of Alice's short nails but also how strong her hands looked.

Janeth grabbed a chocolate of her own. She held it up right before Alice took a bite and said, "To new friends."

Alice grinned, and something flashed in her eyes that made Janeth's stomach flip. Janeth tossed the entire candy into her mouth, savoring the chewy combination of caramel and crisp sea salt. Alice, meanwhile, took a delicate bite, as if unsure how to eat such a thing. Her eyes closed in doing so. In the process, a smudge of caramel dotted her bottom lip. Janeth leaned in at the sight of it, then pulled back. She blinked, wondering at the feeling that had overcome her. She stared a moment more at the caramel, then asked, "Well, what do you think?"

Alice opened her eyes. "It's…like nothing I've had before."

Her words were innocuous, but a flicker of something more laced her tone. Her gaze held Janeth's, and Janeth struggled with the feeling in her chest. It was light, but something deep and distant tugged at her. She felt fraught, like her very body was trying to tear itself in two and hold itself together all at once.

Deciding the only thing to do in such a state was continue their conversation, Janeth scooted back a few inches and asked, "How's your mother?"

Alice was already biting into the second chocolate when she frowned. "My mother?"

"Yes. Has she had an appointment yet?"

Alice glanced down, then said, "Oh. No, not yet."

"Soon, I hope?"

Alice nodded but focused on her chocolate. Janeth, finding she didn't want to leave and continue the tour quite yet, asked, "Where are you living since moving here? Is it somewhere near the medical facility?"

Licking her lip clean of the caramel, Alice replied, "Not really."

It was quiet, and Janeth placed the bag with her last chocolate in her handbag. When Alice still didn't reply, she pressed. "Is your residence near downtown?"

"You could call it that."

Janeth smiled but tilted her head, confused by Alice's elusiveness, as her hand once again went to her pocket. "Alice, why won't you share such things with me? It seems a simple enough question." She tucked a hair behind her ear, glancing around. "I quite enjoy your company, but I'm starting to feel like things are rather one-sided." Alice opened her mouth but closed it, a dark look crossing her face. Her hand returned from her pocket, and a flash of something black caught Janeth's gaze. "Alice?"

Suddenly, she stood. "Thank you, Janeth, for the chocolates. I ought to be going." The flash of black was a pendant stone, and it dragged a gold chain out of Alice's pocket. It fell with a thud on to the grass. She bent to snatch it up, but Janeth, still sitting, beat her to it. Alice reached for it, but Janeth pulled it away from her.

"That's mine," Alice said, but the waver in her voice implied otherwise.

Janeth wasn't sure what to do but decided to stand, matching Alice's stance. "I'm not a jewelry expert, but I was under the impression one wears a necklace here," she said, pointing to her own gold cross. "And one as lovely as this should be worn, I would think." She eyed Alice, a sneaking feeling growing stronger that this necklace had something to do with the handbag from the beach. The muscle along Alice's jawline clenched, and her gaze grew clouded. Rather than shrink back, though, she took the necklace, tugging it away. Janeth let her. "You stole that, didn't you?"

Alice was shoving the jewelry back in her dress pocket. "What do you care?"

The rude question hit Janeth, and she stepped back. "I beg your pardon?"

"I said, what do you care?"

"I care because…" Janeth lost the words as they fumbled from her to Alice, whose eyes swam with hurt and fear and something else. Unsure what to say, she reached for Alice's hand. Gently, she said, "Perhaps I could help."

Alice looked at their hands together but pulled hers back. "There's no helping me."

"But your mother…"

"My mother isn't sick."

"She's…what?" Alice looked skyward, and Janeth shuffled uneasily. A trio of women nearby were watching them. "I don't understand," she said, keeping her voice low.

Alice had tears in her eyes. She took a long breath, shaking her head like she couldn't believe what she was about to say. "I live near the railyard. I'm a swindler, okay?" She practically spat out the words, low and sharp. "My father is a con man. My mother is a thief. I was born a no-good pickpocket. All right? We're swindlers. Crooks. Cheats." She took a heated breath. "Nobodies. I'm nobody."

Janeth's head swam. "I don't understand."

"Come on, Janeth." Alice stepped back. "I'm sure that uncle of yours educated you. Gave you books to read." She gestured to herself, but the look on her face was one of revulsion. "You know the type. Now you've met one in the flesh."

The last word drew Janeth's gaze to the pulse at Alice's neck that was beating rapidly in her agitated state. She licked her lips and tried to recover her train of thought. "But you…"

Alice stared, waiting. A deep, bright glimmer of what Janeth thought was earnest longing burned in the back of her gaze.

You've opened something in me I can't name, she wanted to say. But how could that be, when Alice, the person she'd thought was a friend, had been lying to her this entire time?

When the words still didn't come, the hope died in Alice's eyes, and she lowered her gaze. "I'll see you around, Janeth." Hands in her pockets, Alice walked back toward the beach, leaving Janeth standing in a tangle of thoughts she didn't think she'd ever be able to unravel.

CHAPTER THIRTEEN

A lice couldn't stop trembling, like she'd been stuck on the rumbling trolley for too long and was left disoriented and unsteady. It took extreme effort just to walk. All she could do was focus on her feet as she wound through downtown, bumping into unsuspecting passersby until she made it to the soot-laden railyard. Nearly back home, she steadied herself along the tracks, leaning against a rusted, vacant rail car.

She slowed her breathing, leaning back against the hard metal. What was she doing? She liked Janeth. She knew that. But Alice also knew very well the dangers that came with enjoying the company of another woman. Her right hand found her left arm, and she squeezed it, trying to relieve some of the pressure building inside her.

You're lonely. Loneliness makes you sloppy, makes you forget. From the first moment she had met Janeth, it was clear the effect she had. It had taken mere minutes for Alice to break two rules that governed her life. Now, she had revealed more truths before Janeth. Not even Gladys had known the reality of who she was in this world: a lowly pickpocket with nothing to offer anyone.

Somehow, she'd trusted Janeth with this truth. Like with her handbag, she could have summoned a cop upon learning about the necklace. But she hadn't. It seemed impossible, but perhaps she truly didn't care.

Wishful thinking. Alice wiped tears that had strayed down her cheeks. Fixing her hair, she smoothed her dress and made her way to the house.

"Dinner is on the stove, Dumplin'," her father called as soon as she walked in. He scurried to her, smiling wide and placing a quick kiss on her cheek before finding a seat to tug on his shoes. His aftershave lingered in the air with old cigarette smoke. He and her mother were already dolled up. Another evening in the gambling hall awaited them downtown. Alice had overheard them the other day. They'd lost more than half of what they'd won the week before and were determined to get it back. Additionally, her mother had weaseled her way into a circle of dressmakers and was pilfering material to sell to other shops across town. Per usual, it was a daily roller coaster of "Where is the money coming from?" with their eyes—no, her mother's eyes—set on Alice for an answer.

She trudged to the stove. Pulling off the pot lid, she found bits of stew stuck to the burned bottom. Her stomach rumbled. She had hoped to have lunch with Janeth, but that, of course, hadn't panned out. A boiled egg sat on the table, and she snatched it up, scarfing it down.

"Who put a bee in your bonnet?" her mother asked. She stood across the room, watching Alice in the mirror as she donned a long shimmering earring to match her fitted black dress that fell just below her knees.

"I'm only tired," she replied, which was mostly true. The day with Janeth had seemed to wring her dry. She felt like the frayed end of one of her dresses, ready to come undone at a moment's notice.

Her mother's gaze narrowed. Alice worked to rid herself of even the thought of Janeth. Her parents couldn't know where she'd been or who she had been with. "It wasn't a Holy League day," her mother said. "Tell us, Alice. Where have you been?"

She turned, using the cold edge of the stove to brace herself and face the room. The belief she'd always held in her abilities—her quick thinking, her sharp tongue and crafty lies—shrank away. Damn her, she thought, remembering Janeth. *What has she done to me?* "I was in Seaside."

Her mother, dabbing a drop of old perfume on her neck, turned. "Seaside?" She seemed to consider the notion. "John, did we tell Alice to work a job in Seaside today?"

Her father finished tying his shoes and leaned back in the kitchen chair. He glanced at her mother, then at Alice, who hoped he could read the plea in her eyes. He grimaced, then stood. "I don't recall, my love."

One brow raised, the start of a smile lifted her mother's lips.

Alice could see the words growing in that smile. The words that waited eagerly for Alice to mess up again. They waited for her to show her true colors like she had once before. They waited for the moment her mother could do what she hadn't been able to in Oklahoma.

Anxiety overwhelming her, Alice felt sick. She had to think of something to say but couldn't. She cursed herself and her own cowardice as she pulled the necklace from her pocket.

"There are plenty of wealthy tourists in Seaside." She shrugged, forcing her voice to remain casual. She tossed the piece on the table like it didn't mean anything and wasn't the one thing she had taken for herself today.

Her mother slunk closer, reaching slowly for the jewelry from the other side of the table. The gold chain glinted in the dim lighting. She examined the pendant, and her smile widened. "Well," she finally said, handing the necklace to her father, "what a relief. Here I thought you had wasted another day."

Alice's resolve cracked, and she turned around, pretending to search for a fork to scrape up some of the stew. Closing her eyes, she listened as her parents grabbed their things and headed out for the night.

"Be good, Dumplin'," her father called before they left, and she was alone.

After a bath in the shared yard behind the shanties, Alice crawled into bed. Her stomach ached from the stew, or perhaps the lack of real food, and she tried fitfully to sleep. When dreams did come, they seemed as troubled as her body, twisting themselves around her, wrenching old memories to the front, forcing her to see them once again:

"Gladys," Alice said, tracing her fingers up her arm. They sat on the floor of Gladys's room, leaning against the small bed frame on the patterned rug. Daylight streamed in through an east-facing window, lighting the fine furnishings and shelves in golden rays. Alice had loved Gladys's room; it felt the way she imagined a home should feel: warm, soft, and safe. "When can we go away together?"

Their knees pressed against each other, Gladys grabbed her hand. "Al, you know we can't do that."

Alice chewed her lip, searching the room. The house was quiet. Gladys's father worked in a bank, and her mother was on a trip to Lincoln to visit her sister. Alice had come over after sunup, her own parents under the impression she was begging on a corner downtown near the hospital.

"We could go anywhere," she said. "Just you and me. What about Boston?"

Gladys laughed, high and light, then snuggled into Alice's neck. She kissed below her ear, then pulled back, meeting her gaze. "And what would we do in Boston?"

"Whatever we liked," Alice said, her finger tracing up Gladys's dress sleeve, over her shoulder, then down the front buttons. She grinned, undoing one of them, then another.

Gladys found her hand. "Al, we can't."

"It's all right," she said, leaning closer. Alice kissed her, and she relished the way Gladys's entire body relaxed. She could do this forever. A distant creak made her stop, though, and Gladys put a warning hand on her chest. They both listened, breathing as quietly as they could. Her gaze finding Gladys's lips once again, Alice leaned close.

"Al."

She cut Gladys off with another kiss.

The bedroom door burst open. Gladys shot away from her like a bullet. "Father!"

The next few minutes were a torrid blur. Gladys's father, red-faced, tore into the room. He was shouting, and Alice was being shoved away. She reached for Gladys as he spewed accusations: "You promised you'd never see her again." Gladys was crying. Alice was stumbling to the door, reaching for her.

She was thrown outside. Alice lingered near the elegant brownstone, knowing she wasn't wanted there but desperate to get inside and help Gladys. She stood, shaking, clutching her arms across her chest when the doctor's car arrived.

"No," she said, standing near the streetlamp. The doctor, an old man with shiny white hair, a baggy suit, and rounded shoulders hurried up the stairs of Gladys's home. His glasses perched on the end of his nose. At the same time, a voice came from behind her.

"Dumplin'?"

"Father?" Alice felt sick, throwing a worried look back to the house. "What are you—"

"I was nearby." His gaze was sympathetic but worried. "I had a feeling you were here."

"Father, I'm sorry. I…I had to see her."

He took a long breath. A crashing sound from inside the house drew both their gazes. Moments later, Gladys was being shoved out the door. Her father had a suitcase in one hand as he pulled her by the wrist with the other. The doctor walked behind them solemnly, hands clasped behind his hunched back.

"Gladys!" Alice started for them, but her father pulled her back.

Gladys didn't hear her, though. She was screaming, hysterical, tears staining her cheeks as she pleaded with her father. Her cries fell on deaf ears as Alice saw the unrelenting decision in his cold face as he forced his daughter into the back seat of the doctor's car.

"No," Alice called again, fighting against her father's grip. "No, Gladys, please."

Gladys's father shook hands with the doctor, who climbed into the passenger seat after a brief, muttered exchange. People had gathered across the street to watch. Women spoke behind fans or gloved hands. Men muttered, their prying eyes taking in everything. Alice hated them.

"Alice," her father was saying, "we need to go." From the base of the front stairs, Gladys's father glared and seemed to contemplate coming over. Instead, he only tossed an angry stare to the onlookers, then stormed inside, slamming the door behind him.

The car sputtered to a start and started down the street. "Gladys," she shouted, trying to run after it. This wasn't how it was supposed to be. They were supposed to be together. They were supposed to slip away to somewhere beyond, somewhere where they could be happy. Somewhere, Alice realized as she slammed her eyes shut, Gladys's screams echoing, that could never really exist.

CHAPTER FOURTEEN

"Janeth, love, here's the payment for Hugh's delivery." Maria handed her an unassuming burlap purse. Coins sat heavy in it, and Janeth quickly slipped it into her handbag.

"I do hope this next round will be to everyone's liking. Hernandez mentioned they're from a different ranch known for their blue agave."

"You know it will be a success." She gave a knowing smile. Jorge scampered past where they stood behind the counter, the partition to the rest of the store raised. He sprinted through it, Elena on his heels. The frilled ends of her dress kicked up behind her, her long, dark hair flowing in a determined mane after her brother. "You two, what have I told you? No running in the store."

"Mama, Jorge took my ribbon." She gestured to her hair where one yellow ribbon remained neatly tied around a small braid near her temple. The other braid was unadorned.

Leo emerged from the back room. Besides the five of them, the store was quiet on a Wednesday morning. It had been over a week since her day with Alice, and Janeth had found herself in need of familiar faces. Leo called after Jorge, but it was half-hearted as his son continued a gleeful lap around the store with Elena resuming her chase as an elderly couple entered. The woman wore a cotton dress dyed sunflower yellow, a multicolored shawl wrapped around her shoulders. She playfully chastised Jorge in Spanish as he narrowly missed colliding with her. Her husband, meanwhile, called a greeting to Leo. The men started a lively conversation as Leo managed to corral Jorge, tug the ribbon from his tiny grasp, and return it to a relieved-looking Elena.

Maria, after quickly rearranging the top tier of apples in their display crate, said hello to the woman. Janeth recognized the couple as Mr. and Mrs. Diaz, who ran a restaurant known for their seafood on the other side of the barrio.

Janeth remained at the counter, feeling stuck as the conversations filled the store. She followed each thread of banter fine—Leo and Mr. Diaz discussed the men running for mayor, while Maria and Mrs. Diaz conversed about the weather—but found herself unwilling to interject. The last year had seen her spending less and less time in Logan Heights. Besides that, her native tongue sounded more and more foreign as English conversations with Mr. Mills and his customers overran and overwhelmed her mind.

Elena tugged at the waist of her dress. "Aunt Janeth?"

"Yes?"

"What do you think Uncle Victor is doing in heaven?"

Janeth smiled and knelt as more customers trickled in. "My, what a question." She considered it a moment. "I like to think he's enjoying a fresh mango beneath the leaves of a cypress tree. It's always summer and always the perfect weather for such a treat."

"Are the mangos fresh in heaven?" Elena wore a serious look, and Janeth reached out to brush her cheek, wondering at how like Maria she was.

"Always."

This seemed to satisfy her, and she skipped away to drag her brother to the back of the store. A pang hit Janeth near her ribs, and she found the end of her cross beneath her dress.

"Janeth, can you help Mr. Diaz with their supply?" Leo winked, gesturing to the back of the store.

"Of course." She made her way to the storeroom and found the packages labeled "Fresh bread." Grabbing one to peer inside the wrapping, she found the part that revealed the hollowed loaf hosting a concealed bottle of tequila. She handed four of the packages to Mr. Diaz. In Spanish, he thanked her, adding, "You need to come by the restaurant sometime. Your brother speaks often of you when he's there. It would be nice to see the family together."

She didn't imagine his words were intended as rude, but she stiffened nonetheless. "That's a kind invitation."

Shaking her hand, he seemed to accept the response and turned to peruse a few other items while he waited for his wife to finish chatting with Maria. Janeth had gone back to inspect the rest of Hugh's delivery work—each product seemed in fine shape, as far as she could tell—and was helping to restock some of the bean jars behind the counter when another customer entered.

Leo called out a welcome as he and Maria helped other customers on opposite sides of the store. Janeth noted the furrowed brow on Maria's face at the sight of the new patron.

"Alice?"

Much like she had in the sweet shop, Alice seemed to be taking everything in. *She's sizing up the place*, Janeth thought, though she chastised herself for such a sentiment. *Well, she is a thief.* Attention to detail probably came with the territory. Her inquiring gaze made more sense. The realization was followed by a question: why was she here?

Janeth glanced again to Maria, who eyed Alice as she readied a bag of corn and asparagus for a young man. Janeth felt frozen behind the counter as Alice approached. "What are you doing here?" she managed to ask once Alice was within earshot.

Alice's eyes seemed to take in her hair, done in an underpin today to mimic the short-hair most women wore. She scanned her jacket, her forearms, before answering. "My father had a meeting near the trolley station in town." Now on the other side of the counter, she rested one hand on the worn wood. Her gaze fell as her fingers thumped in an uneven beat. Was she nervous? Unease seemed to radiate from her posture as she stood perpendicular to Janeth, like she was ready to dash out the door at a moment's notice. "I remembered you mentioning your brother's market. This was the first one I saw."

Janeth stood, bewildered and elated at Alice's presence. Finally, she said, "I didn't think you wanted to see me again."

Alice looked up. Shadows had grown beneath her eyes. Had she not been sleeping? "I didn't think I did, either."

"But here you are."

Alice smiled. "Here I am."

Maria appeared next to Alice. Her smile was kind, but her eyes were cautious. In Spanish, she asked, "May I help you?"

Alice stepped back, then looked to Janeth, who felt a small blush creep into her cheeks as she translated. "Is there anything we can get for you?"

A flicker of something flashed in Alice's eyes, something daring that sent a ripple of anticipation through Janeth. She swallowed at the feeling's familiarity. She'd felt something just like it years ago, when Victor had courted her.

"Not today, thank you," Alice replied. Maria smiled. Turning, she shot Janeth a wary look before hurrying after Jorge, who was jumping on sacks of flour in the store room.

"About the other day," Alice said, stepping closer to once again rest her hand on the counter. She gave a slight shake of her head. "The way I spoke to you…"

Reaching out, Janeth rested her hand on Alice's. She kept her voice low as she said, "It's already forgiven." The shift from trepidation to relief on Alice's face struck something in her, and she felt delight at easing her fear. They were to be friends, Janeth knew. Even if Alice was who she said, there was something in the air between them that drew Janeth in, convincing her theirs was a kinship she couldn't let go. Meanwhile, Alice's gaze fell to their hands, still pressed together on the counter.

A warmth swam from Janeth's fingers to her chest. Again, that strange, distant feeling that reminded her of moments with Victor overcame her. She inhaled, then pulled her hand back. Recalling their last meeting, she felt a hundred questions packed tight on her tongue, but this was hardly the place for such a conversation. "Will you meet me for coffee?"

Alice's eyes widened. "Coffee?"

"How's next Thursday?" Janeth ran through her mental calendar of appointments. She could squeeze in an hour with Alice during lunch. She'd have to ask Hugh if he could come by the mansion to ensure their uncle was taken care of. Alice coming to see her after their time in the park was no small matter. It urged Janeth to keep this newfound kinship burning, and she smiled at the excitement stirring within her.

A blond man, his hair thick with pomade, breezed into the store. High-waisted brown pants fell over tan loafers that didn't quite match. His blue collared shirt was rolled to the elbows, no doubt to keep the warm summer air at bay. His eyes lit up at the sight of Alice, and he hurried over to her. "Dumplin', there you are."

"Sorry, Father. I was…I saw the market and thought I'd stop in for a few things."

Janeth noticed the similarities between the two, especially in the way he smiled, a little lopsided, as he said genially, "Good idea." He fished in his pocket and produced a dollar note. "I'm sure this lovely young lady can help you." Alice, whose posture had stiffened at her father's presence, nodded. "Don't be long, now. We've got to get home." He touched his forehead in a salutation to Janeth, then disappeared outside.

"Your father seems nice."

Alice seemed anxious, though, and only pushed the dollar note across the counter. "Eggs will be fine," she said, her gaze fixed on the money.

Janeth packaged a dozen fresh eggs. When she was certain neither Maria nor Leo was looking, she stuffed a pear and two apples into the sack. Giving Alice her change she said, "Next Thursday?"

Tossing a look over her shoulder as if to check if her father had returned, Alice seemed to try to contain a smile. "I know a spot. What time?"

Janeth bit her lip, excitement trilling through her. "One o'clock?"

"One o'clock."

Alice left. Janeth didn't realize she was still watching the spot where she had stood when Maria's voice cut through the air. "Who was that, Janeth love?"

"What?"

Maria scooted behind the counter, leaning against it, a curious spark in her dark eyes. "The white woman you were speaking with. You seemed to know her."

"Oh." Janeth gave a laugh, but it sounded forced. She swallowed to clear her throat. "A friend. A new friend."

"One of your uncle's customers?"

"No. She's new to town. We met in Seaside." She found she didn't want to relay all the details. She knew enough of how Maria felt about white people, and rightfully so. But Alice wasn't like that. She was, apparently, a lot of things, but she wasn't like that. Janeth was certain.

One hand on her hip, Maria looked like she was ready to interrogate her. Much to Janeth's relief, Elena called from the back of the store. "Mama, Jorge stuck a bean in his nose, and I can't get it out."

Maria straightened. "Coming, my love."

Janeth exhaled, brushing back strands of hair as she busied herself with taking down, then replacing different jars along the shelves.

Her movements hardly registered, though, as the only thought that consumed her was the notion that she was going to see Alice again.

❖

Alice walked quietly beside her father, the sack of goods from Janeth nestled in the crook of her left arm. Near the railyard, a train whistle sounded. They stopped. The rumble of the oncoming train shook the earth. Another whistle pierced the midday sky as they waited.

Her father took a deep breath, then said, "She looks like Gladys."

Alice had been watching the pebbles jump over one another from the train's force. She jerked her head up, meeting her father's gaze. Her throat went dry, her heart pounding. The train screeched by, its cars lurching hungrily across the tracks. "She's not like her."

Her father placed both hands in his pockets, his lips puckered in thought. "Is she a Temperance gal?"

"No."

Ahead, the cars sped by, green and blue phantoms flying past. The sound of wheels grating against the track scraped through the late afternoon air.

"You know what your mother would say."

Alice turned, tucking the grocery sack close. "It's nothing. Honest. She's a friend." A lump rose in her throat. "Can't I have a friend?"

Her father's clouded gaze studied her. Alice saw his concern. In his face, she saw the memories replay. She heard the shouting that fated day when Gladys had gone.

The final cars raced past. Another whistle broke open overhead.

He didn't say anything else. He didn't have to. Alice knew the words, knew the warnings. They were the same he'd said to her as he'd led her home that afternoon after Gladys was taken away, ripped from her life. "You have to forget her. Forget…" He'd had tears in his eyes, confusion and fear clear in the lines on his face. "All of it. It's not safe for people…like that."

Like that. She was a person *like that*. Alice hadn't known until she'd met Gladys what that even meant. She had fancied women in moving pictures and advertisements but had imagined all the girls did. Why else would they print their photographs all over newspapers? Her affair with Gladys had seemed natural, but at the same time, she'd known

Gladys had been right in her warnings. Women could show affection to one another. To a point. The way men and women went together was different, though it was everything Alice wanted for herself.

Now, Janeth was rekindling those longings. She was kind and inquisitive. Each look from those eyes was full of care and grace. Alice hadn't thought anyone would, or could, look at her in such a way again. Or want to know her in a way that made her feel special. Like she was more than an ignorant pickpocket. Like she was someone worthy of being cared for. Janeth sparked the urge in Alice to reach out, to brush a lock of hair from her face, to run her fingers down her arm. The image of the day at the carnival returned. The way she had relished the line of Janeth's stockings, dying to follow the seam to its fruitful end beneath her dress.

Finally, the passing train disappeared down the track as the earth quelled its rumbling.

"She's only a friend," Alice said again, shifting the grocery sack to her other arm as if the fragile package needed her protection from the world.

Her father didn't say anything, and they continued home.

CHAPTER FIFTEEN

"Madam Enfield was asking after you, Oklahoma." Dorothy sipped her coffee across from Alice near the back of Baley's Café. "Tardiness is her least-tolerated trait."

Alice pushed back in her chair. The café was busy on a Sunday evening. Families in day dresses and suits looked like they'd come from a church service for an early dinner. She briefly wondered at such a life and how different it was from her own before replying, "I had to help my parents." She had been out late with them, assisting her mother, who was lifting more dress material from a shop's back room downtown, selling it for a pretty penny to unsuspecting competitors. The late night had found her oversleeping today. Her father had woken her and hurried her out the door. By the time she'd caught the trolley and found her way to Coronado, the Temperance protest had nearly ended. She'd been so tired that she didn't even bother trying to pick any of the donations, leaving a pleased-looking Mary to count the contributions.

Dorothy tucked a dark strand of hair back beneath her hat, her gaze on her half-eaten biscuit. A funny look filled her face as she spoke. "Late nights, little sleep…" She let the words hang in the air, a suggestive grin spreading as she met her gaze. "Oklahoma, if I didn't know better, I'd say you've met a gentleman."

Alice coughed to stifle her laugh. She pretended to brush crumbs from the table, then swiped the linen napkin across her mouth to collect herself. Apparently interpreting this as an admission, Dorothy pressed on. "It's exactly like when Harold and I were courting." She sighed, her eyes finding the middle distance. "We couldn't get enough of each other. If my parents had known where we'd been..." She chuckled, shaking her head.

Alice bit her lip, remembering Janeth in the market the other day. The way her dress had clung to her figure had left Alice wondering what lay beneath the fine material. Janeth's eyes had shined with longing during their conversation, as if tiptoeing around the idea of wanting to see her again. Alice still couldn't believe how easily Janeth had forgiven her for her outburst in the park. Such generosity wasn't something she was familiar with, and it drew Alice in. Forcing herself back to the conversation, she said quietly, "I may have met someone."

Dorothy straightened, a satisfied look on her face as she thumped the table. "I knew it. I've got a sixth sense for these things. It's from my aunt on my mother's side. She was a mystic." Dorothy started in on the history of women who possessed "the gift" in her family.

Alice tried to listen, but all she could think about was this Thursday, when she'd get to see Janeth. Beneath the anticipation, though, her father's warning gaze stared from the shadows of her mind. It crept into her chest and curled beneath her heart, urging her to be cautious.

She determined then and there that she would be careful. She'd already laid a lot in Janeth's hands: her name, her identity, her lot in this life. She couldn't risk sharing that other part of her, the part that longed to feel how soft Janeth's lips were, to kiss the inside of her thigh, to press her hard against the wall. No, Alice needed to contain herself.

Or at the very least, try.

Inside Baley's Café on Thursday, Janeth smiled behind her cup of coffee. Midday light landed softly along the tiled floor near the front windows of the restaurant. Besides a nearby table of well-dressed businessmen, she and Alice were the only patrons. Alice was sharing her latest adventure with the Daughters of the Holy League. It was the most she'd heard Alice speak thus far in their time together. Even her posture seemed more relaxed.

"I like the way you explain things," she said when Alice paused for breath.

Alice's gaze narrowed a moment before she grinned. "You do?"

"You're direct."

Laughing, Alice said, "I never knew how to be anything else."

Janeth sat back and listened as Alice regaled her with how her friend Mary, whom she remembered as the tiny redhead, had nearly fallen down a sand dune last week, her protest sign had been so heavy.

A jarring *ring* made both of them turn. The bartender slung a rag over his shoulder before answering the candlestick phone nestled in the back corner of the bar. He ran a hand over his mustache as he listened to the operator. Janeth had refocused on Alice when the bartender called out, "Is there a Mrs. Castro present?"

Alice gave her a curious look. Janeth shrugged at her inquisition and stood. At the bar, she ignored the way the table of businessmen watched her as she took the earpiece and leaned on the bar to speak. "Hello?"

"Mrs. Castro, I'm in dire need of your assistance."

"Hugh?" She glanced across the room at Alice. "How did you know I was here?"

"You're with Miss Covington for coffee, are you not?"

"I...yes."

"Baley's is the most popular spot for the Temperance gals. It wasn't that difficult to imagine where you'd be."

Feeling a flush creep up her neck, Janeth recalled his initial statement and cleared her throat. "What have you gotten yourself into this time?"

His buoyant voice cut through the static of the line. "I've met a lovely dame, see. She's from your neck of the woods."

"Logan Heights?"

"Thereabouts, I think."

She rolled her eyes. "What do you need me for?"

"Isn't it obvious? I am an expert elocutionist in English, Mrs. Castro, but Spanish? I'm afraid I'm lacking."

"You want me to tell you what to say?"

"You're a doll. Now, how would I tell her, 'You have the most inviting and supple—'"

"Hugh."

"Very well. 'You are a divine creature at whose altar I must worship.'"

She shook her head. "Why don't you start with 'What's your name?' or 'Would you join me for coffee some time?' "

Hugh gave a dramatic sigh. "So provincial." He paused. "Very well. What'll it be?"

She proceeded to give him a few introductory phrases to use. Once he repeated them and seemed satisfied, she said, "You've got it. Now, I expect you to be a gentleman about this."

"Aren't I always? Cheers, Mrs. Castro."

She chuckled as the line clicked, then returned the phone to the bartender and rejoined Alice. As she did, she felt the bartender's gaze follow her to her seat.

"Who was that?" asked Alice.

"Oh, only Hugh." Janeth noted their empty cups. "Shall we pay and continue on?" She was eager to show Alice a new boutique. They had just enough time before her next appointment.

At the counter, Janeth opened her handbag. Alice stood behind her, hands in her dress pockets as she seemed to study the other patrons. "Here you are," she said, passing fifty-six cents across the bar. "For the two coffees."

The bartender eyed her a moment, then said, "It's thirty-eight cents a cup."

Janeth frowned. She found the menu overhead. Behind her, Alice drew nearer. Janeth pointed to the prices scrawled in chalk above the back of the bar. "That says twenty-eight cents, if I'm not mistaken."

Not bothering to look, the bartender grabbed a glass and started to clean it. "It's thirty-eight cents for you."

"What are you talking about?" Alice stepped forward. "It has the price right there. Why should we pay more?"

Janeth shifted, muttering a sentiment not unlike the one Leo spoke that day downtown, "It's not *we* he's charging more." Her throat felt dry. She glanced over her shoulder. The trio of businessmen watched them. "Alice, please," she said quietly. They were already drawing more attention than she cared for.

"No," Alice said, either ignoring her or interpreting her plea as one for help. "That's not fair." She turned on the man. "What kind of a business is this?"

Wanting to leave, Janeth fished in her handbag for more coins. No sooner had she started than Alice's hand came down on hers. "You're not paying him."

"Alice," she said again, an urgent warning in her voice. She felt hot. The last few years, Janeth had navigated Seaside like a cat. She moved quietly about her days, remaining out of sight when she needed to. As long as she went where she should, when she should, she was fine. The permanent residents knew or knew of Mr. Mills. But temporary workers passing through didn't know him—and therefore her—from Adam. They only saw her and jumped to their own conclusions. Meeting Alice's gaze, she shook her head. Slowly, Alice retracted her hand.

After paying, Janeth hurried outside with Alice on her heels.

"Janeth, what are you—"

"Stop." She spun around, stepping toward Alice with more gusto than she intended. Seemingly startled, Alice stumbled back onto the sidewalk. "Alice, what did you think you were doing?"

Frowning, she looked flabbergasted at the question. "I was helping you."

"I don't need your help." Janeth tried to keep her voice low as passersby eyed them. Walls she had built upon first moving to the United States sprang up again. She had forgotten they existed, but Alice's actions in the café had exhumed them, leaving Janeth defensive. The last thing she needed was a white woman as a savior. Janeth had worked too hard for too long to get to where she was. Yes, luck had been a part of the draw in San Diego, but Mr. Mills's name wasn't something she liked to throw around for protection. This wasn't like the host not serving Leo. Alice speaking for her implied she was content to hide behind someone else, and that was something she refused to do. She had earned her standing amongst the people of Seaside. Even if, as she was reminded of today, she was still a step behind.

Alice seemed at a loss for words. Janeth heard Leo and Maria's voices in her head: "Who do you think you are, Janeth? Cavorting around town with white people. Expecting to be treated like one. You think you're better than us now, don't you?"

"No," she muttered.

Alice asked quietly, "What?"

Blinking, Janeth oriented herself. "You should go." She cursed herself. What had she been thinking? "I've got to get to my appointment," she added brusquely, unable to look at Alice. She turned to go as Alice reached for her.

"Janeth, I didn't mean to insult you. Please, wait."

"I'll see you another time, Alice," Janeth called over her shoulder. She put her head down and headed toward downtown.

❖

"Good afternoon, Mr.—Oh, Mrs. Aldridge." Janeth straightened, a strange nervousness washing over her. "How lovely to see you."

Mrs. Aldridge was reorganizing a stack of ledgers on her husband's desk. Her light blue eyes found Janeth, seeming to squint in the dim office light. "Mrs. Castro?" Her gaze flitted to a wooden wall clock. "Do I have the time wrong? You were expected at two o'clock."

Janeth grimaced as she read two fifteen. The events at Baley's had caused her to lose track of time. "I do beg your pardon. My last appointment ran long." Mrs. Aldridge didn't say anything. Rather, she only stared, her gaze seeming to take in Janeth's long skirt, the fine earrings she wore. Janeth, for a moment, felt as if she'd gotten dressed wrong thanks to the way Mrs. Aldridge scrutinized her. Wanting out from under such attention, she gestured to the corner where a crate sat unopened. "I trust the delivery was made safely?"

Mrs. Aldridge straightened. Janeth had forgotten how tall she was. They'd met once before, when Mr. Aldridge had joined the business circle. She'd welcomed him and Mrs. Aldridge into the mansion for a meeting with her uncle. Now, she recalled Mr. Aldridge sharing that his wife's family hailed from Denmark. Janeth wondered if everyone there was a light-haired giant.

Presently, Mrs. Aldridge replied, "Yes. I'd just arrived last night to meet my husband for dinner when that lovely young man came by with everything."

"Wonderful." A din of conversation began in the store, drawing Janeth's gaze. A group of middle-aged women had wandered in.

"Well," Mrs. Aldridge said, dipping her hand quickly into a drawer and procuring a twenty dollar note. "Here you are." She remained on the other side of the desk, however, and extended her hand. Janeth hurried to grab the payment.

"Thank you." She didn't miss the way Mrs. Aldridge's hand

retracted quickly. Her gaze flitted over Janeth's shoulder, a look of worry growing on her face.

"If you wouldn't mind, Mrs. Castro…" She let her voice trail off as she gestured behind her. A narrow door which Janeth knew led to the back alley stood closed.

It took a moment for Janeth to understand. She opened her mouth, but the words fell flat. She pursed her lips and forced a smile. "Of course."

Mrs. Aldridge gave a smile of her own, though Janeth knew it was more of relief than courtesy as Janeth moved to leave out the back door. She threw a final glance at Mrs. Aldridge as she hurried to the front of the store, closing the office door so as to obscure any patron's view.

In the alley, Janeth leaned back against the brick. She closed her eyes, trying to ignore the queasiness in her stomach. She clenched her jaw as the smell of dirt and garbage drifted around her. The nerve, she thought, throwing a glare at the brick wall. Slowly, she took a breath, pinching the bridge of her nose to collect herself. Something had to be in the water today. First the bartender, now Mrs. Aldridge. She hadn't had a day like this in a long time. Running a hand over her forehead to ease the tension building there, she recalled the way Alice had acted in Baley's. Admittedly, Janeth hadn't wanted the attention. Thinking about it now, she realized Alice was only standing up for her. Janeth's pride had been at the forefront. The way Alice had acted wasn't because she was white. It was because she cared. She had only cared, and Janeth had pushed her away.

She shook her head, placing the payment in her handbag, and tried to rid herself of the uneasy feeling today had left her with. Then she pulled back her shoulders and headed for the trolley.

CHAPTER SIXTEEN

Three days later, Janeth finally found the Daughters of the Holy League protest. It took three different trolley rides and inquiring at four different businesses, but she tracked them down. She had to laugh. *Look at me, going into the den of the lion. Who would have guessed?*

She'd felt compelled, though, to find Alice and make amends. After all, Alice had been honest with her in the park. Even if it had been a reluctant honesty, Alice had given her that much. She'd even sought Janeth out to apologize. The least Janeth could do was return the favor. Besides, how was she going to hold on to any sort of friend if she couldn't handle someone standing up for her in times of trouble? That was what friends are supposed to do, after all. So Janeth had crisscrossed town, hitting the most common spots she'd known the league to picket. Finally, near the outskirts of downtown, she found them.

Disembarking the trolley, she caught Alice's eye instantly. Her gaze widened as she chanted between her friends. Janeth motioned toward an awning that shaded the front door of a music shop, hoping Alice would meet her there.

Janeth pretended to study the gramophones in the window display when a tap on her shoulder made her turn. She smiled in relief at the sight of Alice. "Thank you for seeing me."

The protest raged on nearby. Alice eyed her a moment, then followed her gaze over her shoulder. "I don't have long. The matron will notice I've disappeared."

"Of course." Janeth sank back more against the building, and Alice followed under the shadow of the blue awning. In the shade, Janeth was overcome with a strange sense of intimacy and was struck at how close they stood to one another. She blinked quickly to rid herself of the feeling that stirred in her stomach. "It's my turn to apologize. I was terrible the other day."

Alice didn't say anything.

"I realized you were only trying to help. I…well, I suppose I'm used to doing things on my own when it comes to…people like that."

"That man was terrible."

Janeth didn't disagree but kept her thoughts regarding the bartender to herself. "That's not the first time something like that has happened. And it won't be the last."

Alice seemed to study Janeth before she said softly, "I know." Taken aback at her gentle tone, Janeth wasn't sure what to say. Alice glanced toward the protest group, now directing their jeers to the cars stopped by the policeman as they waited for a mule cart to pass.

Janeth pulled her attention when she said, "I let my pride get the better of me. You didn't deserve to be spoken to like that. I'm sorry, Alice."

Her jaw clenched, Alice again studied her. Slowly, she smiled. "Sometimes, pride is all we have."

Janeth returned the smile, relief flooding her as she sensed Alice's understanding. Janeth wanted to reach out, pull her into a hug. She almost did before Alice asked, "Do you think it's because he heard you speaking Spanish?"

Reluctantly, Janeth remained standing against the building. She wrung her hands to help them forget the urge to reach out. She took a deep breath. "Probably. And I'm sure my name gave me away."

"I'm sorry," Alice said.

"You're sorry?" Janeth laughed, trying to lighten the mood. "Alice, you did nothing but try to help."

She glanced at her feet. "I'm sorry because I understand." Janeth tilted her head, waiting for Alice to continue. She looked up, a sheepish smile on her face. "Well, I don't understand exactly. But…being treated a certain way because of who you are. Because of things you can't help. Like where you come from or…who your parents are. I understand that."

Janeth was surprised at the confession. She also sensed there was something more behind Alice's words. "I pay people like that no mind," she finally said, hoping Alice would buy the lie. Of course, Alice read people and situations for a living. It shouldn't have surprised Janeth when Alice gave her a knowing grin. She blushed. She should have known better than to try to fool her.

Alice reached up, moving strands of hair that had blown across her face back behind her ear. Janeth noted the concern in the downturned corners of her mouth, in the faint lines around her eyes.

Janeth took a steely breath, then reached out, giving Alice's forearm a squeeze. "Thank you. I appreciate your words. And again, I'm sorry for how I acted."

After searching her gaze, Alice seemed to relax. "It's all right. Though I stand by what I said. Sometimes, people need a good talking to."

Janeth laughed. "Well," she replied, realizing her hand was still on Alice's forearm. She swallowed, then pulled it back. "I'm certainly glad to have you on my side."

A hurried "What are you doing?" came from behind Alice. They both found Mary wearing a worried expression.

Alice turned to Janeth. "I'd better get back."

"Will you come to dinner soon?"

"Dinner?"

Janeth smiled. It was quite sweet, she thought, how incredulous Alice was of every invitation. "Yes, dinner. How's Friday night? My uncle has expressed the need for fresh blood in the house, as he calls it. I think Hugh, his nephew you met, is due for a visit as well." The idea of Hugh being around wasn't ideal, and a bolt of jealousy hit her as she recalled the way Hugh had approached Alice at the protest weeks ago. Raymond was due with another shipment that same night. An evening of good food and good conversation, she decided, seemed a necessary predecessor to a meeting with her least-favorite associate.

"Alice," Mary called again, and Alice replied, "Just a moment."

"Eight o'clock?"

The smile Alice seemed to try and hide filled Janeth with warmth. "Eight o'clock." She hurried back into the crowd.

Janeth watched her go, her body feeling light. Friendship wasn't the right word...something was blossoming between her and Alice. *Now, only to find its name.*

CHAPTER SEVENTEEN

A deep melodic chime echoed within the Mills mansion after Alice rang the doorbell. Standing beneath the gabled front porch, she glanced back at the street below the manicured lawn. Beyond, the seaside cliffs were scattered with people taking in the brisk summer air. One couple had laid a blanket near the cliff's edge, sharing a picnic as the sun began to set beyond the horizon. The sky was just starting to burn a vibrant blush, streaks of clouds cut with ribbons of orange. Alice had never seen such a view. She tossed a glance at the second story. Did Janeth get to see this every night? The ocean seemed calm this evening, listless waves greeting the sandstone when the front door opened.

"Miss Covington." Hugh flashed a charming smile. His pressed pants fell over polished black oxfords, the kind she'd seen her father admiring on other men. A blue-striped dress shirt with a high white collar was adorned with a bold red bow tie. His matching vest was open as he motioned for her to enter.

"Good evening," she muttered, self-conscious of her own outfit. She hoped her dress was classy enough. Upon learning she was meeting friends for a dinner party in Seaside, Dorothy had dragged her to her home near Balboa Park. There, she'd insisted Alice try on several of her dresses. Alice, grateful for the kind gesture, wasn't quite as tall and slim as Dorothy, but they'd decided together on an olive-green evening dress. The material slid a bit around her shoulders, and the straight lines fell wide around her hips. The shimmering beads that lined the feathered hem made her feel like a picture star, and she'd swiveled her hips in Dorothy's mirror, hypnotized by the motion of the material.

"Your new beau won't be able to keep his eyes off you," Dorothy had said with a playful grin.

Now, Alice lifted the mesh material at her shoulders, aware of the plunging neckline that she wasn't used to. Her strapped black heels clicked on the marble floor of the foyer. Light music drifted from a nearby room. Hugh looked her up and down, gesturing as if asking to take a handbag or coat. Finding neither, he smiled and said, "It's lovely to see you again. I'm glad to see the matron lets her Temperance gals out once in a while." His gaze fell to her calves as he added, "I do hope we can get to know one another more in the time we have this evening."

She raised a brow. "Are you not staying for dinner?"

Hugh pulled back his shoulders, catching his own reflection in a large mirror hanging over the entry table to her right. "I've a job to run for my uncle and Mrs. Castro this evening. I'm afraid I'll have to leave before dessert."

She gave what she hoped was a sympathetic smile. She also wanted to ask what the job was when Mr. Mills called from the drawing room, "Hugh, is that our guest?"

"Yes, Uncle." He motioned for Alice to follow him. She scanned the brightly lit entryway, wondering where Janeth was. Her gaze trailed up the grand staircase. Maybe she was still getting dressed. The idea led to a series of indecent but delicious images. She forced herself to focus as she followed Hugh into the next room.

This room, like the entire house, it seemed, was alight with lamps and candles. The drawing room—draped in elegant furnishings that complemented off-white walls and a fine, kelly green rug over the wooden floor, its herringbone pattern gleaming—seemed primed for guests. A drink cart sat full and ready on the table in the room's center, where Hugh poured a glass of red wine for himself. "White or red, Miss Covington? We won't tell the matron about your indulgences this evening if you don't tell on us." He tossed her a wink.

"Secret is safe with me." Alice had tasted red wine only once, when her mother had told her to watch her glass when she'd gone to the powder room at a club. The dark, sweet taste had gone almost instantly to her head, leaving her warm and light. She wondered if white had the same effect, so she asked for that.

"Miss Covington, welcome." Mr. Mills was seated in a high-back green chair in the right corner of the room, next to the doorway that she remembered led to the kitchen.

"It's good to see you, Mr. Mills. How are you?" She took a glass from Hugh, who clinked them together.

"Oh, I've been better, my dear." His pale face did seem tired as he reached for his knee. Alice had noticed the limp he walked with but didn't know how to ask after the cause of his injury.

"You need to keep up those exercises, old man." Hugh leaned casually against the fireplace mantel, his elbow resting between an urn with Asian-inspired prints running around it and a model boat that reminded Alice of the ships that pirates had sailed years ago. Behind him, the source of the music revealed itself in a large gramophone, where a record spun lazily. Alice didn't recognize the song, a gentle piano piece.

Mr. Mills puffed on the mouth of his pipe. "Miss Covington," he said, changing the subject, "I hear you're recently transplanted to California. How are you finding San Diego?"

She took a sip of wine, finding the dry fruity notes quite pleasant. "The weather is incredible."

He raised his pipe as if in praise. "Finest weather in the country."

Hugh raised his glass in agreement. "Hear, hear."

She smiled and took another drink. Janeth still hadn't shown herself. She thought she heard the distant clink of silverware. Maybe she was adding the finishing touches to dinner.

Hugh, perhaps sensing her question, said, "Let me go check on our hostess." He downed his wine and breezed from the room.

Mr. Mills began a brief history of the county as Alice shifted her weight, still standing in the middle of the room, unsure why she felt uncertain of her decision to come here. Yes, Janeth had extended another invitation, but what if she was having regrets? What if she realized Alice wasn't the kind of person she wanted to be around? A terrible thought hit her: what if Janeth didn't really want her here after all?

CHAPTER EIGHTEEN

I'm not a renowned host, Mrs. Castro, but I did think it proper to greet your guests upon their arrival."

Janeth wiped perspiration from her brow. Even with the back window open, the kitchen was stifling hot. A trickle of sweat ran down against the back of her art deco dress. She'd bought it on a whim—not usually one to fall in line with every fashion trend—but had felt the need for something new and eye-catching. The dress was heavier than she was used to, its layered strips of material falling in a dazzling design just past her knees. It was mostly white, but each plate was adorned with blue sequins on its edge. She had pinned a rose from the garden on her shoulder and donned two pearl necklaces of different lengths. Her cross sat quietly beneath one of them. She'd even bought a new pair of satin heels.

Janeth had, of course, heard the doorbell upon Alice's arrival. Yet the sound had done something to her, acted as an anchor, bolting her to this room as if trapped. She couldn't bring herself to leave, so had decided to check, over and over, that the meal she'd prepared was indeed ready. Scooting past Hugh, she added another garnish to the roast duck on its silver platter and bed of lettuce. Roasted rosemary potatoes and seasoned carrots sat in a wreath around it.

When she removed, then replaced, the same sprig of mint three times, Hugh crossed his arms, leaning against the icebox. "Mrs. Castro, are you nervous?"

Her gaze swung to him, and she scoffed. "Nervous? Whatever is there to be nervous about?"

"Beats me." He snatched a carrot from the platter, still watching her. "She's a real doll, that Miss Covington. Wish I could stick around tonight."

Janeth grabbed the platter, though her fists wanted to shove Hugh at his comment. "Yes, what a shame." In front of the kitchen door, she paused, aware of how quickly her heart was beating. Was he right? Was she nervous? Preposterous. What was there to be anxious about? This was a dinner party. She'd hosted plenty for her uncle since living here. This one, she assured herself, wouldn't be any different.

Still feeling defensive, she added over her shoulder, "I do ask you to be more careful, Hugh, with the library door." She kept her voice low, knowing Alice was nearby. "The latch didn't catch earlier. You were the last one down there, if I'm not mistaken."

His brow rose, and a curious look brightened his gaze. To her relief, he only gave a low bow and said, "Of course, Mrs. Castro. My mistake."

Content that the food and place settings were perfect, Janeth took a breath, then walked into the drawing room. "Dinner is served."

Alice sat in a chair near the fireplace, her legs crossed and a glass of wine in hand. The line that ran up the stocking on the back of her thigh caught Janeth's eye. Tearing her gaze away and feeling confused about why she'd done such a thing, she moved to greet her.

"Thank you for having me," Alice said, standing.

Janeth smiled, finding Alice's free hand and taking it between her own. "Alice, the pleasure is all mine. We're so glad to have you join us this evening." They held one another's gazes until Janeth remembered they weren't the only ones in the room. She turned to call over her shoulder, "Aren't we, gentlemen?"

Her uncle stamped his cane in agreement as he headed for the dining room. Hugh wore an inquisitive look but only raised his refilled glass in a salute before helping their uncle to the table.

Turning back to Alice, Janeth found she wanted to say a thousand things. She wanted to express how glad she was Alice had decided to come. How wonderful it was to have a new friend. She tried to take in the way Alice's hair fell in a gentle wave just above her shoulders. She didn't recognize the dress and wondered how she'd come by it. The impulse to embrace Alice washed over her, and Janeth stepped back, fanning herself.

"Are you all right?" asked Alice.

"I fear the kitchen was too warm. I'll be fine." She pointed to Alice's glass, then fetched one of her own. "You have the right idea. Nothing like white wine on a warm summer's day." Janeth took a long drink. Her nerves still vibrated beneath her hands. "Come, let's eat."

Dinner was, to her relief, perfect. Janeth relaxed into her seat as they all sat back, content. The duck was nearly finished, and only scraps of potatoes remained on everyone's plates. The music played on from the next room, and conversation had flowed effortlessly over the past hour as they dined.

Mr. Mills and Hugh ran most of the talk, as she had expected. Her uncle loved to share stories of his younger days. He had been a savvy businessman in his youth, responsible for a large part of San Diego's expansion across the southern stretch of California. He and Hugh compared sailing stories. Janeth indulged their adventures with commentary and laughter but relished the opportunity to watch Alice across the table. She seemed enraptured by the tales, offering her own witty remarks on occasion. Her smile was one that Janeth found unable to look away from as Hugh stood.

"Well, I'm afraid I must be off." He pushed in his chair, then clapped his uncle lovingly on the shoulder. "Mrs. Castro, thank you for the lovely meal. I'll see you tomorrow after tonight's shipment."

"Very good," she said but threw him a look that told him not to share more.

Alice raised a curious brow, then gave a start when Hugh grabbed her hand, kissing her knuckles. "Good evening, Miss Covington. It was a pleasure."

Janeth clutched the arms of her chair at the gesture but forced herself to smile as Hugh replenished their glasses before departing.

Once he had gone, Janeth fetched the fruit cocktail. About to dig into the cherries and mandarin oranges, Alice asked, "You receive shipments for your business at night?"

Janeth's uncle answered in stride. "Yes. It's impossible to have a set schedule when goods come in from other countries. We're at the mercy of the carriers and the great Pacific."

She nodded, but Janeth could see the questions in her eyes.

The clock chimed. "Is it nearly ten o'clock already?" her uncle asked, giving a groan and checking his pocket watch to confirm.

Janeth stood, beginning to clear their plates. "My, how time flies when one is having such fun," she replied. The realization that Raymond was due soon hit her, and she dropped some of the silverware.

Alice bent to collect it. "Let me help."

"No, Alice, it's all right."

"I don't mind." She stood, gathering the dropped silverware and grabbing the platter.

Glancing again to the clock, Janeth said, "Uncle, will you be all right? This will be a faster process with the two of us clearing things."

He stood somewhat gingerly. "It's that time for me, anyway. I'll have a smoke before retiring, Janeth, dear."

"I'll see you to your room once we get this cleaned up."

With Alice's help, the dining room was spick-and-span in minutes. "We'll leave this till the morning," she said, setting her uncle's scotch glass into a large basin filled with soapy water and the other dishes. "One should never scrub in an evening dress, especially one as fetching as yours."

Alice gave her half a grin, pulling up the strap of her dress. "You like it? I borrowed it from a friend."

"It's a lovely color on you."

Alice seemed like she was going to say something as she dried her hands on a rag. They were only a few feet apart, but the walls seemed to press in. Janeth inhaled at the light playing in Alice's eyes as pink filled her cheeks. "You look lovely yourself."

Janeth waved the comment away. "This old thing," but a heat filled her chest at Alice's remark, and she felt pleased the dress had had its intended effect.

They stood across from one another like they had in the drawing room, their gazes locked. Janeth wasn't sure why she felt at a loss for words. This feeling was so peculiar. Finally, she said, "I'll just be a minute. If you'll…if you'll wait in the drawing room while I see my uncle to bed. Then I must meet my associates with the delivery. It shouldn't take long if you…well, assuming you haven't anywhere to be."

Alice tilted her head as if considering. The idea that she did have somewhere to be, or that she'd rather be elsewhere, cut through Janeth's chest. She wished Raymond wasn't on his way. She wished she could sit with Alice in the drawing room, conversing over a bottle of wine about their lives. "I can stay awhile."

Relief flooded her. "Wonderful. I'll see you soon."

In the library, Janeth paced. The grandfather clock upstairs chimed the hour. Practically on cue, the scraping of the cellar door sounded downstairs. She waited for the knock, then opened the door.

"Say, aren't we gussied up this evening?" Raymond stepped out from behind two of his men, their saltwater-stained shirts tight against their muscled forearms as they carried in a large crate.

She kept herself on the other side of the desk. "I'm hosting a dinner party."

One of the men pulled a small crowbar from his back pocket and lifted the crate's edge.

"Our invite musta gotten lost," Raymond said. One man guffawed. The one with the crowbar smiled, but Janeth caught his eye roll at the comment. Reluctantly, she moved around to inspect the latest shipment. This time, large glass perfume bottles sat in the straw. Unscrewing one of the lids, she dipped her finger in. Tasting the full, sweet taste of rum, she nodded. The men replaced the lid and dragged the crate back downstairs.

Raymond watched them, then turned to her. He wore a flat cap tonight and took it off to scratch his head. His eyes roved her body, but she stood stoically, not wanting to show him how his gaze left her skin crawling. "You know," he said, rubbing his stubbled cheek. "Since starting this gig, I've gotten to know my fair share of broads like you." She raised her brows but didn't say anything. "You know," he said, starting to move in a slow circle around her. "Broads of a certain... background."

She swallowed. His predatory steps were frighteningly close.

"Told the fellas I'd never go for a gal like that. I'm an all-American kinda guy, ya see." Behind her shoulder, he leaned close. She could smell his sweat and the scent of seaweed and tobacco. His breath was stale against her neck. "I think I get it now, what Mr. Mills sees in you. But still, there's one question I've yet to answer, and I wonder..." His lips were just below her ear as he whispered, "Do spics taste different?"

She spun, stepping back until she hit the desk. Wide-eyed, she somehow managed to collect herself, pointing emphatically at the hidden door. "You'll find my uncle only too eager to hear about this."

Raymond laughed and replaced his cap. "And what does the old man plan to do about it?" He rested his hand at his hip, drawing Janeth's gaze to the pistol. "We know how that story ends, Mrs. Castro."

Janeth hurried behind the desk. She wished for more than that to fill the space between them as she unlocked the drawer with shaking hands and found his payment. "Here." She shoved it across the mahogany desk. "Now, if you please, I must get back to my guests."

Raymond watched her. For a moment, a terrible vision flashed before her: Raymond cornering her, his men watching and herself powerless to fight him off. The dread left her reeling. Thankfully, he took the payment and started for the door.

"Until next time, Mrs. Castro," he said, then disappeared into the cellar.

Her legs gave out, and she stumbled forward, clutching the desk for support. She pressed her hand to her mouth, trembling. She let out a cry, her arms shaking as she released the anguish Raymond's visit had left behind, a glaring, garish scar on an otherwise beautiful evening.

A knock at the library door startled her. "Janeth?"

It was Alice. Janeth sniffled, quickly wiping away tears. She checked that the hidden door was in place, then tucked her uncle's wallet back into the drawer. "Come in."

Tentatively, the door opened. Alice seemed to hesitate before moving into the room. The wineglass was still in her hand. "I was admiring the art in the hallway," she said. "I know you told me to wait, but I've never been in a house like this. There's so much to see."

Janeth turned, pretending to straighten a row of books as she worked to gather herself. "My uncle has spent years acquiring his collection. There's a stunning Monet upstairs I can show you if you like."

Alice's voice was closer when she said, "Janeth, are you all right?"

Turning, she said, "Of course."

But Alice didn't seem convinced as she drew nearer. "You're crying."

"It's nothing," she said, but even she wasn't convinced as her voice broke, giving her away.

Alice moved around the desk and sat on the corner, her feet dangling above the carpet. She placed the glass of wine beside her, studying Janeth. "Did something go wrong with the delivery?"

"I assure you, it's nothing," she said but found herself unable to meet Alice's gaze. How could she begin to explain the feeling Raymond left her with, the way his presence oozed up from the dark corners of this house to infiltrate her happiness? How to explain the truth of what she did?

"You know," Alice was saying, tracing the base of the wineglass. "I was thinking about the rumors."

"Rumors?" Janeth swiped at a stray tear, frowning.

"About this house."

Janeth swallowed again, wishing she had a glass of wine for herself. Slowly, she sat on the edge of the desk too. She was well aware of what people said about her uncle's home but had hoped it was only that, legends and unproven tales. "Ah, those rumors."

Alice took a slow breath. "Janeth...I think you're swell. You're smart. Kind. Beautiful. A top-notch cook." She flashed a grin, and a blush warmed Janeth's cheek. "But there is one thing you're not very good at."

The words struck her, and Janeth found the cross pendant below her neck. "I beg your pardon?"

Alice reached out, running her fingers along Janeth's wrist. The touch sent a torrid spell of longing up her arm, and Janeth carefully met her gaze. "You aren't very good at hiding things."

Confused, Janeth started to reply but caught the knowing in Alice's gaze. She gave a small laugh. "My uncle's business." Alice nodded, giving her wrist an encouraging squeeze, prompting her to continue. "The Daughters of the Holy League were right to protest here. We're exactly who they think we are. Mr. Mills, Hugh, myself." She took another shuddering breath. "I help my uncle run the most lucrative bootlegging business in San Diego. That's why he asked me to move in. Well," she said, shaking her head, "it wasn't the only reason. But since he was hurt, I've had to take over most of the operations."

Alice frowned, then glanced around the room. "He was hurt by one of those men?"

"The same one who was here tonight." She reached up, rubbing her neck, hating the way the feel of Raymond's breath lingered.

Alice leaned closer. "Did he hurt you?"

Janeth found herself falling into Alice's hazel eyes, the concern in them like a fire she yearned to feel the warmth of. This same look had been a part of her distant past with Victor. Janeth had never imagined it could be something she'd experience again. But here was Alice, looking at her just like that.

"No," she finally said, her voice low. She watched Alice's lips as they fell into a hard line. They looked so soft. She wondered if they tasted sweet, like the wine.

"You're sure?"

The ability to collect herself was growing thinner by the second. Janeth turned to face her better, crossing one leg toward Alice. "Raymond is…he's a brute. But he wouldn't do anything that would be bad for business." She didn't believe her own words, though. The dangers were prominent, lurking on the other side of that hidden door. She'd seen the reality of them with her uncle.

Alice's left hand cupped her cheek. The gesture was so tender, so unlike her interaction with Raymond, that Janeth leaned into it. Tears filled her vision, but they weren't fearful tears like five minutes before. These were tears of hope, of longing, of something she'd never thought she'd feel again.

Alice started to say something, but Janeth hardly heard her. She leaned in, pressing her lips to Alice's. They were soft like she imagined. She pushed closer. Alice seemed to stiffen at first, a startled sound coming from her as she pulled back her hand. But Janeth pressed forward, and Alice, to her delight, pushed back.

The kiss deepened. It wasn't like any kiss she'd shared with Victor. While he had always been tender in his affections, he had also been very much a man, enthusiastic to move things along. Alice seemed to take each touch slowly, and Janeth found herself the eager one. She grabbed the back of Alice's head, bringing her in, willing them closer. Her tongue parted Alice's lips, and Janeth smiled into the kiss, relishing the taste of wine and fruit.

This seemed to change something in Alice, as she moaned and shifted so her right knee was on the desk. She kissed Janeth harder, then pulled back, searching her gaze.

Janeth reached up to trace Alice's cheek, wanting more of this

ADRIFT

feeling. Her breath came quickly. She wanted to chase away the darkness Raymond had given her. She wanted more of Alice.

Quickly, Alice stood. For a moment, Janeth feared she was going to leave. But Alice only took her hand and kissed the top of it. Then she nudged open Janeth's legs, nestling between them, and pulled Janeth close once again.

They kissed fiercely, Janeth wanting to disappear into her lips. While Alice's hands roved up her back, finding her shoulders, her hips, Janeth kept her hands around Alice's face. While kissing her was like a blissful dream, she found herself unsure what to do beyond that. Perhaps sensing this, Alice broke their kiss.

"Have you done this before?" she asked, her eyes hungry, her breath coming fast.

Janeth inhaled and shook her head. "Never." This answer seemed to settle deeply between Alice's brows, her smile falling into a contemplative line. When she looked down, Janeth lifted her chin. "What is it?"

Her gaze fell to Janeth's lips, and for a moment she seemed ready to lean in for another kiss. Instead, to Janeth's dismay, she stepped back. "I should go."

"Go? But..." But what? Janeth had no reason to keep her there, except for the reason that surged through her body, yearning for more of Alice's touch.

"It's late," Alice was saying, heading for the library door. "Thank you for dinner."

Feeling like the desk was at a tilt, Janeth leaned atop it, trying to steady herself. "You're welcome," she managed to say.

"I'm glad you're all right." Alice took a step back into the room, then stopped herself. "I'll see you around, Janeth." The front door opened and closed, and Janeth pulled her legs closed atop her uncle's desk. A stark vulnerability enveloped her. Searching for something to center herself, her fingers bumped the empty wineglass.

Her thoughts from earlier in the evening returned, when she had anticipated another common dinner party. How wrong she had been: this had been anything but like the others. A kernel of truth sprang up as she realized a part of her had hoped tonight would be different. The realization of what she'd done in these last ten minutes hit her: she'd kissed another woman. Everything she had been taught had told her such an act was a sin. A crime. A deviant behavior.

It was also, Janeth thought, running her finger around the glass's rim, imagining Alice's lips, absolutely exquisite.

CHAPTER NINETEEN

The streets of Seaside were quiet as Alice hurried down the stairs. The night air was cool, a nearly full moon shining bright amongst glittering stars. A light from the second story lit a rectangle over the lawn. Alice caught a shadow behind the window shade but didn't wait for confirmation that it was Janeth.

She wound down Osprey Street to the bungalows. Voices echoed within, another summer gathering stretching into the midnight hours. She couldn't go home. She contemplated finding Dorothy's house again but decided against it. The energy needed to weave more lies about the mysterious beau Dorothy had imagined felt impossible. She wasn't sure where to go after what had happened between her and Janeth. All she knew was that it was the one thing that wasn't supposed to happen.

Wrapping her arms around herself, she wandered slowly down the narrow path cut between tall grasses and sand dunes that led to the carnival grounds. The tents were closed. The only sound came from the waves washing upon the shore, indifferent to her dilemma.

Shedding her heels, Alice stepped onto the sand. The moonlight shimmered off the cresting waves, reminding her of the endless candlelight in the Mills's mansion. Far out, a handful of ships' lanterns dotted the black waters. Did one of them hold the man who had frightened Janeth? Alice clenched her jaw, wishing she had been there, wishing to give that man what he deserved.

Wind whipped around her dress. She laughed, the sound breaking over the waves. Did she really wish to fight a man in such a business? Well, why not? While she had never been in an all-out brawl, Alice had had her share of scuffles on the street. A pickpocket against a rumrunner…she liked her odds.

A shrill shadow of memory cut through her, the memory of not being able to help Gladys. Standing outside her home, Alice had been frozen, lifeless as Gladys had been torn from this world. She'd watched, her father's firm hand and her own cowardice pinning her to the ground like a spineless rat.

Swiping at tears, Alice muttered, "Why are you doing this again?" She watched the water, waiting for an answer. An answer to why she was like this, why she loved women, and why—after the heartache of Gladys—had Janeth come into her life? What kind of joke was this to present someone who could reignite the feelings she knew were wrong?

But it felt so right, she thought, closing her eyes and tilting her head to the stars. The way Janeth had kissed her, like it was a most pleasant and startling surprise. Like she craved more. Alice certainly had. But Janeth…she had no idea of the dangers their relationship could bring. What it could become.

Alice couldn't bear to see someone else she cared about hurt because of her.

Turning, she walked silently through the boardwalk until she was standing in front of the Ferris wheel. She lifted the bar to the lowest car and lay back against the cold metal bench. The Milky Way's white mist shone dimly amidst the stars. Alice had never noticed how magnificent the night skies were here. She was always busy, her nose to the ground as her mother kept her watchful eye on her.

Was there a place out there, among the gleaming lights, where she could be herself? A place miles away from this life, where she could be happy and free of the guilt that followed her? The waves crashed along the sand, and she took a deep breath. Could she make it there if she tried? Could she bring someone with her, someone like Janeth?

The questions swirled through her tired mind and eventually, she drifted off to sleep.

"Hey, you deaf, lady? Scram." Someone shoved Alice's shoulder. The same man's voice, gruff and hard, added, "No loitering."

She sat up, a pinch piercing her lower back as she jerked away. Blinking, she found the angry carnival worker whose face was nearly as red as the stripes on his shirt. "Sorry," she said, scurrying out of the metal car, snatching up her shoes, and hurrying away.

The beach and fairgrounds were still nearly empty. Only the workers trudged along to their respective stations, opening the tents for the day. The early morning sky was gray, a soft mist settled atop everything, which explained the chill she felt in her bones.

She walked inland up the main street, passing several shops she'd wandered through with Janeth. A tiny café with outdoor tables looked appealing, until she remembered she didn't have any money. She pretended to window shop next door until the pair of women who had eyed her curiously left their table. Before a waiter could clean it, she swooped in—beating the circling seagulls—and grabbed a half-eaten croissant and a fistful of berries. She jogged as best she could in her shoes up the street toward the trolley.

The food woke something in her. God, why hadn't she gone home? A troubled feeling filled her at the thought of what her mother might think. Maybe, she thought hopefully, her mother was still passed out from last night, or she wasn't even home yet. She clung to that fragment of hope as she opened the door of their home.

Her mother sat at the card table, a lit cigarette between her fingers. "Where have you been?"

Alice closed the door behind her, keeping her back pressed to it as she searched the room. "Where's Father?"

"Out on a job." She took a drag, her gaze roving over Alice. "You didn't answer my question."

She didn't move. She wasn't sure she could. "I was out."

"Out." Her mother exhaled a line of smoke, a sarcastic smile lifting her face. She stood. A silk robe Alice didn't recognize was tied around her waist. It was pink, patterned with blue Chinese women and characters. Alice imagined it was stolen from one of the shops downtown.

When her mother was standing before her, a questioning hand on her hip, Alice attempted to change the subject. "Did you have a good night?"

Her mother gave a low laugh between drags. "Don't play that

with me. You've been acting suspect for a while, honey." She stepped closer, less than a foot of space between them now. "You were out with someone."

"No."

"No?" She reached out, the ash from her cigarette falling just over Alice's shoulder as she picked at the strap of her dress. "My daughter doesn't own anything this snazzy. A dress like this had to have come from someone else. Someone well above my daughter."

Alice considered saying she had stolen it, but her mother would see through the lie. Licking her lips to give herself time to think, Alice cursed this town, this place and its stealthy theft of all her gifts. This place kept taking them from her, always when she needed them most. "It's from my friend. She's in the Holy League. She let me borrow it for a dinner party she threw last night."

Her mother's left brow raised as she seemed to contemplate this. "A dinner party at a house with a woman who owns *that* dress." She gestured again to the fine material, nearly singeing Alice with the cigarette.

Mercifully, the fear in her mind cleared, and Alice stammered, "She's wealthy. I'm…I'm working her. You know, earning her trust, doing a long con. She's got a dowry. I can get my hands on some of it, but it'll take a while."

Studying her, her mother tapped her fingers on her hip, no doubt weighing this potential profit against raking Alice over the coals. Eventually, she said, "And you came back empty-handed from this party?"

Cold ran down her back. "I…"

Her mother exhaled, rolling her eyes. "Pitiful."

"I'm sorry." Alice stammered, though she wasn't sure why she was apologizing. Her mother, back at the table, tipped the end of her cigarette into the ashtray. Alice started for her room, desperate for a warm bath, but her mother called.

"I don't think so."

Alice turned. "I'm tired."

"You think you're the only one? Your father and I work day and night to give you the food you eat, the clothes on your back that you're not even grateful enough to wear." She stormed forward, her gaze taking in the dress again like it was the most repulsive thing she'd ever seen. "We keep a roof over your head, and this is how you repay us?"

"Mother, I told you, I'm—"

"I'll tell you what you are. You're this close, Alice." Her mother's voice rose as she leaned in. Her eyes were wild, her thumb and forefinger an inch apart next to Alice's cheek. "I just need one reason... one thing your father can't turn his cheek to this time." She trailed off, and Alice felt sick at the look in her eyes. She wanted to shrink away, to melt into nothing, anything to get away from this. Her mother spoke quietly. "Get out."

Alice took a shaky breath. "What?"

"There's a Holy League event near the shipyards. You're already late."

"But..." She needed to change. She needed to sleep. "There will be one next week."

Her mother had started across the room, but she turned, a hard glare chilling her resolve. "You'll go now, Alice."

Alice swallowed at the warning fire in her mother's voice. She cut her gaze to the door as if doing so would bring her father home. She wished he was here. She wished for so many things.

As she started to go, her mother added, "I don't want to see you until tonight. And, Alice?" She paused to put out her cigarette. Alice couldn't help but liken the gesture to her own flame, the spark dwindling into nothing beneath her mother's will. "Don't disappoint me again."

Her feet aching and the chill from sleeping outside still on her shoulders, Alice left. She ached to fall against the door. She ached to scream, to run back to Janeth. Instead, she swallowed the disdain her own life thrust upon her and started back for the trolley.

CHAPTER TWENTY

A lice lingered near the edge of the road. The Temperance group was twenty yards away across the street. She'd already dodged three men who thought she belonged to a different group of women. One of them even tried to pull her into an alley. She'd given him a swift kick to the groin and run away.

She'd ignored the looks from passersby as she walked, her chin high, in her fine evening dress and black heels. When Dorothy spotted her, her face wide in disbelief and confusion, Alice gave a meek wave.

Dorothy hurried across the street, looking her up and down. "Oklahoma." Alice was sure she sported dirt from the railyard on her stockings and cheek and probably smelled like the sweat under her arms. "Rough night?"

"You could say that."

Quickly, Dorothy shed her jacket. "Here. You need this more than I do."

Gratefully, Alice slipped it on. "Thank you."

Her voice still low, she asked, "How did dinner go?"

Alice took a deep breath, trying to reconcile the highs and lows of last night. How incredible it had felt to kiss Janeth, and then how terrible it had been with her mother this morning. "It was…not what I expected."

Dorothy rubbed her arms as if to warm her. The gesture was so kind, so gentle, Alice nearly cried. "Golly," Dorothy said, giving an encouraging smile. "Come stand next to me. I'll have Mary keep the other girls off your case."

"Won't she be scandalized?" Alice gestured to the hem of the dress sticking out beneath the jacket and the tear in the calf of her stocking, now gritty with sand.

Dorothy grinned. "Mary may be naive, but she likes you. So do I." She looped her arm through Alice's. "We've got you."

As they moved, people waited outside the cannery near the docks. She thought of Janeth working there. One woman standing in a small group wearing a bold green dress with a matching black hat looked familiar, though Alice couldn't place her. The woman was speaking to someone when her dark gaze found Alice's in the Holy League group. Wondering where she'd seen her before, Alice leaned wearily into Dorothy and reluctantly joined in the chants.

"There you are. Have a nice day." Janeth smiled at Mrs. Gomez as she handed her a sack of goods.

"Your English is better now than my niece. She lives in a place called Iowa." Mrs. Gomez leaned close, lifting a hand to obscure her mouth. "Married a Native man."

Janeth lifted her brow. "My. Well, I'm sure they're very happy. Please give your husband my regards."

Once she was gone, Janeth pulled out the slip of paper from her handbag beneath the counter in Leo's market. Leaning on her elbows, she studied the numbers from this week's payments.

"Someone is lively this morning." Her brother walked behind her, replacing a large jar of sunflower seeds on the shelf.

"Busy, more like," she replied. "Mr. Aldridge talked my ear off for nearly an hour. I still have to go see Mr. Preston in Seaside. I forgot to ask when I saw him earlier, but how did the Cadenas like the latest shipment?"

"If you'd come to the baptism, you'd know," he said, though his voice was mostly teasing.

Janeth felt the back of her neck warm. The baptism had been last night, the date of her latest dinner party. All night she'd sat up, thinking of nothing but the kiss with Alice. At first, she'd been swimming in the warm memories of it, of Alice's soft lips, her hands on her back. *Oh, the idea of it.* How long had it been since someone had held her like that?

Since Victor, of course. The blissful thoughts that had filled her mind in the dark of her room combatted for hours with the guilt of her actions. She'd lain there, staring at the ceiling, then at the wedding band on her finger. The glint from it seemed too bright, reminding her of her husband. But Victor was gone. Had been gone awhile. Everyone had been encouraging her to get out into society again. How many times had Maria invited her to church or to a birthday party to meet a man?

A man. Janeth had never imagined herself caring for a woman in the same way. Once she'd dragged herself out of bed this morning, she had found herself in her uncle's library. She had a million questions and no idea where to even begin finding answers. "Have you any books on…unconventional relationships?" she had asked, hoping to sound casual.

"Unconventional?" Her uncle had hummed thoughtfully from his desk. "Why, I'm not sure what you mean, dear."

She hadn't been entirely sure how to express what she was hoping for. Her uncle had stood, hobbling over to a corner shelf. "This one has several of my friends up in arms." He chuckled. "I hardly understand it. The writing is absurd. But…" He tugged a thick blue book from its place, handing it to her. She read the cover: *Ulysses*. "That's as unconventional as I get, my dear." He laughed to himself and headed back to his desk.

She had frowned at the name of a man on the cover. She was looking for something…something that could put words to what she was feeling. Something that didn't come from the first book she'd ever read and the only one she owned. Her grandmother had instructed her and Leo in the Bible's teachings from a young age. Raised Catholic, church had been a part of life for years in Mexico. Growing up, she'd never fully understood the good book's words. After Alice, though, Janeth had furiously torn through the pages, finding the dreaded verse she knew lay within the fine print.

She had slammed the worn cover shut. "How could something wrong have felt so good?" she muttered to the walls. Surely, she couldn't be the first woman to feel this way. Alice, she assumed, had done this before. She had seemed so confident. How many others were out there, contemplating these same thoughts, these forbidden desires? Janeth had strolled Seaside early this morning, observing tourists and local residents. She would catch a woman's eye, waiting for the same feeling she got when Alice looked at her. While she had noticed the beauty other women possessed and the way their dresses fit their figures, none of them had sparked the same feelings. Was it only Alice, then, who prompted these longings?

Returning to the present, Janeth replied, "I was terribly busy, Leo. You know."

"Well, whatever you've been up to has certainly livened your step." He flashed a smile. "I'm happy to see it."

She returned it, trying to push aside the confusing thoughts in her mind. Maria wandered in from the back room. "Elena and Jorge are with my mother until three. Leo, don't let me forget we're bringing the sides to lunch tomorrow with my parents."

"Yes, my love." He kissed her, then scooped away the paper Janeth was studying. He clucked his tongue. "My sister remains a tragedy at arithmetic."

Janeth gave a playful pout. "Why do you think I am always here when I go over the numbers?"

They exchanged teasing faces for a moment before Leo nabbed her pencil and got to work adjusting the sums. Maria started to sweep in front of the counter, but Janeth noticed her inquisitive gaze.

"What is it?" she asked, reaching up to her hair, once again done in an underpin. She brushed a hand through her bangs, wondering if a lock had gone astray.

Maria dropped her eyes to the floor as she said, "I saw that woman this morning. The one who was in here."

Janeth smiled. "I'm afraid you're going to have to be more specific than that, Maria."

She gave a hearty sweep, bits of dust flying up. "The white woman."

"Oh," Janeth said, pretending to be interested in the empty flour sacks at the end of the counter. She moved, starting to count them. "Her."

Maria was focused on the bristles, and Janeth sensed her attitude slowly starting to match the harsh ends. "She was with one of those Temperance groups."

Janeth met her gaze, swallowing at the sharp look in her sister-in-law's eyes.

"Temperance?" Leo asked, looking up. "The protesters?"

"She was with a large group near the docks," Maria added. "Outside the cannery. I'd gone by to see my cousin before her shift."

Janeth's throat went dry, and her mind felt black. "Oh?"

Maria's face turned incredulous as she stopped sweeping, moving the broom to her left hand while her right flew to her hip. "Oh? Is that all you can say, Janeth? Don't be ridiculous. This woman came into our shop. You claim she is a friend."

"A new friend, yes." She felt hot under Maria's gaze and found the end of her cross beneath her dress. Maria followed her anxious gesture, a curious brow raised.

"Did you know this new *friend* is part of the groups trying to take down your business?"

Janeth blinked. She tossed a glance at her brother. He leaned against the counter, the pencil hovering over his notes, his gaze rapt as he waited for an answer.

"I..."

"Did you know?"

The air was heavy. Janeth opened her mouth, then closed it. This is ridiculous, she thought. Why was Maria interrogating her like this? "I don't see what that has to do with anything."

Her eyes wide, Maria asked, "You don't see?" She scoffed, then said to Leo, "I'm afraid your sister isn't well. How can she not see what is so wrong with this situation?"

Janeth straightened. "Maria, don't talk as if I'm not here. The fact that Alice is a part of that group—"

"The Temperance group."

"—has nothing to do—"

"The group that wants to dismantle rum-running."

"Will you stop?" Janeth inhaled, surprised at the volume of her own voice.

Red swam in Maria's cheeks. Leo said softly, "Janeth, that's my wife you're speaking to."

"And I'm your sister. She's accusing me. Of what, I don't know."

"Of fraternizing with the very people who could ruin you. Ruin *us*."

Janeth felt exasperated. "What are you talking about?"

Maria stepped closer, moving the broom to her other hand as she

ADRIFT

stood on the other side of the counter. When she spoke, her voice was even. "It's one thing to make nice with the white folks in your uncle's world. It's another to befriend them." She paused, seeming to weigh her next words. "It is something else entirely to bring one into *this* world. Someone who could bring you down with a single word if she learns what you do."

Janeth swallowed. Alice already knew what she did. She hadn't even thought about the consequences of revealing the truth to her. It had seemed like the natural thing to do. How else to explain Raymond? Maria didn't understand the situation, didn't understand what she and Alice were building.

"It's fine," she finally said, trying to laugh. "Alice isn't like those other women."

"Alice?" Maria said. "And what if Alice isn't who you think she is? What if she exposes you, tells the world about your uncle's business. Where does that leave us? You know we save our share of the money for Elena and Jorge's future."

Leo held out a hand as if to stop this conversation. "Maria, now..."

But she raised her hand right back, tossing him a warning look. "We help you for the benefit of *our* children. For the benefit of *our* community. You're willing to risk all of that for..." Maria searched her gaze. "For a white woman?"

"That won't happen, Maria."

But her sister-in-law looked bewildered. She tugged off her apron, shoving the broom across the counter to Leo. "You want so badly to be like them," she spat, her gaze boring into Janeth. "You don't even see what is happening." She turned and stormed out the door, leaving Janeth feeling like she'd been tossed like a ragdoll across the waves of a furious storm.

CHAPTER TWENTY-ONE

Janeth had hardly slept. She woke in the morning to an overcast sky. All night, she'd tossed and turned, replaying Maria's words.

"You want so badly to be like them."

Memories of Victor had wrapped around her in the night. At first, it had been pleasant; times from their youth drifting over her mind like a warm breeze. But the images had shifted like the sea, growing dark and wide. Shadows reached out from the unrelenting waves. She watched her vision of Victor's boat being lost again to the cold depths.

She was sitting at the dining room table at nine o'clock, listlessly stirring too much sugar into her coffee, when Mr. Mills hobbled past. He paused, and she glanced sideways at him. He wore his usual attire: high-waisted black trousers and a pressed white shirt with a high collar, looking ever the businessman. His hair was slicked down, and his mustache looked freshly trimmed. "Janeth dear, you look positively dreadful."

She gave a dry laugh, tugging at the collar of her robe. She hadn't even bothered to unpin her hair this morning. "Thank you, Uncle."

He hesitated. She sensed that he wanted to ask what was wrong. They had shared a lot about themselves when she had first moved in. She'd listened as he'd spoken of Lenore, his wife, and their daughter, Abigail. In turn, she had shared about Victor and her family in Mexico. They knew well the scars drawn over each of their hearts. Surely now, her uncle recognized the resurgence of old pain.

Though Janeth found herself facing a new dilemma: was Maria right? Who was she to become as she grew closer to Alice? What did

Alice mean to her, and what did those feelings mean for someone like her?

"Well," he finally said, "I'll be in the library if you need me."

Janeth nodded as he disappeared. She wasn't sure how long she sat there. The doorbell chimed. Leaving her coffee, she brushed a hand through her hair, then remembered it was full of pins. Oh well, she thought. Whoever it is, it doesn't matter.

A policeman greeted her, his navy uniform full of straight lines and sharp angles in contrast to his round face. "Good day."

She started back, instinctively shrinking the space to block his view into the home. "Good day."

He seemed to take in her unkempt appearance. She pulled herself taller at his curious gaze as he said, "I was hoping Mr. Mills may be of assistance today. We're going around inquiring after this man." He held up a small notepad. Staring back from the white page in a well-rendered sketch was Raymond.

Her heart raced, and Janeth forced a smile. "Has he done something?"

The officer seemed to watch her for a reaction. She kept her gaze even until he replaced the notepad in his breast pocket. "That's a worry for the police. Is Mr. Mills at home?"

Now, her heart leapt into her throat. "Yes. Please, come in." The officer removed his hat as she closed the door. "This way."

She led him to the library, each step sending a pulsing beat through her body. *God, what if Raymond has done something to hurt the business?* Her mind raced with possibilities as she called, "Uncle?"

He looked up from his desk. If he was concerned at the sight of a policeman in his home, he didn't show it. "Oh my. Good day, dear boy. Please, come in."

"I've just a few questions, Mr. Mills, if you don't mind."

"Of course," he said. He threw a glance at Janeth.

"Shall I put on some tea?" she asked.

"This won't take long," the policeman said.

She nodded and closed the door, then returned to the dining room table, her entire body heavy. Her mind hummed. What if Raymond had lost a shipment, and the police had found it? No, she countered her own worries, dropping her head into her hands and staring at her coffee.

Raymond was careful and too greedy to be careless with the product. She took a long breath. She was overthinking this. Everything was fine. The business was running smoothly. It was only her personal uncertainties prompting insecurity. She recalled Hernandez's comments regarding Raymond, how he was extending his reach to other rum-running rings along the coast. She ran a hand over her hair, looking into the foyer, staring into the middle distance. "What are you up to, Raymond?"

She pretended to rearrange the clock on the table near the stairs when the policeman left. Once he had, she ran to the library. "Uncle, is everything all right?"

"Of course, Janeth." He opened the wooden box on his desk that hosted his pipe and tobacco. Preparing it, he sat back in his chair.

She frowned at the sight of the false door behind him not sitting flush. Ready to chastise her uncle for leaving it open again, she thought better of it. Besides, it very well might have been her. She had been so preoccupied lately, details like checking the latch seemed to slip her mind more and more. After ensuring it was closed, she sat on the couch across from him. "What did he want?"

Lighting a match, he kept his gaze low. "Nothing you should worry yourself with."

Perhaps it was the lack of sleep, or maybe the policeman's visit had gotten under her skin more than she thought. Whatever it was, her voice came out more curt than usual as she scoffed. "Uncle, don't treat me like a child. I'm as much a part of this business as you."

His blue eyes widened as he held the pipe in front of him.

She inhaled sharply, looking away. "I'm sorry, Uncle."

"Don't be. You're right."

She met his gaze as he took a few puffs. "I'll tell you why he was here after you tell me what has you so sore lately."

Janeth opened her mouth, but it quickly closed. She gave a sardonic laugh. "Is it that obvious?"

He smiled. "You're walking around this place like I used to." His voice fell gently. "What is it, my dear?"

She didn't expect tears. She tried to swallow them, then leaned her head back to keep them at bay. Terrible visions of Victor flew across her mind's eye. Without thinking, she turned the ring on her left hand. The metal felt cold and dull.

Her uncle watched her a moment, then grunted. "You know," he said, "after Lenore passed, I began taking less pleasure in things." He gestured to the surrounding shelves. "Not even these could tempt me from my dreadful stupor."

"No one blames you for that," she said. "You'd lost your wife of over thirty years."

"Yes. I was lucky to have found a jewel like her. The way you were lucky to have found Victor."

She swallowed, swiping a tear away. "Uncle—"

"You know," he said, raising his voice. She sniffled, sitting back to let him speak. "There is an abundance of precious jewels in this world, Janeth. But they're hidden away. Sometimes, they unearth themselves right in front of us. Often, they're not what we expected." He paused, taking another puff. "So we end up missing them, walking right past." He demonstrated, motioning with his pipe. "We go a lifetime without that one perfect jewel. And I don't mean perfect in cut or color. I mean perfect for us."

She wiped her nose, listening.

"If we're lucky, and I mean really lucky, we stumble across that shining specimen. The one intended for us. Once we do, we cling to that fine stone. We make it ours, and we, in turn, become theirs." He took a breath, his eyes growing hazy. "Even after it's grown dull and weathered. Even after it's lost. We cling to what it was, what we had." She waited as he blinked, seeming to collect himself. "Janeth, dear, if we're fortunate to have found such a thing *twice* in this life…" He shook his head. "Well, by Jove, I should hope you would hold tight to it again."

She knew precisely what he was saying. She looked from him to her ring. A vision of Alice at the park came to her. Funny, smart, and sweet Alice. "What about what we had…before?"

"My dear, it's still here." He brought his free hand to rest over his heart. "It always will be. What's next doesn't take its place. It only reminds us of the beauty we had before while shining a light on what's to come."

She let his words settle around her. Was he right? Could she give herself to someone else…someone like Alice? A distant singing in her chest hummed a quiet reply.

"Treasures are so rare. Don't let such a thing slip by out of fear or guilt."

She sat up, shaking her head. "I don't know if it's that easy," she replied.

He barked a laugh behind his pipe. "Nothing ever is, Janeth dear. Nothing ever is."

She laughed with him. The room had grown heady with his smoke. She let the sweet scent envelop her. What she was feeling was anything but simple. But she could feel it, the shifting of her heart. This morning, she had feared it was Victor disappearing, her old life deserting her. But she had been wrong. Victor was still there. He always would be. Her heart was merely making room. A new space was readying itself. Readying her for Alice.

She exhaled, her shoulders relaxing. "Very well, Uncle." She brushed back her hair and wiped her face clean. "Now, it's your turn. Tell me about the visit."

CHAPTER TWENTY-TWO

After the protest yesterday, Dorothy had treated Alice to another lunch at Baley's Café, though she had repeatedly insisted she was fine to go without. "Oklahoma, you're more hardheaded than my husband." She had practically shoved a cheese sandwich and steaming cup of tea at her. "Eat that. Once you're done, you better get home. Your parents will be up in arms."

She had obliged, shoveling the food into her mouth. Dorothy didn't pry, and she even let her keep the jacket until they saw one another again.

It was only twelve o'clock when Alice went to the house to change. Peeking inside, she found no one home. She slept in fitful spurts the rest of the day. She heard her parents come home but feigned illness to avoid their company. The next morning, she rose and quickly washed, jumped into a day dress and more comfortable shoes, ran a brush through her hair, and headed back to Seaside while her parents slept. She hadn't found many places over the years that felt calm, like a harbor to the torrential life she'd always known. Something about this small beach town gave her a sense of peace. Though almost any place was better than home.

She was sitting on the edge of the boardwalk, the trackway closest to the beach, when Janeth's voice floated toward her above the murmur of beach-goers and the waves: "I'll wait right here, Mr. Preston. Once these customers are done, however, I expect Mr. Mills's payment."

Alice watched her standing outside the confectionary tent. The man inside —Mr. Preston, she presumed—wore a worried look while he attended to a family. She took a moment to admire Janeth, simultaneously thrilled at seeing her again so soon but also frightened by her proximity. Still, she couldn't help gazing upon her salmon-colored skirt that fell to her mid-calf, its straight lines matching the vest that fell over her white blouse. The sleeves that landed at her elbows were cuffed wide and trimmed with an elegant red flower pattern that also lined the vest's pockets. These rested below her waist. The collar on her shirt was fashioned with a thin blue bow. Janeth had tucked her pinned hair beneath the blue hat, the pale pink rim allowing Alice to catch a glimpse of her cheek and rouged lips.

Ahead of her on the sand, a group of young boys began a rowdy game of football. One, no older than eight, tried to tackle a much larger boy into a divot. Glancing back at Janeth, Alice found her scanning the beach for the ruckus. Alice waved.

Janeth, whose mouth opened in a surprised O, waved back. She tossed a look to the waves—coming in roughly today—then said something to Mr. Preston before joining Alice. "I didn't expect to see you here," she said, but the smile she wore seemed pleased.

Alice noted the scent of lilac on the wind, then gestured to the beach. "Heard there was a game today."

Janeth chuckled at her joke. "I..." She hesitated, licking her lips. "How are you?"

"I'm all right," Alice replied, using her right hand to shield her gaze from the sun. When Janeth only stood there, seemingly waiting for her to go on, she said, "Business meeting?"

"Oh." Janeth turned, then faced her again, her hand touching her neck. "Yes. I'm a bit behind schedule. I had a phone call with my brother earlier today."

"How's he doing?"

"Fine." Janeth said, but her tone seemed tight. Alice frowned. She was about to ask if things were okay, but Janeth quickly added, "How was the protest this week? The one near the cannery?"

Surprised, Alice said, "Fine." Not wanting to relay the incident with her mother, she cleared her throat. "Care for a stroll?"

"Stroll?"

"Yeah." She unbuckled her heels and stood. "On the beach."

Janeth's face fell, her dark gaze flitting to the water, the people, then back to Alice. "I don't know."

Sensing her trepidation, Alice put on an encouraging smile. "It's just sand." She hopped down from the boardwalk, turning and extending a hand toward Janeth. "We'll make it quick. I know you have to get back." She nodded toward the tent and scanned the stretch of beach. "Just down to the cliffs." She pointed. "Where those changing tents are."

Janeth's mouth was in a thin line as she seemed to contemplate this. Eventually, her smile returned. "All right. Give me a moment." She hurried over to Mr. Preston and said something. He seemed pleased and waved her off.

Alice felt a swelling in her chest. Her head felt light, and she started to remember how little sleep she'd had recently. A strange sensation filled her mind, as if she'd had too much to drink. She leaned into that feeling, still reeling from the last forty-eight hours, and ignored the voice that told her to be careful. She helped Janeth down once she'd taken off her shoes.

They were both quiet for the first few yards. Alice had wanted to loop their arms together, as she saw several women doing the same, but decided against it. She did put herself between Janeth and the water, sensing her reluctance to be near the waves.

Curious about Janeth's hesitation, Alice kept her tone gentle and asked, "Did your husband die at sea?"

The wind picked up, and Janeth reached to hold on to her hat, keeping her shoes at her side with her other hand. Her steps were a bit awkward in the sand, like she wasn't sure how to balance. "Yes," she said. "He came from a family of fishermen. They traveled each month to the coast." She threw a wary look at the water. "It was the last way I expected him to go."

"How long had you been married?"

"Only two years, though we'd known each other since childhood. He began courting me when I was fifteen." A fond smile lifted her face.

Alice smiled too, though she recognized the rising jealousy in her chest. Shoving it aside, she said, "I'm sorry he died."

Janeth waved like she was shooing a fly, a gesture she often used when she wanted to change the subject. "We shared a wonderful life while he was here. And now…well, I've grieved Victor for a long time. It's nice " Her voice trailed off.

Alice's heart skipped, filling in the empty space with her own hopeful thoughts. She leaned closer, feeling safer now that they were twenty yards from the crowds.

"It's nice to have met someone else."

Alice couldn't help her grin. "You mean me?"

Janeth laughed, leaning back her head. Alice relished the sound. "Of course I mean you." She glanced behind them. "Alice, I can't help but think you've come into my life for a reason."

Alice took a deep breath. She'd been trying to reconcile the fact that Janeth had come into her life after Gladys, searching for a reason to explain things. Maybe Janeth had an answer. "You do?"

She reached out, linking their arms together. "I have to. I don't believe in accidents. Even when I'd love nothing more. Meeting you has been…" She glanced at Alice, a small blush rising in her cheeks. "Well, I'm not certain I can describe it."

"Try?" Alice slowed.

Janeth did the same and looked at her, her brows low in concentration. For a moment, her gaze drifted past her to the sea.

Alice reached out, touching her elbow.

Janeth found her again and smiled. "I never imagined feeling anything like what I did for Victor again. But you're unlike any woman I've met. It's so easy to talk to you." She licked her lips, taking a breath. "I've had a hard time meeting friends in San Diego."

Alice raised her brow at "friends" but let her continue.

"When I worked at the cannery, the women were nice enough. They were kind to my face. But I never felt like one of them, or any of the other Mexican immigrants who worked there." She frowned, and Alice sensed her struggling to find the right words. "I heard the way they whispered about me when Mr. Mills took an interest in me. I know what they were thinking." Her voice turned hard, and she paused, collecting herself. "Then there are the women in my uncle's world. The white women. It's mostly their husbands I meet, but the courtesy they extend me only reaches so far. It's like…there are walls everywhere I turn. Every neighborhood, I can only look in upon them from the outside. No one ever lets me in."

She hesitated before adding, "Part of me has given up trying to be a part of any world." Her voice broke a little, and she dipped her chin. "So meeting you was like a dream. You seem to understand what it's like, straddling worlds, drifting between places. But," she said, meeting Alice's gaze, "it was more than that. I find I can't bear long stretches without seeing you. When I'm not with you, I find myself thinking of you. I wonder what you're doing. Who you're talking to. What you're planning," she added, giving Alice a knowing smile. "So many things now remind me of you."

Alice's heart raced. There *were* words to describe what was happening between them. But still…why? "Janeth," she said slowly, reaching to take her hand. "I feel the same way."

Her eyes lit up. "You do?"

"Yes, but…"

Janeth stiffened. "But what?"

Alice was flooded with her parents' warnings, with Glady's screams. It was all too much. Right now, standing here with Janeth with the sun overhead, everything was lovely and warm and bright, but soon…how long did they have until they were found out? Until one of them was struck down, forced away into the dark and cold, shunned from this world? What was it all worth in the end?

"Alice?"

The tears surprised her, but even more surprising was Janeth reaching out to brush one away. "Darling, what is it?"

Alice felt weak at the term of endearment. Overcome, she said, "Come here," and quickly pulled Janeth into a nearby changing tent.

The sunlight vanished in the tight space. Only sparse slats of light crept in through tears and the vertical seams on each corner. Alice felt as if the world had vanished too, and for a moment, her heart skipped at the notion of finding a place like her dreams, a place all their own. She ignored the fact that it was a musty changing tent with a clump of odorous seaweed tangled in the corner of the matted sand.

"Alice, what's going on?"

"I need to tell you something." They stood close. Wind whipped by outside, jostling the tent. It stood eight feet high and leaned slightly to the left. Alice was grateful for the wind, though. It would muffle her next words. "I've done this before," she said, finding Janeth's gaze in the dimness.

Janeth seemed to take her words in. She gave a small smile, then looked down. "I see."

"It's dangerous, Janeth. What we're feeling."

Her gaze lifted, a small vee between her brows. "Dangerous? How?"

"It's not right."

Janeth studied her, then raised a hand to her necklace.

Alice watched her rub the end of the gold cross. "Before," she said, trying to get out the words. "The woman…before you. She…we were found out."

Janeth searched her gaze. "What happened to her?"

"She was taken away. Her father…they came for her and took her away."

Janeth shifted closer. "Alice…"

She was crying. She felt chilled despite the heat inside the small space. "Janeth, I don't want that to happen again."

"Shh." She reached up, wiping away more tears. "I'm right here, Alice."

"For how long?"

A small smile broke Janeth's solemn face. Tears shined in her eyes. "Only God knows that answer."

Shaking her head, Alice said, "What if you get hurt?"

It was quiet a moment before she said, "I've been hurt, Alice. More hurt than I could possibly imagine. My heart has been shattered like the finest glass, broken so intimately, I never thought it would mend." She smiled. "But it did." She studied Alice awhile. "It seems you carry that hurt too."

Sniffling, Alice muttered, "Yes." Uncertainty wrapped around her. The pain of the past, her past, stung sharply. It made her tremble.

Janeth reached out, pulling her into an embrace. "I don't understand why this is happening," she said over Alice's shoulder. "All I know is that it is. I think we were meant to find one another, Alice. To help each other. To…be there for one another."

To love each other? Alice thought, wrapping her arms around Janeth. How soft she felt, how warm. She took a deep, shuddering breath to try to calm herself. She pulled back, finding Janeth's gaze. Even misty-eyed, she was beautiful.

Alice kissed her, pulling her close. A blissful moan came from deep in Janeth's throat, and it opened something in Alice. She kissed her harder, their tongues meeting. There was a small gasp, though she wasn't sure if it was Janeth or her own breath catching. Alice slipped her hands under Janeth's vest, finding her back beneath the white blouse. She pressed her fingers into the supple flesh.

Outside, the wind howled. Inside, Alice held on to Janeth. Time split, opening up and folding in on itself as they kissed. Seconds and endless moments stretched into eternity. Alice wanted to dive into that sense of infinite time, live there forever. Distant voices drifted softly over the sound of the crashing waves, and the tent shook with the wind. This moment was everything. She never wanted it to end.

Eventually, Janeth stepped back, her breath coming fast. She pressed one hand to her chest below her necklace. "Oh my God," she said, a knowing smile lifting her cheeks. She ran her hands up and down Alice's arms, her grip tightening and loosening as if she was deciding whether or not to pull her in again.

Alice grinned, reaching to brush a smudge of lipstick from the corner of Janeth's lip. Janeth laughed, then did the same to her. The elation of the moment filled the small space until reality crashed back down like the waves outside.

Alice's smile fell, and she said, "Janeth…"

She held a finger to her lips. "Alice, please." She kissed her again, quick and passionate. "I need to see you again."

"When? How?" She had so much to do. She needed to learn more about the Temperance fundraiser. What had started as a new target her family had their eyes on now seemed like a distant, desperate hold on a life Alice wasn't sure she wanted anymore. But how could she live differently? It seemed impossible with her mother on her back.

Janeth's words from earlier sank in, how she had battled her own demons with identity and where she fit in this world. Alice swallowed, not having considered who she might be without her parents and this dreary life she'd led since Gladys.

Janeth was chewing her lip, seeming to run through a mental calendar. "It's nearly July," she muttered. A look of defiance crossed her face. "Come to Logan Heights?"

Alice blinked, surprised. "Are you sure?"

"Yes. I'd love to show you around. Next Tuesday? Say you will."

Alice clasped their hands together, searching Janeth's gaze. In it, she found longing and affection. No, she thought, her breath catching again. It was something more. Something someone with their own hurt and grief carried, just like her.

"All right."

"All right?" Janeth said, her tone incredulous.

Alice laughed and kissed her again. Voices sounded closer outside. "We must be careful, but yes. And we had better get back. Your Mr. Preston probably thinks you deserted him."

Janeth's face turned surprised. "Oh God, you're probably right." She stepped out of the tent, fixing her hat that had gone askew. They checked one another for lipstick. Janeth nodded approvingly, and they started back for the beach. Walking side by side, with respectable space between them, Alice felt a sense of something coming. Something that could, just maybe, help her feel whole again.

CHAPTER TWENTY-THREE

That's the local fish market. It's run by Mr. Ruiz." Janeth frowned. "I can't recall if his son has taken over most of the business. He came from Mexico City just last year, according to Maria."

Janeth and Alice walked along the road in companionable silence. Janeth had shown Alice the orange groves at the end of town, where they had wandered between the dormant trees as Alice had asked about the seasonality of the fruit and how the farmers managed to pick so many oranges each year. Now, they wandered back to town toward the family market.

"It's nice here," Alice said, looking around at the sleepy houses. "Quiet."

"During the day." She tossed Alice a smile. "Nights are for music and dancing."

"Do you come here a lot for that? Music and dancing?"

Janeth was struck with the vision of dancing with Alice and found her words deserting her. Ahead, Leo stepped out of the market, jogging toward them. His black shoes kicked a dusting of dirt onto the back of his pants. He waved.

"Leo, good day." Janeth turned to Alice, who stepped away to create more space between them. The gesture sent a longing through her, but she pushed that aside as Leo spoke in Spanish.

"What are you doing here...with her?"

The question surprised her and prompted heat in her cheeks. She was glad such a rude question was asked in Spanish so Alice couldn't understand. "We're walking, Leo. I see no harm in that."

He gave a tight smile to Alice, who looked between them curiously. "Do you think it's smart bringing her here?"

"This is a free nation, is it not?"

"To an extent."

Frustration built, and she clutched her handbag, resisting the urge to shove her brother in the chest. "Alice," she started to say, but she was cut off by a knowing look in Alice's eye.

"I ought to be going anyway." Alice nodded to Leo. "Good to see you."

Janeth started to reach for her, then stopped, remembering Leo was there. "Lunch next Wednesday?" she called after her, hoping to keep the longing from her voice. "At the house," she added quickly.

Alice only smiled, but in it, Janeth saw her acceptance. Then she nodded to Leo.

He bid her a good afternoon in English. They both watched Alice until she disappeared behind an oncoming trolley. When she was gone, Janeth turned and said, "I can't believe you, Leo."

"Me? I'm not the one parading around with a white woman."

"That's not a crime," she countered. Though she hated how hot her face felt recalling thoughts of Alice that *could* be deemed as such.

Leo was shaking his head. "What will people say if she starts coming around more? Here, to our streets? Our homes?" He gestured behind him. "To my market?"

"I'm sure they'd say she has good taste in produce."

He stared, seemingly incredulous. "I didn't want Maria to be right," he finally said.

The air left her lungs as if he'd hit her. "Right about what?" Tension reared in her as she clenched her jaw. She wanted to hear him say it.

He couldn't seem to, though. She sighed, knowing that, ultimately, he didn't need to. She saw it written on his face.

She forced herself to face him, to meet the challenge in his gaze. "I'm not doing anything wrong."

He squinted as if trying to find the admission between her words. Eventually, his shoulders fell, and he found her hand, holding it between his. "I don't want you to forget who you are, Janeth. You spend more time in Seaside than anywhere else. You dress like them, speak like them…"

She pulled her hand back. "You know why I do that. It's part of the business, Leo."

"Is it? Or is it just you now?"

Fire filled her lungs, spewing out with her next words. "If this is what you think, why push me into this in the first place? That was you, wasn't it? You and Maria telling me to take this job with Mr. Mills? The two of you told me to do this. 'Do it for the family. Think of the future.' What did you think was going to happen, Leo?"

He swallowed, his eyes gleaming. "It seems as though those priorities have shifted, Janeth."

She could hardly believe what she was hearing and worked to keep her voice even. "What are you implying?"

"It's one thing to work for someone like Mr. Mills. It's another to abandon the life you lived before."

"Abandon? Leo, I—"

"It's not like when I first came to this country to be with you. It's so much effort to get you to come to an event here. When was the last time you saw Maria's family?" He paused, seeming to consider his next words. "Have you forgotten where you come from?" He gestured to her clothes, her handbag. "It seems that way more and more lately."

She stepped forward, letting a growl seep into her voice. "I know precisely where I'm from. I could never forget that, Leo."

"And Victor?"

She blinked, taken aback. "What about him?"

"You're his wife."

"I'm his widow," she corrected. Taking a breath, she added, "And I'm your sister. I'm only me, Leo. That's all I've been and all I'll ever be." She pressed her hand to his chest, finding his breathing as uneven as hers. Softer, she said, "You can't push me into a new life, then berate me for trying to live it."

His gaze searched hers. For a moment, she wondered if he could see it. Could he see the growing connection between her and Alice? Not even she was certain what such a relationship meant. She only knew it was significant and good.

"Just…be careful," he said, and mercifully, the tension between them began to thaw. Though she could still sense his wariness despite the softness of his tone.

She waited a moment, letting the remnants of their argument

dissipate, then said, "I always am." She kissed his cheek as he squeezed her hand. He turned to go. She hadn't noticed Maria standing in the doorway of the market, watching. There was something in her gaze Janeth couldn't read before Maria turned and followed Leo inside.

CHAPTER TWENTY-FOUR

The following Monday, Alice met Mary at Dorothy's house before the Temperance event downtown. She and Mary waited in the modest parlor of the quaint home until Dorothy thundered down the stairs, exclaiming that her mother-in-law had held her captive at breakfast as she hurried them out the door. Alice had just enough time to hand her the jacket and dress she was returning, at which Dorothy gave a wink.

Dorothy tossed the jacket on a coatrack and grabbed her hat before the three of them started the trek downtown. "Madame Enfield will have our necks if we're late. Good thing today's is within walking distance."

"Dorothy, what if we *are* late?" Mary asked, rubbing her neck, her voice thick with worry as they crossed a busy street. "Madame Enfield is announcing the location of the fundraiser today."

Giving a knowing grin, Dorothy replied, "I already know where it is."

Mary gasped. "What?"

Alice, trying to keep up with Dorothy's long strides, hurried to walk beside her. Their heeled shoes clopped a staccato beat along the sidewalk. "You do?"

"Heard the matron and her biddies last Tuesday during their meeting at Baley's. I was there with my husband for lunch." She halted them on the sidewalk, one arm extended. Mary collided with Alice as they waited for several cars to pass.

Mary practically bounced on her toes, and her eyes were wide. "Well?" she said, her voice trailing expectantly.

"It'll be in the auditorium of San Diego State."

"Oh my," Mary muttered as the officer signaled for them to cross. Alice raised her brows. "Sounds fancy."

"It's a beautiful campus," Dorothy said. "And a good location. Hoity-toity folks love to donate to the school, so it's a good venue to maximize funds for the movement."

Alice nodded, her head starting to spin with the idea of her family getting their hands on more cash than they'd ever had. This feeling filled her up through the protest and got her through the heat of the day. Even under the shadow of a three-story building, she couldn't avoid the layer of sweat that gathered on her skin. Noticing Mary's pale face, she easily convinced her to head to the café with Dorothy to cool down while she handled their group's donation basket. Slipping a handful of dollar notes and sixty cents into her dress pocket was easy.

"Here you are," she said to the matron at the end, most of the women standing under awnings while they waited for the next trolley to leave. Even Madame Enfield seemed ready to be indoors. Her dark heavy dress was even darker at the collar and waist. She dabbed her face with a handkerchief as she took the basket without a word.

At home, Alice relayed the fundraiser information to her parents. The three of them sat around the card table, Alice having found a stool in the railyard that she'd pulled into the house.

"Oh, John dear, it will be grand," her mother said, pulling a fresh cigarette to her lips.

He grinned and lit it for her, shaking out the match. "They'll probably do a collection bin," he said, sitting back, a thoughtful look on his face. "Could be a big check written at the end."

"My Temperance friend said that's usually what happens," Alice explained, taking a bite of a banana. Someone had gone to the market recently; two apples, a carton of eggs, a slab of cheese, and a bottle of milk sat in the center of the table. She figured her father must have done well with the tourists buying into his games last night on a corner downtown.

"Alice, you'll need a new pair of stockings. Can't have you looking like a street urchin at a place like that," her mother said, her gaze roving the ceiling. Alice could see the wheels turning, her mother's plan for their family to walk away with the Temperance fund forming in her mind.

"We'll get you a pair, Dumplin'," her father said, grabbing an apple and taking a large bite.

"You'll come with me this Friday downtown," her mother was saying. It wasn't a question, and Alice waited for her to continue. "The woman I've been stealing fabric from…she has a shipment coming in soon. I'll bring you, introduce you, then I'll have her show me the new stuff. You get into the stockings, pick a pair, and slip it into my handbag."

"Perfect." Her father nodded approvingly. "We'll need to be on top of things for the fundraiser."

Alice nodded, sitting back as her parents dove into a conversation about their recent successes and ways to lift the fundraising money. Her mind drifted to the cigar box under her bed. She'd already slipped half the money from the protest in there, using cramps as an excuse to lie down upon her return home. She had more than twenty-five dollars now and pondered the idea of buying that red dress and matching hat. Not to spite her mother, though. No, Alice thought, a stirring feeling filling her stomach, she wanted to buy it so Janeth could take it off.

"Alice?"

"What?" She sat upright, afraid she'd said her thoughts out loud.

Her mother eyed her. "I asked if you're ready for the protest on Wednesday?"

"Oh," she replied, straightening. "Yes. I may meet my friends at the café after. In case I'm late getting home."

"Sounds good, Dumplin'." Her father stood, then headed out the back door to the privy. She smiled but felt her mother's gaze still on her. Swallowing, Alice met it, determined to keep her cool while her mother examined her. She couldn't let on that it wasn't the protest she was going to tomorrow but Janeth's house. It was all she could think about, but now, in this moment, she kept her face still, her eyes empty until her mother exhaled a line of smoke.

"Don't forget our cut," she said. "Today's wasn't much. We taught you better than that."

"Yes, Mother."

Alice knew her mother was holding back. Her father was the buffer, the wall that kept her unrelenting venom at bay. They'd been icy around one another since their last big conversation, and Alice felt like she had been walking on eggshells. And, God, was she getting tired of that. Glancing at her mother, she wondered if it wore on her, too. Would her mother even miss her, she wondered, if she was gone?

Sighing, Alice grabbed one more bite, then retired to her room.

CHAPTER TWENTY-FIVE

This flan is delicious, Janeth," Mrs. Cadena said, dabbing her lips with a napkin before running off to fetch another piece. Janeth caught Leo scooping pieces on his plate with his spoon, licking his lips.

"Thank you," she called after her, feeling pleased. She watched Leo a moment.

Seemingly reluctantly, he admitted, "It is quite good." She only smiled.

Mrs. Cadena wasn't the only one who seemed to enjoy the dessert she'd brought. Mr. and Mrs. Estevan, Maria's cousin, Helio, and even the host of this birthday party, Mrs. Ruiz, had complimented the dish.

"Papa, can I have another piece?" Elena asked on the other side of him at the circular, six-person table. It was arranged among five others in the backyard of the Ruiz property. Elena wore a dress Janeth had seen Maria working on a few months ago during quiet moments in the store. It was soft pink and matched the stain around Elena's mouth from the cups of punch she'd guzzled with dinner. Jorge had acquired a matching one on his white shirt, much to Maria's chagrin.

"Of course," Leo said, pulling Jorge's untouched piece over to her. Jorge had run off with his mother as soon as the music had started after the meal. Next to the tables, a space had been cleared for dancing. Most of the partygoers were out there now, everyone dressed in their finest garb. A band played an upbeat mariachi tune beneath white and blue paper streamers that had been strung from trees surrounding the modest lot of land. The evening sky was stretching into a canvas of deep blue streaked with pink, the color reminding her of the cotton candy at Mr. Preston's stand. That thought, naturally, transitioned into the fiery memory with Alice at the beach last week.

Someone grabbed her shoulders from behind, jostling her from her thoughts. "Janeth, come dance," a young woman said, her voice playful and light. She turned to find Maria's sister, Rosa, gesturing for her to follow.

She laughed. "I'll be there soon, I promise."

Rosa waved her off, then kicked up her skirt and joined the fray. Janeth watched on. A young man whom she had noticed watching her through dinner was dancing with Mrs. Martinez. He caught her gaze and smiled. She returned it but refocused on Leo.

"Maria didn't think you'd come," he said, taking a sip of beer.

Janeth pursed her lips, keeping her initial retort back regarding her sister-in-law. She was still upset about Maria's, and then Leo's, tirade against Alice. She hadn't known how to act around her or her brother all night. It felt like neither of them was on her side. "I'm happy to have been able to surprise her."

Leo chuckled. "You two are like fire and ice sometimes."

"That's sisters for you." She tapped along to the music, avoiding his gaze. Even she was surprised to have found herself back in Logan Heights so soon. It was Maria's father who had extended the invitation to this party when they'd run into one another on the trolley. Janeth's first instinct had been to refuse. She had been furious with Leo after the way he'd accused her of throwing away who she was. Digging in her heels, and perhaps to prove him wrong, she'd decided to show up tonight.

Presently, he eyed her from across the table. "It didn't used to be that way between you and Maria." She shrugged but felt his expectant gaze. When she didn't say anything, he asked, "Are you still planning to see your friend?"

She took a sip of her own beer, still looking anywhere but at him. She watched Jorge running between people on the dance floor. Another young boy chased him, both cackling with glee. "Her name is Alice."

Leo finished his drink, then leaned his elbows on the table, resting his chin behind his hands. His voice was low as he said, "Janeth, I told you how I feel about the two of you going around together." When she didn't say anything, he tilted his head as if shifting to try another tactic.

"What makes you think you can trust her? If she finds out what you do—"

"She already knows."

Leo went wide-eyed. He scooted his green metal chair closer. She caught the scent of cologne wafting from his neck, gleaming with sweat above his high collar. He whispered, "What?"

"She knows. I told you and Maria…she's not like that. She doesn't care."

"But she's a part of those groups."

"It's for show."

"For show? Why would anyone do that?"

Janeth glanced around. She didn't feel like she had the right to share exactly why Alice was a part of those groups. They'd built a trust. She didn't want to break it. "She has her reasons, Leo. It's private."

His brow was sky-high as he watched her. "How do you expect me to explain this to Maria?" he finally asked.

"I don't. She probably wouldn't hear you anyway."

"Janeth—"

"I know. I understand her worry, Leo. I do. But how many white people does she know?"

He was quiet a moment, then said, "She knows enough, Janeth."

She met his gaze. Her neck warmed at the piercing look in his eyes. In them, she saw the harassment, the broken windows, the judgment hurled at her brother and sister-in-law any time they left Logan Heights. They were right. But so was she when it came to Alice.

"I'm not going to stop seeing her."

Her brother's brow furrowed at this. He seemed like he was ready to ask her another question when someone tapped her shoulder.

"Good evening." It was the young man from the dance floor. He was a nephew of Mrs. Ruiz, she was pretty sure. His pressed pants and shirt looked new. His thick dark brown locks were slicked back with oil as he gave a small bow. "I'm Carlos. Would you honor me with a dance?"

Janeth smiled tightly, then glanced at Leo. Eager to get away from their conversation, she held out her hand and said, "I would love to."

On the dance floor, she let Carlos lead her into the middle of the crowd. The band had shifted to a traditional folk song, the guitars plucking rhythmically while the men's voices harmonized. Carlos pulled her close, and they moved together. She caught the surprised look on Maria's face near the tables. Closing her eyes, Janeth took a breath. Opening them, she found Carlos smiling as he spun them. She looked at him, taking in his kind eyes, his mustache and rosy cheeks. When he twirled her, she turned her focus inward to register how she was feeling. She searched her mind, tuned in to the beating of her heart, searching for a sign of life as she danced with this seemingly sweet young man. She tried to find a fraction of the feeling she had standing in the same room as Alice. She attempted to conjure the kick of warmth that swam in her stomach, the flutter that filled her chest, the buzzing of her mind as it was overrun with thoughts of being close to her. She tried to find it in the whirl of colors as the music lifted to a crescendo, but as she swayed in this man's arms, all she felt was empty.

The song came to an end. The crowd applauded before the next song began. "Thank you," she said to Carlos. He looked ready to take her hand again, but she turned away and hurried back to the table.

"Aunt Janeth," Elena called, speckles of cake on her chin as she sat on her knees to be seen over the tabletop.

She took a drink, her breath coming quickly. "Yes, dear?"

"Your face is red," she said, pointing with her fork.

Leo eyed her, a pleased look on his face. Janeth lifted her palm to her face, feeling the warmth. "My, so it is." She smiled, ignoring her brother's gaze. Let him think it's from the dance, she mused, settling into her seat. It would be her little secret, the true reason of her blush. The realization that she was, inexplicably, falling in love. But not with any man. Certainly not with Carlos. Janeth fanned herself and smiled. She was falling quite hard, she realized, for Alice.

CHAPTER TWENTY-SIX

Janeth could hardly contain herself as the doorbell chimed on Wednesday. She had risen early that day—far too excited to sleep past her usual seven o'clock—and had gone through the entire house to ensure it was presentable.

"Janeth, dear, you've dusted the entire place twice," her uncle had said, amused, as she'd run over his desk with a feather duster. She'd brushed off his shoulders as he'd compared her brother's numbers to his own ledger. Since getting Leo's help with inventory, her uncle had been happily using those sums to balance his books. "Whatever is the occasion?"

"My friend is coming for lunch," she'd replied, feeling the need to reorganize all of the books on the shelves. Realizing the impossibility of such a task in so little time, she'd continued shining the banister and straightened her room once again. In between bouts of baseboard scrubbing and chandelier shining, she'd made deviled eggs and laid out several bowls of fresh fruit for the meal. All of it sat waiting on the dining room table, napkins covering everything to keep flies away. The summer day was hot, and many of the windows were open to keep the sea breeze blowing through.

As she opened the door, her face fell. "Oh. Hello."

"Humph." Mr. Mills's sister came in, eyeing her at the informal greeting.

"Apologies, I've forgotten the time. Uncle is in the library. I'll fetch him." Janeth made her way to the back of the house. Of course, she was acutely aware of the time; it was exactly eight minutes until one o'clock. Eight minutes until Alice arrived. Behind the staircase, she stopped at the black-framed mirror hanging in the hall. She brushed a hand through her bangs, then ran a hand over her hair that she had decided to pin back, most of it sitting in a loose knot at the base of her neck. A few strands had escaped, hanging delicately by her ears where she'd decided to don silver hoop earrings.

Her dress was one she'd worn to an outdoor luncheon with her uncle two years before. The salmon-colored material of her rounded neckline met the black satin of her dress that was patterned with large, pale pink roses. The material was fairly sheer, and she'd donned a slip beneath it. She picked a piece of lint from one of the sleeves that fell just above her elbows. She brushed down the dress's straight lines until they met the asymmetrical skirt that rose higher on her left side. It was her most fashion-forward dress and to her, the most scandalous, as the skirt fell just to her knees. Her sheer stockings ran up beneath it, held in place by clips attached to her girdle over her finest rayon tap pants. She had splashed an extra dab of perfume to the pulse points on her wrist.

"Uncle," she called. In the library, she found him already limping toward the doorway with his cane. "Your chaperone is here."

He continued forward, then looked up upon reaching her. "My, you look lovely today, dear."

"Thank you, Uncle." She reached up, checking again that her bun was in place. Back in the foyer, she held the door open for them and said, "We'll be sure to save you some eggs for your return." But don't hurry back, she almost added, pursing her lips in a tight smile to keep the words to herself.

Waving them off, she watched them go down the stairs to the sidewalk below. She scanned the street, then the sandy cliffside. It was a quiet afternoon. Only one man and his son stood flying a kite on the cliffs. It caught the wind beautifully, soaring higher, then dipping low before finding another breeze on which to climb upon.

The water was calm, a stark comparison to the beating of her heart. Janeth moved inside, closing the door. She rearranged the silverware again, paced the drawing room, then the foyer, until the clock struck one.

She waited. More time passed. Janeth was certain an eternity wrapped itself around the house, lifting her into its endless abyss as a sinking feeling filled her stomach. While there was no clear reason why Alice wouldn't come, her mind reeled with dozens of scenarios. What if the run-in with Leo had scared her off? Finally, at seven past the hour, the door chimed.

She hurried forward, then stopped in front of the door. She took a deep breath to gather herself. "Breathe, Janeth."

"Sorry I'm late." Alice stood beneath the gabled porch looking divine. Her light hair held a shine to it. She wore the same dress as on their venture to Seaside, though it looked freshly laundered. Even her heels looked like they'd been polished. Janeth felt light at the clear effort Alice had put into her appearance, feeling less silly for how long she'd spent getting ready this morning.

"It's perfectly fine. I hardly noticed the time," she said, stepping aside to let her in. A flutter filled her stomach, and she felt at a loss for words. Turning, she looked at Alice, who was taking in the house as she always did.

"How's your uncle?" she asked, her gaze darting momentarily to Janeth's hemline.

"He's all right, thank you for asking. The doctor is afraid he's not moving enough. God only knows what having a bullet stuck in you will do. You know, I've heard stories of people living for years with something lodged in their arm or leg."

"A lot of Civil War soldiers did, I reckon."

"Yes, though my uncle doesn't have the benefit of being young with such a malady." She shook her head. "He'll be back in an hour after his walk." She threw a glance at the mantle clock on the table near the stairs. "Less than, now."

Alice raised a brow at her comment. Janeth cleared her throat. God, was she being too obvious? She wanted nothing more than to spend time with Alice, get to know her even more, and here she was complaining about the time passing.

"Well, lunch is ready," she said, quickly running her hands down her dress to rid them of the clamminess that had gathered. She gestured toward the dining room, starting that way.

Alice stepped forward, grabbing her hand. "Wait."

Janeth turned. "Is something wrong?"

Smiling, Alice nodded toward the stairs. "You promised me a look at that painting, remember?"

The blood rushing in her ears nearly drowned out Alice's words. Janeth's throat went dry, and she swallowed before saying, "Of course.

The Monet." She smiled. "I remember." She tossed a look around the entryway, confirming they were alone, aware of how empty the house was. She led them upstairs and worked to ease her breathing. She found she was keenly aware of Alice's presence, one step behind her, as they moved. It was as if she could feel her, the air between them heavy.

Reaching the landing, Janeth waited for Alice. Her gaze roved over the vast space in the long hall that ran in opposite directions.

"Down there is the guest quarters and my uncle's room," Janeth said, pointing to the right where a peacock blue carpet snaked over wood floors. Fine white walls framed the hallway. "He refuses to relocate downstairs, even though it'd be easier on him. Then there's the upstairs drawing room. Here's the study." She pointed to large French doors in front of them.

"Where's your room?" Alice asked, her voice even as she eyed a bust of George Washington tucked against the far wall.

"The southwest corner," Janeth explained, hoping Alice didn't notice the catch in her voice. For a brief moment, she envisioned taking Alice by the hand and pulling her into her room, closing the door behind them. The vision was bold, and she grabbed the banister to steady herself. Blinking, she regained her senses and said, "The painting's in here."

In the study, Janeth pulled open the heavy yellow curtains on the far walls. Soft midday light cast itself over the space.

"Golly," Alice muttered, stepping into the large room. The white walls held hardly any vacant space.

"My uncle is an avid collector. Well, he was. He can't get to the museums or auctions as often now. Hugh will go for him on occasion." She followed Alice onto the thin blue rug that hosted a brown, high-back chair opposite a green chaise lounge. A coffee table sat between them. Otherwise, there was no furniture in the room.

"People need space to stand back and admire these works," her uncle had said when she'd moved in. "A masterpiece should be appreciated from precisely the right distance."

She watched Alice slowly circle the room. Her face fell into a look of concentration as she moved. Feeling the need to fill the quiet, Janeth explained, "Most of these are replicas, but he has a few originals, like that one." She pointed to the one Alice stood in front of in the middle of the southern wall. "It's called *Wanderer Above the Sea Fog*, painted by Caspar David Friedrich."

Alice turned. "Do you know about all these painters?"

Moving to stand beside her, Janeth laughed. "I didn't know any of these works before moving here. I had some schooling in Mexico but stopped when I was twelve to help my family on their land." She caught Alice's gaze. "Did you go to school?"

Alice snorted. "What do you think?"

Janeth put her hands up. "I would never assume."

"No," Alice said, returning to study the painting. "No time."

Alice resumed her circle. Janeth, a restlessness stirring in her, directed her toward a painting in the corner. "This one is my favorite."

Alice eyed it, then another one across the room. "They look the same."

"They're both Monets," she answered. Alice raised her brow, seemingly in recognition of the name. "I adore the colors. The sun dabbled over the water like that…" She let her voice trail off as she gestured to the work.

It was quiet a time before Alice said, "Does it remind you of your husband?"

Janeth opened her mouth to respond. She'd never told a soul how the blurry image of the man in the canoe ignited memories of Victor. The entire painting had been a salve on her heart upon moving here. She had come in here often in those first few months to stand and stare at it, imagining Victor on the water. She pictured him out at sea, happy, content, at home.

She blinked back tears. "It does, yes."

Turning to her, Alice reached for her hand. "It's a beautiful painting."

Janeth took a breath, smiling at the warmth resonating from Alice's touch. "Here," she said, "let me show you the others." She started past Alice, but like she had downstairs, Alice gripped her hand and turned her so they were standing in each other's places. Janeth searched her gaze.

"Janeth," she said, "are you really going to show me more paintings right now?" In the hall, the clock struck the quarter hour.

Janeth's heart hurried its pace. "I—" Alice waited, a small smile lifting her face. God, Janeth loved that smile. "No," she finally said, her voice low. "I'm not." She stepped forward, pulling Alice into a kiss. She felt Alice's smile melt against her lips. Janeth still couldn't comprehend how soft she was, how absolutely delectable kissing her could be.

Alice pressed closer, and Janeth wrapped her arms around her, pulling her in. Her lips parted, and she met Alice's tongue with her own. The sensation kicked up a yearning in her stomach, and that feeling quickly trailed lower between her legs.

Janeth pulled back. Alice, seemingly reluctantly, opened her eyes to meet her gaze. Her bottom lip was swollen from their kiss. Her chest rose and fell, and Janeth stared openly at her bosom.

Another grin crossed Alice's face. She took Janeth's left hand in her right, lifting it to kiss her knuckles. She slowly stepped backward toward the chaise. As she did, Alice kissed the tip of Janeth's forefinger, then her middle finger. She felt utterly dizzy, trying to walk and reckon what her body was doing as Alice kissed her.

"I don't…" Janeth started to say, licking her lips. "I don't know how…"

She didn't need to finish her sentence. Alice's eyes burned with understanding. Janeth felt hot as Alice lifted her hand, taking the same two fingers she'd kissed into her mouth. Janeth gasped as Alice held them there, then slowly, sensually, pulled them out.

Pushing forward, Janeth crashed into another kiss. She hadn't felt like this in years, this overwhelming, nearly uncontrollable desire to be close to someone. Alice had surprised her in so many ways. Her sweet, beautiful, honest thief. Everything about the two of them seemed contradictory, and yet made perfect sense. Alice made her feel alive again, made her feel seen in a world that demanded she dull her flame to fit in. She kissed Alice hard and relished the fierceness with which Alice returned the kiss. They found the chaise. Alice broke their kiss but only to lay her lips upon Janeth's neck.

"God," she muttered as Alice trailed kisses against her. Alice inhaled near her pulse, making Janeth smile.

"You smell incredible," Alice mumbled between kisses. Janeth reached up, running a hand into Alice's hair as Alice stepped back. Her hands roved over Janeth, reaching below her skirt. She found Janeth's hips, gripping them. The sensation elicited a groan.

Smiling, Alice sat back against the head of the chaise, motioning for Janeth. Glancing at the door, Janeth climbed on top of Alice, tugging up her skirt to straddle her hips. "I can't believe this is happening." Alice leaned forward, kissing the material over her breasts. Meeting her gaze, she asked, "Is this what you wanted?"

Straddling Alice, Janeth cupped her face. Her beautiful face, her eyes—so often filled with such concern and sadness—were bright as they gazed back at her. The look in them made her shudder. "Yes," she said, leaning down to mimic the kisses Alice had given her along her neck. In her ear she whispered, "This is exactly what I want."

Alice reached down, and Janeth helped her unclip the strap keeping her stockings in place. She reached for Alice's hand, slipping it beneath her skirt. Pushing down the waist of her tap pants, she directed Alice to her center.

Janeth heard Alice's breath catch and could hardly stand the little space left between them. She moved Alice's fingers over her, brushing gently at first, feeling her arousal build. Alice continued the rhythm, and Janeth moved to rest one hand on her shoulder while the other tentatively cupped her breast. Alice smiled, bringing her other hand on top of Janeth's, showing her how she wanted to be touched.

They kissed again. Janeth found herself eager to taste as much of Alice as she could, using her tongue to search her mouth. As she did, she felt Alice's hand stop. She groaned but only for a moment before Alice's fingers pushed gently inside her.

"Oh God, Alice." She kissed her again, deeper. Alice moaned too, starting a steady motion inside her. Janeth leaned back, her gaze locked on Alice. She moved her hips to match the rhythm, feeling Alice move within her. Her heart raced, her breath came fast, and heat rushed to her center.

Janeth's arousal continued to build as she rode Alice's fingers. She closed her eyes, but only for a moment, to center herself in the bliss coursing through her. "Alice," she said, opening her eyes again and pulling her close. Their foreheads pressed together. Alice stroked her as Janeth bucked over her fingers. Moments later, the pressure rose, and Janeth cried out into a kiss.

Trembling, Janeth slowly pulled back, her lips already missing Alice's. Slowly, Alice withdrew her fingers, then wrapped her arms around Janeth.

"Are you all right?" she asked.

Janeth's breathing finally slowed, her mind coming down from the heaven Alice had sent her to. "I'm more than all right." She moved to lie beside Alice, who stretched out on her back while Janeth wrapped her left arm and leg over her. They lay quietly together for a time. Alice pressed a kiss to her forehead. Janeth ran her fingers over Alice's abdomen, imagining what lay beneath her dress. She had never considered how wonderful being with a woman could be. Alice had seemed to know exactly where to touch her, how to elicit absolute ecstasy with only her fingers. A desire to return the favor struck inside her chest, along with a flurry of nerves. She'd never done such things before...what if she didn't do it right?

In the hallway, the grandfather clock struck the half hour. They both raised their head to the doorway. Janeth had forgotten the outside world even existed.

"We should probably get to lunch," Alice said, her chin resting against Janeth's head as she stroked her hair.

Looking up to meet her gaze, Janeth wondered at the look swirling in Alice's eyes. How had this woman undone her, broken her open to a world of new possibilities? In a time when Janeth felt like she was being stretched, forced into a thousand different boxes, here was Alice, showing her there was life outside of the restraints thrust upon her. Telling her how she felt was valid and real. Seeing her for everything she was.

Willing herself to be brave, she shifted onto her right elbow, lowering her hand to the hem of Alice's dress. She lifted it, finding the rolled end of her stockings. Raising it higher, she revealed the peach bloomers. Gingerly, her fingers traced the waistband, her gaze going back to Alice.

"Janeth," Alice said, her voice barely a whisper, "you don't have to."

The words were sincere, she knew, and she loved Alice for it. Janeth leaned forward, kissing her hard. "I know," she said. "I want to."

❖

To Alice's delight, Janeth was a quick learner. At first, Alice had directed her fingers where to go, how to move, what kind of pressure to apply. But she had only given a few directions as she lay back, relishing the feel of Janeth's strokes on her center. Her breathing grew staggered, her left arm wrapped around Janeth over her, her grip tightening on her waist.

Janeth leaned down, kissing her. Alice lifted her hips, encouraging Janeth's movements. She moaned into her mouth, and Janeth's strokes grew faster. She couldn't make out what Janeth muttered against her neck as she kissed her there, continuing her movements. The only thing that registered in her mind was her own desire, racing in a languid heat across her body. Leaning back, Alice cried out when her orgasm crashed over her. She rode it out, then found Janeth's hand, pulling it up to kiss.

Almost timidly, Janeth asked, "Was that all right?"

Still breathing hard, Alice reached up, cupping her face. "That was amazing."

Janeth smiled, kissing her again as the clock—to Alice's surprise—chimed a quarter till the hour. "Oh," Janeth said, turning to the doorway. "They'll be back soon."

Alice lay back, feeling satisfied as Janeth scampered up, adjusting her tap pants and trying to fix her hair that was an adorable mess. Pulling an arm to rest behind her head, Alice watched her re-clip her garters, then straighten the coffee table that had been perfectly untouched. She laughed.

"Alice," Janeth said, "what's so amusing?"

"You," she said, feeling warm and light. This feeling that had once been so familiar was back. She recognized it and knew its name. But the idea of falling in love again wasn't an option. That heavy truth pushed out the wonderful feeling in her body, bringing her crashing back to reality. Slowly, she stood, adjusting her own dress and undergarments.

"I need to wash up," Janeth said. "Meet you in the dining room?" she asked, closing the curtains before she headed for the doorway.

The darkness that fell over the room was like the gloom in Alice's mind. Was that all this was, a brief moment in time for them? A fleeting dream restricted to stolen moments that couldn't last. It couldn't... could it? If anyone found out...

"Alice?" Janeth said. Alice blinked, realizing Janeth was standing before her.

"Sorry," she said, shaking herself from her thoughts. Janeth kissed her, brief and sweet. "See you downstairs."

Smiling, Janeth hurried out the door. Alice watched her go, a part of her heart going with her.

Chapter Twenty-Seven

K eep up, Alice," her mother called, dashing ahead of her on the crowded sidewalk on Seventh Avenue.

Alice darted between passersby, men and women out in their glad rags for a night on the town. Word was, a new speakeasy had opened in the Gaslamp District. The buzz of anticipation was evident as the sun set over the city streets. Cars honked as folks headed to the theater, to dinner, and a night of summer fun. Alice envied them as she caught up to her mother. She imagined walking arm in arm with Janeth on their way to a show or hunkering into a booth in a dark bar. Images from another life swam before her. The daydream parted as she collided with her mother, jostling her as she checked her reflection in a storefront window.

"Jesus, Alice, watch it."

"Sorry." She adjusted her hat as her mother smoothed the ends of her short hair. She looked the part tonight: homely, approachable, the only hint of flair in her bold red lipstick. Otherwise, she looked like a working-class woman heading home for the day.

"Shape up now. Bernice is inside. After I introduce you, head to the front. Stockings are in a bin just inside the window." She pointed behind the glass to the dimly lit corner. "Be quick." Her mother's gaze roved her figure, then her hand found Alice's pocket. "Keep these loose against your hip so as not to draw attention. Bernice knows every inch of her store like the back of her hand."

"Yes, Mother."

Seemingly satisfied with her reflection, her mother pulled open the tall door and led them inside. A bell rang overhead.

"Margaret, is that you?" a woman's voice called from the back of the shop. The boutique was small and absolutely packed. Her mother moved easily through the maze of mannequins and haphazardly placed tables filled with stacks of fabric. The walls seemed like they were closing in, each one draped with an assortment of patterned fabrics hanging like curtains. Alice felt as if she had fallen into a basketful of sewing materials. The air smelled musty.

Her mother called, "Yes, and I've brought my daughter."

"Oh, your girl is here?" A tall, slender woman appeared from the back room. She had sharp features and high cheekbones. Her sleek brown hair was styled in a chic bob, and she wore exorbitant amounts of rouge. Greeting her mother, she planted a quick kiss on each cheek. The hint of an accent that Alice couldn't place laced her words. "My," she said, greeting Alice with a handshake and cheek kisses. "You look nothing alike."

"She takes after her father," her mother said, and Alice was sure she was the only one who noted the cutting tone of the words.

"My girls are just the same," Bernice said. "Come," she said to her mother, "the new fabric is in. The pattern you had your eye on is even more stunning in person." She led her mother toward the back.

"You'll be fine, Alice, dear, for a moment?" Her mother's gaze was hard and challenging.

Alice replied, "Yes, Mother. Take your time."

Her mother smiled and followed Bernice into the back. Alice waited a moment, then maneuvered toward the corner and found the waist-high bin packed tight with rolled stockings. She studied it first, noting the varying shades. They were organized from sheer to dark, a few striped patterns featured here and there. She ran her fingers over them, gauging the material. In doing so, her mind flashed with memories of Janeth. She bit her lip, imagining lowering Janeth's stockings, kissing her way down her leg.

Outside, a cop's whistle sounded. Alice forced herself to focus. She glanced over her shoulder to be certain no one else was there. Deciding on a pair of sheer rayon, she slipped it into her pocket, then carefully rearranged the bin so as to fill the empty space. When she was done, it looked just as it had before.

She spent the next ten minutes browsing the store until her mother and Bernice returned. "I'll be by again next Tuesday," her mother was saying.

"Wonderful, Margaret. I look forward to it." Bernice sidled up to Alice, who was studying a dress on a mannequin. "It's lovely, isn't it?" Alice nodded. "I'm sure your mother would consider it for a Christmas gift, no?"

Her mother laughed, then, to Alice's surprise, pulled her into a side hug. "Anything for my girl," she said, kissing her temple, then rubbing the lipstick away. Alice didn't know what to do with the unexpected gesture.

They said their good-byes and headed outside. Once they were two blocks away, her mother asked, "Well?"

Alice dipped her hand into her pocket in acknowledgment. "Success."

They paused beneath an awning. Her mother smiled, then discreetly turned to open her handbag. Alice dropped the stockings inside. Her mother pulled a cigarette from her case. She lit it, seeming to savor the long drag while Alice waited. "Well done."

Despite herself, the compliment lifted Alice. For a moment, as she stood with her mother as she smoked, Alice fell back into the times they'd spent working jobs together. They'd been a great team once upon a time. Alice had stayed by her side when she was little, her mother pleading with people on street corners to support her in their plight to survive. Single mothers were more likely to garner sympathy, she had explained. Alice had been the pawn in so many schemes, she'd lost track. Back then, her mother had applauded their efforts together. When had things changed?

When I grew up, Alice realized, watching her mother. When Alice had become a woman and drawn the attention away. That was when things had shifted, when her mother had begun sending Alice on her own, leaving her to fend for herself.

A new idea sprang to her mind: was her mother jealous? Surely not. Her mother could have anything she wanted. She had Alice still in her grasp, a puppet on a string. The strings had pulled tighter since Oklahoma City. And that, she knew, had been the recent reason for her intensified scrutiny.

"You hungry?" her mother asked.

Alice returned to the dark shadow beneath the awning, finding the burning end of her mother's cigarette. "Yes."

Her mother took a final drag, then stamped out the cigarette on the sidewalk. "Dinner's on me tonight." She started across the street toward a small café. Stunned, Alice wondered at her mother's demeanor and rare good mood. What if they could reach a turning point, a way back to how things used to be? Things were certainly moving forward with Janeth…could she find a way to balance her lives, her growing love for Janeth and her life with her parents? As her mother called for her to follow, Alice thought maybe, just maybe, she could.

CHAPTER TWENTY-EIGHT

Two weeks after her lunch with Alice, Janeth whistled a tune as she cleared the dining room table. It was Friday night, and they'd had Hugh over for dinner. Their uncle had retired for the evening after light conversation in the drawing room. Now, Janeth filled the washbasin in the kitchen with soapy water.

Hugh, lingering and enjoying a bowl of sugared plums in his usual spot in the doorway, watched her. "You're jolly lately."

She shot him a look but continued to rinse dishes. "I'm always jolly."

He barked a laugh. "You, Mrs. Castro, are many things, but jolly is not one of them."

"Well, you, Hugh, are a wandering scoundrel."

He bowed slightly. "Your words flatter me." She couldn't help but laugh. He grinned, eyeing her. "I didn't want to ask at dinner," he started, brushing back a lock of hair that curled over his forehead, "but I couldn't help noticing your ring. Or rather, the lack thereof."

Janeth slowed her movements. In the basin, she found her left hand.

"I've never seen you without it. And as you know, I find you quite the dame." He didn't move closer, but when she looked at him, he grinned and tossed a plum into his mouth.

"I'm not interested, Hugh."

He straightened. "I was afraid you'd say that." He sighed dramatically. "Well, come on then, who's the lucky chump?"

"You wouldn't know him," she replied, trying to focus on scrubbing the plates.

"I know a lot of people, Mrs. Castro." He set the glass bowl on the counter, then moved behind her to lean against the open window sill. "Is it one of your brother's friends?"

She thought for a moment about lying. Carlos came to mind. She was certain she could convince him to come to the house if she extended the invitation. But the very thought felt like a betrayal to Alice. "Like I said, you wouldn't know him."

Hugh's voice dropped to a hushed tone. "It's not one of those men, is it?" His brow raised. "The runners? I never took you for a woman to walk on the dangerous side of life. But your husband was…" He moved his hand in a prompting gesture, trying to conjure the right word. "You know, like that."

She shot him a look. "Victor was a fisherman. Not a runner."

"Pardon me," he said, his right hand going to his heart. "Well?" he said, waiting.

She rolled her eyes. "Give it up, Hugh."

"Some of those men are due by tonight, if I'm not mistaken." He hummed thoughtfully. "Is this why you sent Uncle to bed so early?"

"He was tired. You saw him." She set the plates on a rack and dried her hands. "Now, if you please, I've got to get ready to receive tonight's shipment."

"I'll bet you do."

She slapped his arm at the comment and pushed past him into the dining room. She turned off the lights. Hugh followed her into the front sitting room. As she closed the curtains, he said, "I see the way you're moving about, Mrs. Castro. Someone has torn off that stuffy facade of yours."

She huffed but didn't answer. If you only knew, she thought, images of Alice swimming in her mind. She held on to those images as a visit from Raymond loomed. For a moment, she considering having Hugh stay. Their last meeting had been so tense, a small fear had kindled in her gut at his next arrival. She tried to push that fear aside, though, reminding herself of her own capabilities. She had handled him so far. Surely, she could continue to do so.

"Don't you have a date to get to?" she asked, dimming the foyer lights. It was already quarter to ten. Raymond would arrive soon.

He grabbed his jacket from the coatrack. "Yes, I suppose so. You don't think Uncle will mind if I take the Bentley again?"

She waved him off. "Just be careful."

"I always am, Mrs. Castro." He winked and disappeared down the hallway. When she heard the back door close, she exhaled, relieved Hugh and his questions were gone.

In the library, she settled on a chair, the key to the desk drawer in her hand. As she waited, her mind drifted back to Hugh's comment. Of course he had noticed she'd taken off her ring. She had only done so last night after a long bath and an evening at the piano. The music had calmed her mind, clearing her thoughts. She'd thought of Victor, of the time they'd shared as man and wife. It wasn't like what she had with Alice. Victor had been so familiar, like an easy friend she had grown to love. Their marriage had been a natural step in their knowing each other. The wedding night, too, had been lovely, his touches like a warm embrace.

Being with Alice was startlingly carnal. She had never even imagined being with a woman, and while she'd been utterly terrified at the prospect, their time together thus far had been shockingly intuitive. The passion wasn't like anything she'd experienced before. Victor had been comfortable. Alice was like the raging sea, pulling Janeth in and taking her down into a realm of desire she'd never known. It left her wanting, no, needing more.

So last night, she'd snuffed out her candle and lain in bed, recalling Alice's touch. She accepted the shifting of her heart, and she had placed her ring on the bedside table beside Victor's photograph. The act was like setting a key into a lock, opening her up to a new kind of love. An unexpected love that prompted deep longing and an aching need for Alice.

The cellar door scraped open, and Janeth sat up in her chair. The mantel clock on the southern wall read ten o'clock. Raymond might have been a brute, but he was punctual.

A few minutes later, she opened the door. The same two men from before dragged in a crate. They greeted her in Spanish, bringing the shipment to rest on the rug. As one of them used the crowbar to open it, Raymond appeared.

"Mrs. Castro," he said, a slight shine to his eyes, his voice a little too loud. "What, no evening dress tonight?"

"Not tonight," she said, standing and moving to the crate, keeping Raymond's men between them. One of the men shot the other a look as

Raymond guffawed. They lifted the lid off, and she found what looked like bags of flour packed inside. Pulling one out, she felt for the bottle inside, then opened the drawstring to find the tequila.

As she ran her tongue over her teeth, savoring the taste, one of the men said in a low voice in Spanish, "Madam, I have a message from Hernandez."

She glanced at Raymond, who was running a hand over the books behind Mr. Mills's desk. "A message?"

"He said they're getting ready for war. War to take down the one who thinks he's a king." She followed his gaze to Raymond, who finally seemed to remember they were there.

"I told you," he said, "English only." He took a stumbling step forward, a warning in his eyes. Janeth gave him a demure smile before the men replaced the lid and carried it downstairs. Her mind buzzed with the cryptic message.

"Hope you don't mind," Raymond said, moving to sit against the edge of her uncle's desk. "I had a taste of this week's product." He brought his fingers together, kissed them, then opened them in a showy gesture. "Delicious."

"I'm glad it was to your liking," she replied, keeping a wide berth as she moved to the desk to get the money. She bit her tongue at his offensive theft of the product. It wasn't worth the fight, though, and she knew he wanted to egg her on.

"How's the old man?" he asked as she pulled out the money.

"He's fine, thank you."

She replaced the billfold, closing the drawer. As she slid the money across the desk, Raymond turned, trapping her hand against it. A nudge of fear pulled near her ribs, and she worked to keep calm.

"I had hoped to see you dressed up again tonight, Mrs. Castro." His imposing figure loomed over her as he leaned down. His grip was strong as his fingers curled around her wrist.

"No dinner parties tonight." She gave a tight smile and tried to pull her hand back. His gaze lowered to her breasts. She could smell the drink on his breath. Fear rose into panic as a new look filled his eyes.

Before she could think of what to do, he pulled her wrist up and moved around the corner of the desk, tugging her toward him.

"Raymond, it's time for you to leave," she said, looking up at him, willing her voice to be even. His chest bumped hers, and she tried in vain to create some semblance of space between them.

He still had her wrist in his hand and raised it higher. "Is it?" He turned her hand over. "Where's your ring, Mrs. Castro?"

She tried to yank her hand back, but he was too strong. Pulling harder, she stepped back but couldn't break free. His grip tightened on her wrist. "Let me go."

"I was serious about what I said before," he said, ignoring her. He licked his chapped lips. His blue eyes blazed with something that conjured a terrible dread in her body. It locked her in place, paralyzing her. "About wanting to know how you taste. You're so...intriguing."

She worked to twist her wrist to loosen his grip, trying again to pull away. "Uncle," she shouted.

Raymond sneered and shoved her against the desk. He overpowered her, pinning her arms behind her. She shouted again, leaning as far back as possible, loathing the way he eyed her lips, her neck. "Keep quiet now, Mrs. Castro." He tightened his grip on her hands behind her back, stepping between her legs.

"Excuse me."

Teary-eyed, Janeth turned to the library door. Hugh stood there, his hat in one hand. She'd never been so happy to see him in her life.

Raymond seemed to study Hugh a moment. Finally, he released her and stepped back.

Hugh kept his eyes on Raymond as he moved into the room. "I forgot my hat, Mrs. Castro."

She hurried around the other side of the desk, wiping away tears. Her body shook. She found the chair, putting it between herself and the rest of the room. "Did you?" she managed to ask. "Well, I'm certainly glad you found it."

He gave her a smile but burned a glare into Raymond, who cleared his throat and snatched up the money. For a moment, he looked like he was going to say something. Instead, he only saluted Hugh and left.

Hugh was at her side in a flash. His voice was the most concerned she'd ever heard it. "Mrs. Castro?"

"I'm fine," she said, though her voice, like her limbs, trembled terribly.

He helped her sit, then went to their uncle's drink cart and poured two tumblers of whiskey, handing one to her. "Here, drink this."

She did, closing her eyes as the liquid quelled her nerves. Hugh knelt beside her, searching her face. "I'm fine," she said, uncomfortable with the attention. For some reason she couldn't fathom, she felt embarrassed at what had just transpired, at what Hugh had witnessed.

"I know," he said, a gentle smile lifting his lips. "You can handle yourself."

She found the cross around her neck, gripping the pendant as she slowed her breathing.

After a time, Hugh sighed. "My uncle is naive to think a woman can handle these sorts of things."

She met his gaze but was too weary to respond. Was he right? Tonight could have gone a very different way had Hugh not returned.

"What am I to do?" she asked. "Uncle isn't well enough to handle these meetings. I think part of him is scared, which I don't blame him for." Hugh nodded. "You can't be at the house each night. Soon, you won't even be here."

He frowned. Over dinner, he'd revealed he was going abroad in the fall. They'd have to hire someone new. "You should arm yourself, at least."

"Arm myself," she said, wondering at the thought. Her uncle had purported the business to be exactly that, a business, somewhere where men acted with decorum. There were rules to this business, he had explained, even if it was a dirty one. Raymond, though, didn't seem to care about such things. Perhaps it wasn't a bad idea.

"Uncle has a case of firearms in the car carriage." Hugh stood, downing his glass and taking hers to be refilled. "Have you ever fired one?"

She shook her head. "I imagine it's easy to learn?"

He chuckled. "Aim and fire, Mrs. Castro. Aim and fire."

She fell back against the chair. Hugh passed her another drink. When she reached for it, he pulled it back, drawing her gaze. "You're sure you're all right?"

Downstairs, the cellar door scraped open again. When it shuddered closed, she exhaled. "Yes, I'll be all right." She took the glass. He donned his hat and headed for the door. "Hugh?"

He turned. "Yes?"

"Thank you."

He smiled. "Not bad for a wandering scoundrel, eh?"

She smiled, relief washing over her. "Not bad."

He left, and she fell back against the chair. She wasn't sure how long she sat there. Eventually, the feeling like she'd been holding on to the edge of a cliff dimmed, her body still tense but able to move once again. She hated the fact that this dangerous job was the source of her income. How could something that had given her so much come with such evil? How had she been so ready to take on such a task?

A quote from Proverbs flew to her: *an inheritance claimed too soon will not be blessed at the end.* Was this a punishment for her work? Had her uncle's business sent her on a spiral of greed and wanting, blinding her to the dark underbelly of such a world? Had her own pride brought a demon like Raymond upon her?

Janeth wrapped her arms around herself, still shivering. She thought of Maria, of the women in the cannery. How many stories had she heard? How many women were taken advantage of by men like Raymond simply for existing? Maria's ire for white men burned as bright as Raymond's eyes.

Those women didn't have the security of a great house when they were turned away for missing work after such an incident. Janeth trembled at her privilege. How foolish she'd been; her bravado had carried her through her uncle's injury, her fierce resolve secured in order to succeed among these men and their world. But now…

Her gaze lifted to her uncle's desk, then fell to her nightdress, her fine slippers. She'd grown too comfortable. Her tenacity wouldn't save her the next time Raymond tried something, or a deal went wrong. And now, with Hernandez's warning… No, she decided, wiping her face clean of tears. Now she needed to be smart. She needed to be prepared.

Taking a shaky breath, Janeth stood and checked the lock on the drawer. Turning off the lamps, she watched the smoke from the gas leave its marks upon the wall. For the first time, she wondered at the dark marks this life had left on her. And for the first time, as she carried her exhausted body upstairs, the idea of moving away from such dangers began to form in her tired mind.

CHAPTER TWENTY-NINE

After the evening at Bernice's shop, Alice's parents kept her working nonstop. Her days were either spent tagging along with her parents or with the Temperance group. Sometimes, she was her father's assistant on street corners, wrangling unsuspecting customers into his grasp. Other days were spent helping her mother push stolen merchandise to black-market buyers. When she could get away, under the guise of working her wealthy friend in the fictional long con, Alice spent time in Seaside with Janeth.

On a Wednesday in August, her mother—once again in a startlingly good mood—treated them all to lunch in Coronado after a morning of pickpocketing wealthy tourists.

"Cheers, darling," she said to her father as they clinked glasses of beer. Alice scarfed down her eggs and toast while her father cut into a ham and cheese sandwich.

"Margaret, dear, you are doing fabulous work," her father said, leaning one arm around her mother's metal chair on the restaurant patio. The ocean broke calmly over the sand twenty yards away. Seagulls soared lazily overhead. "You too, Dumplin'," he added, reaching over to nudge her shoulder.

She smiled into another bite of food. "Thanks."

"I see a new pair of suspenders in my future," he said, biting into his sandwich. "Margaret, another hat for the gambling halls?"

She lit a cigarette, flashing her silver case at them. "Perhaps."

He laughed, then looked at Alice before asking, "And somethin' for our little dumplin'?"

Alice slowed her chewing, shooting a look at her mother, who studied her half-eaten bread roll as if not wanting to look her way.

Then her mother leaned forward, dropping ash into a tray. "She did just get new stockings, John."

"Aw, come on, love. She's earned it. Pulled in nine dollars alone this week."

A waiter came by and refilled their water glasses. The silence that filled the space between the three of them grew thick. Alice tried to focus on her food, but a sense of anticipation filled her at her mother's thoughtful gaze.

Finally, she said, "I reckon we could find her a new dress."

Her father clapped and shouted, "That's the spirit." He took a long swig of beer. "We'll be the most fashionable family in town."

Joy swirled in her chest at the prospect of new clothes. Since spending more time with Janeth, her priorities had shifted. She had to laugh, recalling the idea of stealing treasures from the Mills's home. It had been Janeth, it turned out, who had been the thief, running away with Alice's heart. And now, Alice found herself dreaming of buying something for her. Alice wanted to treat her to something different. Not to mention, she couldn't recall the last time her parents had thought of *her* in their spending. Everything they stole went to them and their needs: cigarettes for her mother, the latest hat for her father, the next costume for their next scheme. She was always an afterthought. Now, here she was a part of their plan. Her mother's good mood had lasted longer than it ever had. Maybe things really were changing.

On Friday, her mother opened her bedroom door with a clang. "Rise and shine. Wear the dress you wore to Bernice's." She scrounged the small space for her black heels. "Pair it with these. We're heading to National City bank. You're Bernice's daughter, Ellen. We're dipping into a savings account."

Alice sat up, rubbing her eyes. "A bank?" She'd never posed as somebody else to pull money from an account. Her mother and father, yes, but Alice? Never.

"We've a debt that needs settling quick." Her mother stood with one hand on her hip, eyeing her. "Your father says you're ready."

Hurrying out of bed, Alice swelled with pride at the notion.

Her mother stared at her, a wary look in her eye. "We'll see if he's right," she said, then turned away.

The trolley ride to National City was bustling at midday. Alice followed her mother off at James Street, where the bank stood tall on the corner. It's three-story brick front looked imposing. The door seemed to never stay shut more than a minute as men, and some women, hurried in and out.

"People collect their pay before the weekend," her mother was saying, pulling her onto the sidewalk and turning her to study their reflections in a window. "Bernice let slip her daughter is the one who does that for them. Her English is good. She comes at two o'clock every other Friday. We're going to beat her to it."

"But what happens when she does come at two o'clock, looking for her money?"

"I've gotten all I need out of Bernice," her mother said. "She thinks I live in Chula Vista. She'll never find me if she gets the notion to look."

Alice's stomach flip-flopped. She swallowed, adjusting her blue hat and smoothing her dress.

"Ellen is blond like you, about your height. I saw a photo. Keep your head down, your voice low, and they'll never know."

This seemed more and more dangerous by the moment, but Alice didn't want to let her parents down. Especially if her father thought she was ready for such a job. Something like this was what she'd been preparing for, wasn't it? She glanced sideways. Her mother knew how risky this was. A small part of Alice wondered if it was her idea, a way to get Alice in trouble once and for all. She shook the thought away. She didn't have time for such thinking. Taking a deep breath, she asked, "Where will you be?"

"In the market next door." She passed her handbag to Alice. "Put the money in here, then come find me. Drop it beside me, then leave." At Alice's frown, she sighed and explained, "This is in case you're followed. We'll meet up on the trolley in half an hour."

She nodded, but nerves stirred in her stomach.

"Well, get going," her mother said, then disappeared into the crowd, headed for the market.

Alice did exactly as she was told. She had to wait in line for five minutes, but at the teller, she kept her head down and asked for ten dollars out of Ellen's account. When the teller asked how her mother was, Alice had a moment of panic, then shared what she could about the boutique and Bernice. The teller seemed to only be half listening anyway as he gathered her money and handed it through the cutout in the glass partition. She thanked him, her heart racing, then hurried out of the bank.

A notion like she weighed nothing, light as a feather, overtook her. She grinned, pulling back her shoulders as she headed to the market, glancing back to make sure no one from the bank had followed. At the door, she hesitated only a moment. She was struck with an idea: hide the money and tell her mother Ellen had already been there. Run home. Grab her savings and fly to Janeth. The idea was wild. She knew her mother would, very likely, see right through it. But a ring of opposition clanged in her chest.

The feeling faded at the sight of her mother. The strings of fear plucked at her limbs as her mother's power overrode her whims, dragging her back down to earth.

Inside, her mother conversed with a clerk near the produce bins. Alice walked casually toward her, moving the handbag to her left hand. Passing her mother, she dropped it at her feet without breaking stride. The act brought back memories of a different handbag at Janeth's feet. She tried to contain a smile at the thought of their first meeting as she pretended to study the bags of flour for a time, then made her way back outside.

Relief and pride washed over her. She'd done it. Oh, how good it felt. She imagined the type of dress she might choose, maybe something with a large collar. She imagined Janeth's dress from their last lunch. Distracted, Alice didn't notice the person standing near the corner of a dime store and collided with them, hard.

"Easy there, tiger."

Alice turned, grabbing her shoulder at the quick pain that ran through it. The voice was a woman's, but the person was dressed quite masculine. She wore men's trousers. A white, collared shirt stuck out beneath a brown sweater. She even wore a fedora, her hair shorter than Alice's and slicked back with pomade. "I…I'm sorry. I didn't see you."

The woman leaned casually against the wall. She reached into her trouser pocket, producing a cigarette case. She held it out to Alice, her blue eyes playful.

"Oh, no, thank you."

The woman situated one between her lips, striking a match against the sole of her shoe and lighting it. Alice stared at the men's oxford, her mouth open.

"Something wrong?" the woman asked, but a teasing grin played beneath her eyes.

"No." She shook her head, unsure why she felt tongue-tied. She'd seen women dressed like men before but not since Oklahoma City, in an underground bar she'd been shocked to find in the first place.

The woman straightened, one hand in her pocket as she replaced the case. People hurried by on the sidewalk, and Alice sidestepped to stand closer.

"Say," the woman said, "what's a dish like you doing later? I'm meeting some friends downtown for dinner. Place called Uno's." She reached out, touching the end of Alice's hat. "Wanna join?"

Alice balked. How did this woman know? How did she know she was…like that? How could she sense what Alice worked each day to keep buried deep inside her? How could she meet Alice and in only seconds, note the kindred spirit between them?

Janeth filled her mind. She imagined showing up at this restaurant later, arm in arm with her. She pictured a roomful of people like this woman, people who felt free to be themselves. People Alice yearned to be like in a roomful of lives she wished to lead.

"I—"

"Alice, there you are." Her mother cut between people on the sidewalk like a serpent cutting through tall grass. Her gaze grew wide when she spotted the woman, who put out her cigarette and tipped her hat in greeting.

"Maybe another time," she said, leaving Alice with a smile before she went into the sundry store.

Alice watched the spot where she stood until her mother gripped her arm, hard.

"What the hell was that?"

"What?"

Her mother's eyes burned, and she pointed to where the woman had stood. "That," she said, spitting the word, then seeming to struggle to say anything else.

Worry wriggled in Alice's gut. "Nothing. That wasn't anyone."

Her mother looked around as if everyone was watching. "That's not part of the deal, Alice."

She shook her head, her fear growing tall now. "No, Mother, we were just talking."

Her mother lowered her voice, practically hissing, "That's how it started with Gladys." Grabbing Alice's elbow, she led her down the crowded sidewalk.

"Ow," Alice said, trying to pull away. "You're hurting me."

"I'll do more than that, Alice dear."

She struggled to break free, her mother's hand like a vise. "Let me go."

"Not a chance." Her mother dragged her, unrelenting. A few people turned to look, but no one said anything as her mother found an alley and shoved her into it.

She fell against the grimy wall. Sewage and garbage filled the space with a rank odor. Her mother stalked forward, shoving her farther down the narrow path between the back of buildings. Fire escapes snaked overhead. Alice scrambled against the slimy brick.

"I knew it. I knew those filthy thoughts were still there." Her mother pointed at her accusingly, her face twisted in disgust. "I knew you couldn't change."

"Mother—"

"Your father is a fool. I don't know what he thought was going to happen." She stalked closer and shoved Alice against the wall, hard. "You're as sick as the day you were born."

Tears stung Alice's eyes. She felt just like she had in Oklahoma, and that Alice readied a timid, complacent response.

New anger, though, pushed that aside, and images of Janeth filled her with courage. Courage to bite back. "Why bring me here?" she asked, trying to keep her voice even. "If I'm so wrong, why not leave me behind?" She took a shuddering breath. "You wanted to, didn't you?" Her mother's eyes widened but only for a moment. Alice was sure she hadn't expected a reply, let alone such an honest one. Wiping her nose, she stepped forward. "Do you even want me here? Do you even care what happens to me?"

Nostrils flared, her mother's fiery gaze narrowed. "You dare speak to your mother like that?" She stepped forward, forcing Alice back.

She slipped and fell against the brick, then landed with a thud in a muddy puddle.

Her mother only sneered, crouching to meet her gaze. The look in her eyes was terrible and dark as she studied Alice for what seemed like forever. "Your father will wonder where you are," she said to herself, like she was making a reluctant choice. "You'll take the next trolley back. Once you're home, go straight to your room." Her mother's gaze roved over her like she was searching for the part of Alice she loathed, the part she couldn't understand. "I don't want to look at you tonight." She stood. "And you can forget about the dress." She turned back to the street, her heels clopping against the wet pavement until she slipped into the crowd.

Alice sat there, her chest heaving. Eventually, the fear subsided, overrun by despair. Tears came before she could stop them. She tried to keep her cries quiet, covering her face in her elbow.

Why had that woman been there? Why did Alice have to stop and talk to her? It had been like some spell had been cast over her, keeping her in place. No, she realized, not a spell. A veil had been pulled back. Their brief interaction had shown and reminded her of a life she knew existed but had no idea how to reach. An unattainable reality that lay just on the other side of this one. A life her mother would always make sure she could never have.

When she made her way home, filthy and exhausted, Alice slipped quietly into her room. Her parents weren't home, thankfully. She changed, washed, and crawled into bed after pulling out the cigar box. She counted her money and started to wonder if there was another place this money could go. There was a time she wanted to run away with Gladys. Would Janeth be willing to leave? Could she even ask such a thing? Janeth had her own life. But what they had was growing. She felt it. She didn't want to leave Janeth. Ideas kicked up in her mind as she hugged the cigar box tight.

How much more of this could she take? How much more of this life of fear, this tightrope she walked under her mother's thumb, was really possible? How long until the rope snapped, and her father wasn't there to catch her?

Alice cried into her sheets, wanting nothing more than to escape.

"Thank you, Mr. Preston. Mr. Mills will be pleased the payment was ready today." She shook his hand before turning to go. The boardwalk was packed; the final weeks of summer evident in the families milling about between tents. The Ferris wheel was full, shouts of glee and awestruck calls coming from the cars as they rose higher. The beach was elbow to elbow with people spread out on blankets, beach chairs, and beneath umbrellas.

She walked slowly down the boardwalk, taking in the sights and sounds. The scent of roasted chestnuts wafted on the late afternoon breeze. A lone figure sitting on the sand caught her eye.

"Alice?"

She looked up, and the look on her face made Janeth hurry toward her.

"Alice, what's wrong?"

Tired lines sat beneath her eyes. Without a hat, her hair blew every which way. She sat with her knees to her chest, hugging them close. Her stockings featured a tear near the back of her thigh. "Nothing," she finally said, looking back at the water as it ran up the sand, landing only a foot from where she sat.

Janeth swallowed, tossing a look to the waves. She hadn't realized how close she was. Her only concern had been Alice. Ignoring the unrest in her chest, she sat, not missing the surprised look on Alice's face.

"You hate the water."

"Well," Janeth said, scooting back slightly as the next wave came in. "I'm trying to be brave." She looked around. Certain no one was paying them any mind, she squeezed Alice's arm. Alice only flinched. Studying her furrowed brow, her tear-filled eyes, Janeth asked softly, "What is it?"

Swiping at her nose, Alice sniffled and kept her gaze on the ocean. "Have you ever thought about…escaping?"

Janeth frowned, not liking the tone Alice's voice took on. She looked to the water. The horrible visions she'd made up of Victor and his family during their last moments at sea came to mind. Fear filled her at the look on Alice's face. "Alice, what happened?"

"I don't know if I can do this anymore."

Trepidation curled into dread. Janeth licked her lips, reaching again for Alice, then deciding against it. "Darling, please. Tell me what happened."

After a moment, Alice took a deep breath and turned to meet her gaze. In it, Janeth saw despair, desperation, and something else. Love looked back at her, but it was distant, fighting, clawing against the pain.

Sniffling again and taking a shaky breath, Alice spoke. "I've lived my whole life by my parents' rules. They taught me how to survive, how to do what I do." She shot a look sideways, almost sheepish. "I broke those rules—and part of me knew I would—the moment I saw you." She shook her head. "This life, my parents' guidelines and schemes, are all I've ever known. I can be anyone they need me to be." She held Janeth's gaze. "Anyone but myself."

Janeth took in her words. She recalled the way Alice had spoken of another woman, someone from her past.

"After my parents caught me with a woman, I promised it would never happen again. I had to. My mother…" Her voice trailed off, her face falling into a hard look. "My mother is waiting for me to mess up again." Her right hand reached for her elbow, rubbing it, her gaze going unfocused.

Janeth could put together what might have happened. Fury filled her at the idea of someone hurting Alice. She took a breath to suppress it, chasing it away with thoughts of gratitude at Alice's openness. "Alice," she said carefully, "thank you, for sharing that."

"I don't know what to do," Alice said, looking back to the ocean. "Janeth, what do I do?"

She started to answer, then realized she had no good reply. Alice was a thief, a swindler. What could someone like that do? Well, if she could reinvent herself in the United States, why not Alice? But how to tell her that in a way she would hear?

"The other night," she started, "Raymond came by with a shipment." Alice turned, her gaze clearer. She clenched her jaw, and Janeth wondered at the fight in her eyes just from the mention of his name. "He…well, he tried to…" Her hand moved to her necklace. She couldn't finish. As before, she didn't need to.

Alice pursed her lips, then moved closer. Their legs brushed. "Janeth—"

"He didn't. But…it was bad, Alice. Hugh intervened, thank God. But if he hadn't been there…" She gave a small laugh. "He's teaching me how to use Uncle's shotgun, believe it or not." Her cheeks warmed. "I've been silly, thinking I could handle myself against men like Raymond."

Alice gave a small smile. "I'd like to see you with that shotgun."

Janeth laughed. "Here's hoping you never will. But," she said, turning to face her, "I need to be more careful. At the same time, I've started thinking." She searched Alice's gaze. "I've been wondering if there's something else out there. I've been drifting like a boat at sea ever since coming here, moving between worlds. Between people." She pictured her family, her work. "I don't know where I belong anymore. My sister-in-law resents me." The tension with Leo resurfaced in her mind. "My brother doesn't know how to feel about what I do or who I spend my time with. I've essentially cut myself out of Logan Heights. The white people in my uncle's world never seem to know how to approach me." She blinked back tears. "So, yes," she finally said, "I have thought about escaping. But I've no idea where. Or how." Finding Alice's gaze, she felt elation at the look in her eyes. That distant love was closer now, sparks of hope dazzling in them.

Alice looked for a moment like she was going to lean in. Janeth yearned to kiss her and used all her willpower to keep her distance. Quickly, she said, "Come back to the house with me? Uncle loves the company." She feared Alice returning home and wanted to keep her close. "We can prepare the guest quarters for the night. Please," she added as Alice looked ready to protest. "Just one night?"

Smiling, Alice said, "All right. One night."

CHAPTER THIRTY

"A unt Janeth!" Elena ran to her, colliding into her knees and wrapping her in a hug.

"My," she said, laughing, "you're getting strong."

Elena looked up, still hugging her. "I can pick up Jorge and carry him."

A small voice hollered from behind the counter, "No, you can't."

"Yes, I can," Elena countered, releasing Janeth and scrambling back toward her brother. Squeals ensued as they ran toward the back room. Maria, who had been stocking a corn bin along the left wall, eyed her.

"Hi, Maria." Janeth slowly approached her. "Where's Leo?"

"He'll be here soon. He had to help Helio with his wagon."

Janeth stood wringing her hands. She hadn't seen Maria since the party. The air was still thick between them. Their last conversation crawled out between the floorboards, pooling tension at Janeth's feet. She studied Maria's green dress beneath the apron speckled with bits of tomato and flour. Her short hair shined in the morning light.

Janeth cleared her throat, about to speak, when Maria said, "Carlos has been asking about you." Her gaze flickered to Janeth but refocused quickly on her task.

"He's a sweet young man."

Maria raised a brow. "He wants to escort you to Leo's birthday party next month."

Janeth blinked, wondering at where the summer had gone. Was it really almost September? "I don't know, Maria."

"You turn down every invitation from the nicest men." Maria

spoke quickly, her words curt. "Do you want to be a widow forever?" Her movements turned aggressive, practically slamming the corn into the crate. "Oh, right. I suppose you can afford to be one. Silly me."

Janeth opened her mouth to protest, then took a breath. Carefully, she set her handbag on the counter. Part of her hoped Leo would walk in and be the peacemaker again. But then, she thought, nothing would change. Did she really want to be fighting Maria forever?

Ignoring Maria's glare as she reached to help stack husks, she said, "Carlos is very kind. I wish I was interested in him." She hesitated, then said quietly, "I'm interested in someone else." Maria stopped, her gaze flying to her, wide-eyed. "It's new," Janeth explained, weighing her words. "But it's…" She smiled. "It's breathtaking."

Maria seemed to study her. She could practically see Maria's mental list of all the eligible men in the neighborhood, could see her trying to recall if and when she'd seen Janeth with any of them. She tilted her head, the hard look softening just a little. "Well, if it's not Carlos, who is it?"

Janeth rested her hand on Maria's, halting her work. She held her gaze. "I'd rather not say. It's delicate. Can it be our little secret?"

Lifting her chin, Maria seemed to contemplate this. "It's a white man, isn't it?"

Laughing, Janeth shook her head. "No, I promise you, it's not." Maria's brow furrowed in thought, and she retracted her hand, returning to her work. "Please, Maria."

All of the corn placed perfectly inside the bin, Maria cleaned her hands on her apron, then rested them on her hips. "Fine," she said. "But you know how your brother is. He wants to see you with someone more than I do."

"I'll talk to him eventually," she said, though she had no idea how that conversation would even go.

"Janeth." They turned to find Leo strolling in from the back room. "It's good to see you." He looked between them, a wary glint in his eyes at the two of them in the same space. "Doing some shopping?"

"Actually, yes," she said. "Alice is coming for dinner. I need some things for tonight." She felt Maria's gaze find her at the mention of Alice's name but ignored it. She followed Leo to the shelves where he dropped large bags of sugar to refill the jars.

"She comes around a lot," he said pointedly. Janeth ignored him, and he sighed. "Very well. Take what you need. I'll help you settle up the bill."

"Wonderful. Also," she said, "I wondered if you'd be open to a meeting with JP."

Leo straightened. He and Maria shared a look. "A meeting?"

"Yes. I…" She adjusted the handbag. "Well, I'm considering other opportunities. You practically already handle the books for me. I'd like for you to be able to fully oversee the financial side of things, to make sure my uncle doesn't fall into the red, as they say."

Leo, looking surprised, only stood there. It was Maria who asked, "What are you trying to say, Janeth? You're not working for Mr. Mills anymore?"

"Not necessarily. I'm not completely sure myself, but I think there should be some changes." At their expectant silence she explained, "It's a dangerous business, as you know." Without thinking, her hand found her cross, and she was lost for a moment in the terrible memory. She glanced to Maria, trying to explain what had transpired with Raymond in a gaze. Maria, her face serious, inhaled knowingly. Swallowing, she continued. "You both know I take pride in this work. This work you both encouraged me into."

Leo studied her. "What makes you think Mr. Mills wants to meet with me?"

"He asked for the meeting. He sees your numbers, Leo. He knows what you already contribute to the business." She licked her lips, readying her next words. "You've always been curious about what I do. I know you wonder what it looks like from the other side. Now's your chance to step into my shoes and truly be a part of it."

Her brother crossed his arms, surprise settling over his face. He seemed to gather himself before saying, "I don't understand. What's changed?"

What hadn't changed? This summer hadn't been like any other. She was different. A new awareness had taken hold of her, featuring views of a world she'd never known. A vivid world, its colors bold and bright, beckoning to her. Joy had found its way to her among the fervor of those ridiculous Temperance protestors, an improbability in itself. Nothing made sense, yet everything did. Alice had shown her a new happiness, and it was a happiness she wanted to treasure. This new way of being, of loving, had to be cherished. Like her uncle had said, it was a rare chance she was being given, this second opportunity for love. She had to take it.

To do that, things had to change.

"Leo," Maria interjected when she still hadn't answered. "A woman has the right to change her mind at any time." She met Janeth's gaze and smiled. Janeth's chest warmed. The tension that had plagued them the last month wilted at the understanding in Maria's eyes.

"Janeth," Leo said, pulling her attention. "I have the store." He gestured around, then to Maria. "My father-in-law trusted me with managing things. I can't just leave."

She caught something else in his voice, though, and braced herself as she finally said what she never thought she would. "Jealousy is a sin, Leo. Yes," she continued at his wide-eyed look. "Jealousy. That's why you pushed your envy aside when Mr. Mills came into my life. You hid it well. But it's risen and reared its ugly green eyes. It's shown itself in how you've spoken to me. To Alice." His mouth fell open, his face matching Maria's stunned look. "It's difficult, isn't it, to have it both ways? To not understand something and want it at the same time? To walk a line as you're being pulled each way. Well, now you can have it your way, Leo. But you have to choose it. You have to admit that you want it." She thought of Alice and her own courage to face the life she was dealt. "You have to choose your own happiness. So what do you say?"

The only sound was that of a truck ambling past outside. She quieted her own breathing as Leo and Maria exchanged looks. She pressed on, lightening her tone as the room seemed to shake with the truth she'd laid bare.

"It won't require a lot of time. Once, maybe twice a month, you meet with Uncle. But that's something that can be discussed. Someone else can receive the shipments in my place." She had no idea who, but someone else needed to be there. A feeling like a fever overtook her standing there in her brother's market. Her face grew hot, and she trembled with the idea of starting something different, something new, with Alice.

The front door opened. Mrs. Ramirez entered, greeting them in turn.

Janeth moved closer while Maria saw to her. "Think about it?" she asked Leo. His face was still a mask of guilt and confusion. She could hear the questions. And in him, she saw the distant glimmer of happiness at what she was offering him. The terse comments, the strange intonation each time he spoke of her uncle…she thought it was because it was something he wanted too. It was why he'd pushed her into this in the first place. He was as stubborn as she was, though, and would never say as much. But it was out, and she sensed his gratitude.

Now, a new sense of urgency filled her. Things were changing quickly. Deep in her bones, she knew it was a change for good.

CHAPTER THIRTY-ONE

A lice sat back in her seat at the dining room table, utterly content. If she had thought the lunch several weeks ago had been grand, she hadn't been prepared for dinner.

Janeth had gone all out. They'd started with an appetizer of spinach dip and soda crackers. Alice had balked at the idea of spinach, recalling a rather disgusting childhood memory, but decided to try it at the look on Janeth's face when she took a bite. It turned out to be pretty decent. The baked ham for the main course was nothing short of extraordinary.

"Donated one of my finer bourbons for it," Mr. Mills announced proudly as Janeth had served each of them under the bright candelabra. She'd gone on to explain how she had brushed the ham with the liquor before baking it. The flavor, with hints of clove and some other seasoning Alice couldn't name, was delicious. Potato salad was served alongside it, followed by an icebox cake for dessert.

Alice scooped another spoonful of layered wafers, sweet milk, and whipped cream as Janeth stood and said, "My, I simply can't eat another bite. Uncle, more cake?"

"No, no." Mr. Mills wiped his mustache, then reached for his empty glass. "I will take another sidecar, though Janeth, dear. If you don't mind."

She grabbed his glass, then paused on the opposite side of the table. "Are you sure we can't tempt you with one?" she asked Alice, one brow raised, a playful smile on her face.

Alice shook her head. She'd tried a taste of the drink Janeth had prepared for herself and Mr. Mills before dinner. While the fruitiness had been nice, the cognac had been too much for her tastes. "I'll stick with wine," she replied. "Thank you."

Janeth disappeared into the drawing room for a moment. Alice glanced at Mr. Mills, who pushed his plate forward to lean his elbows on the table. Alice mulled over what topic of conversation to bring up. They'd spent the hour between her arrival and the meal going over the best and worst parts of the Seaside carnival. Apparently, Mr. Mills was considering buying it and wanted honest opinions. They agreed the Ferris wheel was a solid main attraction, and the location was sublime, but some of the vendor tents could use a shake-up. She had enthralled him with her tale of seeing one of Buffalo Bill's Wild West shows as a child. "Maybe something like that, some sort of entertainment, could be good." He'd wholeheartedly agreed.

Prior to the meal, Mr. Mills had shown her around the library and the prize rosebushes in the back garden. Once again, she managed to skirt questions of her family. Her mother was the last person she wanted to think about. She'd returned to her icy self since the aftermath of the bank job. Alice had told her parents she needed to attend a social call of Dorothy, whom she'd dubbed the wealthy Temperance friend her parents thought she was playing. Her mother had only grunted a good-bye when she'd slipped out of the house earlier today.

When Alice had commented on Mr. Mills's ability to move around pretty well throughout the tour of the grounds, he'd chortled. "This is the most I've walked in ages, my dear. Besides my daily constitutional." His eyes had softened. "It's nice to have more life in the house. It keeps this old man going."

Alice had held the door for him as they'd returned inside, recalling Janeth's story of how she'd come to live in this house. She wondered at Mr. Mills's desire to be among people and how difficult it must have been for him not being able to live like he once had.

"When did you get into collecting?" she asked presently, sipping her white wine.

A small smile lifted behind his hands where he rested his chin. "Oh, some twenty, twenty-five years ago. My father had an interest in marble art, statues, and that sort of thing. That's where all the busts come from." He pointed to one in the corner. "I inherited it all when he and mother passed on." He frowned and sat back. "I kept some but sold others. My appreciation always lay in painting. Have you seen the works upstairs?"

"I—"

The drawing room door swung open. "Here we are." Janeth placed a full cocktail glass next to his empty one. Alice watched her return to her seat. Just as she went to sit, Mr. Mills grabbed his cane, which rested on the table's edge. "Uncle, wherever are you off to?"

"Let's take the drinks upstairs, Janeth."

She looked from him to Alice, a vee between her brows. "Upstairs?"

"I've got to show this young lady my art collection." He hobbled quickly into the hallway.

When he was gone, Alice pushed out her chair, keeping her voice low. "I didn't have a chance to tell him."

Janeth moved to grab his drink, her own in hand. She smiled. "That you've already had a tour?"

Alice grinned and, checking the door, pulled Janeth into a quick kiss. "I think I got my money's worth."

Janeth laughed and gently pushed her away. "Very well, then. Let's go."

After helping Mr. Mills climb the stairs, they turned on all the wall lamps of the gallery room. The sun had nearly set, and the east-facing windows showed the dark outlines of hills. The light was different than last time, and Alice sipped her wine at the memory of sunlight splashed over Janeth's face.

They politely listened while Mr. Mills crisscrossed the study, at times using his cane to point to different parts of each painting. Alice did appreciate his passion. It was clear he'd studied certain techniques and knew a lot about each work's history. It wasn't his fault that as hard as she tried to listen, her mind returned to the last time she was in here. As he talked, her gaze drifted to the green chaise. She licked her lips, recalling the feel of Janeth on top of her.

The grandfather clock chimed the hour. "My, is it ten already?" Mr. Mills checked his pocket watch to confirm. "Well, ladies, thank you for indulging me." He finished the last of his drink. Janeth took it as he said, "I better be off to bed."

"Yes, Uncle." Janeth helped him to his room. Alice lingered near the banister that overlooked the foyer downstairs. When Janeth closed the door to Mr. Mills's room at the end of the hall, stepping quietly in the dim light, she said, "I'll just clean up downstairs. First, let me show you your room."

Alice wanted fiercely to go into Janeth's bedroom. She yearned to know what it looked like. She ached to fall into the bed she slept in. Somehow, she restrained herself and only followed Janeth to the other end of the hallway. At the end of the narrow space was an equally narrow door she hadn't noticed before.

"This is the bathroom, should you need it. If you like, you're welcome to draw a bath."

Alice stepped closer, opening the door. Janeth squeezed past to light a wall lamp. The orange glow fell over a seven-by-eight tiled floor with a claw-foot tub in the middle. A small table sat beside it with an assortment of bottles that Alice presumed were shampoos and lotions. A long-handled scrub brush dangled from the silver faucet.

"That's the nicest bathroom I've ever seen," she said, turning to Janeth.

Her smile was kind. "Well, you should definitely draw yourself a bath. I'll find a spare robe and leave it on the bed in your room, just in there." She pointed to the doorway opposite the room Alice knew was Janeth's. They'd be so close, separated only by a three-foot stretch of hallway. The inevitable agony of it rocked her, but she shoved the feeling aside.

"Thank you," she finally said.

Janeth kissed her cheek. "I'll see you soon."

Later, Alice lay back against the porcelain, pushing her feet out of the sudsy water. She groaned at the relaxed feeling settling into her limbs. Hot baths, even warm ones, were few and far between in her life. She lifted her leg, running the scrub brush from her toes to her thigh. She'd uncorked a bottle of something that smelled like magnolias and watched several droplets fall into the water. Now, sinking deeper, Alice let the cocoon of warm bubbles and soft light envelope her.

A gentle knock on the bathroom door startled her. "Alice, are you all right?"

She pulled herself up. "I'm fine." The clock chimed forty-five past the hour. She'd lost track of time, feeling so at peace. "Sorry, I'll be out soon."

Opening the drain to let the water run, she stepped carefully out and found a towel. "God, even this thing feels good." She dried the ends of her hair, then wrapped the towel around herself. Turning off the lights, she opened the bathroom door. There was a small line of light cast near Janeth's room; otherwise, the hallway was dark. She tiptoed to the guest room and closed the door.

As promised, the robe waited for her. It lay on the teal blue sleigh bed that was draped on all sides with a blue and gold-patterned skirt. The bedding was cream-colored. Burgundy carpet ran the length of the floor, and a matching desk set sat across from the foot of the bed, against the large windows. She pulled the drapes—the material matching the bed skirt—and slipped into the silk robe.

"Alice?"

Turning, she found Janeth pushing open the door. She carried a candle in its tray.

Tying the robe, Alice ran a hand through her hair, aware of how stringy it must look. "Hi."

"I brought you some pajamas." After closing the door, Janeth crossed the room to set a pair of long silk pants and a matching top on the desk.

"Thank you."

Janeth turned but seemed to hesitate coming any closer. "Was the bath to your liking?"

"Very much so." She grinned, giving up on fixing her hair and deciding to give off what she hoped was an air of freshly cleaned confidence. "A girl could get used to this."

A smile lifted Janeth's lips, and something lit itself in the back of her eyes. Alice wondered if she, too, recalled their last conversation on the beach. The conversation about escaping, maybe even together.

"I've arranged a meeting between my brother and Mr. Mills," Janeth said.

Alice frowned at the subject matter but said, "Oh?"

"Leo's great at numbers. He oversees the inventory books I take from the shipments, as well as afterward, once we've moved the product to buyers."

Starting to understand, Alice stepped forward. "You want to have Leo step in?"

Janeth wrung her hands, then found the cross at the end of her necklace. Alice was drawn to the glint of gold, then to the dip in Janeth's cleavage in the V-neck of her peach pajama top. "I want—" Her voice broke, and she seemed to search the room. "Alice," she said, stepping forward. She stopped just in front of Alice, next to the bed. "I want more of this, more time with you. This business…it's dangerous. I knew that. But now…" Her voice trailed off, her eyes searching. Alice felt like caged birds were fighting against her ribs at the look in Janeth's eyes. "Now I have something I want more than this business. I want something I never thought I would again." Alice held her breath as Janeth reached out, finding her hands and pulling them toward her chest. "Alice, I want you."

It was like a clap of thunder shook her mind. At once, the memories of Gladys roared. Alice had wanted something then she could never have, trying in vain for a life that Gladys wouldn't, couldn't, give her. Now, here was Janeth standing in front of her, wanting her. Choosing her.

Love filled her; it flowed between the cracks of hurt left behind from Oklahoma. It warmed her veins and reached into her broken heart, daring her to offer it once again. She reached out, pulling Janeth close. Kissing her sent a sensation she knew well through her body. It nestled in her abdomen, then into the space between her legs, igniting a desperate ache.

Janeth kissed her back, moaning into her mouth, and Alice smiled at her eagerness. She pulled her into a deeper kiss. Alice reached beneath Janeth's pajama top, finding her breasts.

Alice broke their kiss but only to lean down and press her lips to the soft skin between the cut of Janeth's neckline. She leaned her head back, and Alice did as she was beckoned, leaving kisses up her neck.

"I love that," Janeth muttered. Alice found her lips again. Janeth pushed her toward the bed. Her calves bumped the frame. Janeth's fingers ran around the waist of her robe, teasing.

"You know," Alice said between kisses. "I don't know why you gave me this, Mrs. Castro, if this is what you had in mind."

Janeth breathed a laugh, then pulled back. She bit her lip, and Alice wasn't sure if there was anything more attractive. "But, Miss Covington, then I couldn't do this." She tugged the robe open, and the material parted to reveal Alice's breasts, her stomach, and her center.

Stepping back, Janeth seemed to study her for a moment. Alice lifted her chin, but a small insecurity filled her. Years of hard living seemed to scream from the scars on her knees and arms, the leanness of her figure, the uneven cut of her hair. But when Janeth closed the space between them, framing her face, those fears vanished.

"You're beautiful." Janeth kissed her, and Alice fell into it. She lost herself in Janeth's lips. Janeth's fingers grazing her center was everything, the only thing she could feel. She found Janeth's hand, encouraging her. As her fingers found Alice's arousal, Janeth kissed below her ear and said, "I want you terribly, Alice."

Something different took over. Alice kissed Janeth hard, turning her so that she was against the bed. Janeth quickly lay back against the pillow. Alice shed her robe, and Janeth took off her top. Alice remembered the candle she'd brought in. Quickly, she retrieved it and placed it on the side table. As she'd anticipated, Janeth looked utterly gorgeous in soft candlelight.

She climbed into bed and straddled her. They kissed, a throbbing need building between her legs. Janeth's hand found her there as Alice ran her own fingers through Janeth's dark hair, loosening the braid she'd fashioned.

Janeth turned them over so Alice lay beneath her. She reached for the waist of Janeth's pants, but Janeth caught her hand. Alice smiled at the look in her eye. "Not yet," she said, then reached down to stroke Alice's slick folds.

Alice leaned back, relishing her touch. Heat rose in her cheeks as Janeth's mouth found her nipple. She bucked her hips when Janeth's tongue caressed her breast, then bit gently. "God." She wrapped a hand behind Janeth's head, gentle but firm.

Another buck of her hips elicited a low laugh from Janeth, who kissed across to her other breast, her tongue teasing her there too. When her fingers slipped inside Alice, she cried out.

"Shh." Janeth kissed her. "We have to be quiet, darling."

Alice could only groan in response. She knew Janeth had been hesitant their first time in the study. She remembered what it was like the first time she'd been with a woman. But like before, Janeth seemed to learn quickly. Her fingers moved in a rhythmic motion. She kissed Alice's breasts, her stomach, then her lips in a dizzying whirl.

"Janeth," Alice said, pulling her into another kiss. Their breathing came fast, and for a moment, Alice wasn't sure where her breath ended and Janeth's began. Finding her gaze, Alice felt a desire she thought might overwhelm her. Kissing her again, Janeth pressed her forefinger to Alice's lips a moment, a lover's challenge as she dipped between Alice's legs.

"Oh God," she whispered as Janeth's tongue stroked her. She shook, trying to keep from wriggling as Janeth started another rhythm with her mouth. Reaching for her, she found Janeth's shoulder, her hair, then her arm, and held on as pleasure built within her.

She raised her hips, wanting more, wanting this forever. Janeth gripped her thighs as she licked, sucked, and left Alice utterly bewildered with waves of bliss. When her orgasm came, she found the pillow and cried out.

Slowly, Janeth kissed her way up her body before lying with one arm and one leg over her. Sweat lay in a fine sheen over both of them. Janeth kissed her cheek. They lay in the dark for a time, Alice collecting herself as her breathing slowed. "Was that all right?"

The trepidation in her voice threatened to lift Alice off the bed and carry her away. She turned, reaching to brush her fingers through Janeth's hair. "That was more than all right."

Janeth gave a shy smile. Alice kissed her again. She pressed her forehead to Janeth's, keeping her eyes closed. If she tried hard enough, she wondered if she could will them into that space between night and day, that dreamscape where things like happiness and true love could live out.

Janeth's hand on her cheek was cool. She opened her eyes. "Stay here, darling," Janeth was saying, her voice soft. "Be here with me."

Emotion rose in her throat, and Alice felt another tremble overtake her limbs. But this feeling that rocked her was one of stark reality. Janeth *was* here. This wasn't a dream. She was lying in her arms. The woman who made her feel whole again saw her for everything she was and still wanted her.

Alice took a shaky breath. It seemed like an eternity that the words sat on the edge of her tongue, her lips parted, ready. Janeth smiled softly, waiting. "I love you," she said, a tremor running across her shoulders and through her voice.

The room seemed to shrink in upon them as Janeth leaned in and kissed her. "I love you, too, Alice."

CHAPTER THIRTY-TWO

A lice wasn't sure how she tore herself away from Janeth the next morning. Upon waking, she remembered she had to meet her father on Coronado. He was going to set up on a corner across from the famous red-roofed hotel. It was her job to wrangle tourists into his reach, entice them with the idea of winning big at his shell game.

After kissing Janeth good-bye, promising to meet her in two weeks' time to help her plan Hugh's going-away party, she threw on yesterday's dress and caught the trolley. Along the way, she replayed the conversations she and Janeth had about escaping. What would that look like? She wasn't sure, but a new determination filled her as she disembarked at National Avenue. Janeth's willingness to make a change was inspiring, and Alice wanted to follow suit.

She found her father looking like the everyday man in high-waisted brown pants and a blue button-down. The white collar was unbuttoned at the neck, his suspenders tight on his broad shoulders. His flat cap sat slightly askew over his blond hair. The approachable showman, Alice had dubbed this outfit. When he spotted her, he waved. "Hiya, Dumplin'."

"Hi," she said, assessing the passersby and the expansive hotel across the street. She could hear the water beyond it, the waves lapping gently on the shore.

"It's a beautiful day," he said, arranging the three shell halves atop his apple crate, rehearsing the patterned movements with such ease, Alice was sure he could do it blindfolded.

Deciding there was no good way to broach the topic of conversation she wanted to bring up, she took a steely breath and dove headfirst. "Why did you keep me from going to Gladys that day? After…when the doctor came for her."

He looked up, squinting at first as she stood with the sun behind her. He lifted and adjusted his cap, and she could tell he was trying to understand where this question had come from. In true swindler fashion, he answered with a question of his own. "What do you think would have happened, Dumplin', if you'd been caught up in that?"

She held his gaze. She knew what would have happened, about the terrible conditions she would have been subjected to in an asylum, the awful days spent in a place that believed her heart and mind were corrupt and needed to be set straight.

Her father pulled a deck of cards from his pocket. He shuffled once. "We wouldn't be where we are, Dumplin', without you."

She blinked. "What?"

He shuffled again, his tone light and casual. "You pull in as much as I do, sometimes more. You're a real chip off the old block, if I do say so." He looked up, grinning proudly.

Feeling sick, Alice fell back into memories of that day. She forced herself to relive the screams, the agony of watching Gladys ripped from her life. She saw herself trying to go to her, but her father had held her back. He'd held on, keeping her away from Gladys's father, kept her out of harm's way. He'd kept her safe.

Kept her with him.

Her throat dry, Alice tried to swallow the realization. All this time, she'd thought he'd been there to protect her because he loved her the way a father loved his child. She could feel his arm around her that day, directing her home as she stumbled, inconsolable. Now, the hushed conversations from that night came back to her, unveiled behind the fog she'd let drift over that part of her memory:

"Margaret, I won't let you send her to that place."
"She's sick, John. You always had your suspicions."
"I won't hear it."
"She's not right. Somebody has to do something. John—"
"No." His next words crept out of the mist, creeping across against the black canvas of her mind. *"We need her, Margaret. You may not want to admit it, but we do."*

Tears slid down Alice's cheek as the street began to teem with people. Someone bumped into her, startling her into the present. Her father's words, though, lingered.

"Why did you help me?"

He looked up from his stool, shifting the gum he chewed to his other cheek. "Come on, Dumplin'." His grin widened, but Alice saw right through it. It was the same smile he used on customers, willing them to bet higher, wager it all on something they could never actually win.

"Was it because you love me?"

A flicker behind his eyes shone in the sunlight. Was it affection? Worry? No, just the careful calculation of his next response. "Dumplin'—"

"Don't." She raised a hand. Her father gave a nervous laugh, glancing around. "You saved me in Oklahoma for your own needs. You wanted to keep me working for the two of you. You needed someone to clean up the mess you always make wherever we go. Tidy up the debts. That's the only reason I'm still here."

The flash of acknowledgment in his gaze was all she needed. Swiping at her nose, she turned to go.

"Alice." Her father stood. "You can't..." She faced him, her gaze unwavering. He shrank a little beneath it, then straightened his shoulders. "We still have the fundraiser."

She took a long breath. After studying her father, there was a moment of glaring truth, like when the tide went out near the cliffs. What typically lay beneath the churning waters was exposed, and she saw the man who bent to her mother's will, who used Alice as leverage, who needed her around to bear the brunt of her mother's cruelty. He was many things, but his true self lay open before her on this street corner. He was just as afraid of her mother as she was. Alice, though, had found the nerve to break free.

"Fine," she finally said. "I'll help today. And I'll be at the fundraiser with you in October. But that's the last time. After that, I'm done."

He swallowed, seeming to accept this. Was that admiration shining in his eyes? "Where will you go?"

She smiled. It blossomed before her, the image she'd started to build in quiet moments on her own. Images of a life she called the shots in. A life with Janeth. "Anywhere I want, Father. Anywhere I want."

❖

"Oklahoma." Dorothy embraced her as she descended the trolley. "Long time, no see."

"I know. Been busy."

Mary, perpetually at Dorothy's side, asked, "Can you believe it's the last protest of the summer? I can hardly believe it's September already."

Alice shook her head as Dorothy muttered, "Thank goodness. I'm going to enjoy this month. My suffrage group is marching through Seaside next Tuesday, and I cannot wait to spend time with those ladies again." She nudged Alice's arm. "You should join."

Alice had been spending more and more time with Janeth and would probably be in Seaside anyway. They spent hours wandering through the quaint shops or sitting together in the park. She was even staying overnight more frequently. Alice had been able to sneak home for clothes when she knew her mother would be gone, even moving her precious cigar box and its savings to keep beneath her guest bed at the mansion. While staying the night in the railyard felt like a chore, she still did so to keep up appearances and fend off their inquiries. She'd leave ten cents for her parents here and there to keep them off her back. It was almost as if her mother had sensed the shift, too. She wondered if her mother knew she was planning her escape, and a smaller part wondered if her mother even cared. Her father, for his part, remained quiet after their conversation in Coronado. A stunned reverence from her declaration seemed to overcome him, leaving him subdued in her presence.

Hugh, when not giving Janeth target lessons in the sprawling back lawn of the mansion, had introduced Alice to croquet. "You're a natural," he had said last Sunday as Mr. Mills and Janeth had sat watching from beneath a covered patio table, all of them sipping lemonade. "A regular Suzanne Lenglen."

They'd formed an unexpected household, the four of them. A going-away party for Hugh was to be thrown at the Mills Mansion the third Friday of the month. It was the first party Mr. Mills had hosted since his injuries, and anyone who was anyone was going to be there. "I feel better than ever," Mr. Mills had told Janeth when she'd asked if he was really up for such an elaborate shindig. "This is a new chapter, Janeth, dear. This old man is ready for his last, great act."

Presently, Alice swam with the warmth of finding people who felt like what she'd imagined family could be like. People like Dorothy and Mary, who had become good friends, something she had once thought she'd never be able to have again.

"I'd love to join," Alice replied. "Can I bring someone?"

Madame Enfield gathered them into a group to assign locations. Dorothy smiled. "Of course." She gave her arm a squeeze, and Alice swelled with the warmth of friendship. She relished the faint but growing light of a new way to be, a new way to live that was all her own. She could see it, still on the horizon, but each day brought it closer. Soon, Alice knew, it would be hers.

CHAPTER THIRTY-THREE

L eo, come in." Janeth stepped aside, letting her brother into the foyer.

He took off his cap, glancing around. Whistling low, he said, "I always imagined it was grand, but this is somethin' else."

"How was the trolley ride?"

He shrugged. "A few looks but no one said anything. I'm glad he was willing to meet me early. I don't think I'd have had the same experience coming here after lunch."

Janeth would have to agree. People in Seaside, though outwardly friendly most of the time, could turn cruel toward unfamiliar folk as the sun started west. Leo wandering these streets wouldn't be safe. She was already planning to accompany him back to Barrio Logan after his meeting with JP.

"Uncle is in the library." She motioned for him to follow, not missing how his eyes roved over the rooms. Despite invitations to join her for lunch over the past year, Leo had never been willing to set foot in the Mills mansion. Janeth didn't understand it at first; why encourage her to live here if it was going to create an obvious separation between the two of them? When he'd telephoned a few days ago, they'd finally aired everything out. He confessed he hadn't known how to feel at times about her position in Seaside. He begrudged her ability to slip into white society with ease. And, yes, he feared she would leave him behind. She had listened, realizing she'd let the comfort of this new life blind her to the ugly truth of the world.

"Leo, I didn't mean to make you feel as if I'd abandoned you," she'd said when she'd invited him.

"I know," he had said. As she'd listened, she'd realized that his eagerness to see her in a better life could stand alongside his discomfort. Her privilege didn't extend to him and Maria.

Their egos set aside now, here was Leo, crossing that often frightening, unspoken line between people and places. She would do what she could to help him navigate such fearsome waters.

In the library, her uncle looked from his desk where he scribbled notes on an open ledger. "Janeth, dear, this must be the infamous Leonardo."

Hurrying across the room, Leo reached out to shake her uncle's hand. "Mr. Mills, it's nice to meet you officially."

"The pleasure is mine. Janeth speaks often of you." He leaned back in his chair, running a finger over his mustache, seeming to take both of them in. Janeth was sure he wondered at the stark physical contrast between them but to his credit, didn't say anything. "I hear you're the secret keeper of my books," he said to Leo, thumping the pages in front of him.

Leo gave a small smile and dipped his chin. "I help where I can. Janeth has been sharing the last year's inventory with me. I clean things up here and there."

Standing beside him in front of the desk, she gave him a playful shove. "Don't be modest, Leo. I would have things backward if it weren't for your keen eye. You're a valuable part of this operation too."

A nervous look crossed Leo's face as he glanced from her to Mr. Mills. She gave him an encouraging nod. "Sir, I hear you're looking for someone to help keep the numbers on a more regular basis."

"That's right. Janeth is stepping away from her responsibilities, it seems." Mr. Mills leaned forward, placing a hand over the side of his mouth as if to share a secret but kept his voice so she could hear him. "I theorize she's met a gentleman friend and won't have the time."

"Uncle," she exclaimed, but her tone was light at their easy laughter. "I'll still be around, at least for now. But I'd like Leo to be the one who handles the books for Logan Heights and the surrounding neighborhoods. We can find someone else for the coastal towns and will need a new runner when Hugh leaves. But one step at a time." She gestured to Leo. "He's a wonderful candidate for the job, Uncle."

Mr. Mills smiled. "I have no doubt. Janeth, I'd like to speak with your brother one-on-one now, if that's all right?"

SAM LEDEL

"Of course. I've got lunch to make." She gave Leo a quick kiss on the cheek. "See you soon."

Nearly an hour later, Janeth was munching on cucumber sandwiches in the dining room when Leo appeared. "Well," she asked, standing. "How did it go?"

In the doorway, Mr. Mills's cane echoed, and he appeared behind Leo, clapping him on the back. "You're looking at the latest partner in the highly acclaimed JP Mills bootlegging corporation."

Leo beamed. Janeth collided into him with a hug.

"Mr. Mills has agreed to meet me downtown once a month to go over everything."

She stepped back, about to ask if her uncle was really up for such a task. Apparently expecting this, he explained, "I need to get out more, Janeth dear. My sister will help me get there. She knows how to drive, believe it or not. Of course, you're always welcome to accompany me by trolley if you're up for it."

She smiled. "You know I will as long as I'm around."

"Splendid," he said, thumping his cane on the floor. "Now to find a replacement for Hugh. Who knew that boy would end up being so good at his job?" He turned to head back to the library, muttering about Hugh's departure along the way.

Leo turned to her. "So," she said, "you're doing this."

"I'm doing this," he echoed, a mild look of disbelief in his eyes.

"How does Maria feel?"

"Oh, you know Maria." He turned his hat over in his hands. "But we talked a lot. Your uncle will pay me for my time. It would give us more savings, more for the kids. Maybe I can even take her on a trip somewhere."

She swelled with happiness at the idea. "That's wonderful, Leo. Thank you for doing this. I know it's a big task."

They wandered toward the front door. "Why *are* you stepping away?" he asked carefully, replacing his hat.

She looked at him, recalling the awful feel of Raymond on top of her. She still hadn't told anyone but Alice about what had transpired that night. She knew how Leo would react if she did. "I need something else," she finally said. "I've been too focused on this work. I need..." She found her necklace as she opened the door. The breeze blew through, gentle and warm. "I need people, Leo. I'm ready to be out there again, ready to see what the next part of this life holds."

His gaze held hers, knowing settling between his brows. "I'm happy for you." He kissed her cheek. As he started to go, he hesitated. "Your uncle invited me and Maria to some sort of party next Friday."

"Hugh's party." She laughed. "He's going abroad at the end of the month. We're having a big bon voyage gathering. You're more than welcome to join."

She saw the hesitancy on his face. "We'll see, Janeth."

Knowing that was all she could ask for, she found her hat and jacket and walked with him to the trolley.

CHAPTER THIRTY-FOUR

"Hugh, your mother is looking for you in the drawing room." Janeth squeezed between a pair of middle-aged women dressed to the nines near the back wall of the dining room. The room was utterly packed with partygoers gathered around the equally crowded dining room table. One hat with an elaborate feather kept tickling the cheek of a nearby gentleman. Janeth was glad she'd opted for her simple black dress, as there was enough razzle-dazzle to last a year, thanks to Mr. Mills's many guests. Men shined in black coattails, and women looked radiant in their elegant evening gowns.

Hugh popped another deviled egg into his mouth, then grabbed a glass of shrimp cocktail in one hand and a full champagne flute in the other. "What does Mother want now?" he asked.

"Unclear," she replied, raising her voice to be heard over the din of conversation. "However, I do think she's had more than her share of champagne."

Through a satisfied chew, he replied, "Ah. She'll be wanting to regale me with the story of my childhood, followed by the sacrifices our pioneering ancestors made to give us this life. I better hurry." He scooted between people and managed to find his way out of the room.

Meanwhile, Janeth checked that all the food trays were sufficiently filled, noting the ones that needed restocking. She'd done most of the preparation herself over the last several days. Alice had helped, and Janeth had to purchase a few things outside of her usual scope: oysters to keep on ice being one such item.

"The oysters are a smashing hit, Janeth dear," her uncle had said two hours into the party when she refreshed his drink. He sat regally in a high-back chair in the sitting room, guests floating past him in greeting or pulling up a chair to relive old memories. Since the door had opened at eight o'clock, Hugh and several of his friends had continuously circled the dining room table like ravenous hounds.

"These boys eat like they've never seen food," she muttered, sneaking past Alice in the kitchen while she poured more punch into a crystal bowl.

Everyone floated between the three vast corners of the mansion, drifting from the drawing room, across the foyer to the sitting room, then toward the back of the house and the dining room. Crates of champagne had been stocked in the cellar, and it flowed like gold through the house. The late September evening was brisk, and all of the windows stood open. The house itself was lit like a beacon. Janeth imagined any passing ship could spot them along the dark coast. Music played nonstop from the gramophone that Mr. Mills's sister insisted on being in charge of. The house had come back to life, and it pleased Janeth to see her uncle in such good spirits.

"Won't this draw attention?" Alice had asked not long after guests began to arrive, gesturing to the dazzling chandeliers and loud record starting to play. "You know…this is technically illegal."

"Parties aren't illegal, darling," Janeth said before answering the door again. "Just what we're imbibing. Uncle has it taken care of."

She had raised a brow as she'd taken a guest's coat. "Did he pay the cops?"

Janeth smiled. "Let's just say, their patrol won't take them past this house tonight."

At ten thirty, the telephone rang. Janeth managed to move through the guests into the front sitting room. The earpiece pressed close, she answered, "Hello?"

"Call from thirty-four seventeen, Logan Heights."

"Yes, put it through."

Leo's voice was dim through the static. "Hi. I wanted to say we won't make it tonight."

Janeth grabbed the candlestick phone and pulled it so she could sit in a corner chair, the long cord trailing after her. A group of people floated through the room, admiring the mantel decorations while she spoke. "That's all right, Leo. I had hoped you and Maria could make it, but I understand."

"Maybe another time."

She knew there likely wouldn't be a time when Maria, especially, would be ready to travel to Seaside. Sighing, she accepted that, knowing the trepidation she carried was completely valid. It was a big deal for Maria to even let Leo take on this new work. They couldn't ask her for any more than she was already giving. "Tell Maria and the kids hello from me," she finally said. "And thanks for calling, Leo."

"Don't have too much fun," he teased. "Unless it's with that new suitor of yours."

At that moment, Alice stepped into the room, seemingly to search for her. Catching her eye, Janeth smiled. "No promises, Leo," she said. "No promises."

Minutes later, everyone formed an impromptu dance floor around the grand staircase. Streamers hung from the upstairs banisters, tied to the overhanging chandelier. "It looks like a great octopus," Hugh had commented upon arriving.

Janeth had shot him a glare as she had finished tying off the final white balloon she'd added to the collection of gold and black ones for decorations. Now, those same balloons lay scattered about as Mr. Preston from the boardwalk danced a jig with his wife, his normally nervous nature seemingly at ease after some good food and drink. At one point, Janeth pulled Alice into the fray, and several others followed. Laughing, she bumped into Mr. Aldridge, who was conversing with someone in the corner.

"Apologies," she said, laughing and letting Alice pull her back for another dance. Mr. Aldridge only lifted his glass in a salute. Beside him, his wife eyed Janeth, a wary look on her face. But Janeth didn't care. Not right now. Mrs. Aldridge, Maria, the rumrunners, Leo…the ceaseless whirlwind of who she should be and where she belonged came to a halt as she danced with Alice. She anchored herself to their love. Twirling, Janeth allowed the party to sink into her, let the joy careening off each wall lift her up, filling her with a happiness she never thought she would know again.

Laughing and dancing with Alice, Janeth felt like she could do this forever.

❖

"I need some water." Alice pulled Janeth into the kitchen after several more minutes of dancing. She filled two glasses from the sink, handing one to Janeth while downing the other.

"My, you were thirsty." Janeth drank from hers, but a different sort of craving filled her gaze.

Alice grinned, wanting nothing more than to get Janeth out of that delicious dress, but the party was in full swing at eleven o'clock, and surely, someone would see them or notice they'd slipped away. "Thank you," she said, pulling the glass to her chest, cupping it gently.

Janeth used the back of her wrist to catch some water running down her chin. Her brow furrowed. "Whatever for?"

"For this." She gestured around. "For letting me practically move in these last few weeks."

"Alice—"

"I know. 'I'm more than welcome anytime.'" She glanced down, studying the black toe of her high heel, pushing it into the floor. Her heart sped as she gathered the courage to ask, "What if...what if I stayed...permanently?"

Janeth blinked. Her eyes flashed with confusion, then excitement gave way to hope. "You mean..."

"I mean," Alice said, "what if I was a permanent guest of Mr. Mills?"

Janeth straightened, setting the glass aside as she listened.

"It wouldn't be the first time he took in a young woman in need. The timing is spot on. The Temperance fundraiser next Thursday. I promised my father I'd be there, and I will. But..." Alice swallowed and took a deep breath. "I'm done, Janeth, with them. I'm done with my father. I'm done with my mother." She felt ire rise in her throat and worked to keep her voice even. "I have to do something, one last thing for them. But then, I want to leave. I want out of that life. I want a different one...with you." She exhaled, relieved she got the words out.

The look on Janeth's face was so happy, Alice didn't think she could love her more. Janeth threw a quick glance to the swinging door, then kissed her. She framed her face, practically squeezing her.

Alice laughed when she stepped back. "Is that a yes?"

Janeth pulled her into a hug. Over her shoulder she said, "Yes, darling. Utterly and absolutely yes."

Alice found it hard to keep her eyes off Janeth for the rest of the party. When she helped Mr. Mills to the staircase where she'd set up a chair for him in preparation for farewell speeches as the night came to a close, Janeth spoke to the guests as the ultimate warm and accommodating hostess.

Hugh's voice made Alice turn. "I had a feeling about the two of you."

"What?"

He leaned casually against the drawing room doorway looking smug. "She's different around you, Miss Covington."

Alice glanced across the foyer. Janeth, holding Mr. Mills's right arm, helped him stand behind the tall seat. She found Alice's gaze and smiled. Blushing, Alice whispered to Hugh, "I don't know what you mean."

He snorted, then downed his champagne. "Your secret is safe with me, Miss Covington. Besides, I knew there had to be a reason the two of you refused my advances." He grinned and joined his uncle, Janeth, and the crowd that gathered near the stairs. Alice scoffed but was grateful for Hugh's kind nature. He had certainly grown on her since their first meeting all those months ago.

Behind her, the gramophone stopped, and everyone turned their attention to Mr. Mills as the clock struck midnight.

He trembled slightly, and Janeth offered him the chair. He shook his head and remained standing, facing over sixty of his closest colleagues, friends, and family. His voice wavered a little when he spoke. "Thank you, all, for being here this evening. While tonight's event is to celebrate my nephew, Hugh, and wish him well on his voyage across the sea for yet another European sojourn, it is also the first time in a long time I've gotten to see so many familiar faces."

A soft utterance billowed over the room. Several clapped. One man shouted, "You're the top, JP."

Alice lingered in the doorway as Mr. Mills, eyes shining, continued: "These years have been good to us. Things haven't always been easy, but I firmly believe that if you have people in your life…" He looked around the room. "If you have people who care, who lift you up when you feel like throwing in the towel, well, by Jove, you need to keep those people around. People are everything." He raised a fist. "People are what we need."

Whistles and cheers filled the house. Somewhere, another

champagne bottle popped. Mr. Mills steadied himself against the chair. Alice caught Janeth's gaze, and that same warmth from earlier swam deeper within her. She could see it beneath the shining lights: their new life together.

"Before I carry on too long, let's hear from the man of the hour. It's his final days on this side of the Atlantic, after all. Hugh." Mr. Mills stepped sideways, motioning for Hugh—who had been sitting halfway up the stairs—to join him.

Hugh shook his hand, then waved to everyone. "Thank you, Uncle, first and foremost for this absolutely incredible evening," Hugh exclaimed, raising a toast to the room. His college friends whooped and hollered from their corner. "Europe has a lot to offer. Wonderful food, beautiful women…" He let his voice trail off suggestively, leading to more whistles from the crowd. Hugh's mother, wearing a disapproving look, fanned herself nearby. "Another adventure awaits. At the same time"—he lowered his glass, taking a sip and seeming to take in the crowd—"I've started to understand how life's adventures can take unexpected forms." He turned to Mr. Mills. "Take this old man, for instance." He reached out, resting a loving hand on his uncle's shoulder. "This man lives an adventure every day doing what he does for all of us. I've learned a lot from him. He's a savvy businessman with a generous heart." He shot a look to the crowd. "Two things one doesn't find together very often. This world could use more people like him."

Alice, this time, was the one to say, "Hear, hear."

"I can't thank you all enough for being here," Hugh said after a moment, turning his attention back to the group. "Even those of you I don't know." He pointed to a gentleman who looked at least ten years older than Mr. Mills. "You, sir, for instance. I have absolutely no idea who you are, but by golly, I am glad you are here." Laughter murmured over the crowd. Hugh sighed. "My mother will be shocked to hear this, but I'm actually going to miss this place." Alice caught a look between him and Janeth. She knew how Janeth's feelings had changed when it came to Hugh. She, too, had to admit that he wasn't the rake she'd imagined him to be.

"So," he said, turning back to the party and taking a long breath, "that is why I've decided *not* to leave Seaside this year."

Confusion broke over everyone. Several people called out, "What do you mean? What's going on?"

His mother, looking pale, shouted, "Hugh, what in heaven's name are you talking about?"

Alice was just as bewildered as everyone else seemed to be and met Janeth's confused gaze across the room.

"Hugh, son, what are you talking about?" Mr. Mills asked.

Hugh grinned, holding up his hands to quiet the crowd. "I like it here, Uncle. I'm staying on…in every capacity." He winked at Janeth, who looked like she was ready to drop her champagne flute. "Sorry, Mother," he added, "you can't get rid of me yet."

The crowd was incessant now, everyone buzzing electric as people tried to make their way to Hugh or Mr. Mills. Someone shouted, "What the hell is this party for, then?"

Hugh hopped onto the stairs to be seen. "Please, everyone, eat, drink, be merry. We have much to celebrate. Cheers!" Half the crowd applauded and drank while the rest continued to shout over one another, asking for an explanation.

Alice wove through people to the stairs as Hugh was tugged down them by Janeth. "Hugh," Janeth asked, "did you *just* make this decision?"

"Oh no, Mrs. Castro. I knew weeks ago that I was staying here. Canceled my ticket last month."

Janeth's mouth fell open. Alice could only laugh. "Then…" Janeth seemed to struggle to find her words, gesturing around the room. "What was all this for?"

Hugh took another drink offered him by a friend. "It's for me, of course. Go and ask my mother, she'll tell you. I can never resist a good party."

CHAPTER THIRTY-FIVE

G ood night, Uncle." Janeth closed his bedroom door. The house reverberated with jarring silence following the party, the quiet vibrating between the walls and over the floors scattered with fallen streamers and stray balloons lying in listless heaps. The guests had thinned out after Hugh's speech, though a few had lingered beyond the midnight hour. Now, at nearly one in the morning, only her uncle and Alice remained.

Downstairs, Janeth found Alice in the library. She sat on the leather couch across from her uncle's desk. Janeth watched her a moment. She sat quietly with her legs curled beneath her, the ends of her dress stretched over her knees. Her eyes roved the bookshelves, the fine wallpaper.

Stepping into the room, Janeth asked, "What are you thinking?"

Alice turned, a look of mild surprise on her face, like she'd been caught doing something she shouldn't. "Nothing."

Raising an incredulous brow, Janeth sat beside her, kicking off her heels and pulling Alice close. "You can tell me."

Alice leaned into her, and Janeth relished the feeling of their close bodies. "I was just thinking..." She glanced down, running her fingers gently over Janeth's forearm. "I wish I knew more for you."

Frowning, Janeth studied her forlorn look. "Darling, what do you mean?"

She gestured to the books.

"Alice." Janeth reached up, tugging Alice's chin so she had to meet her gaze. "You know so many things." Alice scoffed and started to reply, but Janeth continued. "You know more about people than I ever could. You have to in order to do what you've done for so long."

"Steal?"

"Survive."

Alice's eyes shined.

"You've learned how to read people and situations. You know what people will say, where they're going to be, how they'll react. You knew Hugh was up to something at the start of the party tonight."

She chuckled. "He looked more smug than usual."

"Precisely." She reached for Alice's knee, giving it a squeeze. "You have so much to offer, my love. More than you even know."

"I just..." Alice swallowed. "I just want to be enough...for you."

Janeth's chest felt tight at the break in her voice. She understood what Alice was doing, giving up her parents. She was breaking away from a life of limitation, but doing so took a leap of faith that was more terrifying than anything. Janeth remembered doing such a thing when she left Mexico to come to the United States.

"You're more than enough for me, Alice. You're..." She found a piece of Alice's hair and ran her fingers down it. "You're a jewel, Alice Covington. I'm the luckiest woman to have you in my life."

A smile broke over Alice's face. She leaned in, kissing her. Janeth held her tight, pouring as much love into their embrace as she could. Eventually, Alice pulled away. "I guess I ought to draw a bath."

Janeth bit her lip. "Maybe I can join you?"

Alice looked surprised but quickly replied, "Yes, please."

Giggling, Janeth kissed her again before Alice stood to go. At the same time, Janeth thought she heard the distant scraping of the cellar door as Alice said, "See you up there?" She turned from where she'd been watching the book shelves. She started to ask if Alice had heard that, too, but she was already in the doorway.

"See you soon," she called as Alice disappeared.

Janeth went to the wall lamps and turned them out. She was straightening the cushions on the couch when the secret door opened, and she spun around. "Raymond?"

He was dressed in his usual high-waisted pants fastened with suspenders over a weathered blue shirt. His boots looked damp, like he'd had to tug the boat he'd come in on into the shore of the cave beneath the house himself, something his men usually did. But no one else came through the door, and his predatory gaze bored into Janeth. She swallowed. How had she not noticed the door had been left ajar? God, it must have been that way all night. They'd gone down to fetch supplies in preparation for the party. It could have been Hugh, or her... *Damn that latch.*

When he stepped closer, the dim light revealed that his left eye was swollen shut, the skin puckered and red. His bottom lip was cut, and a bruise sat on his right cheek. He looked disheveled, and his breathing was heavy, like he'd been running.

"What happened?"

He glared and swiped at the trickle of blood on his chin. He lurched toward her uncle's bar cart near the southern wall and found the ice bucket. Tossing off the lid, he reached in, his dirty hand finding a melting fistful of ice. He brought it to his lip and said, "They're gonna pay for what they did."

Janeth looked around, wondering what to do. She tried to think of a plan, something to get Raymond out of her house. Alice had already gone upstairs to draw her bath. Her uncle was in bed, and he slept like the dead. Unease pricked along her spine. Raymond shouldn't be here. Not tonight. She had a feeling she knew what had happened to him.

He quickly confirmed her suspicions when he said, "Hernandez and his pals have another thing coming."

She moved slowly around the couch toward the corner where her uncle's shotgun rested. "Hernandez is a good man. The others are honorable and hardworking. Whatever they did, I'm sure they had their reasons." It was the truth, but she grimaced at the sneer on his face from her comment. Perhaps it wasn't the best plan to upset him.

"Honorable." He guffawed, then spat into the ice bucket, tossing the pieces back in. "Nothing about this business is honorable. It only matters who's willing to take what they can get."

She lifted one brow, feeling behind her for the back wall. Then again, she thought, maybe an angry Raymond would signal his arrival. Someone upstairs might hear his shouts. *I can only hope.* It was risky, but it was a plan. She took a breath and said, "And you tried to take more than your share, I imagine."

He snarled and kicked the cart. Janeth looked to the door. Surely, Alice could hear that, even over running water. She swallowed a spike of fear and asked, "Why are you here?"

"Because you're going to help me."

"Help you?"

"They'll be here soon," he said, and for the first time, worry flashed through his piercing gaze. "You're going to call them off." He reached for the holster on his hip, drawing her gaze. When he found no pistol, he growled. Janeth wondered if he'd lost it in the fight he'd clearly gotten into, or perhaps as he'd fled. He pulled himself up, clearly trying to intimidate her. "Those men respect you," he said through gritted teeth, the words pushing out like he was trying to hold them back. It wasn't a compliment. Only a rueful, reluctant admission from a desperate man. "They'll listen to you."

She knew it was true. If she asked Hernandez to leave Raymond alone, he would. But she recalled their last conversation, when he had asked her to stand with them. Blood pounded in her ears as Raymond's fury seemed to flood the space between them. Fear drowned her mind. She conjured a lie, an easy excuse that it was Mr. Mills who Hernandez listened to, not her. She kicked herself for such a thought. Yes, she could lie, but then where would she be? After everything she and her uncle had been through, after the respect she had gained from Hernandez, from all the runners, from herself. She couldn't betray that now. Steeling herself, she said, "I'm sorry, Raymond. I can't do that."

"Can't or won't, Mrs. Castro?"

"It doesn't matter," she said, gesturing for the hidden door. "Leave now, Raymond."

He didn't seem to hear her. His gaze grew glazed, and a torrent of worry swept over her as he stepped forward. "I think you misunderstood, Mrs. Castro." He swiped at his lip again as she retreated, bumping into the globe in front of the window. "I wasn't asking."

Her heart raced as she found the heavy curtains, realizing the shotgun must be tucked behind them next to the case.

Raymond was moving around the end of the couch, never taking his eyes off her. "Come on, Mrs. Castro. You're a generous broad." He licked his lips. She hated the way his eyes traced her body. "Help a fella out."

"You've done enough damage to this family, Raymond. I won't stand for more of your brutish ways. You're a horrible scar on this business." She could hardly believe the words tumbling out of her mouth. All of the things she'd yearned to say to him since that fateful night rushed forward. His gaze burned red as she continued, but she didn't care. "I won't be a part of this. Not anymore."

"I would hate to see another bullet in your uncle, Mrs. Castro." He paused at the back of the couch, five feet of space between them. The air was dark and thick with tension.

She fumbled behind her back, searching for the shotgun. He stared at her for what seemed like forever. Her breathing was coming quickly as she thought of how to get rid of him. Was she really prepared to shoot him? Was he being chased? Were others on their way? She glanced over his shoulder to the secret door. She thought she heard distant voices, but that could have been wishful thinking. Taking a deep breath, she whirled around and grabbed the shotgun.

He barked a laugh. "Come now, Mrs. Castro. You can't be serious."

She cocked it and aimed at his chest. "I'm very serious, Raymond. Get out of my house."

His lip curled, another flicker of desperation in his gaze. He stepped forward, muttering, "Have it your way."

The reality of what she needed to do froze her, and Janeth could only step back into the window before he was on her, grabbing the barrel of the gun. He yanked it away, tossing it over the side of the couch. He started forward again, pinning her against the wall. Her body shook with the impact.

He sneered. "This didn't have to be so hard." His breath burned her cheek.

She needed to get out of here. She cried out, but he slammed his hand over her mouth. She brought her knee up into his groin. He grunted, and his grip loosened. She dove away from him.

He recovered quickly, grabbing her wrist and tugging her back. His face was wild, a wide grin lifting his stubbled cheeks. "I love a feisty dame."

She spit, hitting him just below the eye. This only seemed to motivate him more as he grabbed for her. She shoved his hands aside, but he found her again, his grip firm on her arms. He pulled her toward him, wrapping a hand over her mouth to keep her quiet.

Shoving her onto the couch, he straddled her. She tried to scream again as she fought beneath him. *No!* His suffocating weight came down on her.

His voice singed her senses: "You're going to help me, Mrs. Castro, or I swear to God, I'm gonna..." Still trying to fight, she screamed against his hand as a sound like shattering pottery came from overhead.

Raymond fell forward with another grunt, then slumped off her shoulder. Blinking, trying to see in the dark, she found shards of an urn scattered over the couch and floor. Alice stood at Raymond's feet and promptly kicked him, eliciting another groan.

"Alice." Janeth scrambled up, scurrying over the couch, racing for the shotgun.

Alice went to the fireplace and found a poker. She brought it up over her head like a baseball bat as Raymond stood, but Janeth positioned herself protectively in front of Alice, her chest heaving.

Raymond looked haggard as he said, "Mrs. Castro, you found a friend."

Before he could take a step toward them, Janeth readied the shotgun against her shoulder. "Don't," she said, drawing his gaze.

He looked surprised at the double barrels once again aimed at his chest. Laughing, he said, "Are you really going to shoot me this time? That kind of thing can create tension in a business partnership, I'll have you know."

Her breathing came fast, and she tried to steady it as she stepped closer.

He guffawed at the tremble in her arms.

Through gritted teeth, she said, "Get out, Raymond."

He studied her awhile. All three of them stood frozen in the dark library. For a moment, as her finger hovered over the trigger, Janeth shook with the memory of that fateful night nearly three years ago. She heard Raymond's pistol fire; she saw her uncle fall. She felt the rush of blood as she worked to keep pressure on his wounds. How much pain had Raymond brought them? They'd had enough. *She'd* had enough.

Alice's voice pulled her back into the present. "Janeth, we need to move."

Raymond rubbed his chin, eying Alice now.

Janeth kept her focus on Raymond. "I said get out," she repeated. Something came over her, a strange sense of wild abandon, coupled with the need to take action. The need to fight back. This was her home. This was her life. This complicated, wonderfully messy world she'd fallen into was hers. She wasn't going to let anyone take that away from her. Slowly, she smiled. The way Raymond's face fell made her heart leap as she added, "I wasn't asking."

The bang from the shotgun shook her terribly, and her ears rang. She stumbled back as Raymond's strangled cry broke the air. She had no idea where she'd hit him. The arm, maybe? Damn, she had hoped to do better than that. She didn't have time to try again, though, as Alice pushed her away while he staggered around the room.

"We have to move."

Janeth pulled Alice with her, shotgun still in her left hand, as they ran for the library door. She was certain, this time, she heard voices downstairs, but Raymond's heavy footsteps weren't far behind her.

In the foyer, lit only by the dim lamp at the base of the stairs, they fumbled over errant balloons. Janeth tried to step between tangled streamers when Alice started upstairs. "No," Janeth said, pulling her away.

"Then where?"

"This way." She started for the front door. The last thing she wanted was for Raymond to get his twisted reunion with her uncle. She had to lead him away. Over her shoulder, she found Raymond bursting from the library. Alice ran out the door, bounding down the front steps. Janeth followed, trying to balance the shotgun in her arm. The ocean was midnight blue, but a nearly full moon cast a glow from among a sky of stars. Clouds shrouded the street below in mist, a nearby streetlamp shining from twenty yards away. She started to yell, then remembered her uncle had paid the police to stay away, and her heart sank.

"Keep running," she told Alice, who dashed across the street toward the cliff's edge. Janeth stopped, facing the house. Raymond leapt after them, landing awkwardly at the base of the stairs onto the sidewalk. Blood trickled from the left side of his chest near his armpit. It stained his shirt in a slowly growing pattern.

"I'll take them down, Mrs. Castro. Hernandez, his men. You and your uncle. Unless you call them off."

She scoffed at his delusion. "You made your bed, Raymond. Lie in it." She gripped the butt of the shotgun tightly.

He lunged for her, and she swung the shotgun upward. The barrel struck his face, sending him backward for a moment. She turned and ran, her feet slapping across the paved street. All she could think was to get him as far from the house as possible, away from her uncle. With any luck his wound would leave him faint soon enough. "Alice?"

"Janeth!" She appeared in the mist. The ocean roared, loud and angry on such a quiet night, from beyond the cliff's edge. She tried to pinpoint where that was as they hurried onto the gritty sandstone. Their harried breaths came fast. Janeth peered back into the fog, but everything outside of a two-foot radius was obstructed by white.

"Where is he?" Alice asked.

"Right here."

Janeth spun, but Raymond swung, his left hook meeting Alice's jaw. "Alice!" Blood spewed from her mouth as she whirled and fell.

Raymond reached for her. She ducked, and he stumbled forward. She struck him again with the shotgun, but he recovered, meeting her next strike and catching the barrel with his right hand. Grimacing, she tried to pull back, but he overpowered her, snatching it away. She watched helplessly as he tossed it into the mist.

She stepped back. The water was louder now. She was close to the edge. She just didn't know how close. Alice's limp figure lay a few feet away. Raymond, his breathing haggard, lumbered toward her.

"Raymond," she said, putting her hands up and looking behind her, trying to measure the curved edge of the cliff. One wrong step and she would fall to the churning waters below. "Think about what you're doing."

His thumb came up to his lips. He wiped at a new cut, then swiped at one near his temple. Alice's doing, no doubt, from the shattered urn.

Alice. Janeth glanced to her again. She thought she saw her move, pulling a leg closer. Rage filled her. She clenched her fists, for once letting the crashing waves penetrate her mind. She let the rumble of the sea beckon to her. She accepted the truth of her life, her work. The world was not stark columns of black and white. It was a whirling eddy of ever-changing colors, choices, and emotions. It left her dizzy and uncertain.

But that was life, wasn't it? She didn't have to know the answers, but she knew what was right. Pulling herself up, she knew that even if she was different, even if her life didn't look a certain way, no one could tell her how to live it. Men like Raymond wanted to control her and those like her. They wanted the world to bend to their will. But no one could tell her what to do. She was in charge of her fate.

Raymond yelled, a futile war cry, as he dove for her. She lunged to meet him and managed to shove him away. They both fell, tumbling awkwardly. Her foot found the cliff's edge, and she reached over the slick sandstone for something to cling to, just managing to pull herself up. Raymond found his feet a yard to her right. He sneered and stepped forward.

She was certain her face matched his in the moment he realized there was nothing beneath his feet, only the unforgiving air. He clawed at the sky, but it was fruitless, and he fell.

Janeth knelt, leaning over the cliff and its twenty-foot drop into the tumultuous waters. The fog was less dense over the water, but sprays of foam and fighting waves swallowed Raymond. She held her breath. His arm came up first. His head bobbed above the water, only to be swallowed again by another wave. He'd fallen into a whirlpool, spirals of relentless waves trapping anything that came into its grasp between the cliffs and surrounding rocks. She thought she heard him scream before he was underneath the water again. She waited a minute. Then two. He didn't resurface.

"Alice." She hurried to her. Alice muttered something, and Janeth carefully helped her sit up. "Oh, darling." She reached for her face, then stopped before touching the already dark bruise on her jaw. Her bottom lip was swollen.

Alice ran her tongue over her teeth. She grunted, then said, "Still have 'em all."

Janeth laughed through her tears. "Come on," she said, helping Alice to stand. "It's over."

Rocking on her unsteady legs, Alice searched her gaze. She looked to the mist-shrouded cliffs. "You mean…"

"He fell," she said, swallowing the tremble in her voice. She helped Alice to the cliff's edge. A dory with a lantern was navigating the cliffside. One man rowed while two others pulled a lifeless Raymond from the waters.

"What are they gonna do with him?" Alice asked as they watched the macabre scene play out below.

"I don't know," she said. "But it's done."

Alice nodded slowly, then let Janeth help her back toward the house. At the top of the stairs, beneath the gabled front porch, Alice said, "Janeth?"

"Yes, darling?"

She met her gaze, taking a long breath. "You're a terrible shot."

Janeth barked a relieved laugh as Alice, swollen lip and all, grinned before heading inside.

CHAPTER THIRTY-SIX

Alice was pouring coffee when Janeth ran in to the kitchen, telling her officers found Raymond's body two miles down the beach early Saturday morning. He had no identification on him, but they didn't need any to identify a wanted man known for his dealings in rum smuggling. When the police came by the Mills Mansion to inquire if they'd noticed any suspicious activity, Alice remained out of sight while Mr. Mills explained that he'd seen Raymond lurking around the last few months.

"He had an altercation with some fellas in town, though I can't say what about," Mr. Mills said, puffing on his pipe in the drawing room while Janeth stood behind his chair. Alice stayed in the next room but listened quietly at the door. The police would surely have been curious about her swollen lip and bruised cheek, so she stayed out of sight.

Mr. Mills spoke again. "They told him not to come around here anymore. My guess is he did, got into a brawl somewhere out there, and had an unlucky fall out on the cliffs. Between you and me, he may have been intoxicated."

"There was a bullet wound near the top of his left ribs," the officer said, his bushy brows furrowed as he read from a small notepad. "Cuts and bruises along his face."

"I imagine a deal of some sort went sideways," Janeth said.

"Interesting characters in that business, as you know," Mr. Mills added, and Alice could imagine the pointed look he gave the officer.

"If there was an altercation, whoever he argued with is gone. Wind washed away footprints on the cliffs. Tide cleared everything on the beach." The officer hesitated. "You sure you didn't see anything?"

Mr. Mills replied, "We were all in bed, my good fellow. My nephew's going-away party was last night. What a time that was, wasn't it, Janeth dear?" Again, Alice imagined the look between him and Janeth. She and Janeth had told him everything when they'd woken him last night after Hernandez had come up the cellar stairs. He and his men had indeed gone after Raymond. Alice had sunk into the couch, ice on her face, as he had thanked Janeth for standing with them. With a trembling hand, Janeth had shaken his before Hernandez had slipped away, back into the night to place Raymond's body on the sand several miles away.

After relaying all of this to Mr. Mills, he had helped them plan out exactly what to say when the police came by, and it was he who reminded them to fetch the shotgun from the cliffs, leaving no trace they were ever there.

"Yes, quite the event, Uncle," Janeth replied presently.

The officer cleared his throat. "Very well, then. We've been after this guy for some time. He was no good. Left a nasty trail everywhere he went." Alice thought she heard relief in the officer's voice. "Thank you for your time, Mr. Mills. The San Diego Police are always grateful to helpful citizens."

"Of course, dear boy."

❖

A week later, things had returned to normal in the Mills household. All that remained from that night were the marks left behind from the fight. Alice stood in front of the mirror of the bathroom while Janeth applied makeup to her chin. "This is the best I can do, darling."

She scanned her reflection. A faint purple was still evident where Raymond had hit her. Her lip wasn't as swollen, thanks to a steady routine of cold rags. She'd looked better, she decided with a sigh, but she had definitely looked worse.

When she took the trolley to the railyards, Alice's stomach fluttered. Today was the Temperance fundraiser and the last day she was to ever spend with her parents. It was strange. She had expected to feel a little sad, but all she felt as she opened the shanty door was relief.

"You're late," her mother said, standing from her seat at the card table. Her father was in the middle of the room; it looked like he had been pacing, waiting for her arrival. They'd both donned modest attire: her mother in a brown day dress and matching hat, her father in an equally drab suit. They looked utterly unsuspecting.

"I just need to change," she said.

"Make it fast." Her mother didn't even meet her gaze as she brushed past. Her father gave her a sad smile before he followed. She caught his arm and turned him, wanting to ask what he'd told her mother. He seemed to read the question in her eyes and gave a small shake of his head. She exhaled, then hurried to her room.

She changed into the only dress that was left in there, the dress she'd come to San Diego in. In the pocket, she found a crumpled dollar note and laughed. What were the odds her mother hadn't found that for herself? She shoved it into her bra, smiling as she imagined adding it to her savings. The money, now safely at the mansion, was her starting point for the next chapter of her life. All she had left to do now was turn the page.

The three of them were quiet on the trolley ride. She went over their plan in her head. The fundraiser featured the presentation of a check to Madame Enfield at the end of a keynote speech that would be given by the mayor. Dorothy had said that the matron always placed the check in a Bible for safekeeping, which she kept firmly under her arm the rest of the event. Alice was to distract the matron while her mother knocked the Bible from her, replacing it with one of her own. They'd had to comb several bookstores to find a matching copy that fit Dorothy's description. The matron would be none the wiser, and her parents would make off with hundreds of dollars.

That, anyway, was the plan.

Alice took a deep breath when they arrived at the sprawling institution of the University of San Diego. She'd never been on a college campus before. The lawns were pristine, rows of trees lining the sidewalks that formed a vast web connecting each building over the expansive acreage. People milled about the lawns, but most headed toward the towering auditorium where the event was to be held.

"Oklahoma!" Dorothy waved and hurried to her, Mary at her heels. Alice glanced at her parents, who hesitated alongside her. "This is her," she said under her breath, referring to the supposed wealthy friend Alice had been working the past several months. Her mother's gaze turned shrewd, but both her parents made their faces the picture of kindness as Dorothy wrapped her in a hug. "You made it."

"I did," she said. "Mary, you look lovely. New dress?"

Mary blushed and simpered, running a hand over the red skirt. "Why, yes, it is."

Dorothy said, "Mary's met a gentleman, believe it or not." She grinned teasingly.

"Dorothy," Mary replied, her blush growing.

"Oh, Mary," Dorothy said, swatting her playfully, "I'm happy for you."

"As am I," Alice said. "That's wonderful."

"He'll be here soon," Mary said. She and Dorothy looked from Alice to her parents, who had yet to say anything.

"These are my folks," Alice said. Before she could introduce them, her mother reached out.

Her voice was sweet but confident as she said, "Charmed." They shook each other's hands in turn.

Dorothy's smile faltered, no doubt curious about them not sharing their names, then said, "Well, it's nice to meet you. Always good to see new faces at these things."

Her mother gave a tight smile, then patted her father's arm. "We had better head inside."

"Right you are, my love." He tipped his cap to each of them. "Alice?" he asked, turning to her.

"I'll be there soon," she said. She caught her father's gaze as her mother turned to go. A pang of guilt flared in her chest, but she ignored it, remembering what she was here to do. She'd decided on this plan weeks ago while sitting on the beach with Janeth. It was time, and she knew it.

When her parents were out of earshot, she turned to look between Dorothy and Mary. Dorothy seemed to notice the amount of makeup on her face. She squinted and leaned closer. "Oklahoma, what happened here?" She gestured to her chin.

Alice found herself on the verge of tears at the concern in her voice. How had she ended up in a place full of such warm people? "Dorothy," she said, clearing her throat, "can you promise me something?"

A worried look filled Dorothy's eyes, followed by a register of understanding. "Mary," she said, "I think you'd better go find that gentleman of yours. I'm sure he's here."

Mary, who had been glancing between them, a mildly confused look on her face, nodded. "Yes, I suppose so." She squeezed Alice's arm. "So glad you're here," she said, then scampered away.

Dorothy stepped closer, lowering her voice. "What is it, Alice?"

She took another breath to steady herself. "I may…" She licked her lips, trying to find the right words. "I'm going to do something, Dorothy, something that will leave me in dire need of a good friend. If you won't stand by me, I understand. I have other people…" She searched Dorothy's gaze. "But I would love to still call you my friend when all is said and done."

Dorothy blinked, clearly trying to pick apart her words and find the meaning behind them. "Oklahoma," she said quietly, "what are you saying?"

"You'll see." Alice turned, searching the grounds. "How many policemen will be in attendance?"

At this, Dorothy's face grew worried. But she only pointed near the auditorium's entrance. "There will be one at the door and two inside to oversee the attendants."

Alice found her hands and squeezed. "Thank you. I'll see you after."

In the auditorium—a room that encompassed three stories and was twice as long as the Mills mansion—Alice spotted her parents. Rows of chairs were already half filled with people as folks trickled in, and her mother and father had found seats near the back, leaving one empty for her. She looked at them a moment. Again, she waited for sadness to overwhelm her. She waited for something akin to regret or fear or even anger to fill her. She waited, but none of that came. She found her seat.

The fundraiser played out as expected. The speeches were rousing, though Alice hardly heard them as she ran over what she was about to do in her head. Standing, she waited a few minutes, then found the matron after the check was handed to her and slipped carefully into her Bible.

"Congratulations, Matron, on a successful fundraiser."

Madame Enfield, as dowdy as ever, looked down her nose at Alice, much as she had the first day they'd met. "Yes, thank you."

"I had a few suggestions, if you don't mind, about ways to improve the protests for next spring."

Madame Enfield raised a brow. Several other people were coming over to give them their regards. Alice spotted her mother among them, reaching into her handbag. Her father's voice bellowed to their right. Many in the crowd turned to see him captivating a small audience with an impromptu card trick, gasps from a few of the guests trickling over the room at his sleight of hand. When the attention was firmly away from the matron, Alice's mother bumped into her. As a result, the Bible fell. Alice called out, drawing the matron's confused gaze. Quickly, her mother placed her own copy on top, then slipped the matron's into her handbag.

"I beg your pardon, but did you drop this?" her mother asked, handing Madame Enfield the book.

"Goodness, yes. Thank you."

"It's my pleasure," her mother said, bowing slightly, then disappearing back into the crowd.

Taking a moment to gather herself, the matron turned back to Alice. "What were you saying, young lady?"

"Nothing," she said, "it can wait. Congratulations again." She hurried back through the crowd. At the open doorway, she found the cop.

Alice tapped his shoulder. The man—tall, with a brown mustache and light eyes—faced her. "Good afternoon." She swallowed the rapid heartbeat threatening to climb up her throat. "I just saw two people steal the funds from the matron." She pointed toward an unsuspecting Madame Enfield.

His brows furrowed. "What do you mean, miss? Nothing looks afoot to me."

She pointed to her parents. "There. That woman in the brown dress walking toward the man doing card tricks. Check her handbag. There's a Bible in it that she switched with Madame Enfield's. It has the check she was presented with not fifteen minutes ago."

The officer frowned, then told her to wait there. She stepped back, finding the doorjamb to steady herself. In the sea of people, the cop approached her mother and father. Alice watched her mother's face go from demure to incredulous as he asked to see her handbag. Her father moved closer, but there was nothing he could do as she had to hand it over. The officer pulled out the book, flipping through it. The crowd had moved to give them room, and the fundraiser check drifted listlessly to the floor.

The officer whistled. Two others stormed forward from the corners of the auditorium. One grabbed the check while the other two apprehended Alice's parents.

Her mother's protests screeched over the crowd. "This is absurd. I have no idea what that's even doing in my bag. This is ridiculous." Her father only stood solemnly as the cop cuffed him, then shoved him forward to follow her mother. Alice hurried outside as the crowd watched and whispered.

Outside, the officer forced her mother to walk as she shouted, "Alice? Alice, where are you? You did this, didn't you, Alice?"

Alice shrank behind people but kept her gaze on her mother. Distress and liberation battled in her chest. She closed her eyes, forcing the sound of her mother's voice away and clinging to the fact that she had done it. She'd chosen a life, a world, where her mother couldn't hurt her anymore.

"Alice, you rotten girl, where are you?"

Someone stepped behind her. She turned to find Dorothy watching the arrest unfold. When Alice met her gaze, to her relief, she saw understanding. Dorothy wrapped an arm around her, steering her away from her mother's shouts as her parents were taken away.

C<small>HAPTER</small> T<small>HIRTY</small>-S<small>EVEN</small>

Janeth and Alice walked the boardwalk in Seaside. The early October day was cool but sunny, blue skies overhead lined with a smattering of white clouds. The skirts of their long dresses hugged their legs as they passed Mr. Preston's cotton candy stand. Janeth had already offered to buy Alice some roasted chestnuts, which she knew were her favorite, as she'd been in a quiet mood all morning. Janeth didn't blame her. After all, she'd had her own parents arrested just yesterday. When she'd returned to the house last night, Janeth could nearly see her coming to terms with such a choice. "How are you feeling?"

Alice gave her a sideways look above a small smile. "The same as I was when you asked me half an hour ago. I'm all right, Janeth." She squeezed her arm.

"Are you sure? I know it must have been a lot..." She let her voice trail off, the rest of her concerns catching on the breeze.

Alice took a deep breath as they stopped near the boardwalk's edge. The final weekend of the carnival was here, and the crowds were thick. People sat on the sand: families, children chasing dogs while their parents enjoyed a refreshing shaved ice. Others strolled the boardwalk like them, taking in as much of the attractions as they could. "It was," she finally said, "but it was what I needed to do."

Alice had told Janeth how Madame Enfield, along with Mary and several other Temperance members, had been shaken by the incident at the fundraiser. "I'll see those two receive the maximum punishment," the matron had said, holding a shaky finger up to her followers after Alice's parents had been taken away.

"What is the maximum punishment?" Dorothy had asked quietly.

"Six months in county jail."

Now, Janeth studied her. "Where will they go...after?"

Alice shrugged. "I don't know. Wherever they can to start fresh, I suppose."

They were quiet a long time. Janeth reached over, finding her arm. "I'm proud of you, Alice."

Alice turned, the wind pulling some of her hair across her face. She reached up to tuck it behind her ear and smiled.

They spent the next hour walking around the boardwalk. They even took a ride on the Ferris wheel, hands clasped at the very top as they seemed to float above the world together. After, they returned to the house for lunch. Hugh came by around three to check in. They'd told him about everything that had transpired with Raymond. To Janeth's surprise, he'd since taken on the role of protective big brother to them both.

"Mrs. Castro, we have got to work on your shooting skills. My friend's grandfather has land south of here. The three of us should go one weekend. You can try your hand too, Miss Covington, if you like."

"Are you sure you're up for it?" Janeth asked. "You really want to be here, teaching us how to shoot, rather than jaunting around Europe?"

It was still difficult for all of them to believe Hugh had given up his boat ticket. The wandering scoundrel, it turned out, was keen on their unconventional, family-run business and wasn't ready to give it up quite yet. Janeth had a feeling he wanted to be here, too, in case anyone else like Raymond ever came along. His parents, at first wary of his decision to stay, seemed pleased when he requested to move into the mansion. Mr. Mills let him take the guest room upstairs, across from his own quarters.

"Mrs. Castro," he said, lighting a cigar in the drawing room where he leaned against the mantle, "I am a man of honor, believe it or not. I am committed to this work of ours and refuse to abandon you or our clients."

Once the cigar was done, he bid them good-bye with the promise of returning later to oversee tonight's product delivery from Hernandez. During dinner—roasted lamb with cranberry salad—the telephone rang. Alice met Janeth's gaze.

Mr. Mills grunted from his seat at the head of the table opposite her. "Probably another police follow-up."

Janeth wiped her mouth and stood. "I'll get it, Uncle." In the drawing room, the operator patched through a call from Logan Heights. "Leo?"

To her surprise, it was Maria's voice that came through the line. "Your niece has something to share with you," she said, hardly able to finish before Elena's voice squeaked through the airwaves.

"Auntie Janeth, I lost a tooth. It was a big one."

Chuckling, she replied, "Is that so?"

"Jorge pulled it out for me."

"My, what an exciting time."

"Papa says it will grow back bigger and stronger."

"He's right."

Elena shouted something, presumably to her brother, and Maria's voice came back through the telephone. "She had to tell you right away."

"Thank you," Janeth said, "for letting her."

The line was quiet a moment. There were so many things Janeth wanted to share. She longed to be in the place they used to be, when they spoke candidly, poking fun at Leo and sharing gossip. Janeth wanted to tell her about Alice, about their plans, and about everything that had happened recently with Raymond. But how to even begin?

"You should come by for lunch next weekend," Maria said, breaking the silence.

Janeth inhaled sharply, emotion tightening the words on her tongue. "I would love that."

"Good," Maria said, warmth clear in her voice. "We'll see you then," she added before the line went static.

That evening, Janeth helped her uncle to bed early. All of the excitement from the last few days had taken its toll on him, though he was loath to admit it. "I'm nearly caught up on rest," he explained as she helped him upstairs.

"Of course, Uncle."

"I'll be right as rain by tomorrow," he added, but she noted the relief on his face as he climbed into bed.

The sun was just setting when she came back downstairs. Alice was in the drawing room, the gramophone playing a record softly. She sat in one of the high-back chairs, her legs tucked beneath her.

"Come on," Janeth said, reaching toward her. "It's going to be a beautiful sunset tonight."

Alice smiled but didn't say anything as she took her hand. They walked quietly down the front steps and crossed the street to the cliffs. A young couple stood about fifty yards away, wrapped up in each other as they watched the sun dip closer to the horizon. Janeth let go of Alice's hand as they crossed the space where Raymond had chased them. They studied the sandstone, both searching for evidence of that harrowing night, but, of course, finding none.

They stood side by side a few feet from the edge. The wind had calmed as the sky burned a fiery orange. Scattered clouds above the water were lined in bold pinks, while overhead, splashes of blue deepened. All of it was reflected off the sea, calm and quiet.

Alice spoke over the breeze. "I'm surprised you wanted to come here."

"Because of what happened?"

"Yes." Alice turned to face her. "And because you don't like the water."

Janeth gave a small smile as she looked from Alice to the waves. "I *didn't* like the water," she said, emphasizing the second word. At Alice's raised brow, she explained, "My fear came from anger and sorrow. The water took so much away from me, once upon a time. But," she said, reaching for Alice's hand, "it's also given me so much. It gave me my work, which gave me this…" She paused, searching for the right words. "This unpredictable, messy, wonderful second chance at life. This life that brought me you." She squeezed Alice's hand, blinking back tears.

"So," Alice said, nodding to the sea, "you're saying you're up for a swim lesson? I hear there are stunning lakes in Washington."

Janeth smiled, imagining traipsing through the northwest with Alice. She had purchased tickets a week ago, when Alice had shared her plan to escape her parents. Hastily, she'd bought return tickets, mostly out of worry at leaving her uncle in Hugh's hands for so long.

Of course, her uncle had waved her concern off when she'd told him about the trip. "Go explore, Janeth. I'll be perfectly fine. Hugh and I have a business to run. And that brother of yours will be helping, too. Nothing to fret about."

She had eyed him, searching for a sign that he needed her to stay. Not finding it, she had said, "We'll come back, Uncle."

"When you're ready to, Janeth, dear. When you're ready."

Now, she blinked back tears of anticipation, laughing at Alice's proposal of swim lessons. She gave her a playful shove. "I wouldn't say I'm quite ready for that yet. One step at a time."

Alice laughed too, the sound breaking into a thousand joyful pieces over the breeze. Janeth knew she could listen to that sound forever.

They stood quietly for a time. The sun sank lower, the skies darkening as the final light of day descended below the water.

"I can't believe it's all done," Alice said quietly. "My parents, Raymond, it ended, just like that."

Janeth took a deep breath. Glancing around, she reached to pull Alice close, wrapping one arm around her. "Yes. It is over." She placed a gentle kiss on her cheek. "But this," she said, pulling Alice's gaze, "you and me? Darling, this is just the beginning."

About the Author

Sam Ledel grew up in the sprawling DFW metroplex of Texas. After graduating with her BA in creative writing, she found a calling in education and has worked in the field for more than a decade, including during her time in Peru serving in the Peace Corps.

Her debut novel, *Rocks and Stars*, was a Golden Crown Literary Society finalist for Young Adult fiction. *Wildflower Words*, a historical romance, was a 2023 LGBTQ+ finalist in the Next Generation Indie Book Awards.

Ledel enjoys being able to write in her free time, usually with a cup of coffee in hand and her Jack Russell Terrier snuggled close by. She currently resides in Denver and is working on her next novel.

Books Available From Bold Strokes Books

A Heart Divided by Angie Williams. Emmaline is the most beautiful woman Jack has ever seen, but being a veteran of the Confederate army that killed her husband isn't the only thing keeping them apart. (978-1-63679-537-9)

Adrift by Sam Ledel. Two women whose lives are anchored by guilt and obligation find romance amidst the tumultuous Prohibition movement in 1920s California. (978-1-63679-577-5)

Cabin Fever by Tagan Shepard. The longer Morgan and Shelby are stranded together, the more their feelings grow, but is it real, or just cabin fever? (978-1-63679-632-1)

Clean Kill by Anne Laughlin. When someone starts killing people she knows in the recovery world, former detective Nicky Sullivan must race to stop the killer and keep herself from being arrested for the crimes. (978-1-63679-634-5)

Only a Bridesmaid by Haley Donnell. A fake bridesmaid, a socially anxious bride, and an unexpected love—what could go wrong? (978-1-63679-642-0)

Primal Hunt by L.L. Raand. Anya, a young wolf warrior, finds herself paired with Rafe, one of the most powerful Vampires in the Americas, in an erotic union of blood and sex.(978-1-63679-561-4)

Snake Charming by Genevieve McCluer. Playgirl vampire Freddie is on the run, and a chance encounter with lamia Phoebe makes them both realize that they may have found the love they'd given up on. (978-1-63679-628-4)

Spirits and Sirens by Kelly and Tana Fireside. When rumored ghost whisperer Elena Murphy and very skeptical assistant fire chief Allison Jones have to work together to solve a 70-year old mystery, sparks fly—will it be enough to melt the ice between them and let love ignite? (978-1-63679-607-9)

Aubrey McFadden Is Never Getting Married by Georgia Beers. Aubrey McFadden is never getting married, but she does have five weddings to attend, and she'll be avoiding Monica Wallace, the woman who ruined her happily ever after, at every single one. (978-1-63679-613-0)

A Case for Discretion by Ashley Moore. Will Gwen, a prominent Atlanta attorney, choose Etta, the law student she's clandestinely dating, or is her political future too important to sacrifice? (978-1-63679-617-8)

The Broken Lines of Us by Shia Woods. Charlie Dawson returns to the city she left behind and meets an unexpected stranger on her first night back, discovering that coming home might not be as hard as she thought. (978-1-63679-585-0)

Flowers for Dead Girls by Abigail Collins. Isla might be just the right kind of girl to bring Astra out of her shell—and maybe more. The only problem? She's dead. (978-1-63679-584-3)

Good Bones by Aurora Rey. Designer and contractor Logan Barrow can give Kathleen Kenney the house of her dreams, but can she convince the cynical romance writer to take a chance on love? (978-1-63679-589-8)

Leather, Lace, and Locs by Anne Shade. Three friends, each on their own path in life, with one obstacle…finding room in their busy lives for a love that will give them their happily ever afters. (978-1-63679-529-4)

Rainbow Overalls by Maggie Fortuna. Arriving in Vermont for her first year of college, an introverted bookworm forms a friendship with an outgoing artist and finds what comes after the classic coming out story: a being out story. (978-1-63679-606-2)

Revisiting Summer Nights by Ashley Bartlett. PJ Addison and Wylie Parsons have been called back to film the most recent *Dangerous Summer Nights* installment. Only this time they're not in love, and it's going to stay that way. (978-1-63679-551-5)

All This Time by Sage Donnell. Erin and Jodi share a complicated past, but a very different present. Will they ever be able to make a future together work? (978-1-63679-622-2)

Crossing Bridges by Chelsey Lynford. When a one-night stand between a snowboard instructor and a business executive becomes more, one has to overcome her past, while the other must let go of her planned future. (978-1-63679-646-8)

Dancing Toward Stardust by Julia Underwood. Age has nothing to do with becoming the person you were meant to be, taking a chance, and finding love. (978-1-63679-588-1)

Evacuation to Love by CA Popovich. As a hurricane rips through Florida, so too are Joanne and Shanna's lives upended. It'll take a force of nature to show them the love it takes to rebuild. (978-1-63679-493-8)

Lean in to Love by Catherine Lane. Will badly behaving celebrities, erotic sex tapes, and steamy scandals prevent Rory and Ellis from leaning in to love? (978-1-63679-582-9)

The Romance Lovers Book Club by MA Binfield and Toni Logan. After their book club reads a romance about an American tourist falling in love with an English princess, Harper and her best friend, Alice, book an impulsive trip to London hoping they'll both fall for the women of their dreams. (978-1-63679-501-0)

Searching for Someday by Renee Roman. For loner Rayne Thomas, her only goal for working out is to build her confidence, but Maggie Flanders has another idea, and neither is prepared for the outcome. (978-1-63679-568-3)

Truly Home by J.J. Hale. Ruth and Olivia discover home is more than a four-letter word. (978-1-63679-579-9)

View from the Top by Morgan Adams. When it comes to love, sometimes the higher you climb, the harder you fall. (978-1-63679-604-8)

Blood Rage by Illeandra Young. A stolen artifact, a family in the dark, an entire city on edge. Can SPEAR agent Danika Karson juggle all three over a weekend with the "in-laws" while an unknown, malevolent entity lies in wait upon her very skin? (978-1-63679-539-3)

Ghost Town by R.E. Ward. Blair Wyndon and Leif Henderson are set to prove ghosts exist when the mystery suddenly turns deadly. Someone or something else is in Masonville, and if they don't find a way to escape, they might never leave. (978-1-63679-523-2)

Good Christian Girls by Elizabeth Bradshaw. In this heartfelt coming of age lesbian romance, Lacey and Jo help each other untangle who they are from who everyone says they're supposed to be. (978-1-63679-555-3)

Guide Us Home by CF Frizzell and Jesse J. Thoma. When acquisition of an abandoned lighthouse pits ambitious competitors Nancy and Sam against each other, it takes a WWII tale of two brave women to make them see the light. (978-1-63679-533-1)

Lost Harbor by Kimberly Cooper Griffin. For Alice and Bridget's love to survive, they must find a way to reconcile the most important passions in their lives—devotion to the church and each other. (978-1-63679-463-1)

Never a Bridesmaid by Spencer Greene. As her sister's wedding gets closer, Jessica finds that her hatred for the maid of honor is a bit more complicated than she thought. Could it be something more than hatred? (978-1-63679-559-1)

The Rewind by Nicole Stiling. For police detective Cami Lyons and crime reporter Alicia Flynn, some choices break hearts. Others leave a body count. (978-1-63679-572-0)

Turning Point by Cathy Dunnell. When Asha and her former high school bully Jody struggle to deny their growing attraction, can they move forward without going back? (978-1-63679-549-2)

When Tomorrow Comes by D. Jackson Leigh. Teague Maxwell, convinced she will die before she turns 41, hires animal rescue owner Baye Cobb to rehome her extensive menagerie. (978-1-63679-557-7)

You Had Me at Merlot by Melissa Brayden. Leighton and Jamie have all the ingredients to turn their attraction into love, but it's a recipe for disaster.(978-1-63679-543-0)